THE SHADOW BRIDE

THE SHADOW BRIDE

ROY HEATH

PERSEA BOOKS
New York

The Shadow Bride was first published in the United States by Persea Books in 1996; originally published by William Collins Sons & Co. Ltd., in Great Britain, in 1988.

Persea Books, Inc.
60 Madison Avenue
New York, New York 10010

Heath, Roy A. K.
        The shadow bride/Roy Heath.
            p.   cm.
        ISBN 0-89255-213-1
        1. Mothers and sons—Guyana—Fiction. 2. Married people—Guyana—Fiction
3. Physicians—Guyana—Fiction.   I. Title.
PR9320.9.H4A53 1996
813—dc20   95-33733
                                                                            CIP

Manufactured in the United States of America
First U.S. Edition

For Mohammed Umar

CONTENTS

BOOK 1   The Doctor   1

BOOK 2   The Mother   87

BOOK 3   Hangers-on   139

BOOK 4   The Exclusion   261

BOOK 5   The Return   387

          Epilogue   419

BOOK I
THE DOCTOR

Chapter 1

Dr Singh was helped to the front of the house by his wife, who held his left arm while he eased his frame into the armchair by the window. The Lamaha canal, which once ran along the other side of the street, had now been filled in. When the work was finally completed he would not allow his wife or son to take him to his seat because he could not tolerate the sight of the 'mall', the improbable name given to the filled-in canal. This, the first day on which the doctor made up his mind to contemplate the structure that covered *his* canal, he looked sadly across Church Street to the mall, flanked by two narrow trenches, the remains of the once handsome waterway. On the farther side of the twin trench was North Road, where houses were not as uniformly elegant as those on Church Street and, in fact, remained resolutely old-styled, even when rebuilt.

Dr Singh's home was neither in the old nor the new style. The open front facing south had not a single window and was protected from any freak rainstorm by a curved extension of the roof, an unnecessary arrangement, he felt, since the wind never changed direction.

The doctor's status as a retired physician was finally acknowledged by the authorities, who had twice 'hauled him out of retirement' – a phrase he had used more than once – because of the shortage of doctors. He was ill, he protested, and after fifteen years in public service should be left in peace for the short time still allowed him on earth. But on each occasion he gave in on being reminded that a department had its eye on his house, which was suitable for use as government offices. In the end, when his failing health was evident and he took to turning up at the hospital in house slippers, the authorities gave in.

Dr Singh's wife was many years younger than he and was, like him, an East Indian. They had married when she was sixteen and he in his early thirties at a ceremony that was followed by the interminable beating of tablas under a cloudless evening sky. The immense yard of beaten earth, strewn with raised concrete squares for threshing paddy, was filled with guests who stood around in groups or sat on stools while consuming rice and mutton served on plantain leaves. Whenever he recalled that day, the ritual lifting of the bride's veil so that he would see her face for the 'first time' – he had met her on many occasions at her parents' house – he was invariably overwhelmed by the weight of a tradition to which he had yielded unquestioningly, the wreaths of brilliant flowers round his neck and the scattering of silver coins at his feet. He recalled a sky vividly streaked with white and the fall of night when he was a prey to an unaccountable shyness in the presence of his taciturn bride. He had already been practising for some time in conditions that admitted of no prudishness or reserve; yet then, and even today, his wife managed to overpower him with a terrible mystery.

Mrs Singh's devotion to her husband was suspended on days when she declared life to be unbearable, because she longed to go away to a country where there were no food shortages and she could walk her crippled son by the sea without fear of being molested. How could she endure a diet without roti, the unleavened bread she had eaten since she was weaned? The importation of flour had been banned a year ago to save foreign exchange and the general outcry had failed to move the Government, which insisted that the country must make do with the foodstuffs it produced.

Dr Singh had had a series of attacks with the classic symptoms of angina pectoris, which made him think that he was about to expire. The electro-cardiograph tests carried out at the General Hospital having proved negative, he had come to the conclusion that he was suffering from cramp in the region above the heart, a condition that often preceded angina. In the beginning he could reduce the severity of the attacks – or so it seemed – by eating three or four young coconuts a day, but of late the seizures were as bad as ever and made him think of death and the final parting from his wife and son, now in his mid-thirties.

He could now hear him feeding the dog before he unchained it and let it have the run of the yard.

Since his two daughters had qualified as doctors in Canada and remained to practise there, he could concentrate his anxieties on his son, who suffered from a speech defect and walked with the gait of a drunkard. While he and his wife understood him when he spoke strangers could not, so that he had never been able to find work. Dr Singh adored his son. He recalled the moment when he learned that he was suffering from an abnormality which confirmed suspicions aroused by an unusual expression in his eye. He recalled the feeling of utter desolation a patient once tried to communicate to him on discovering that his daughter was afflicted with a stammer and his own qualified sympathy. His wife had accepted their son's affliction more readily, with that resilience of certain women who, having buried their husbands, mourn them for a week and then pursue their daily chores as if nothing untoward had befallen them.

But against all expectations Arjun had learned to walk and talk well enough to take part in lengthy conversations with his sisters and his parents. And it was Dr Singh's endless reflections on his son's condition and his ability to make himself understood that led him to ponder on the need of humans to develop such sophisticated speech.

During his final retirement the doctor devoted most of his time to looking inwards and backwards. He reflected on his numerous trips along the rivers at the dead of night, watching the paddlers' shoulders dip with each stroke, while mosquitoes drew blood from exposed parts of his skin; on the many faces of poverty on the sugar estates, enclosed worlds where East Indian immigrants were required to reside, as in a kind of purgatory, before striking out for one of the towns or finding temporary employment in a village. His own father – so his mother claimed – had found a chest of Dutch guilders, gold coins in mint condition which had lain hidden at the base of a silk-cotton tree. With the money he had built himself a mansion capped with a weather vane where he had retired in his thirties. Thereafter the family moved every few years to a larger house, always by the sea to take advantage of the nourishing wind, first to Mahaica, then to Mahaicony, then to Belfield, Anandale,

Goed Verwagting, Ann's Grove and finally to the outskirts of
Georgetown at the corner of Vlissingen Road and Dowding
Street, to a mansion of the old style with many Demerara
windows and a spacious porch. There he used to sit and watch
for the afternoon train from Rosignol, trailing a black plume and
slowing down as it passed between the gates protecting the
crossing on Vlissingen Road. Occasionally he would set out on a
journey to India or Mexico and return with tales of golden
temples on Ganga Mai or sumptuous courtyards behind drab
exteriors. Although he came of sober stock he grew 'tetched' on
his wealth and took to drinking spirituous liquors with names
new to everyone and labels of superior design. According to
Betta's mother one night when he had locked himself away with
his bottles and cylinders of bamboo in which he kept his hoard
of gold and jewellery he fell into a drunken stupor and passed
away soon afterwards.

Dr Singh was four when his father died. His mother, whom
his father had married on one of his trips to India, said when the
paternal estate had been wound up, 'He was a secretive man. I
don't know if he was always a secretive man.'

Soon after his father died his mother took to wearing trousers
like a man. People he had never seen before began visiting them
and one teacher of whom she was especially fond was installed
in a large room under the house which, until then, had been used
to store rice and split peas and bunches of plantains which hung
from the floor above. 'He's the Mulvi Sahib,' his mother had told
him. 'He's a Mohammedan and I'm Hindu and come from
Kerala; but I respect him. He's your teacher from now on. You're
not going to one of these schools where the white boys sit in the
front and the East Indians at the back. Do you understand,
Betta?' He said he did only because his mother thought it was
right that he understood. His father had planned that he should
be sent to Queen's College at the age of eleven, but his mother,
who had raised no objection while her husband was alive, now
made known her violent opposition. She had not come to the
country as an indentured labourer and had no intention of
suffering either directly or vicariously the humiliations heaped
on the children of estate workers. Besides, *she* had had a private
education, a fact betrayed by her often stilted English.

Despite his wealth, her husband could not live down his past and she was astonished that a man who had dazzled her family with jewellery and his knowledge of foreign parts should have turned out to be a nobody in the country from which he came. But then she had discovered other things as well, that his Hindi was as poor as his English. Allowed no say in the way he had planned their son's education, she was now determined to put that right, and entrusted his upbringing to the care of the Mulvi Sahib, whose reputation for success with children overcame the objection that he was not a Hindu. He would teach her son not only the obligatory school subjects but prepare him for a career in medicine as well.

In the turmoil of his home life since his father died, the coming and going of countless friends who, impressed by Mrs Singh's hospitality, dared not criticize her freedom, Betta's father soon became a vague memory for him. He began confusing him with the Mulvi Sahib who, like his father, never wasted his words and expected to be obeyed. Yet his mother never mentioned his father without suggesting that he had been a hero. His trips abroad became perilous voyages, his visit to her family in Kerala the arrival of an intrepid traveller. Her mother, captivated by his courtesy, asked him to remain in India after his marriage to her daughter, whose father would find a place for him in his coconut-rope-making business. But he took her away across the Indian and Atlantic oceans to the country which bore a striking resemblance to Kerala, with its landscape of coconut trees and the sea never far away. Not once did she speak to Betta of her loneliness so far from home, of her loneliness made doubly hard to bear on account of his father's withdrawal from the world. The same wealth that had brought them together had separated him from the humble estate Indians both in distance and in his way of life. The villages he had lived in successively were stations in the journey to isolation, each house being larger and more sumptuously appointed than its predecessor. And finally the house near the train lines, which stood in the shadow of a massive saman tree with branches that spread towards the paling fence. That property, with its water tank set on a lofty tower, represented at once the summit of his ambition and despair. When passers-by stopped to admire the wide driveway and the shuttered mansion so far back from the asphalt road he would smile bitterly to himself. Some inner force had obliged him to make the journey and now he could not return to a village where everyone addressed him as 'neighbour'.

This was the house in which Betta's earliest memory lingered. He was not yet two years old, of that he was certain. He recalled that a man was bending over a trunk in the drawing room near the passageway that led into the kitchen. It was not his father. Even as Dr Singh sat in his chair by the window of his own house, an old man entirely dependent on his wife's attentions, the recollection of that mysterious figure possessed a mesmeric quality of some vivid dream.

All those years of toil, travelling up and down the coast and occasionally into the interior, had given him little time for reflection. Often at bedtime, determined to take stock of his years of practice, he would rest his head on his hands and look down into himself, only to be overcome by sleep. Perhaps he had lost the art of deep reflection, the ability to make those sustained voyages on which the heroes of books embarked with such an enviable facility, and he was destined to spend the better part of a day watching the road, the cars fleeing east, a solitary passer-by with her umbrella raised against the sun, or listening to the predictable radio programmes, the obligatory religious services and quizzes or a political speech about the country's achievements. It was only as dusk fell and the road began to blend with the shadows of fences and trees that he had some success in achoring his will to the bedrock of his memory. And even then his thoughts would invariably turn to his wife and son, as though *they* were the past, his earliest memories, his student years in Dublin, his year at the School of Tropical Medicine in London, his return to the country of his birth, his bachelorhood and eventual marriage, the epidemics of malaria, the sugar-estate morgues filled with the corpses of small children in the years of terror. His wife and son were like two instruments he had learned to play and was unable to put down. His wife, like his mother, was a prisoner of her past and a recurrent dream that followed her to the various houses they had lived in along the coast. In the dream her younger sister would come to visit her and, before she left to go home, she would promise to give her all the saris that languished in the wardrobe. But whenever she opened the wardrobe door to let her sister choose from the array of garments there was nothing but the faint scent of camphor wood.

'Meena, Meena!' he often exclaimed when alone. 'What will happen to our son when you die? He walks like a schooner in a storm.'

He would no doubt be passed on to his wife's relations, from one hand to the other, in the wake of a death. Betta's father's relations had all returned to India at the end of their indenture. His mother had none in the country, and Betta's five brothers and sisters had been stillborn following severe attacks of malaria.

Wife, son. . . . He thought of them more frequently than the pain in his chest which would sever the thread of his life one night after the cicadas had stopped singing and the frogs had stopped whistling in the twin trenches that flanked the twin roads.

He remembered well the afternoon he learnt the results of his final examinations in Dublin. For the first time since his arrival he dared walk about the town, for until then he could only think of his studies, his lectures and examinations. He was incapable of describing the terraced house in which he lived until that evening when he scrutinized it for the first time and found it attractive as he found the public house in which he celebrated attractive. His study companion, a young man from Bombay, drank beer – like him for the first time – and after one pint spoke more freely than he had ever done. Why did Guyanese Indians speak such execrable Hindi, while Fijian Indians spoke so well? They fell to insulting each other cordially and decided to repeat the drinking bout once every week. Yet, he never got to know Dublin, despite the year's internment that followed, the long brilliant summer, the easy public-house acquaintanceships. He was to have the same experience in London, where his most vivid recollection was the display of a flower seller huddled in her overcoat, surrounded by a mass of yellow and red bloom, the bleak afternoon sky and the silent public houses. Not once in the seven years had he sat at a family table or even seen the inside of a home. He began speaking in glowing terms of 'his' country, while excluding from his mind any thought relating to his reasons for falling in with his mother's plans to study medicine, inspired from stories of East Indians dying like flies at Mara.

This city of brick and inscrutable faces with its tall omnibuses, its long nights and grey prospects made such a profound impression on him he began to arm himself against it every morning before going out. Even the flower seller's display he once admired only appeared attractive because of the grey background that set it off. Then he was afforded the opportunity of attending the surgery of a certain Dr C for six weeks and came to recognize his warmth and diagnostic skills.

Then came spring when the heath on the edge of his lodging house burst into bloom. There was singing in the public houses, a muted choir of voices unlike those in the Dublin drinking places. And one late April evening when he was passing by one through whose opaque glass he could make out the shadowy figures of men standing at the bar, he heard a group singing a song he had heard in Dublin:

> 'There was a soldier
> A Scottish soldier . . .'

And suddenly all was well and even he could detect the spring in the air about which everyone seemed to be talking.

But when he returned to his own country to practise he realized how little relevance his London stay had had for his own experience. The London School of Tropical Medicine was preoccupied with diseases found in Africa and the East. And as for the six weeks' observation of private practice, he had learned much about the treatment of bronchial complaints and other diseases associated with damp, cold and a temperate climate, but little that would serve him later on.

On the eve of his return Dr Singh called to mind the Mulvi Sahib, under whose spell he had fallen when he was fifteen years old. Although he had been the teacher's pupil since the age of six it was not until the age of fifteen that he discovered something in himself which had come alive and required instruction of a different sort from rules of grammar and differential calculus. When the Mulvi Sahib spoke of his soul, of God and the meaning of life he was roused, as if a part of himself had been asleep and was destined to be awakened precisely at that time. He began to reflect on death, on his feelings for his dead father and on many other matters which he raised with his teacher. The Mulvi Sahib instructed him with the same zeal and authority that had won his mother's respect. There was one God and one gate through which He could be reached. A man must keep himself clean and do good at all times. He had a special duty to his family, his friends and the poor. When some months later he learned about the death house that was Mara sugar estate, from a visitor to his mother's home, he saw the news as confirming his mother's plans for him and the opportunity to put into practice the Mulvi Sahib's philosophy of personal service. He had told his mother none of this, since there was a tacit understanding between herself and his teacher that the latter would not teach Betta anything regarding the Muslim religion. But the seven years abroad had given Betta an independence that was intolerant of the pupil–teacher relationship he had once valued so highly. He did not look forward to seeing the Mulvi Sahib, just as he did not look forward to giving an account of his experiences to the visitors of his mother's home, many of whom he hardly remembered. There were no doubt others who had gained a foothold in the house since he went away, acquaintances who began arriving late in the afternoon and after dusk. So it was before he left, and from his mother's scant letters little had changed. All these people would have heard of her son who went away and came back a stranger to his mother's house with its many windows and camphor-wood furniture. He had lost the art of meeting people and would be intimidated by the greetings and admonishings of strangers, the excessive respect shown by the poor and the curiosity of his mother's hangers-on.

At the same time there was a deep longing to return to a landscape of bamboo and coconut trees and eat the food he had been eating since he was weaned. He even missed the newspapers with their confident horoscopes and pale, unevenly printed photographs displayed in reading rooms and in barber shops. But always his thoughts returned to the Mulvi Sahib. He would overcome conflicts with his mother, with her friends and acquaintances, simply because he was to set up on his own. But his struggle with the bearded teacher would match the one with his dead father, a myth because he was dead. It would be a struggle for his dignity as an individual who had travelled to countries so unlike his own and had arrived at another plane of understanding. His dread of meeting the old teacher once more became an obsession that haunted him during his voyage home.

Dr Singh nodded off and in his half-sleep saw images of islands floating down the Courantyne river, hospital beds with three patients, the illusionist who extracted white down from a hat and money from your hair, mosquitoes that drew blood, himself stepping from a cinema in New Amsterdam one moonlit night into a street deserted except for a solitary drunk. When his wife woke him he muttered incoherently, believing that he had been awakened by Sister Pearl in whose house he used to drink scented tea in diminutive cups. He began to weep softly, tormented by the thought that he had wronged his wife in insisting that he stayed to the bitter end.

Moonlight, houses tiled with slate, the reassuring barking of his dog. . . . His wife busied herself around him with the confidence of those women who ran the Salvation Army teashop behind Water Street, where round tables and wicker-seat chairs were redolent of verbena and an unostentatious elegance.

Chapter 2

Dr Singh's mother was angry when he declared that he intended remaining in private practice for no more than two years. He would then seek a post as an estate doctor so as to help in the fight against malaria.

'But people're dying of malaria in and around Georgetown!' she objected.

He reminded her of Mara.

'Mara! What do you know of Mara?'

He answered her with the gentle firmness he had adopted since he came home from abroad, driven by the impulse seven years of independence had kindled in him.

'It's on the estates that people suffer most,' he said, pained that his first important decision should be opposed as though he were still a child.

Secretly she felt she was capable of persuading him to remain with her. She did not believe he could abandon the camphor-wood chairs and chests or the coming and going of servants and guests, or even the traffic on Vlissingen Road.

Several days later Mrs Singh went to the Mulvi Sahib's house to ask him if he would persuade her son not to bury himself in the countryside. The teacher lived in a Kitty street, the only one lined with trees. Just before she came to his house she was obliged to get out of the way of an approaching horse-drawn dray cart. The sari she wore – she would not have dared go to the teacher's house dressed in trousers – was spattered with water from a puddle which had not evaporated, in spite of the dry, cloudless day. She turned on to the bridge over the un-weeded gutter and rattled the semicircle of metal that secured the gate.

'Is who you want?' a thin voice called out.

'Mulvi Sahib. Is he there?'

'He there, yes. Is who?' the unseen voice enquired.

'Tell him Mrs Singh wants to see him.'

The voice appeared from under the house in the guise of an old woman wearing a misshapen dress.

'Open the gate an' come in, ne?'

Mrs Singh undid the latch, opened the gate and slipped into the yard, which was so overgrown with fruit trees that the house was only visible in parts.

On reaching the foot of the stairs Mrs Singh waited for the old woman to show her up, but she just stood watching her from head to foot.

'He not there,' came the woman's voice when Mrs Singh, losing patience, began climbing the stairs without prompting.

'But. . . .'

Then, overcoming her exasperation, Betta's mother asked when the Mulvi Sahib would be coming back.

'He gone for his walk.'

'Can I wait?'

'You can wait, you can go; you's a big woman.'

The visitor took a seat on the porch, resting her feet on the first stair.

A good hour and a half later, long after the cicadas had fallen silent, Mrs Singh got up to leave, thinking that her informant had no knowledge of the Mulvi Sahib's whereabouts. An overpowering scent of vegetation came up to her and bats darted from the eaves of the cottage to circle the fruit trees before disappearing among their branches.

'It's not possible! It's not possible,' she whispered to herself, reflecting on all she had done for her son, on her abstinence, even while he was abroad, and on her loyalty to his dead father. She had even faced the scorn of her fellow Hindus for availing herself of the Mulvi Sahib's teaching skills. She was not accustomed to arguing with Betta. Until he went away he obeyed her without question, while displaying signs of independence which he practised on others. 'He's got a mind of his own,' the Mulvi Sahib had said more than once; and she approved silently, believing that without relations he needed a mind of his own.

She had always kept Betta from other children and, had she been honest, would have admitted that that was another motive behind her decision not to send him to the public secondary school. How, then, did he acquire his passion for burying himself among the poor? Could the teacher have put the idea into his head? When she went to see him again she would find a way of putting the question to him. Back home she went straight up the front stairs, at the head of which sat Aji, the oldest of her hangers-on, whom her husband had taken on to help her run the house. Aji waited until Mrs Singh reached the porch before speaking to her.

'Betta goin' be long tonight. You see how much people he got?'

Mrs Singh looked back involuntarily, then recalled the knot of patients waiting in front of the surgery.

'I went to see the Mulvi Sahib,' Mrs Singh said.

'You see that crazy woman, then.'

'You know her?'

'Yes. She get on as if she does own him.'

'You think Betta's changed since he went away?'

'Yes. He skin not so dark. You in see that you'self? They say something does suck you blood over there.'

'You know he wants to work as a doctor on a sugar estate?'

'Who, Betta?'

'Yes.'

'Why?'

'To help East Indians.'

'Good.'

Mrs Singh took the old servant's lack of understanding calmly. Aji was one of the few people who did not listen to her with that exaggerated show of respect which flattered her, but often served to emphasize her aloneness.

'He's going to end up like other estate doctors,' Mrs Singh said, 'moving from one place to another without anywhere. . . .'

Aji did not take her up, so she sought refuge in her own reflections. She must not despair, she told herself. The Mulvi Sahib had performed miracles in the past and she had often enough acknowledged his debt for the period of years he had lived in her home. Besides, a man who prayed several times a day would be in a better position than anyone to help her. No, she must not despair, for if the Mulvi Sahib could not find an answer she could not face the thought of losing her son.

Without a word to Aji, she went through the open door into her vast drawing room. It was empty, for the two young women who lived there were talking on the back stairs. Seeing that she was alone Mrs Singh decided to sit at a window overlooking Dowding Street. On that side of the house there was little space between the house and fence and you could lean out of the window and look down on the street, which was separated from the palings by a deep, concrete gutter. It was her husband who hired men to weed the verge running along it because all the municipal gutters were neglected and used to be the haunts of goats which devoured anything that grew, even the breadnut leaves from the tree she had cut down.

If Betta let her down, she reflected, she would go back to India, to the place of longboats that returned at morning to auction off their catch to middlemen. It was he who had anchored her to this land where the sand burnt your feet when the tide went out. Until now she had not complained about her husband's home. Now she feared its interminable coastline and above all the poverty of those who came and would not go back.

She heard Betta closing up downstairs and, on an impulse, decided to return to the teacher's house. He was almost certainly back now. She did not want to see her son and knew that he would seek her out before he settled down to making up his accounts and patients' records.

'I'm going to see the Mulvi Sahib again,' she told Aji, who was sitting where she left her.

'Again?'

She hurried down the stairs without answering, afraid that her son would catch her before she was on the road.

This time she walked straight up Vlissingen Road and turned into the tree-lined street. The narrow wooden bridge across the trench with bollards at the entrance was blocked by two youths in conversation with a young woman accompanied by a small girl who stood some distance away. They stepped aside and allowed her to go by. Then, as she penetrated deeper into Kitty she passed more people until, on crossing Alexander Street, there were as many standing about as in the centre of town at that time of evening.

From the street she could see the teacher's profile rimmed with a line of light from a pale kerosene lamp.

'It's me, Mrs Singh . . . from Vlissingen Road!'

'Come in!'

She opened the gate, went up the stairs and greeted her son's teacher on the porch.

'Salaam!' Mrs Singh said respectfully.

And he returned the greeting with the gesture of clasped hands.

She followed him into the modest gallery and then into the drawing room. She had not seen the unusual furnishings on her first visit, the rug secured to the partition dividing it from the bedroom and a framed print of an illuminated script, because she had not bothered to look through the half-open door.

'You came earlier and I missed you. I always come by Sandibab Street when I go to the mosque.'

'Your housekeeper said you went for a walk.'

'She never listens. I said I went for *my* walk. And she knows what that means. She looks you in the eye, but doesn't listen. I used to teach a boy who was always fidgeting when all the others devoured me with their eyes. "Tell me what I said last!" I'd challenge him. And, surprised at my question, he'd always tell me exactly what I said. The housekeeper listens but doesn't hear.'

The Mulvi Sahib talked, disarming her, as he always did, knowing that when she was ready to speak she would be vulnerable. And when she was indeed ready to tell him why she came he interrupted her and called out to the housekeeper, to whom he spoke in Hindi. Then, turning to his guest, he said, 'You must have some lime juice before we talk about what's bothering you. You never came to see me once since I left your house.'

'How could I come alone? There was no man. And now that Betta's back he says he's going in two years' time.'

'I know. He told me.'

'Ah. . . . You advised him to go?'

'Tell me, Betty,' he said, using the term of endearment to mollify her. 'When you read the lives of outstanding people don't you admire them for their sacrifices? Sacrifice is at the very heart of human experience. . . . No, I did not advise him to go away, but only because I knew you would not be pleased.'

'You didn't encourage him, then.'

'No, I didn't,' the Mulvi Sahib replied. 'You should have had many children, Betty.'

She stared at him. Was he mocking her?

'I did, Mulvi Sahib. They all died because I was always down with the shivering sickness.'

She related the story he had often heard, how once, when they were living on the West Coast, Berbice, she took the ferry at Rosignol. On the boat she was seized with such a fit of shivering, that on arriving at New Amsterdam she was unable to dis-embark. Back and forth she went with the ferry, weak, tormented by the thought that she would fall over. In the end one of the sailors plucked up the courage to ask if the lady in the saffron sari and gold bangles was in some sort of trouble. She was helped off the boat and taken to a local official's house. Later that month she lost her first child. And she was to lose others until Betta came.

Her voice faltered. And while the Mulvi Sahib was waiting for her to recover the housekeeper came with a tray on which were two glasses three-quarters filled with a clouded liquid.

'He's not a boy, Betty.'

'How many sons go off to live on their own. . . ? And the family, Mulvi Sahib.'

'Why not suggest to him that he goes for five years before coming back to live with you?'

'Five years!'

'All right, all right. Do you want me to talk to him?'

Mrs Singh looked at the teacher suspiciously, thinking that she was no longer certain she could rely on him to help her. He himself did not believe he could help her either, but had already made up his mind to suggest to Betta that he extend his private practice by a year.

'What will you tell him?' she asked.

'I'll tell him to stay three years with you instead of two.'

'Mulvi Sahib. . . .'

She threw herself at his feet.

'Betty!' he said, confused at her lack of restraint.

In turn submissive and domineering, she had been an enigma to him while he lived under her roof, and he gave up his original idea of guiding her in the only way he thought seemly for a woman living alone.

'How could I do any less after I've known you so long?' he told her. 'Betty, you must control yourself. My housekeeper is a light-headed woman . . . and you're not much better. Get up. Get up, please.'

She took her seat again and accepted the glass of lime juice in water he offered her, but winced at the taste of the unsweetened drink, which was a staple of the teacher's diet.

Mrs Singh drank the concoction to the last drop and then began talking as though she had consumed a glass of alcohol. She confessed that she had no close friends among those who frequented her house, that Aji was ageing and could only speak lucidly about the old days when Mr Singh was alive and brought her back presents from abroad. She spoke of Betta's birth, that she was in labour for forty hours and even in her worst moments was determined that she would bear her child alive. Since those terrible hours she had never been afraid of physical violence. She spoke to him of her childhood and her passion for her husband before she met him. After his death, when she altered her way of living, the Pujaree spoke of her re- birth; but she knew that she had not changed.

The Mulvi Sahib, embarrassed by these confidences, took the first opportunity to say goodbye to his erstwhile employer. He saw her to the gate, where the willow-like branches of his clove trees discharged a heavy, sweet scent. She reminded him of his promise to speak to Betta, before setting out for her house by the way she had come.

Chapter 3

It was about a year after he came back as a qualified doctor that Betta met Neil Merriman, a dispenser practising at Anna Catherina. The year was 1930 and placards on the stelling exhorted people to 'Welcome in the Thirties'. Anxious about his handling of the new car his mother had bought him he carefully edged it on to the narrow planks connecting stelling and boat which undulated on the flood tide. The stranger, judging that he had only recently learned to drive, offered to take the car on to the boat for him. They talked afterwards in the first-class saloon and Dr Singh was able to offer the pharmacist a lift to his home along the coast.

On his way back from visiting his patient at Leonora he stopped as he had promised. He was to make many friends on the coast, in the bush and on the savannahs, but never again was his spirit to be in concert with another in the same way. He found in Merriman someone with whom he could share his prejudices, who lived in a household so different from his own every visit was like crossing a frontier into another country. It was a household of tie-pins and linen jackets soaked with sweat, of books on shelves – there was not a single book in his mother's house, except a copy of the Mahabharata, his old school texts and medical books – and magical devices set up by Merriman's father, a retired schoolmaster who taught music. In place of the obligatory metronome on the piano was a glass case with a celluloid ball miraculously suspended in mid-air, which the old man used to inculcate in his pupils a level of concentration which, in his view, was necessary before a pupil could even begin to play.

Merriman introduced Betta to his wife, a lady somewhat older than himself. She said that the old man was picking fruit in the yard and would come up when he had put his basket away. Then she left the two men, returning soon afterwards with home-made lemonade and black cake.

Later Betta was to wonder that neither Merriman nor his wife told him that she was well known along most of the West Coast, Demerara, for the private court she held once a week, at which she attempted to solve the problems of couples and neighbours. Years ago she had persuaded a man whose wife had run away to cut up the clothes she had left behind rather than burn down his house, which he had been threatening to do. This and other successes achieved such notoriety that she became known as the counsellor and soon found herself with so much to do that she set aside one day in the week when anyone could seek her advice. Many people gave her nothing in return, while others brought gifts of ground provisions, cloth, candles and whatever they could lay their hands on, anything except money, which she would not accept.

Before Betta returned home that afternoon he was made to inspect Merriman's drug store, which was a few hundred yards away from the house. It was a small, well-kept establishment in which the score or so of drawers were labelled with the names of their contents in gold and black letters: Cascara Sagrada, Senna, Tincture of Iodine, Lanolin, Petroleum Jelly, all so perfectly aligned and so appropriately setting off the grained wood that they seemed an extension of the Merriman household.

'I call this the "abscess room",' Merriman said, leading him into the dispensary in the back shop. 'A lot of people come to get their abscesses lanced. What I can't understand is why somebody doesn't set himself up as a lancer of abscesses.'

He and Betta laughed. Then they fell to talking about the ravages of malaria and deplored the small amounts of money spent by Demerara Sugar Estates, Bookers and other estate owners on drugs like quinine.

'If they only allowed their workers to cultivate the plots in front of their ranges their diet would improve,' Merriman said, 'and with it their resistance.'

'They're not allowed to do that?' the doctor asked, surprised at the revelation.

'No.'

His resolve to 'lose himself on a sugar estate' was fortified by this disclosure. He was convinced that his meeting with Merriman was not an accident. When he disclosed his plan Merriman's approval, like the Mulvi Sahib's tacit encouragement, made him see his mother's objection as wilful and provided him with a convenient reason for the dissatisfaction that had crept into their relationship.

Betta heard from his acquaintance about life on the coast. Indians had lost caste in their journey across the water, a constant complaint of those who claimed to be Brahmins; and the swift dismantling of the caste system which delighted many had left others bewildered and confused. He found it difficult to relate what he was hearing to the men and women he had seen from his car disappearing into the depths of villages that merged into one another with no perceptible boundary, to the shave-ice seller surrounded by a crowd of children, to the women ambling along with trays balanced on their heads, to the faded prayer flags hanging limp in the windless afternoon. He listened avidly to Merriman, whose work had provided him with a knowledge of domestic life that rivalled that of any postman.

'Well,' Merriman said, when Betta remarked on what he knew. 'Teachers know as much as I do, but their knowledge only confirms their prejudices.'

According to him the constant complaint of teachers was about the stupidity of East Indian children. The fact was that, unlike the creoles, they were kept home by their parents at sowing and harvest times. Their performance at school was, necessarily, less good than those who attended regularly.

Merriman spoke of the extreme jealousy of East Indian husbands, of the alarming vengeance taken on lovers caught with their women, traditionally smaller in number than the immigrant men.

'Mind you,' Merriman said, 'things aren't so bad among the young people born over here.'

The cutlass was the favourite murder weapon, he said. And the sight of an East Indian man sharpening his cutlass was the source of many jokes among creole estate workers.

Betta in turn recounted his experiences abroad and was able to speak of matters that would have been of no interest to his mother or the Mulvi Sahib or anyone without a technical knowledge of his craft. He spoke of his time as a houseman, the things he was required to do in that hectic year, the checking of a patient's fluid balance, the taking of his pulse and blood pressure. So much had to be borne in mind, and one error in the assessment of the patient's fluid balance could damage his pancreas irreparably. Once, while himself recovering from an operation, he became aware of himself as a 'case', that all those patients prostrate in their beds were *himself*, at the mercy of a god-like figure. Armed with the despairing knowledge of the workings of his own body he began to call to mind events from his childhood, those tranquil days, always by the sea, always with his mother whom he confused with the objects surrounding him and with the stars from which he knew his dreams came. And later he was to ask himself what it was in Merriman that emboldened him to speak as he had done.

He lingered in Merriman's drug store, unwilling to tear himself away until, alerted by the number of taxis and bicycles on the road, his acquaintance observed that the boat had come in. And when Betta drove off he felt that he had leapt over an unseen obstacle, in the manner of those healers who purport to cross invisible boundaries before being fit to cure a grave sickness.

The tide being low, Betta was able to cross the gangplanks without difficulty. He remained in his car for the crossing which, with the slack tide, only lasted a quarter of an hour. Then he drove off to his home in the outskirts of the town, keeping to the main thoroughfares and turning up Vlissingen Road towards the train lines where he was obliged to stop at the level crossing. Soon the train from Rosignol went by, scattering a fine rain of fire that settled on the allotments beside the lines.

If he had learned so much in one afternoon, he thought, as he drove the couple of hundred yards home, was he not living in a state of dangerous ignorance? Could anyone be called wise? Was Merriman wise? Was the Mulvi Sahib wise? These two men were, in different ways, perfectionists. The Mulvi Sahib was a fanatic for bodily health and mental accomplishment. Merriman, on the other hand, from the little he knew of him, seemed to be striving for knowledge of a practical formula to set the world to rights. And the Pujaree, Ma's priest friend? Betta thought. He kept his eyes on the ground, not wishing to crush any living thing. Was the anopheles mosquito, which saws through one's epidermis to make a pool of blood so that she can drink enough to lay her eggs, to be spared at the expense of the patient who succumbs to the madness of delirium? Did not man's wellbeing presuppose a continual war on animals?

Betta parked his car under his mother's mansion and watched the score or so of patients waiting for him, most of whom were ultimately victims of poor diet and an infected water supply.

The earlier anxieties about his inadequacy as a doctor were now behind him. Besides, when he made mistakes there was no one to judge him. With his growing confidence and increasing knowledge of local conditions he had no doubt as to the value of his work.

The Indians idolized him and many came after the sun went down to sit under his mother's house and listen to the lore about Betta, who 'tek he moder money an' mek somet'ing o' heself'. They admired his suit, the tailored jacket he wore during surgery hours. 'If you don' got nuf paisa 'e put de fee down in a book an' you don' got fo' pay till neverwerry mawnin'.'

On certain days his mother distributed food among the throng under the house, encouraged by her priest friend, the Pujaree.

She had got to know him when the Mulvi Sahib was discharged as Betta's teacher, when there was no ostensible reason for keeping him by her, even though she needed his guidance. The Pujaree had replaced him. He taught her many things without assuming the didactic tone the Mulvi Sahib used. He taught her where the salt went when the sea penetrated the rivers and why nothing grew on the sand washed by the sea and why water in the coastland wells rose and fell periodically. He came from Madras and she from Kerala and she resisted his claim that they were from the same part of India, the south, for she knew that there was no land like Kerala.

He had more than once recounted how he had cured a young leper. The patient's father was prepared to sacrifice a cow in the Kali Mai puja ceremony, but he protested that Kali Mai had singled her out as her victim. The man said he was still prepared to go through with the puja. The young patient was cured and the villagers helped him to expand the temple in which the former patient became a devotee.

That same evening after surgery Betta joined his mother and the Pujaree and heard the story for the first time. He could not help thinking that it was meant to inform him that there was a limit to the usefulness of his drug medicine. He wanted to say that such a spontaneous recovery in the early stages of leprosy was not uncommon, that there was a village where people pay no attention to the spots on their children's faces, knowing that few of them would develop a serious form of the disease. But he was not certain how his mother would take this show of resistance to the Pujaree's wisdom.

Betta was, in fact, interested in the limits of each type of medicine and was prepared to discuss the subject at length when he and the Pujaree knew each other better.

Aji joined the company, drawing up a chair next to Mrs Singh's. Although she tried to concentrate on the men's talk, she soon gave up and fell into her habit of dreaming her evenings away. Betta never ceased his attempts to engage her in conversation, but to little purpose. He was not even certain if she remembered who he was sometimes.

Mrs Singh called for one of the young women to make the company tea, for everyone was perspiring in the humidity, in spite of the wide-open windows and the two electric fans, which were always put on when visitors came.

The men talked and Mrs Singh never tired of listening to them. She hoped Betta would come to like the Pujaree. He now visited regularly, encouraged by his hostess, who felt the need of the company of someone as imposing as the Mulvi Sahib, but whom she was not obliged to obey.

When the tea was brought in little glass cups on a tray of brass Mrs Singh herself drew up a low table which she placed nearer the men than herself and Aji. They each began sipping the beverage. The night was singing around them, but Betta took no notice. While abroad he used to recall its song during the long winter nights when he studied in his Dublin room. On going out into the street he would imagine that the bleak landscape of naked trees and identical brick houses had been transformed into his beloved wooden cottages with their jalousies and elevated porches. Now he heard nothing, saw nothing, thought of little else except his work and his patients. He had never felt at ease in this man's company and could not decide whether he resented his influence over his mother or was contemptuous of his intellectual pretensions.

'Do you want more tea?' his mother asked the Pujaree, who declined with a gesture. 'You, Betta?'

She then asked Aji, who only grinned at her in reply.

And the men continued to talk while Mrs Singh remained to supervise their comfort through the intermediary of the two young women who were never far away, always ready to abandon their conversation on the porch and serve, like those immobile butterflies that suddenly take flight and disappear among the trees to reappear as abruptly as they had fled.

Neither the Pujaree nor Betta thought of asking Mrs Singh's opinion on anything, yet both would have been unable to continue their conversation in her absence.

The longer the Pujaree talked to Betta the less arrogant he found the young man, whose predilection for jackets and laced shoes seemed to him a dangerous affectation. He saw his mother, on the other hand, as a child of nature, embodying much that was the finest in South Indian culture. She never failed to change into her sari when he came and ran her household with the assurance he expected of a great woman, while placing little restriction on the conduct of those around her, provided all went well.

When Betta requested another cup of tea the Pujaree put the question he had wanted to ask since the doctor came upstairs.

'You think East Indians should go back to India?'

Betta reflected for a moment before answering.

'I don't know. Probably they have no choice.'

'A third of them already gone back.'

'As many as that. . . ? I bet nearly all of them were first generation though. The young people won't go.'

'True,' the Pujaree agreed. 'But should they?'

'I think you can make out as good a case for them going as staying. The death rate among them is high, so they should go. On the other hand the young people wouldn't want to, so they shouldn't. What do you think?'

'Me?' asked the Pujaree, pointing to himself. 'I think the question don' have sense.'

Betta looked at him in surprise.

'Why did you ask it, then?'

'Because your mother did ask me earlier on and someone else did ask me the same question a few days ago. I don't think is a accident when two people say the same thing in a few days.'

'So the question is not pointless,' Betta retorted.

'I think is fear that making them ask it.'

'Fear of what?' Betta demanded, determined to pin him down.

'Of everything. Of becoming beggars in town. Of . . . of losing control over the children and of the hold Christianity taking on the younger generation.'

'And from your point of view isn't that important?'

'No,' said the Pujaree.

Betta judged him to be evasive, but they continued talking even when Aji fell asleep and the young women retired without saying goodnight, for fear of interrupting the men's conversation.

In the end the Pujaree went home and Betta picked up his stethoscope from a nearby table before bidding his mother goodnight. She would not go to bed before one or two o'clock, for during the day she slept two hours with unfailing regularity

26

after the eleven o'clock main meal, when the house fell into a hallucination of muffled sounds and the young women dropped off on the interior staircase or under the house.

Chapter 4

Dr Singh, although he was rumoured to be doing well for a young man who had been in practice for just two years, was in fact heavily in debt to the bank, which had given him a substantial loan to cover the purchase of a motorcar, medical books, instruments, several suits of clothes and all the paraphernalia needed to set up a practice. His mother would have bought everything for him, but he refused to be helped any further. The patients who flocked to consult him paid for the most part in ground provisions or not at all. Most of the plantains, tanias, sweet potatoes and cassavas, once the household needs were satisfied, found their way back to indigent patients who had brought nothing and could afford to bring nothing.

All this had not been foreseen by Betta or his mother. Infuriated by the patients' attitude – many saw in their visits to the surgery not only an opportunity to be treated free of charge, but to receive a meal for their families, according to her – she would have turned away those who were unable to pay, if Betta had allowed her. No one else in the 'family', neither Aji nor the young women, saw anything wrong with the patients' conduct. Her objections perplexed them, especially as more people seemed to be depending on her largesse than ever before.

Apart from the problem of payment, Betta was concerned at his mother's apparent indifference to his decision to seek work on one of the sugar estates. Could it be that she had hatched a plan to outwit him? She was not one for sulking, preferring to yield when she could not have her own way. But in her avoidance of conflict with him there was something unreal, especially when he called to mind the period of his childhood and adolescence, how she thwarted his slightest wish to deviate from his timetable of study.

One afternoon, on going downstairs to take surgery, he found only a few patients waiting for him. He called to one of the two young women and asked why there were so few people in the waiting room, but she was visibly embarrassed by his question and claimed she did not know.

'Come down, Rani,' he told her. 'What is this? You know something?'

'No, Betta. I don't know anything,' she answered, averting her eyes. 'I don't know anything.'

'You mean you won't tell me,' he said, impatient with her readiness to deny any knowledge of the matter.

'I don't know anything, Betta! Why should I know anything?'

'Very well, Rani,' he said, powerless in the face of her stubbornness.

She ran up the stairs to get away from him.

When his first patient, a middle-aged man, came into the surgery at the sound of the bell on the table, Betta said to him, 'Anyone came down to talk to you while I was upstairs?'

'Nobody talk. I in' see nobody talkin'.'

'Mrs Singh came down here?'

'The missie? She come an' gi'e awee food.'

'And what she said?'

'She chase some people out o' t' yard before she give out the dhal pourri.'

'All right,' Betta said, calming the man.

On the enquiry as to what was wrong with him, the man answered that he had a life-sore.

'It 'pon me foot.'

Betta examined the sore on the man's left leg and wrote him a prescription for an ointment.

'It's not a life-sore,' he assured him. 'Don't wear long pants till it's healed up. Have you got money?'

'Yes, Doctor, I got money.'

'It's a dollar.'

The man pulled out a wad of notes and gave one to Betta, who entered his name and address on a blank page of a register he kept on his desk, before doing the same on a sheet from a loose-leafed accounts book which he headed with the day's date.

As the man got up to leave he said, 'I got to tek the prescription to the doctor shop?'

'Yes.'

'Which one?'

'Any dispenser will fill it.'

Every patient he treated that day was able to pay cash and with each examination his agitation grew.

It was a humid evening and the sweat ran down his neck, under his armpits and down his back in cooling, uneven runnels. Through the single window in the room came the chattering of birds in the trees, the last rays of sunshine and the chanting of a solitary voice; and with the arrival of every bus on the edge of town could be heard the coughing of engines and shouting as passengers got off and on. All pleasure had gone out of his work, Betta reflected, and the very idea of dedication seemed absurd, like the immature impulses of a callow youth.

On closing the surgery door he thought of going to see the Mulvi Sahib before he acted hastily. He could not bear having the matter out with his mother; on the other hand he was determined to put an end to her interference.

Then, for no apparent reason, Betta felt ashamed of the need to consult his teacher. He locked the room and, stethoscope in his right hand while carrying the accounts book in his left, he mounted the front stairs. Rani, who was sitting on the porch with her companion, turned away.

Betta looked down into the yard on hearing the thud of an object falling in the recently cut grass. He then looked up and saw a young man picking coconuts, evidently on his mother's orders. It was not the time to talk to his mother, he decided with some relief, and remained standing on the porch to watch the heavy young fruit drop beside the palings.

The coconuts came down, one by one, at long intervals, but with the regularity of a blacksmith's hammer; and with each thud there was a slight reverberation of the earth. Two small boys stopped on the road to watch and hear the falling fruit.

'Gi'e me a coconut, mister!' one of them shouted.

'They got centipede up there?' the other one asked.

The man, around whose feet a belt was attached, ignored them and went on with his work.

Dr Singh entered the house and, not seeing his mother, imagined she was in the kitchen or upstairs. He laid his account books and stethoscope on a round table in a corner and went into the kitchen to wash his hands. Then, undecided as to what he should do next, he went back to a front window.

His practice had turned out to be entirely different from what he had expected. Apart from problems of payment he was taken aback by the hypochondria afflicting many patients. Any sore that did not heal readily was described as a life-sore. Besides, he was surprised to discover that there was a high incidence of diabetes among East Indians, while creoles frequently complained of constipation. He could not help feeling that, far from being equipped to practise, his university studies had done no more than equip him to learn. But what astonished him more than anything else was that he had come across only a few cases of malaria, the demon that had drawn him to medicine. The swampy East Coast as far as Buxton, the area from which nearly all his patients came, was a notorious breeding ground for the anopheles mosquito. He intended to get in touch with a colleague to solve the mystery, for the time was approaching when he was to apply for a job on one of the estates, where most of the country's East Indians were concentrated.

The coconuts had stopped falling, but he had not noticed the man come down from the tree. The young women were gathering the fruit, which lay pell-mell in the yard.

'Here's one,' one of them would say, and the discovery would be accompanied by laughter.

Over the grass verge between the gutter and the broad pitch road candleflies lit up the dark with brief bursts of light. He could not quarrel with his mother, he thought. 'Impatience is the devil of fools; patience is the devil of cowards.' Thus the Pujaree had spoken, like a dealer in mystifications whose customers know not what to make of his words. However many patients were turned away he could not quarrel with her. The day he declared he was leaving was approaching inexorably, like the coming of the seasons, the waning of the moon and those bursts of lightning above a distant horizon.

He found himself thinking of women. Throughout his youth and early manhood he had had no time to do so. Now, in his twenty-eighth year, there was just as little time, he told himself, knowing that it was not true. In his teens he dismissed anyone approaching the age of thirty as old. In a couple of years he would have crossed that threshold without having resolved so many things he once discussed passionately while at university. The students never discussed marriage, he now realized. The subjects they avoided were as revealing as those that occupied their talk in the refectory or in the hour before sleep when they lay awake, unable to ignore the noise made by students whose lectures began later than theirs. He confessed to himself that he was attracted to Rani, who never failed to leave her bedroom door ajar when she was brushing her hair and knew that he had not yet retired for the night. And he found himself timing his ascent to bed in anticipation of seeing the band of light across the banister. He was ashamed of 'behaving like a boy'. Far from being impulsive, he could not bear to catch himself out in conduct he would have despised in someone else. He knew that the seat of his disturbance lay in that head of hair especially when lit by an unshaded electric bulb. And each night he staggered past her room to his own, where the noise made by the Delco plant disturbed his thoughts.

In his mother's opinion his mind was preoccupied with working on an estate. For the two young women he was the authoritative doctor-son of the authoritative mistress, who had forgotten how to tackle a meal of crabs and would be one day as rich as she was. Who could have imagined that one corner of his mind was obsessed with a mass of black hair, like those men who do not work and spend all their time thinking of women. A doctor who received letters sealed with red wax was not capable of such obsessions! One only had to look at the way he carried himself, at the slow, deliberate manner of turning his head when a question was put to him to realize that he inhabited a superior plane of existence. He, like other doctors, drove around in cars, wore fine suits and had even learned a special doctor walk. And if that was the way many people saw him it was more or less the way Betta saw himself. Acutely aware of his position, especially among the East Indian community, he had rarely been able to relax. And, with some anxiety, he noticed that his gestures, even when he was alone, were taking on the same stiff, puppet-like definition he assumed for his public appearances. Aware though he was of what was happening to him, he could do nothing to arrest the process. Indeed, he was beginning to question the very reality of those impulses that declared themselves as a boy and even as late as his early twenties. Now, considering his feelings for Rani, he decided they were an embarrassment. Like a tree denying the existence of its roots because they were invisible, he concentrated on the contemplation of his public conduct, the trunk and the leaves that shook when the wind blew.

Betta put his stethoscope away in its case, and, deciding he could not face anyone, began to prepare for bed. But, not being in the habit of retiring at such an early hour, and uneasy about a feeling of something left undone, he put on his clothes again and left his room with the intention of visiting the Mulvi Sahib. He had not seen him for several weeks, except on one or two occasions when he passed by the house on his way from the Church Street mosque.

Betta shouted out to his mother that he was going into the village to see the Mulvi Sahib, hoping that she had not heard him. But no sooner was he on the stairs than she put her head out of an upstairs window – the window of the room next to his own – and called, 'Betta, where're you going when you haven't eaten?'

'I'll be about an hour or so.'

'Eat first, ne?'

'When I come back,' he answered, without stopping.

She spread out her hands in exasperation and watched him walking up the road, wondering whether he was so angry at her interference with his practice that he was refusing to eat at table. Earlier on she had gone upstairs to avoid meeting him when his surgery was over, and when he called out to her she was sitting on the bed, trembling in anticipation of a quarrel. Expecting him to seek her out at any moment her agitation had grown until, on hearing him call, she started involuntarily. Now she felt sure that he was angry and had gone out walking, the better to collect his thoughts. Their quarrel would come later, when he returned, with his words carefully prepared.

Mrs Singh came downstairs.

'Lahti! You paid the coconut man?'

'Yes, Miss Singh,' Rani's companion answered, surprised at Mrs Singh's sudden appearance downstairs.

'How was the doctor?'

'How you mean?' Lahti asked in turn.

'Did he look vexed?'

'No. He look in a hurry to go out.'

'And he said where he was going?'

'He shouted up he was going to the Mulvi Sahib,' Rani answered this time. 'You didn' hear him?'

'Would I have asked if I had?'

She stood in the middle of the drawing room considering what to do next.

'How you girls can sit all night doing nothing is beyond me,' she declared in the end. 'I'm perspiring like a horse and the two of you sit around as if nothing . . . as if the wind was blowing.'

She began opening the windows, each one as wide as possible, and, as if to give weight to her words, stopped from time to time to fan herself vigorously with her hands.

'It's all these trees round the house,' she continued. 'I must cut down some of them to let the air through. 'What's the point having all these windows if you can't breathe?'

She wanted to howl with impatience at her impotence in the face of events she could not control; and it did not occur to her that her agitation was the direct result of her action in turning away patients who could not afford to pay her son cash.

So he's gone to the Mulvi Sahib, she reflected. Why? To ask his advice? No, Betta wouldn't do that. He's too proud.

'Rani!' she called.

Indolently, Rani turned round, unimpressed by the excitable tone of her voice. She was the only one in the world who would scream for a person only a few feet away and was also capable of hearing a name uttered in a whisper. The effect of the scream on Rani was far less great than that of Dr Singh's demand to extract information from her with regard to the missing patients.

'Child,' said Mrs Singh, 'you are untrustworthy. You told Betta I sent away those spongers . . .'

'I didn't,' Rani answered.

'She didn't, Miss Singh,' Lahti confirmed.

'How can you know?' Mrs Singh snapped. 'If she told him under the house and you were upstairs how could you know? I take you in and feed you and you . . .'

'It was only a few patients today,' Rani persisted. 'The doctor must've noticed right away.'

'You're devious, child. You'll end up like your mother.'

Mrs Singh did not believe a word of what she said, but nonetheless continued insulting Rani, who kept her eyes fixed on her benefactress.

'Everyone must be judged by their deeds,' Mrs Singh continued, then went on to speak of her father, who once lost a copper coin while he was a little boy, and was ordered by his father to look for it on the village road, even though rain was falling hard. She had told the tale several times and usually dragged it up as a sop to her fury when Rani or Lahti upset her.

'My father had to look in all that rain for *one* copper coin. You young people don't know how easy you've got things. Ask Aji,' she shouted, nodding towards the upper storey, where she thought the old woman might be.

Rani and Lahti knew the storm would subside, that Mrs Singh would then go to her bedroom and pace up and down diagonally from wardrobe to door, from door to wardrobe until her son came home, and then interrupt her wandering to gaze out of the window in order to catch sight of him.

When, ashamed of the absurdity of the charge she had laid at Rani's door, Mrs Singh broke off in the middle of her tirade, she stood near the two young women, astonished by her conduct, by the realization, after all these years, that her husband was really dead and by all that had befallen her since her marriage as if it had all happened to someone else and she had just heard tell of it. She listened to the silence created around her by her dictatorial voice and was ashamed that Rani's irresponsible smile had vanished and that Lahti seemed cowed by her outburst.

'I can't stand ingratitude,' she said quietly.

Then, with a gesture of desperation, she went off to her room, reflecting as she went that as a girl she never defended herself, that as a wife she never raised her voice, that soon after her husband's death she had her long hair cut, took to wearing trousers and discovered the tumult behind her expressionless face and a terrible desire to exercise power over Aji and her husband's hangers-on.

The Pujaree had advised her months ago to give a fête for the poor in order to relieve the pain that came with the anticipation of her son's departure for the countryside; but she was still convinced that he would not leave her. The Pujaree had warned her not to act foolishly when he heard how some patients, far from paying their fee, went away with provisions her son had given them. Besides, the poor had to borrow money from a relation or from a moneylender in order to consult a doctor. She had not taken his advice and was now certain that to keep Betta by her she would be obliged to resort to desperate measures.

Soon afterwards the young women heard the footsteps above their heads; and although that was what they had been expecting they could not break their own silence, which had been imposed on them by Mrs Singh's accusations. They took up positions on the ample porch to watch the outlines of passers-by on cycles, like ghosts under the racing clouds. Rani, offended by Mrs Singh's reference to her mother, would not speak to Lahti of her resentment, but let it grow until it blotted out all the respect she had for her. Even Aji, despite her dotage, would not have offended her so. Tomorrow, perhaps, her resentment would pass; but perhaps it would not. Whenever she was beset by troubles she would sleep on her back. Tonight she would sleep on her side, while not caring to forget the insults she had been obliged to endure.

Rani and Lahti kept each other company without uttering a word, until the silence gave way to the late hooting of owls hunting between the trees and the crackling of decaying branches.

Lahti fell asleep, unable to sustain company without conversation, while Rani, at a loss for the reason why she was incapable of maintaining an angry posture, gazed in the direction where the sun sank without trace, thinking that one day she must find someone to oust the doctor in her secret affection.

Chapter 5

Aji had fallen into a confusion of hours in which 'now' and 'soon' were little distinguishable from time past. She slept in the same room as Mrs Singh, who was in the habit of speaking to her after the light was turned out, without expecting to be answered. Occasionally the old woman broke out into a monologue, usually a long complaint against Rani and Lahti who lacked respect for her and called her 'old lady' when Mrs Singh was out of earshot, or against the inhumanity of time which mocked her by presenting Mrs Singh's husband as if he were still alive and gave her gifts of jewellery and prints of Indian gods. It was Aji who first suggested setting aside a day for feeding the poor. Mrs Singh might have done so later in the year in any case, but her relief that Betta had not quarrelled with her was so great she decided to take the advice at the earliest opportunity.

Having decided to enlist the Pujaree's assistance in rounding up as many destitute Indians as could stand in her yard she mentioned her plan to Aji who, she thought, might have fallen asleep. But the old lady's answer came promptly, 'Kiss me ass!'

So accustomed had she become to this sort of treatment from her dependant-servant that it no longer offended her, provided no one was there to witness it.

The next day Mrs Singh sent the two young women to the Pujaree's home with a note in which she explained what she had in mind and suggested a Friday afternoon. They left early in the morning for Campbleville when the scent of decaying vegetation and wild flowers was still strong. Empty dray carts went past them, heading for the train lines, their horses wearing hats against a sun that had only just risen. On the porches of large houses children and servants were beating mats and hanging sheets out of side windows.

Soon they arrived aback where the canefields had been

recently burnt and harvested and stumps of cane rose out of the blackened ground like the remnants of a disaster.

On arriving at the Pujaree's house they caught sight of his boy-nephews, who often came visiting with him. They disappeared as one through the doorway, but were soon back to take up their former positions in a manner that suggested they were guarding the entrance to the house. Rani recalled how as a girl of twelve the twins came with the Pujaree to apply a heated glass to Mrs Singh's belly, as a cure for the nahra which had afflicted her for weeks. But contrary to Aji's expectations the twist in Mrs Singh's intestines slowly unwound under the upturned glass.

'The Pujaree there?' Rani asked.

'He coming,' they answered in unison.

'Ah, yes,' he said, on learning about Mrs Singh's plan. 'Tell Miss Singh any Friday would suit me. Two weeks from now, eh, girls? Two weeks from now. She's a good woman. Look at you girls, eh? Look how you so filled out, as if she fattenin' you up for market, eh? A good woman. When you get married she goin' give you a good dowry, you wait and see. All you got to do is behave good. Tell her two Fridays from now. Wait here till I come back.'

He left them with the twins, who were staring unashamedly.

Young sea-island cotton shrubs dotted the yard, which was surrounded by high grass among which two goats were grazing. The girls were surprised at the simplicity of the Pujaree's dress and way of life for whenever he came visiting he was always attired in well-laundered dhoti, shirt and brown shoes. They were both saving up impressions for the journey back home and the time after dark when they sat on the stairs and discussed everything that came into their mind.

The Pujaree returned carrying a paper bag.

'The bag in the bag is for you girls,' he said. 'But the big bag is for Miss Singh. In it you goin' find simatoo and sea-grapes. They don't grow in her yard.'

He gave Rani the paper bag and dismissed them with an unambiguous gesture which meant, 'You are young girls. I'm a grown man with work to do'.

'We can't sit down a little bit?' Lahti asked, disappointed at having to leave so quickly.

'If alyou want,' he said drily.

Once he was out of sight Lahti thrust her hand in the bag and took out one of the cakes. They sat at the door in silence, eating the contents of the paper bag and listening to the clucking of the Pujaree's hens, unseen in the surrounding bushes. In their estimation he was a man of lesser stature than the Mulvi Sahib, who lived by the money he earned and not by handling sheep and fowls and spinning his own cotton.

The poor began arriving at about eleven in the morning, the hour of the main meal. Mrs Singh, anticipating this, had got Rani and Lahti to put the pots on two mud stoves under the house which some of the male helpers had made ten days ago for the purpose; and by midday the two young women, Mrs Singh and Betta were sharing out dhal pourri on sections of plantain leaves.

Word had got around that food was being given out and in a couple of hours after the first sharing the bottom house was full of people standing in line, waiting to be served. A few had even brought their own piece of plantain leaf and in their eagerness to get near the food some of them lost their tempers, accusing others of elbowing their way forward. But when it became evident that there was enough for all, the two lines of bare-footed, scantily clad people settled into that monumental patience which the well-off thought proper to their condition.

A chance remark, that in the pots tended by the two women kitri was being prepared, led one toothless lady to say that she did not come three miles to eat poor people's food, to which the man behind her said that she should not be there anyway, since the share-out was for people living in the district.

'Paisa na bah!' the woman protested, declaring her poverty in a whining voice to make up for her blunder.

Betta, while ladling out the dhal pourri, was thinking of surgery and of taking blood samples of two patients he had asked to come back. He looked over to his mother from time to time, wondering at her glistening sari and youthful appearance. Early that morning he had been asked to examine a cartman's lame donkey which was tethered to a tree some way down the road.

He sutured the animal's lame leg and only then was he told by its owner that he could not pay. Angry at what he saw as a deception he walked off in a fit of rage without bothering to take the man's name. Now, confused about his rôle as a doctor, the difficulty in collecting his fees, about clients' belief that he was as agreeable to treating their animals as he was to attending their children, he cast his eyes around the crowd waiting to have as much put on their plantain leaves as they could hold. Could his mother's resistance to being 'taken advantage of' be the way he would see things after a few years of practice? Then, of a sudden, he realized that on a sugar estate he would be paid a salary, and his resentment vanished at the thought.

His attention wandering at that moment, Betta spilled a ladle full of food on the ground. A middle-aged woman who had already eaten offered to clean it up and Betta told her that she would be given a broom upstairs. She could go back up and rest afterwards if she wished.

A crowd had gathered at the front gate and Betta was already giving thought to a decision he did not think he would have to take: it would have to be closed when the throng grew beyond the capacity of the yard.

The woman came back downstairs, accompanied by Aji, who was carrying a pointer broom and an empty sugar bag. Dressed in her best sari, she sailed through the crowd ahead of the woman.

'Le' me do it. You hold the bag!' she ordered.

In the same regal manner she made her way to the bins behind the back stairs, emptied them, then returned to the centre of the crowd.

'Aji,' Betta told her, interrupting his work, 'can you get one of the bigger men to shut the gate and tell him only to let in patients. I'll be starting surgery in about half an hour.'

'Is only you they goin' listen to, Betta,' she said.

But she went all the same to seek out any tall man who was willing to act as a watch at the gate. And, although reluctant to undertake what she had been asked to do, she soon found two strapping men and posted them at each side of the front entrance.

And so, with the sound of the gate creaking from time to time to let in those who claimed to be patients and the protests of those who had been locked out, the crowd in both streets stood watching the extraordinary spectacle of victuals being shared out in private grounds.

The sun had long passed its zenith and cast louvred shadows beyond the palings along a path cleared by the watchers at the gate. Aji, seeing her opportunity to make an impression on the poor with full stomachs, began telling them tales from the time when Mrs Singh's husband was alive. But she soon retired to the surgery in order to hold forth in greater security. In a vengeful voice she informed the waiting patients that Mrs Singh did not feed her properly, in spite of her years of service in the household. If Mr Singh were alive he would not put up with it, because he had never once failed in his duty as her protector, even though she once slandered him when some spiteful person poured rum in her cup of cha and made her lose control over her words. Mrs Singh had always been jealous of him and could not bear to hear talk of his good deeds towards the poor, because she believed she could match him in his concern. While he was dying she promised him she would build a Dharam Sala for the destitute, but promptly forgot her undertaking once he was buried in a Christian cemetery where no one had 'died', but only 'passed away' or 'fallen asleep'. He was always constructing something, and in the months before he died he had been making an apiary of glass, for he believed it would be easier to entice a queen back into a transparent structure where the swarm would follow her. He thought he would live to be a hundred because he drank a pint of water daily from his lignum vitae cup, while *she* had always been sickly and caused him much distress because she would only take medicine that had been sent her from Kerala. No one believed she would outlive him, even though she was much younger.

'She does go on as if the Pujaree is God. An' you should see him when he at home an' don' got no shirt on. But in this house he does behave like I is dutty powder or somet'ing.'

She wandered from subject to subject, and when Mrs Singh, her suspicions aroused, came and listened at the surgery door, she was reassured that the old lady was in the midst of a description of the bonanza of fishes that was washed up on the seashore twenty years ago when people collected mullet and queriman in baskets and middlemen raised a rumour that the fishes were poisoned.

Mrs Singh went back to sharing out the new pot of food to the last of the unfed. She quickly surveyed the crowd, spread out like a colony of birds, and congratulated herself that all had gone well. Had Betta appreciated her gesture? Deep down she felt dissatisfied, as if the result of her day's work was not what she had intended. Perhaps the only way to attain all the things she wanted was to arrange to sacrifice in a puja under the Pujaree's direction.

'Miss Singh, me wan' more,' an old man was begging her.

'I saw Dr Singh give you food just now,' she told him, annoyed above all at his subservient posture.

'Me know, miss, but me hungry.'

She scraped the bottom of the pot for him. There was a burst of laughter from the surgery and Mrs Singh looked over in the direction of Betta, who was on the point of loosening the makeshift apron that protected his shirt. Sitting on the ground next to him was an aged woman with her skirt tucked between her legs and surrounding her four young children who had eaten but were waiting to be taken home. She had heard a false rumour that bread would be given out as well and like most of the others had no intention of going away until they were certain of having received all that there was to come.

'Ma,' Betta said, coming over to her. 'I'm going up to get ready for surgery.'

'Things went well, eh?' she said questioningly.

He smiled at her, but said nothing, leaving her to wonder if he was pleased or displeased, to reflect endlessly on the enigma of the silence he had brought back from abroad. She stared beyond the yard at the sky and the passage of fragmented clouds and on the surface of her skin there was a coldness like some great grief.

Another burst of laughter came from the surgery. Aji was now in full flight, hopping about between the benches on which patients were ranged. She had exhausted the subject of the dead Mr Singh, had slandered Mrs Singh as well as she knew how and was now saying whatever came into her mind.

'He's a good doctor, the best on the whole coast. He goin' go away in the bush where they in' got roads and you got to travel by river and creek. He goin' go and cure the sick like Jesus Christ when the people was too poor to pay money. He goin' raise people from the dead, too, you watch. I telling you 'cause I see him do things only his father could do.'

Aji continued her interminable monologue, encouraged by the Ahs of her ailing audience. She told them how she had been received into the Methodist Church, which her father had joined to secure advancement in his job, against the wishes of her mother, who continued teaching her Hindi in secret.

A man squatting on the floor opposite her interrupted the account: 'Me hear you does fo'get when you eat. Is so you say, I hear. You fo'get everyt'ing. Is true?'

'Me? Forget? Me? I remember the day I come to Mr Singh house as if was yesterday. Kiss me ass!'

A woman, anxious that the entertainment should not come to an end, said reprovingly, 'Lef she, ne. Don' bother with he, Aji. He does always get 'e story wrong.'

Aji, encouraged by this support, adopted a regal stance and surveyed the audience as though she were doing them a favour.

'Who say I does fo'get? I remember the doctor when he was a lil boy, how he did wan' to go to school like the other children and how she say no, 'cause he was too good fo' bakrah school and she family was proud and how she father was a rope maker in Kerala and use to buy thousands o' coconut every month to spin the fibre 'pon a wheel. But she lie! Lie? When she mouth open is only lies does come out. Me? Forget? I did say in them days the boy goin' grow up to be a great man. I could tell from the cut of his jib. When she allow him out of the yard in the afternoon he use to gather the children round him an' say, "You do this! An' you, you do that!" And they did do it an' like it. An' them same children did bring him fruit as if he was Lord Krishna 'self. Me? Forget? But *she*, soon as she open she mouth is . . .'

Aji's audience had fallen silent and she instinctively looked round, to find Mrs Singh standing in the doorway; and in her confusion she began gesticulating aimlessly.

'I din' say nothin' bad,' she said defiantly.

Then, turning to the patients, she pleaded, 'I say anything bad? Is wha' you lookin' at me like that for? If Mr Singh was alive you couldn' look at me like that.'

Aji's confusion was now complete and she suddenly turned and flounced off from the spot where she had delivered her last sentence, past Mrs Singh and into the crowd outside.

'You sit there and encourage her in her lies,' Mrs Singh told the patients. 'But it doesn't stop you from getting free medicine from my son.'

No one dared look at her, and when she left them many of them worried lest the result of her anger might be that the doctor would not take surgery that afternoon. But Betta arrived on time to find the waiting room flooded with the late afternoon sunlight and his patients more subdued than they had been for some time.

Outside, the yard and bottom house were strewn with the debris of the sharing and Mrs Singh had already sent word to a neighbour to bring over her dogs to eat the food that had been spilled lest it attracted rats.

The gate stood abandoned and from time to time the few people under the trees and in the bottom house would stir either in expectation of some occurrence or to take leave of someone who had decided to depart for home.

Rani and Lahti, unaware of the scene between Mrs Singh and Aji, found it odd that she had left them to put the yard in order on their own. They were both looking forward to bed after their day's work and neither of them was thinking of the day's incidents, which they would discuss the following evening when they sat alone on the porch: the gluttony of some older people, the family who sat in a corner of the yard waiting to be served and, eventually, had to be fed from the family pot upstairs, and the threat of anarchy in the early stages when it was believed that there was not enough to go round.

Soon the electric bulbs cast their light on the front stairs and the hum of the Delco plant joined the drumming of a tabla from under the trees.

Mrs Singh sat alone, nurturing her resentment at the way Aji had behaved. Once before she had all but thrown her out, but at the last moment the thought of her stretched out on a pavement in Water Street or huddled in the corner of a yard at the mercy of fierce dogs had caused her to change her mind. It was curious that now, when she needed her protection more than ever, the old woman was at her most dangerous. From the porch she could see, beyond the train lines, the lights of Georgetown like an enormous ship in the dark, an immobile vessel her husband would approach but never board, intimidated by the things his money could buy, by its markets crammed with merchandise he did not need, by its perfumed smells he associated with the boudoirs of whores, by its teashops where, he had heard, the sugar bowls were of blue stoneware, and by its languorous air which made him take alarm. Only the down-and-out East Indians from the estates went to live there, he believed, taking that fatal step across the train lines as an alternative to the voyage back to India at the end of their indenture. Where did the stragglers under her house live? With whom? And why were they reluctant to go home? She knew what her conversation with the Pujaree would be that night. She could even imagine him sitting opposite her now. She would say, 'You don't know what I've had to put up with since my husband died. I've had nothing ... no love, no understanding. People claiming to be my husband's relations come to see me to borrow money. "Le' me tell you how to mek more money, daughter. Le' awee invest you money fo' you, ne?" And they grow with every year and become bolder with every year. ... No, I won't come to the temple. ...' She would then pull her achal down over her face as in the time of her subservience. And he would talk of rebirth and the three nights of ceaseless activity which would end when he threw water upon water when the sluice gate opened. And would he not try and wrench from her a promise to prostrate herself before Durga's image on the occasion of the next puja, the self-same Durga who had robbed her of her children? And they would talk on, accompanied by the barking of tethered dogs in the adjacent yard.

Chapter 6

With the onset of the rains, the extensive fields opposite Mrs Singh's house were flooded. Sultry days succeeded one another and all activity seemed to be affected by the languor of the mornings, when a red sun rose behind the trees in the back yard. In the humidity the towels, hung out from the rear windows, were covered with a fungoid growth, and the women despaired of drying the linen.

Stories were featured in the newspapers of a plague of rats that were destroying the rice crops, especially in the backlands of the Courantyne where there had been a campaign to rid the area of labaria snakes. The rats had even migrated down to the sea in search of food and had taken to robbing the fishermen's nets.

'The world comin' to an end,' Aji kept saying to Rani and Lahti. 'Youal don' listen to me and you goin' regret it. Why you think the towels don' dry? An' you ever see sun bleeding? You read what happen to the lady down the road? How she been walkin' through the burial groun' and a concrete grave next to the road suddenly collapse an' a swarm of rats run out from under it? You tell me all these things happening normal?'

As the old woman spoke Rani nudged Lahti, but the latter, frightened by the ancient voice intoning disaster and by her recollection of the rat she had seen the day before scurrying for shelter under the bridge over the drainage trench, did not respond. It was a season of portents. Everything was possible; everything was believed. Rani had seen rats on more than one occasion, always near the water; but it had never occurred to her that they were any more dangerous than mice or lizards. Indeed, the chicken hawks whose shadows sent hens scurrying around the neighbouring yards seemed infinitely more threatening. Yet Aji's words and the newspaper reports roused a slumbering unease about the secretive rodents, which were seen only infrequently because they usually foraged at night.

Lahti was foolish beyond words, Rani reflected. She could talk to her about her feelings for the doctor, about Mrs Singh's plans for marrying her off or about her desire to have many children. But she could discuss nothing beyond her experience. And it was at such times she felt that Aji, with her impertinence and unpredictable behaviour, was a better companion.

'The price o' rice goin' go up, mark my words,' Aji predicted. 'It happen when I was a girl. Alyou don' believe me when I talk. Is 'cause all these things happening that . . .'

'Stop talkin' nonsense!' Lahti said, interrupting her.

'You talkin' to me?' Aji asked. 'To *me*?'

Aji slapped Lahti so hard that she lost her balance and nearly fell.

'You talkin' to me?' she repeated. 'I goin' to complain to Miss Singh 'bout you, girl.'

Lahti dared not say what she wanted to say and Aji saw the look of contempt on her face. But before the old woman could react Lahti left the kitchen, consumed with anger.

'You know what a rat is?' Aji asked Rani. 'How you goin' know? You never leave this house except to go on errands *she* send you, or to do shopping when the cook late. Well, my girl, a rat is a whore. That's what they call them in town. You're all rats an' *she* is the biggest rat of all. An' your friend Lahti is Princess Rat. Alyou two think you does run this house since you grow up!'

'Aji,' Rani said gently, 'nothing's wrong.'

After looking at her long and affectionately, Aji smiled as though they had been enjoying a pleasant conversation.

'You not a rat, Rani. I'm a rat. I'm the rat in this house.'

When Aji heard the cook's footsteps on the stairs she left Rani without a word.

It was early morning and the cook was dropping in to pick up her shopping list. Having enquired of Rani if the lady who sold greens had come, the cook took the list from the top of the meshed storage safe where Mrs Singh always left it.

Rani sensed that things were not well in the house. Mrs Singh no longer engaged in lengthy conversations with her son after surgery hours and since the gentleman from Anna Catherina came to visit him the gulf between them seemed to have grown. The two Saturdays since he came the doctor went off immediately after morning surgery and did not return until late at night. He had never been in such high spirits. Rani confided in Lahti that she was jealous of the people he was going to visit. Why should he dress so well if a woman was not involved? He never failed to tell his mother goodbye and she would rush upstairs after he left the house and watch from a window to see his car drive off in the direction of the train lines. Then, as if commanded to be discreet in a house where someone was gravely ill, they all went around on tiptoe.

The portents and Dr Singh's Saturday outings were all connected in some way, Rani told herself. She went downstairs to feed the chickens. Several boys had congregated on the bridge connecting the house with Vlissingen Road. One of them was running along the edge of the trench with a large basket in his hand, uncertain whether to defy Aji, who was shouting at them to get off the bridge. So it was whenever the trench was swollen with the rains and shrimps found their way into gutters that fed the alleyways. Rani would have gone to her assistance, but was afraid of offending her, for she, too, was affected by Mrs Singh's uncertain mood.

The yard, built up long before old Mr Singh's death, was rarely affected by the heavy rains, and rose like the road itself above the flooded field opposite and the surrounding yards. While she threw a mixture of paddy and maize to the hens and cocks Rani wondered where the rats lived and considered the possibility of Mrs Singh's house being invaded by an army of the underground animals. Then, without any transition, her thoughts turned to Dr Singh. It was Saturday and he was due to come down to the surgery, where a few patients were waiting for him. Would he be going out again, she wondered. Up to a few weeks ago her love was quiet, protected by the realization that nothing could come of it. But since the visit of the man from Anna Catherina she had been seized by an unreasoning dislike of anyone who might attract him away from his mother's home, just as though she were married to him and they had come to an arrangement that they would tell each other where they went. His occasional visits when he was called to a sick bed were bearable, but these sorties about which not even Mrs Singh dared to speak left her helpless. At no time in the past did Lahti appear to her so childish and insensitive and she could not understand how she had ever confided in her the secret feelings that now tormented her. If Mrs Singh did find her a husband how could she enter into a marriage in that state of mind? She was terrified lest Mrs Singh suspect her feelings, believing that at a time like that when she herself was not on good terms with her son, she was capable of guessing what was passing through her mind. She had lost her appetite, but was obliged to eat as heartily as Lahti did at table, with Mrs Singh supervising meals and sharing out the food.

Rani admired her benefactress's ability to suffer while be-having like someone untouched by suffering. In fact she had never managed to understand her, her relations with the Pu-jaree and the Mulvi Sahib, her son and Aji. All of them were close to her in one way or another, yet she seemed capable of suffering alone, while she, Rani, could not resist the urge to confide in Lahti for long, or were she not there, in Aji.

Rani's jealousy of the doctor had given her an insight into his behaviour no one else suspected to be otherwise than forth-right. Why should he not be visiting the Merrimans if he said so? And how could an association with a woman remain undetected for long, since a car parked regularly in a certain place would not fail to attract attention? But such questions did not occur to Rani who relied on her observations of his eagerness to leave the house and on a quality in his deportment she could not define.

Rani's suspicions were entirely justified. Betta had become friendly with a family who had moved to Georgetown some years ago. The father, now dead, had taken one of the familiar routes from estate to town, working first as an interpreter in the Assize Courts and various Magistrates Courts, then as a revenue runner, a badly paid post which allowed him to buy his groceries at cost price, as a reward for warning shopkeepers of impending visits to check their weights and measures. Both he and his wife died during the great malaria epidemic of 190x. Their daughter, the object of Betta's visits, had grown to maturity with an uncle and aunt, her mother's brother and sister-in-law, who had seized the opportunity to apprentice her to a neighbour who repaired cane-bottomed chairs.

When Betta was first called to attend the young woman he now visited nearly every Saturday, he was surprised at the trivial nature of her complaint, for even well-off Indians did not send for a doctor when common ailments were suspected. While filing down the tip of a metal nail she had received a surface cut, which most people would have washed and treated with tincture of iodine. The concern shown by her numerous aunts and uncles was so clearly out of proportion to the negligible wound that Betta could not help asking the most senior uncle why she did not treat the cut herself.

'She so nice-looking, Doctor, how we goin' take the risk?'

A rank, pervasive odour, out of place in town, hung on the atmosphere and made Betta think of those remote hovels beyond the back-dam, whose thatched roofs harboured all manner of insects. The walls were bare and, as far as he could tell, the only furnishings were the numerous beds scattered about the bedroom and drawing room.

Betta was asked to return and assured that they would not hold back his fee. They knew about the numerous patients who owed him money and had no intention of paying.

'Come an' examine Betty again, fo' make sure,' the senior uncle urged him.

Puzzled by their exaggerated anxiety he returned to the house a fortnight later and found Betty in the drawing room in the midst of stacks of cane, which filled the area with the same rank odour he had noticed on his last visit. She was sitting on a bed, bent over a half-caned, straight-backed chair, holding in one hand a length of rattan beneath the seat while she inserted a wooden plug in a hole through which it had been drawn with the other.

Betty's delight at seeing him was so touching he was tempted to make some extravagant comment on her appearance, but restrained himself, mindful of the people present. He recognized none of them and asked Betty where her uncles and aunts were.

'They all uncles and aunts. Some does live here and some does got they own place.'

'Is that the nail you were filing down when you cut yourself?' he asked, noticing the nail she had just picked up after securing the length of cane in the hole.

'Yes. I need it to do this.'

Betta watched her manipulating the cane with rapid movements of her fingers.

'That's the tool you use?'

'Yes.'

'The only one?'

'Yes.'

'Let me see your finger.'

She glanced round the room at her assembled uncles and aunts, as if seeking approval; but, receiving no encouragement, she assured him that it had healed completely. Then she applied herself to her task once more with deft, almost manic gestures.

In spite of her puppet-like appearance in the midst of her greying relations there was an indescribable repose in her manner, so that Betta found it difficult to keep his eyes off her.

'I'd better go,' Betta said, seeking by some sign confirmation that he was welcome.

Betty stopped working and sank her head.

'Since you're better . . .', Betta began.

'We didn' give you anything to drink.'

The words came like a plea, challenging Betta to depart. He sat down once more on the bed which two uncles and an aunt were sharing with him.

'Please to get the doctor a cup of tea,' Betty said without addressing either of the two beds of uncles and aunts.

The aunt sitting on his bed stood up and went to the back of the house. In the ensuing silence Betta could do no more than watch his patient threading the cane through the holes on the edge of the chair seat and recalled the tea house in Stabroek with its genteel air and the unhurried service of two middle-aged women. Here was the same repose, due not to the impeccable style of its furniture, nor the absence of any conflict, but solely to the unusual young woman who worked with the tireless application of someone possessed.

When he left he knew that he would return, in spite of the innumerable aunts and uncles whose idleness seemed a curious counterpoint to their niece's ceaseless labour.

The next Saturday, although he could find no excuse for visiting, he went and knocked on his patient's door, which opened at once.

'Yes?' an uncle from his first visit said.

'I've come to see my patient.'

'She say she in' sick no more.'

'Doctor?' came the young woman's voice.

She appeared at the door with the same welcoming expression that had seduced him the last time and he followed her in, past the disobliging uncle. And she herself brought him tea in an enamel mug, a sweet concoction of lemon grass. Then she set about her task of caning a bent-wood rocking chair whose runners were propped up at the back by a length of wood.

Almost at once they were joined by three men, summoned no doubt by the uncle who had come to the door. They sat down next to one another on the third bed and began staring at Betta.

'Do you ever stop working?' he asked her, pretending not to notice the unannounced arrival of the men.

'Sometimes.'

'When?'

'When no work come.'

Their meagre conversation resembled those of his past and future visits, doing no more than signalling each other's presence, as though they were in a pitch-dark room. Suspicions swarmed like a nestful of marabuntas in Betta's mind, above all about relations between the young woman and her elders. But with every visit a portion of the mystery was to be illuminated, rousing in him resentments on her behalf. Did his compassion for a woman he had only known a short time arise from her plight or had it sprung from within him, reflecting a need to attach himself to the distress of others, as the Mulvi Sahib had told him in words at once blunt and solicitous.

Betty was the mainstay of her uncles and aunts. They had come from the country, attracted by the money she earned and by her house where they were able to stay until they found work and a place of their own. With the installation of every uncle and aunt as a permanent member of the household Betty was required to work longer hours. Like the aboriginal women in the bush she got up at foreday morning when the cocks started crowing and stray dogs no longer barked. Her only instruments were the blunted nail and an extraordinary skill which managed to infuse new life into discarded chairs. Betta discovered all this from snatches of conversation over a period of weeks, and what surprised him most of all was her conviction that her uncles and aunts were entitled to rely on her as they did, since she was the only one possessing a skill that could be turned to account.

'Don't you ever want to go out?' he asked her.

'I don' have no time.'

There occurred to Betta the idea that he should propose to the young woman, but he immediately dismissed it as absurd, for reasons he did not care to examine. Instead, he gave her money, which she would not take in her hand, content to leave it beside her amongst the strands of cane that lay lengthwise on the bed.

Betta went back every Saturday night, except when he visited the Merrimans on the West Coast. He would then go on the Friday. And it was on these Fridays that her uncles and aunts met him with an unconcealed hostility, as if he had intruded on a special occasion.

One Friday, as he was about to get into his car, which he had left in a nearby road, a man stopped and addressed him.

'Doctor?'

'Yes?'

'You don' remember me? You got to remember me.'

'Should I?' asked Betta, who was put off by the stranger's brash manner.

'You din' treat me. Was me wife.'

'I see. . . . Well, goodnight,' Betta said, reaching for the crank on the floor under the front seat.

'I goin' crank it fo' you, Doctor. You heal me wife. We din' forget.'

'Thanks, but there's no need.'

'Le' me do it,' the man insisted, and took the crank out of Betta's hand before he could protest again.

But as he bent down he hesitated, then stood erect again.

'Doctor, is none o' my business, but it in' a good thing to go visiting in that house. They's bad people.'

'Thanks for the advice,' Betta said, indignant that he had not been firm with the stranger.

He seized the crank and turned it once, only to stop dead when he thought he had caught the man's next remark.

'What did you say?' he asked, turning and looking up at the figure which had moved no more than a foot away from him.

'She married. . . . The lady you does go visitin' is a married lady.'

'Look! Who are you?'

'You did treat me wife.'

'But who *are* you?'

'I'm nobody, Dr Singh.'

'And why are you telling me this?'

'Doctor, I helpin' you,' the man declared, apparently hurt by Betta's continued hostility.

Betta hesitated, then said, 'Get in.'

The man complied at once, entering the car by the door Betta had opened to take out the crank.

The two men sat next to each other without a word. Betta headed east and brought the vehicle to a halt at the point where D'Urban Street met Vlissingen Road.

'Did you say . . . the young lady was married?' Betta asked, looking straight ahead of him.

'She married. Everybody know how she married 'xceptin' you, Doctor. The uncles say the husband been playin' around an' they do fo' him.'

'How do you mean?' Betta asked.

'The story in' for the ears of decent people, Dr Singh. They not people like you an' me.'

Betta could not help looking at the man, who, like him, was an East Indian.

'What do you mean, "not like you and me"?'

'You wouldn' depend 'pon a woman to feed you, Doctor. Not me neither. . . . You know how much people she supportin'? Fourteen. And five o' them depend 'pon she en-ti-re-ly. They couldn' stand no husban' interferin'. The husband did want to keep only one uncle and a aunt, the two that bring she up after the father and mother dead, but not the others.'

The man went on to tell Betta how they tricked Betty's husband into lying on the narrowest bed in the house; and when he had fallen asleep they tied him down with ropes and threatened to burn away what was between his legs if he soiled their niece's bed again. When the man was released he lost no time in fleeing. He had avoided that part of town ever since and now only spoke in whispers.

'I was not told she was married,' Betta said, after a pause during which the man measured his reaction.

'I don' know,' the man replied. 'They probably think she would vex if they tell you. Without she they in' nothing! But *she* frighten of them too. She so frighten she don' dare find another man.'

The man stopped and waited for Betta to speak, but he simply stared ahead of him at the dark, empty road with its islands of light in the distance.

'You remember the lady with the eczema, Doctor? About a year ago? All she hands was cover in it an' she had was to wear long, long sleeves as if she been wearin' she sister frock. You make she bathe in sea water for six weeks every day and cure she without givin' she no medicine. Remember? That lady was my wife. And you cure she.'

Betta hardly listened to the man, but remembered the case. It seemed such a long time ago, like some recollection from a life from which he was irrevocably cut off. His informant evidently had no other disclosures to make, yet he was reluctant to let him go, lest there was something else. And, for a moment, it seemed as if he *did* want him to drag up something else to quicken the distaste he felt for the tenuous relationship between himself and Betty. He recalled the story of the woman who had tied up her boat to an island in the Berbice river and fallen asleep, thinking to complete her journey the next day. When she woke up she found herself in the open sea, her boat still moored to the island, which was no more than a floating mass of vegetation.

'Thank you,' Betta said to the man. 'I am grateful for what you told me.'

'Is me got to thank you, Doctor. Me an' my wife. "Han' wash han' make han' come clean."'

He laughed, out of satisfaction that he had done his duty and also that he had managed to find an appropriate saying to express his feelings about the mutual favours that bound Betta and himself together.

It's so foolish, Betta thought, as the man walked away down the street. What is there between her and me? She owes me nothing, no explanation. I can't say, 'Why didn't you tell me you're married?' when there was nothing between us. And yet . . . and yet . . .

Betta saw the man turn a corner and was filled with loathing for him. He looked like the kind who went around sowing false rumours, listened in to other people's conversations and then left to 'do his duty', when his real aim was to spread as much confusion as he could. Nevertheless he would not go back to Betty's house. If anything the stranger had confirmed that he was unwelcome to her numerous dependants. Was their surliness not of a piece with the description the stranger had given of the threat to maim her husband? He imagined Betty swiftly threading the cane through the holes on the edge of a chair whose varnish was cracked from frequent exposure to the sun, the strands of rattan laid out on the bed beside her and numerous relations guarding her waking hours lest she fell prey to a bout of illness.

On the way home it occurred to Betta that what he had learned that night was not unconnected with the portentous events of the last few weeks, the plague of rats, the floods and the bloody sunsets. It was possible that the stranger, after all, had saved him from a damaging experience.

And in that way he consoled himself for what, in the coming months, was to appear as an irreparable loss.

On arriving home Betta found the house in darkness although it was only nine o'clock. To his surprise, the front door was locked. He changed his mind about calling out and hurried to the back where, however, a vigorous shaking was enough to bring Sukrum to the door. He and Bai – his mother's most recent hangers-on – bedded down on the kitchen floor after the rest of the house retired.

'Where's Mrs Singh?' Betta asked, irritated at the difficulty he had in getting into his own home.

'They . . . she gone to bed, sah!' declared Sukrum, in that half- obliging, half-impertinent voice that never failed to annoy Rani.

To reach the passage leading to the drawing room Betta had to step over Bai, whose prone figure seemed twice its length.

Anxious to know why the lights were out, Betta nevertheless held back from asking Sukrum, who remained standing in the dark.

'You can go to bed,' Betta told him, speaking from the entrance to the vast drawing room, across which the closed gallery windows shone dimly from the streetlamp.

'It's you, Betta?' he heard his mother's voice as he began mounting the stairs.

'Yes, it's me.'

'Why don't you put on the light?'

'I thought you were in bed.'

'I was waiting up for you.'

'Why aren't the girls up?' he asked, his irritation returning, as he expected his mother to offer an explanation for everyone's unusual behaviour.

'I told them to go to bed,' she replied.

Betta threw the switch at the foot of the stairs while his mother came down to meet him, dressed in her nightgown and a shawl thrown round her neck.

'I want to talk to you about Rani,' she told him.

'Rani?' he faltered.

'The Pujaree's found her a bridegroom.'

Betta took a wide chair opposite his mother's, his heart still racing at the thought that she might have suspected his flirtation with Rani.

'I want to know,' his mother continued, 'how much I should give her as a dowry. The boy's father came this afternoon and I didn't know what got into me. I couldn't bargain with him. I wish you were home. You go out so much nowadays. You've got a job?'

'It looks as if I'll take over from the doctor at Anna Catherina.'

'It's not sure yet?'

'From the letter I got and the interview at the Medical Department it looks as if they'll give it to me.'

'And when would you start?'

'Three months.'

'Three months!'

He could think of nothing to say and, without realizing what he was doing, began tapping his right foot on the polished floor, initiating a habit that was to last him all his life.

Betta reminded her that he had stayed on a year to please her and that he had never once said anything to make her believe he had changed his mind about serving the East Indian community.

'Serving the community!' she said scornfully. 'You mean the Bais and Sukrums who're too lazy to work and can't afford to pay you?'

'I'll be paid a salary on the estate,' he informed her, knowing full well that the most carefully chosen words would not placate her, that she was as unconcerned at the conditions of service he would enjoy in his new post as she was in discussing Rani's dowry with him.

'Since your father's death,' she said, 'I've had to face the world alone . . .'

He interrupted her so abruptly she made no attempt to arrest his words.

'And I? What do I know of the world? I know more about Kerala than my own country. I don't know whether I'm an Indian or a Guyanese. When the Mulvi Sahib wanted to teach me the Hindi script you stopped him, yet you filled me with stories about India. You wouldn't let me go to the public school and did all you could to prevent me mixing with other children and now I'm a freak. . . .'

'If you were a freak would Rani go around mooning over you? And your patients? They think you're a freak?'

'I'm nearly thirty years old,' he said, making every effort to avoid words he would regret having spoken. 'If I stayed in this house I would die a bachelor and you would see nothing odd about that.'

'So that's bothering you, is it? If that's why you want to leave . . .'

'I wanted to be a doctor since I was sixteen, and I told you why then. . . .'

All of a sudden he felt he was losing respect for his mother and for the first time he saw her bereft of her mysterious power, which was derived, not only from the wealth she possessed or from her habit of giving orders, but from something within himself. As a small boy he used to associate her with the colour blue, after an illuminated print of Durga in her benevolent aspect. Then, one night after she had petted and fondled him while putting him to bed, he dreamt of her with staring eyes and a long tongue which hung over her lower lip. And soon afterwards, among the numerous old calendars she kept in her camphor-wood chest, he discovered a picture of Durga in her terrible aspect, the devourer of children. The picture was red and baleful. And what remained of the experience, what lingered until his childhood was overtaken by his youth, was the ascendancy of red over blue. Now he felt pity for his mother, realizing that her power was illusory, that he no longer cared to explain in detail why he was obliged to leave as soon as he could, before he was overcome by a complacency which in Merriman appeared admirable, but in him would be a kind of death.

'I don't want to quarrel with you,' he told her, for she was staring at him as though she expected to intimidate him with her stony silence.

'I didn't know your father when we married,' she said. 'Rani will hardly know her husband. But I'm sure you'll be in love with your wife from the start. You'll buy her presents before you're betrothed, visit her home, take her out to a picture house once a week. And when you marry you will not need to lift her veil. But you won't be happier, mark my word.'

Betta was, in one way, relieved to hear these words, believing that they were evidence that his mother had given up the struggle to keep him. Yet, he was disturbed by 'You'll buy her presents before you're betrothed', for he could not envisage any other type of marriage than a Hindu one, arranged beforehand through the intermediary of parents or relations.

'I'd like to tell you a hundred things,' he said, choosing his words carefully, 'but how can I talk to you about them? Anything I say you'll see as a mark of disrespect. I don't even know if a mother and son can talk seriously.'

And no sooner did he utter these words than he recalled the easy manner in which Merriman spoke to his father.

'Tell me things like what?' his mother asked suspiciously.

'About my practice, the people I meet; about the Merrimans . . .'

'The people you meet? Who did you meet when you were a boy? You didn't complain then. I'll be a laughing stock if you worked somewhere else . . . and with Rani going who'll help me look after the house? You should've heard what the Pujaree said when I told him; but he never had much faith in you. He saw through you . . .'

'What he said?' enquired Betta, whose instinctive dislike of the priest flared up at the mention of his name.

And she answered without concealing her relish at his contempt for someone close to her.

'He said that if you were confident about belonging to the Indian community you would not need to throw away your prospects by working among the poorest of the Indian poor.'

Betta smiled bitterly, recognizing that there was probably some truth in the remark, but hated the Pujaree all the more for his discernment.

'Yes, I don't deny it.'

And he went on to tell her that while he was haranguing the local children – a favourite subject for her boasting whenever she spoke about him as a boy – he felt that they possessed something denied him, that the most deprived of them were superior to him, inasmuch as they were familiar with the byways of the village, the alleyways where villagers took their goats to eat leaves fallen from overhanging fruit trees, and the streets skirting the wine-coloured water of drainage canals; that his rare glimpses into other people's houses aroused longings he could hardly define; that as a student abroad he dreamt not only of his opulent home, but of public latrines over the canals by the river at Ruimveld, of burnt clay roads, of creole women with stockings rolled up just above their knees. And all the things he felt he dared not say to her because she was his mother he now spoke with a kind of glee on account of her willingness to take advice from the Pujaree who was not deserving of her hospitality and was feared in the village only for his association with Kali, whose celebrations culminated with the burning of effigies of Ravana by his twin nephews, two waifs with no fixed home.

Mrs Singh listened to her son's jealous outburst, uncomprehending. And if she understood little of its source, she understood nothing of his fascination with the murky corners of the village in which they lived.

'You are from India,' he said, judging that if the words were not said today they would have to be said another day, 'and I was born here and have as little attachment for Kerala as for the moon. When you and Aji quarrel she packs her bags and pretends she's going to India where she wasn't even born. Yet it is only Aji who understands what I want to do.'

'Is that surprising? She's in her dotage!'

Their quarrel had already woken up Rani and Lahti, who were sitting up in bed, disturbed at the way Dr Singh was speaking to his mother. For them, she had not lost her power to command. They listened to the raised voices and dared not exchange words across the gap between their beds, lest they were heard downstairs.

'All right, all right,' Mrs Singh continued. 'You're going? Then go! But when you get malignant malaria or teh-teh don't come back to this house because I won't take care of you.'

She turned her back on him, leaving him to face the reality of a rift he had long thought to be inevitable. Yet why could he not go away with her blessing? He was certain that, had his father been alive, he would not have objected to his plan, and that she would have dutifully swallowed her chagrin.

Nothing short of complete submission would satisfy his mother, the kind of obedience she received from her protégées and the two male hangers-on. And this recognition of his mother's determination to have her own way came as a surprise to him, in the manner of someone who, late in life, comes to discover a blemish on the nape of his neck which had been apparent to all who knew him.

Betta went out into the yard to switch off the Delco plant and to check that the gates were secure. On the way up he stood on the porch where Rani and Lahti spent their evenings before going to bed as part of an unfailing routine. He looked over at the Vlissingen Road and beyond to the drowned fields where gaulings and gulls foraged in more favourable times and children occasionally organized games during the long August holidays. They were all marked by the coastal floods and the alluvial soil laid down by the sea, by the very things that alarmed islanders who came visiting. Was not the inability to see these features a protective trait? The endless wall, the countless drainage canals were evidence more of their blindness than their understanding, for they were only a matter for surprise when contrasted with countries that looked down on the sea. The discovery of his mother's single-mindedness could do him no good. Yet she was his mother, the male and the female, who brought all things to pass. If she had accepted his going away he would have showered her with presents and endearing remarks. But, knowing her intention to thwart his plans, he was prepared to destroy every connection with his home.

The clock stopped when my father died. Why can't I even recall his features? She said he was left-handed, as if it's important, as if that's important. There was a plague of rats when I was a boy, but they only ate the sugar cane, which was already eight months old. Forty-two acres of cane were destroyed on a single estate. Now they're going for the rice and even the fish. Something must be wrong with the world. How little we understand! I accused her of indifference to the poor and diseased, yet she supports Aji, the girls and two good-for-nothing liars who collapse from exhaustion after a half-hour's work. What is wrong? What is right? Does the arrogance of my convictions give me away? When I was young was I more moral then?

The longer Betta reflected, the more convinced he became that he was an instrument of a process that disregarded him, his mother and every other individual they knew. There was no need to ask questions. It was sufficient to yield to the demands of the working of fate, the superior destiny in which he believed in spite of his denial of any connection with India.

On entering the house he felt the draught through the fixed jalousies under the closed windows.

On waking up the next morning Betta immediately recalled what he had learned about the woman he had been visiting, and his resolution not to see her again, which he now rejected as hasty. Suppose the man's account was false? He might well have been put up to it by her uncles who, it seemed, would stop at nothing to protect their niece from any man who showed an interest in her.

It appeared to Betta that the very obstacles to a relationship with the woman – her want of time, the watchers surrounding her – acted as a spur to his passion. And now the most daunting of all impediments, her marriage, had put him off for a period of no more than a night's sleep. In spite of his suspicions about the informant he believed, deep down, that she was indeed married and, while hoping that she was not, had already decided that whatever the truth he would try to get close to her.

He had always visited at evening. Perhaps she did not work on her chairs in the morning. She might even escape supervision then, when people were continually coming and going on the pavement a few yards away and any harshness towards her was unlikely to escape the attention of neighbours. Betta, grasping at this unlikely possibility, decided to prepare himself for the trip. He took a shower and dressed as quickly as he could, fearing that the telephone might ring and he would be obliged to go and visit a patient.

When he set out, leaving his morning meal on the table, there was little traffic on the roads and he drove more slowly than usual. A truck with municipal workmen went by in a cloud of dust as he took the turning into Irving Street. He looked up at the houses of the few well-to-do East Indians who had moved into Queenstown, mansions in whose yards there was not a single prayer flag. At the entrances to one of the well-maintained alleyways a man with a canister on his back had begun spraying the gutter with oil against mosquito larvae.

Catching sight of a young woman hesitating before she ventured to cross in the path of the oncoming car immediately brought his mind back to his visit at this unusual morning hour. And, in an instant, the solution to a mystery concerning the object of his passion occurred to him. On seeing Betty for the first time he had associated her with the scent of lavender oil; now he remembered the woman who sold it in small bottles clad in basketwork, and her daughter who bore such a strong resemblance to Betty she might have been her sister.

On approaching the house on foot Betta stopped a few yards from the gate, his resolution to knock boldly on the door faltering before the knowledge that this was the time of day when women were on the way to market or were attending to domestic chores.

'I can wait an hour,' he told himself, and directed his steps towards the town centre in search of an eating place. The cloth stores abutting on the pavement were empty, but in each cook shop he passed people were seated at long tables, eating or waiting to be served. He chose one in which there were no more than a handful of customers, their backs turned to the street, and ordered a cup of coffee. And soon he was lost in thought, attempting to pin down fugitive reflections and build a coherent picture of his undertaking.

Now Betta had no doubt that it was not his sympathy for the young woman that drew him to her, but rather the crudest of impulses, which ensured the survival of the large numbers of stray dogs in town. And as his reflections succeeded one another he avoided dwelling on what he saw as the most serious aspect of his position, the effect any scandal was likely to have on his standing in the community and, in consequence, on his practice. His thoughts flickered like an uncertain fire and, in the manner of a patient who, having taken a tablet of phenacetin, yields to the illusion that her pain has vanished for good, he consoled himself with the belief that nothing could possibly happen to him since he was protected by his status as a physician. Yet, beneath the conviction of his inviolability, there lurked the equal conviction that Betty's uncles and aunts were like those voracious animals that preyed on others of their kinds and would not hesitate to harm him.

'White sands and a profusion of coconut trees.' Yes, she reminded him of his mother, who must have had the same thoughts in the early years of her marriage while encompassed in a kind of prison. And this train of his reflections led him to things he believed he had forgotten, to the seller of lavender oil and her daughter, who would not look him in the eye, to stories he had heard as a child from Aji and a huckster responsible for supplying green vegetables to St Rose's Convent, of a sadistic Mother Superior who possessed a talent for reducing her girls to tears and once expelled a pupil because she never cried, on the pretext of a trifling misdemeanour; of the strictures on crossing their legs except at the ankles, and of the sad, kind nun who kept a secret collection of red cornelian earrings.

Under the window looking out on to the yard was a score of large, earthenware ink bottles, an incongruous sight in a cook shop whose clients were mostly illiterate.

Betta took out his watch and saw that he had only been there for fifteen minutes. Impatiently he got up, went over to the counter where he paid for the cup of coffee and left, unable to wait any longer.

In that short time the traffic of people and drays had doubled and the air was filled with the ringing of bicycle bells and the sound of car horns. He went past a display of huge fishes arranged on the grass verge, past his own motorcar parked in Bourda Street, until he arrived in front of the house he was visiting. He crossed the bridge and climbed up the stairs. Hesitating a moment, he then knocked on the door and waited.

'Is who you want?' a middle-aged male voice came from within.

'I've come to see the lady who repairs chairs.'

'Who?'

'Betty.'

'Come in, ne.'

Betta pushed the door and saw the young woman in her usual place, a length of buff-coloured cane in her hand.

'It's you?' she said, and looked around her.

'It's me.'

'Go . . .'

'I want to know one thing, please. You're married?'

She bowed her head.

'Why didn't you tell me?'

'Yes, I'm married,' she answered in an unnaturally loud voice.

'Do you want me to come back?' he asked without hesitating, as if the first question was no more than an excuse to put the second.

'No, you musn't come back here,' she answered, speaking more loudly than ever, but with an expression of such despair Better understood at once that there was someone on the other side of the partition for whom her words were meant.

In fact all the members of the household were inside, thus accounting for the empty beds Betta could see around him. On hearing that he was on the stairs they had fled, relying on their bread-winner to give the answers they had warned were necessary to discourage the doctor from returning.

Betta and the young woman faced each other, he, incapable of conveying how she disturbed his sleep, and she not daring to speak of her bondage lest she be overheard. She longed to reveal her affection for him and, with that, her inability to live apart from those who had enslaved her, that she envied those creole women who could look their men boldly in the eye and stand alone. And Betta, sensing her anguish, pushed aside the bundle of cane and sat down on the couch next to her; but, frightened out of her wits by his boldness, she drew back suddenly, so that the upturned chair on which she was working fell from her hands. They both looked down at her unfinished handiwork as though they had done a terrible deed and were contemplating its evidence on the floor below. A strand of rattan, trailing beyond the point where it had emerged from a hole in the rim of the chair, lay like a pale serpent in repose, with the blunt nail she used as a tool as its head.

'I. . . .' Betta began, but did not know what to say. 'If you are sick or if you need help you know where I live.'

She nodded, her eyes averted.

'Goodbye,' he said, standing up slowly, hoping all the while that she would hold him back.

But she looked away stubbornly, almost defiantly, it seemed to him; and he gave up the idea of making some sort of contact with her, be it by way of a formal handshake.

He stood at the top of the stairs, looking down at the busy street with its clanging drays, its noisy motorcars, the erratic flow of pedestrians and cyclists, and saw them as through a pane of opaque glass. But when a van drove up with bundles of cane and timber and the chauffeur leapt out Betta pulled himself together and hurried down to the street, passing the man on the bridge.

The strident sounds, the bustling crowds around the market, the incessant coming and going of vehicles on the road made no impression on Betta as he walked along the pavement, instinctively avoiding pedestrians approaching him. How many times he had driven past the house he had just left without even glancing at it, uncaring about those who went in or came out! Now his thoughts were fixed obsessively on it, on the shadowy uncles and aunts who had thwarted his plan to get near the young woman, on the piles of cane and the nail she used as a tool, on his lack of honesty in not acknowledging at the outset his real interest in her, at the boundaries between honesty and self-knowledge.

The sun had risen above the trees on the edge of the town and many women were carrying open umbrellas and parasols. When one of them brandished hers at Betta from the other side of the road and called out he did not notice; and it was only after she shouted, 'Doctor! Is me!' did he wave, while failing to recognize her as an erstwhile patient. And it was that simple greeting which brought him down to earth, reminding him of his obligations as physician to a whole community which regarded him as being superior to ordinary mortals.

Chapter 7

The Pujaree began by reading from the Sutras to the assembled invitees and those living in the house. Then he introduced the musicians, the Omar family, father, son and two daughters, who were hired for functions in Georgetown and the suburbs. Mrs Singh would have preferred to avail herself of the services of the man who played the transverse flute after she had fed the scores of people in her yard, but no one could tell her of his whereabouts.

'Admit it, ne,' Aji had taunted her the day before. 'Admit that the Mohammedans do things better than the Hindus. Admit you does admire them!'

But Mrs Singh had not answered, desiring to maintain her calm until the function she was holding to mark Betta's departure.

Mr Omar and his son squatted on the ground at the back of the drawing room, the father with an ivory-inlaid sitar across his lap and the son, his hands resting on the tabla before him. His two daughters, fifteen and seventeen years old, were sitting on high chairs behind their father and brother. Under the hanging lamps the arched frets cast shadows on the neck of the sitar, contrasting with the reflections from electric bulbs on the resonating gourd. Mr Omar began playing alone, a raga of such strange beauty that Mrs Singh was cut to the heart, recalling how she married from her parents' home and came across the sea to a land where the poor drank mar water from strained rice. Unannounced, the son started drumming on his tabla.

Around the drawing room candles had been placed at intervals, and wax falling from their spent tops made blobs on the necks of the green bottles from which they grew under flames immobile in a slow air that penetrated the door and open windows.

Betta was sitting on a chair near to his mother who held a fan on her lap. On her left the Pujaree and the Mulvi Sahib sat side by side, and from their position next to Betta and his mother were seen to be the guests of honour. Against the opposite wall of the room squatted the young people, Lahti among them, while Rani, whose marriage was to take place in a fortnight's time, had taken up a position where Mrs Singh could not see her staring at the doctor. The quickening rhythm of the tabla did not affect her in the slightest and she stood, arms folded among a group of women guests, praying that the young man to whom she was betrothed would not arrive. She was staring at Betta unashamedly, not only because she believed she loved him deeply, but because she knew she could feel no affection for a nondescript youth who would judge her on her ability to turn roti on a tawa. Lahti had described him as a pagla, thus obliging her to defend him. But that had been her opinion, too. Occasionally she cast her eyes round at the assembly of people, many of whom were invited on the Pujaree's account. Most of the women had married as she would marry, without having been consulted by their parents, some of them to old men who had lied about the property they owned. And yet none looked bitter, as she was certain she would be after a few years of marriage. Mrs Singh had advised her to spend the first year anticipating what would please her husband and avoiding any action that might offend. Whatever she thought of her mother-in-law she must not answer back. And as Mrs Singh heaped axiom upon axiom the face of Rani's future husband had kept coming back to her, as though mocking her. The only man she had come to know well since she was taken in by Mrs Singh eight years ago was Betta, who possessed all the qualities she imagined a husband should have. She would have spent a lifetime pleasing him. But a boy, hardly nineteen, who had apparently never shaved, who stared at his mother whenever she spoke and bowed his head when his father addressed him, how could she please him a whole lifetime?

When Rani looked over at Betta's seat he was gazing at the musicians. The music came to an abrupt end and there were cries of 'Panditji! Panditji!' One man shouted out a request for a gazal and immediately the elder daughter stood up from her chair to go and kneel by her father, who whispered into her ear. And now both instruments began playing, to be joined by the plaintive, high-pitched voice of the young woman singing in Urdu. She had taken her seat beside her sister once more and sang with the assurance of an older woman, while her father took pleasure in drawing many notes from a single string and her brother's hands trembled like dark butterflies over the diminutive drums. Rani, moved by the girl's song, could not bear to think that Betta would be practising across the river. Was it possible? She would be married to a boy, would be expected to observe the rules of purity to satisfy him, while her tiger was practising beyond her reach. A sudden, uncontrollable sobbing escaped her; and at once all eyes were turned towards the spot where she was standing. Involuntarily she looked over at Mrs Singh, who ordered her out of the room with a peremptory gesture. Lahti followed, believing that she was expected to go and assist Rani if she were needed.

'Wha' wrong?' Lahti asked, finding her at the foot of the front stairs.

'Go back up!' Rani ordered her. 'You hypocrite!'

Lahti backed away, angry at being dismissed as she had been, but at the same time cowed by the unaccustomed violence in her friend's voice.

Tomorrow I've got to explain why I came down, Rani reflected. And the thought of her impotence roused her momentarily to rebellious thoughts.

A noise at the top of the stairs made her take heed of the

consequences of a lengthy absence and of Mrs Singh's probing questions and suspicions about the cause of her flight.

Rani wiped her eyes and followed Lahti to join the company, who turned their heads once more as she came through the open door and took up her position against the wall. She dared not take her eyes off the family of performers. The two young women were now dancing with the jerky, unpredictable movements of articulated puppets, while father and son played more loudly than ever. The interest of the audience in the performance had abated, and while earlier the music imposed itself on a rapt silence, it now possessed the quality of a feature of the night, like the whirring of crickets or the faint scent of orange leaves from the yard. A few children had begun to fidget while adults kept changing position on the floor or the chairs ranged against the wall. For some, however, the very repetition of one or two musical phrases created a web of sound into which they delivered themselves with closed eyes and limp bodies.

From time to time Mrs Singh turned to look at Rani, fearing that she might do something foolish and interrupt the performance; but on each occasion she appeared so engrossed in the music that the older woman was forced to the conclusion that her ward had broken down because she had been moved by the sound of the instruments and the unusual voice of a young woman of her own age.

When the performance was over, the caterers began sharing out spiced cakes made of coconut and wheat flour. Many guests gathered round Betta to find out where he was going and why he had decided to give up a practice that promised to be lucrative. Some of them had never heard of Anna Catherina or Leonora nor been on a sugar estate, while others were surprised to learn that the country's doctors were not concentrated in and around Georgetown. Betta answered as best he could while waiting for a chance to take the Mulvi Sahib aside and apologize for his surliness on the occasion of one of their conversations a few weeks before.

The very poor, a number of whom had been invited by the Pujaree, stood aside, not daring to approach the doctor while he was talking with people whose manners were so superior to theirs. *They* were the ones who would miss him since, if they wanted free medical treatment, they would be obliged to wait for hours at the Government dispensary and, as likely as not, see a bad-tempered pharmacist whose diagnostic ability was more limited than the stock of drugs at his disposal. One woman took courage and advanced into the midst of Dr Singh's well-wishers. She placed her hand on his cheek and said, 'I in' got nothin' to gie you, an' I tek nuf medicine from you. But wha' fo' do? Is God sen' you an' is God takin' you away.' And before he could think of something appropriate to say she turned aside and was threading her way through the crowd.

Betta, when he managed to speak to the Mulvi Sahib, had to do so in the company of the Pujaree and the goblet maker, who was holding forth on the status of barbers in Madras, where they were treated like lepers, while in North India they enjoyed the confidence of the rich and often became keepers of their most intimate secrets.

'The only thing that does make status in this country,' he intoned, 'is money. The son of Mookesh the barber does sit on the same high-school bench as my son. That could not happen in Madras.'

The goblet maker had managed to bring out what he was keen on letting everyone know, that his son went to high school. He was as little interested in whether Mookesh's son sat next to his as he was in the height of the next spring tide and, had Mookesh offered his daughter as a prospective wife for his son, he would have agreed, without hesitation, provided the dowry was substantial and was to be paid in advance. Those listening knew this well enough, but endured him for courtesy's sake. Betta listened to him monopolize the conversation, realizing that he would have to go and see the old teacher at his house in the avenue of flamboyant trees where he found conversation more embarrassing, because there he felt he was a pupil again.

The men continued talking and from time to time were joined by others who, judging themselves to be out of their depth in the company, soon went off to speak to their wives or acquaintances.

It was only when Mrs Singh sat with them that the goblet maker, in deference to her – he saw her as one of the grand ladies of East Indian society – stopped talking. She invited the three men to stay after the others had gone and asked if she might introduce them to the family of musicians, who had not left the area in which they had been performing. When she came back with Mr Omar and his three children everyone was surprised at their youthful appearance, for, isolated from the audience and carrying the burden of their fame, they had seemed older and more formidable. The young women did not behave as naturally as while they were singing or dancing and the younger one especially was shy to the point of timidity. The boy on the other hand greeted everyone with an open smile and looked at his sisters as much as to say, 'Why bother to talk with them? They're only girls.'

Finally the musicians left and the house began to empty rapidly until only the goblet maker and the guests of honour remained. The young women made green tea and served it with sugar cakes, then stood by with calabash bowls from which the Singhs and their guests could wash their hands without being obliged to leave the low table.

Both the Mulvi Sahib and the Pujaree avoided the subject of Betta's going away, only to hear the goblet maker ask as Rani replenished their cups, 'What you think of your son being the doctor on a sugar estate?' He was answered for his interest with a chill silence, which was broken by Betta, who said that his mother was not certain what to think.

'I *do* know what to think,' she put in, disregarding a rule never to butt in on the men's conversation.

Rani and Lahti immediately withdrew.

'And Dr Singh knows what I think,' Betta's mother continued in order to leave the goblet maker in no doubt as to her feelings.

'Oh,' he rejoined weakly, cursing his folly and deciding belatedly to let the talk be led by the other men.

'Well,' declared the Mulvi Sahib, 'we will no longer have the excuse of neglecting Mrs Singh from now on.'

And the Pujaree, accepting the cue, went on to praise the way the evening was organized.

Betta nearly yielded to the temptation of making a consoling gesture towards his mother, but suppressed the impulse because of the goblet maker, who was a stranger to the house.

Soon the men were talking as if nothing untoward had

happened. The Pujaree made fun of Betta because he used words he had picked up abroad instead of their Guyanese equivalents. He spoke of 'squash' instead of 'lonky' and 'egrets' instead of 'gaulings'; and an argument ensued as to whether egrets and gaulings were the same bird. Then the Mulvi Sahib told the story of the Mohammedan who bought a large house with many tenants in Garnet Street, Newtown, attracted by the low asking price. The first Sunday he set off to collect the rent, armed with a list of the tenants' names, but only managed to secure money for one room, since the people occupying the other eleven claimed that the true tenant was away. So it went on for several weeks until, in exasperation, he took out summonses to recover the premises from his tenants for non-payment of rent, but found that personal service on any of them impossible. They were never at home and no one would disclose where they worked.

The men talked long and Mrs Singh served them herself after allowing Rani and Lahti to retire. They spoke of the world recession which had brought widespread unemployment to the country; of the tram workers' strike and the closure of the system by the American company which owned it. They spoke of the epidemic of malaria that came in the wake of the floods; and their conversation went on late into the night, which was now so still that the faint whispering of the coconut branches could be heard. No one wanted to retire, perhaps on account of the tranquillity, or because everyone was aware of the unusual nature of the occasion, or yet out of fear that in bringing the conversation to an end he would be responsible for an unseemly act, like interrupting a meal or an affecting song.

Mrs Singh drew her achal over her head in an involuntary gesture. She was always anxious that her entertaining should pass off without a hitch. And in spite of her bitterness towards her son she never ceased peering into the diminutive glazed cups to see if someone needed more tea or into the face of the goblet maker, who had not spoken for some time.

When the Mulvi Sahib got up to go at about three o'clock, she signalled the Pujaree to remain.

'Betta, take the Mulvi Sahib home,' she said, while accompanying the teacher to the head of the stairs.

'I'll come and see you as in the old days,' he told her. 'You remember when I used to live here? When Betta was that high? Now look at him! He's taller than I am, and stronger.'

At the gate he turned and waved, thinking that fateful events often drew little attention, while those of little significance might be the subject of discussion for weeks on end.

Left alone with the Pujaree Mrs Singh sat down opposite him, tight-lipped. Then, as if calling to mind that her son would be back in less than a half-hour, she began telling him what she had been waiting to say all night, throughout the singing and dancing, when she had been playing host with bitter thoughts.

'Sometimes I believe I'm just a weathercock and that all I can do is clatter in the wind. . . .'

'Don' torture yourself,' the Pujaree said kindly. 'Betta care for you.'

'Yes. Like Rani and Lahti and Aji and those rebellious men who eat me out and give nothing in return. . . . I told Rani she had to live here after she married; and do you know she protested. . . . Protested!'

'Now how do you expect her husband to agree with that?'

'Oh, his father agreed all right.'

'But who does do that?'

'Is it better for her to be a slave in her mother-in-law's home? I'm doing it in her interest.'

It was not wise to argue with her or give her advice when she talked like that, the Pujaree thought.

Then, looking upwards as though Rani could be listening through the floorboards, she went on, 'You can take a person out of the gutter, but you can't take the gutter out of a person. When she was a child I nursed her through long bouts of malaria when the doctor thought she'd die. Yet she's prepared to abandon me in this big house with Lahti, who can't tell the difference between an egg laid by a fowl and one laid by a duck. But what do you expect of young people nowadays? They do what they like. I mean you see it yourself, don't you?'

'I do, I do,' the Pujaree reassured her. 'But it don't do no good to work yourself up.'

'Yes, you're right,' Mrs Singh said, realizing that she had got carried away.

The Pujaree was the only one to whom she could speak freely, with whom she never felt ashamed. His calling and his humble origins allowed her to look up to him and at the same time to retain a feeling of superiority towards him.

'You did tell me,' said the Pujaree, 'that Rani was "going away" and you wouldn't have anybody except Lahti and Aji in the house when Betta went. Why you did change your mind?'

'I told you I did it in Rani's interest. When I met the boy's mother I knew she would suffer.'

'Then let Rani decide. You're a fair-minded woman.'

Mrs Singh remained silent while the priest waited for an answer.

'I thought of that too,' she said at last. 'But if she wanted to live with her mother-in-law I would never allow her to come back here. I gave her a dowry of two thousand dollars. She's had food, shelter and an education *and* a dowry, more than most East Indian girls. What more does she want me to do for her? She'll be unhappy. I know it. I'm saving her from herself.'

'I say what I had to say,' answered the Pujaree, unwilling to place her in the humiliating position of facing her own despairing lies.

A cock-crow rang out in the early morning and it was followed immediately by the crowing of several cocks announcing an illusory dawn.

'Another day,' the Pujaree said. 'I got to go.'

'Stay until Betta comes back, please. Until he goes to bed . . . I couldn't stand . . . I couldn't stand it otherwise. In the morning I'll be able to speak to him, but not now.

'Sometimes,' she said after a long pause during which the Pujaree reckoned it was unwise to speak, 'my strength is a burden. But I know that if I showed the slightest weakness now they would devour me.'

'Who?' the Pujaree asked.

'The people in this house, the Ajis, the Lahtis, the Sukrums and Bais . . . and my husband.'

'Your husband? Does he visit you?'

'Not any more. But I know he's judging me for the way I dress, the way I think . . . and my failure with Betta. The other day when I was driving in town I nearly had an accident because my attention was drawn to a man who looked exactly like my husband. Oh, I know what you're going to say. But it wasn't only his face, you see. His manner. . . . He just swung round and looked at the passing car. I was so frightened! What do we know, when all is said and done? And is anything as it used to be? I respect the Mulvi Sahib so much, yet I know he despises me.'

'No, no! The Mulvi Sahib and me are like chalk and cheese, but I can't let you say such things.'

'Then why he abandoned me when Betta went abroad to study?' she asked, a certain vehemence in her voice.

'He's a Mohammedan and didn' think it . . . right to come and see you here.'

'I don't think so,' she said, pacified somewhat by his words. 'Many people think there's something disgusting about a widow. She's like a used cloth. I can see it in the way some people talk to me. A woman without a man.'

The Pujaree knew she was right, that even though she was capable of attracting a host of suitors it was solely for her money and house that they would have married her. But he was astonished that none of this had come out before, that she had succeeded in concealing her unease behind a self-assurance so complete that no one, except perhaps the Mulvi Sahib, was capable of detecting it. He recalled how the teacher had said, 'Poor lady,' in addressing her, and other remarks, apparently of little significance at the time. He knew as well that the Mulvi Sahib considered her the strongest woman he had ever met and, for that, did not care to cultivate her company.

'For a long time,' the Pujaree said, 'I been telling you to come to the temple at Kali Mai puja. Even if you don' want me to arrange a special puja for you.'

'I'll see,' Mrs Singh replied, giving him hope that at last he could attract her into the growing circle of those whose forebears had come from Madras and, abandoning the sugar estates, had settled in Kitty and Newtown on the outskirts of the city where they could find occasional work or take a stall within the confines of the Kitty and Bourda markets.

'You'd like some more tea?' she asked.

And as she went off to brew him another cup he heard what seemed to be Betta's steps on the stairs.

Chapter 8

Betta had learned of his mother's insistence that Rani should
live in from Rani herself and saw it as yet another piece in the
jigsaw of her personality which had unfolded before his eyes
since he returned from abroad. The discovery that she believed
she was entitled to her own way in everything, and her attempt
to influence the manner his surgery was run, had disclosed
hidden features of a landscape he knew well when young, but,
like a familiar contrivance that bursts open unexpectedly to
reveal an alarming complexity, he had never understood. He
recalled that distant time, her strength, her ability to persuade
people to do what she asked of them, 'because I'm a widow'; and
it occurred to him that the extraordinary feeling of security he
experienced in those early days had been the consequence of the
very qualities he now disliked so intensely. What else would he
learn about her if he did stay on in the house? Looking back on
those days so long ago when he sat beside her in a carriage
swinging his legs in order to make patterns in her muslin sari,
everything was a reflection of her presence, the sun's
penetrating warmth, an evening breeze from the sea, the sound
of clothes being beaten at the trench side, a dying tree
smothered in the dung of roosting birds. It was the age of
primordial ignorance, of implicit belief in the power of words, a
time that ignored the message of dreams in which the beloved
appeared in the accoutrements of terror.

How could he assist Rani, whose betrothed would almost
certainly agree to live in his wife's house only because he was
poor and on account of a dowry so substantial his will to resist
had been destroyed? Betta felt that any help could only be given
at some time in the future, when he had put aside sufficient
money, for at the moment he could do no more than add a few
hundred dollars to his mother's dowry, while assuring Rani of
his friendship.

In spite of his thrust towards independence, in spite of his scientific training, Betta's understanding of his mother's character was as imperfect as when he was a child. In the Kitty community she was highly regarded, even though there were men who shared the Mulvi Sahib's view that 'she thought she was a man'. Rarely was a request to hold a fête or build a tajah in her yard refused. In fact, on the occasion of the Mohammedan festival of Hussein and Hassan, the tradition was all but established that the tajah was to be built in her ample yard; and when the glistening structure set out from the grounds of the house, followed by a crowd of hundreds of people from all sections of the community, small children who were not permitted to follow it through the streets were in the habit of occupying her staircase, believing it to be communal property. At other times, on finding strangers squatting under the saman tree, she had no thought of asking them to leave, for that was the way of her parents in Kerala, whose compound was never empty; where, by day, the rope makers spun their coconut fibre on wooden wheels, and in the evening the men who could not afford to frequent the tea houses or travelling drama booths, congregated to talk. Like the immigrants from Uttar Pradesh who used their skill in rice planting to establish a thriving industry in the country, so she had brought from her homeland a tradition so firmly implanted in her character that any enquiry into the extent to which it was a part of her natural bent would have been pointless.

At a time like this Betta, preoccupied with her effect on his way of life and Rani's, saw her influence as a reality that could not fail to bring in its train the most terrible consequences, since Rani's betrothed would enter into a marriage threatened at the outset by a pool of resentment. And, far from being annoyed at his mother's refusal to enter into the sort of lengthy conversation in which they often engaged after he returned from abroad, he was glad to avoid any meeting during which he could not trust himself to refrain from accusing her of hypocrisy and much else.

In the end Betta fell asleep and did not even hear when the Pujaree set off home and his mother came up to bed.

The next morning Betta woke up to sounds from the yard, words trailing away into incomprehension. He imagined his mother haggling with the hucksters, Sukrum and Bai engaging in one of their mock quarrels and the two young women exchanging remarks in an improvised gibberish. The sun was so bright he believed that the eight o'clock train must have gone a long while ago and he fell to thinking that, as a student in Ireland, he had been robbed of a certain awareness, something indefinable, that could be only expressed by its loss, and that it had been replaced by an obsession with clocks and the passage of time. The trinket seller, who had been in the habit of calling to see his mother up to a year ago, insisted that he was selling time, that his cheap watches did no more than record it and were therefore not the object of his sale. The fantastical element became a reality when he believed he had failed his first medical examination and would have to wait another year before he was able to retake it.

If the eight o'clock train had gone why had no one woken him up? Then he remembered the previous night, the long session of conversation with the Pujaree and the Mulvi Sahib, over which his mother had presided with her discreet attentions; she would not allow the young women to wake him up after such a get-together, more a vigil to mark his departure that afternoon than a meeting of acquaintances and friends.

The words penetrating his window were interrupted by an outburst of laughter, which could only have come from a creole, probably the ice-man or the mender of iron pots, wandering traders armed with soldering iron and ice pick, men of uniformly tall stature whose appearance filled small children with terror, and earned the respect of adults in spite of their resemblance to ill-clad demons.

On hearing someone sweeping the landing Betta got up and dressed hurriedly, hoping that it might be Rani. When he opened the door he found her with a pointer broom raised above her head while she wiped the sweat from her forehead with her left arm.

'Rani, it's you I want to see.'

'Your tea's been on the table long ago, Doctor.'

'I want to talk to *you*.'

'Me? Why?'

'Don't be foolish, Rani. You've been avoiding me.'

'Who said. . . ?'

'Stop pretending!' he told her. 'I said to Mrs Singh I'd add something to the dowry she's giving you. Did she say anything?'

'No,' Rani replied.

'Aren't you glad?'

'Yes, Doctor,' she answered, still avoiding his eyes.

'What have I done you?' he asked, remembering how he had ignored her after his mother announced her intention of marrying her off, but now anxious about the possible consequences of his neglect.

'Nothing,' she said. 'But I don't want any money.'

'For God's sake, why?'

'Doctor, I've got to get the sweeping done or Mrs Singh'll want to know what I was doing.'

'Tell her you've been talking to me. . . . Are you angry about having to live here after you're married?'

And no sooner had he spoken than he realized how insensitive the question had been. But she did not reply.

'Why don't you object, Rani? It's your life.'

Everything he said seemed to be spoken by someone else, as if he was so keen on not letting her go he let out the first thought that came into his mind.

'Mrs Singh did train me to obey,' she declared.

'Do you want me to speak to her?'

'No!' she exclaimed.

'I don't understand you or Lahti. Especially you. Don't you have a mind of your own? If she told you to drown yourself, would you?'

'Lahti would,' she rejoined promptly.

'What? And you?'

She looked away, then, as if saddened by the turn the conversation had taken, said, 'Aji said you're a great man, and I believe her. But I don't . . .'

'Go on,' Betta urged her.

She did not answer and Betta, impatient at her manner, said, 'You love the man you're going to marry?'

'I love him more every time I meet him. And he does bring me presents, things I never did see before. . . .'

She looked at him with an expression of despair and he could only wonder at her eighteen years. He recalled how, in his student days, he went walking alone among the dead leaves, where summer lay extinguished in the breath of an autumnal wind; and his longing for the dark folk, for women whose faces were hidden, not by a veil, but by their own hair, women who beckoned to him in his sleep, but seemed to retreat farther and farther, the nearer he approached. How strange, that the closer they came the more inaccessible they were! He discovered something else, something about himself, about the gulf between himself and students from India he knew, and his soul's longing for the country of his birth.

'Rani,' he said, taking care to speak in a way that would not intimidate her, 'I . . .'

But, with a swift gesture to which he was incapable of reacting she seized his hand and began covering it with kisses. He looked down at her, dumbfounded at her behaviour. Then as he was about to lift his hand to her face there was a noise on the staircase and Rani, taking fright, picked up her broom and fled into the bedroom she and Lahti shared.

There was no one on the stairs. Betta was about to return to his room and heard the whistle of the eight o'clock train pierce the morning calm. It was earlier than he thought.

Downstairs his morning meal was laid out on the dining table. Aji, who was sitting at one of the front windows, called out, 'Betta! I goin' warm up you chocolate. It mus' be cold.'

He felt the jug and declared it to be warm.

'You want anything?' she asked.

'No, Aji. I'm all right.'

'You goin' out this morning?'

'No.'

'Now you's a big man. You leffin' you mother house to live on you own. You got woman?'

'No, Aji.'

'Only men that got woman does do that. . . . You mother was vex bad yesterday.'

As he ate the old woman kept staring at him; and even when

he turned to look towards the drawing room she did not turn away, as though she was no longer capable of embarrassment. And while she was staring she was talking to him without uttering a word, believing that after an acquaintanceship of so many years it was no longer necessary to open her mouth in order to communicate her reflections. If *she* heard them inwardly, so must he, especially as he was one of the great doctors of the world, with his father's gift of comprehension.

'Where's Ma?' he asked her.

'She in the yard. Jus' now she goin' come upstairs an' ask me why I don' help the girls shell the peas or help cook grind the massala. But me hands like me drawers: they got holes. Ha ha!'

She laughed heartily, displaying her few brown teeth, which presided over the interior of a mouth so wasted with age it had lost its definition and like a plantain ball under a wooden pestle kept altering its appearance by the second.

Betta joined her when he finished the meal and they talked about anything that came into Aji's head, the girls, the new car bought by another East Indian doctor, Dr Wharton, with a horn capable of playing a recognizable tune that frightened the dogs; about the blind veena player who had recently moved into a nearby house and was in the habit of performing evening ragas at all hours of the day; about her imminent departure for India, in preparation for which she had packed her grip early that morning.

'When I firs' come to your father house he was proud to talk Hindi to anyone who did come visiting. I was raw, boy, raw, raw, raw. You wasn' born yet. I remember when he get a Delco plant and he tell me to put out the electric light. You know what I do? I try to blow out the light, "Phew! Phew!" But you t'ink he laugh? He din' laugh. He show me how to turn the switch halfway round. And I 'member when the telephone come an' everyt'ing. Yesterday you mother shout at me 'cause I say I din' eat and the girls them say I did eat already and your mother say she see me eat sheself an' I in' got no memory lef' but if I in' got no memory how I remember all them things 'bout the Delco plant and the telephone and the people who uses to talk Hindi with your father?'

From the way she spoke Betta was no longer going away. Indeed, at times, she behaved as if he were still a small boy and she expected him to gawk at her, open-mouthed with admiration for her evocations of the past.

Unexpectedly she broke off her monologue and it seemed to Betta that she thought he had already left.

Suddenly Lahti ran into the room.

'Doctor! Is Mrs Singh. She's got fever.'

'Where's she?'

'In her bedroom.'

Betta found his mother lying full-length on the bed. There was a smell of bay rum in the room from which the sun had been shut out by a black cloth hung over the window. Rani, seated on a chair with a bowl of unshelled peas on her lap, looked up at Betta as if she had not expected him to come through the open door.

'Ma, what's the matter?' Betta asked softly.

'She's got bad feelings,' Rani answered for her.

Betta placed the back of his right hand on his mother's forehead and, feeling nothing unusual about her temperature, declared that he was going to fetch a thermometer.

When he returned the girls were no longer there and his mother was covered with a blanket normally folded over the clotheshorse behind the bed.

'No, Betta,' she told him, as he was about to bend over her, 'I don't want you to take my temperature.'

'Why?' he demanded.

But she dismissed his protest with a wave of her hand.

'You know I'm going away this afternoon.'

'Go,' she said, not disposed to argue or too weak to engage in any further exchange.

'How can I go if you're unwell?'

She did not reply, and Betta, in exasperation, left the room. He went and sought out Lahti, whom he found in the kitchen. She told him that Mrs Singh had fallen ill soon after settling with the hucksters.

'How was she with the hucksters?'

'She was all right,' Lahti said, wondering why Betta had singled her out for questioning when he would have been much happier speaking to Rani.

'You're sure you're not hiding anything from me?' he asked.

Then, with a mischievous expression, she said, 'I don' believe

Miss Singh sick, Doctor. One minute she been talking with the people downstairs and another minute she lie down as if she been in bed for days.'

'That's enough,' he told her.

The old cook, a slow-moving, grey-haired East Indian woman who had started working with Mrs Singh two years ago, came through the back door carrying a bucket of water.

'Marnin', Dactor. I hear Miss Singh sick.'

'Yes, Cook, so I hear,' Betta answered. 'Did she give you orders about what to cook today?'

'Yes, Dactor,' she said, 'she does always do dat. Fus' thing in the marnin'.'

'Did she tell you to cook anything special for her?'

'No, Dactor . . . Dactor, you know the Pujaree come jus' now.'

'My God, who sent for him?' Betta asked.

'Miss Singh.'

He saw her filling the clay goblets and a cooking pot from the bucket of crystal-clear water she had drawn from the vat, and the vague realization came over him that he knew little of what went on in his home, the daily chores shared by the women, the mysterious hangers-on like Sukrum and Bai weeding the yard. Even the objects strewn about the yard, the defunct beehive, the washing lines crossing one another under the saman tree, the glazed stoneware bottles that bordered the two flowerbeds, even these he saw without noticing them.

Betta left the two women and went to sit out front to reflect on the best course of action in the light of his mother's refusal to have him by her side.

There was something unusual in the sunlight that penetrated the opaque glass of the squared windowpanes and the distorted shadows trailing away to expire on the floorboards. Much as he tried to put the offending presence of the Pujaree out of his mind, he found himself recalling the priest's features, the intense, unreasoning dislike he aroused in him, and the fact that his mother had chosen him, of all people, to wound his pride.

Betta went upstairs as quietly as he could, and even at some distance from the bedroom door he could hear the priest muttering words he knew to be Sanskrit because the pujas were always accompanied by formulae in the ancient tongue. Burning incense had replaced the odour of bay rum. His father, of whom Aji spoke continually, what would he have done? Would he have left and risked being branded as the doctor who abandoned his mother? Betta was certain that his mother's indisposition was a contrivance. Having come so far he was not prepared to submit to the feelings it aroused, whatever name they bore, loyalty, fear, uncertainty, jealousy, or simply hatred for a man who could change places with Sukrum as a hanger-on and who did not earn his keep.

Betta decided to lose no time in leaving. He went to his room and fetched twenty-four dollars from his wallet. Then he came down to the kitchen, where he found Rani, Lahti, the cook and Aji huddled together as though a calamity had descended upon the house. Betta embraced Aji and gave her four dollars; then, turning to the young women, he handed each of them four one-dollar notes, saying the same noncommittal words to both: 'I'll miss you, Rani. I'll miss you, Lahti.'

The cook, whom he hardly knew, had to be content with a smile and a weak joke about keeping the household alive with her food. She took her four dollars and said feelingly, 'Dactor, Dactor! Oh, Dactor!' while wiping her eyes.

'Behave you'self!' Aji ordered her, at the same time dragging Betta out of the kitchen.

'You musn' go without tellin' you mother goodbye,' she said to him on reaching the staircase. 'You din' go without tellin' me; how you goin' go without tellin' you mother? I don' even know how ol' I be and you tell me goodbye. Lord Krishna wasn' proud. You so proud you kian' say "I gone" to you mother?'

'She doesn't want to let me in the room, Aji. The Pujaree's attending her.'

'Wait here! Don' move till I come back.'

Betta watched her ascending the stairs, dragging herself up by means of her right hand with which she grasped the banister at every step. A stranger to the house would have seen her as a comical figure, ungainly, loquacious, irreverent to the point of absurdity. But Betta, who had known her all his life and saw her as none of these things, simply believed that she was an indispensable member of the family who ate only unsalted food during the first half of the month as a penance on her way to immortality, who in the last third of her life was like a traveller stopping from time to time at a street corner to discover where she was going or why darkness had overcome her suddenly.

She came back to fetch him upstairs with a solemn gait and a solemn expression and, taking hold of his arm, led him to his mother's room where the smoke from the burning akiari incense was thick in the pale light of two wax candles whose flames swayed inperceptibly in the upward draught from below the sash window with oblong panes.

'Kiss you mother, Betta,' Aji enjoined.

'Goodbye, Ma,' he said, bending down to kiss her on her damp forehead. 'I'll be back to see you soon.'

The Pujaree stood aside at the foot of the bed where the offering to Kali had been placed on the floor, an oblation of coloured water, sweetmeats on a tray and an iron pot whose contents were not exposed by the sunlight flooding through the window.

Mrs Singh did nothing to detain Betta, and on seeing him standing by her bedside after his whispered goodbye, turned towards the Pujaree who signalled him to go. But Betta stood his ground, wondering how his mother could be reduced to that condition in the space of one hour.

When he left the room Aji did not accompany him; but after everything had been packed in the car she came out on to the porch and watched him speaking to Rani and Lahti, who had helped him to fold his suits and collect the things that were to be packed last. She saw the car drawing away and the young women facing the direction in which it went, towards the train lines and the large-wheeled koker dividing town from country, towards the crossroads, one street of which led to the secret village, where on the evenings of weddings Muslim girls danced together in back rooms, protected from the inquisitive gaze of men. Aji watched Lahti and Rani screening their eyes from the sun, while holding down their dresses in the wind blowing up the road. And the smoke from the stubble field across the road went where the wind drove it. Incapable of the effort needed to reflect, Aji watched as caged birds watched, seeing only the bright objects picked out by the sun and the familiars who came and went incessantly in a circumscribed room. The young women came in eventually side by side, as they sometimes went out on early-morning errands, and finally disappeared under the house where the hucksters were in the habit of congregating in a kind of market and Mrs Singh, in spite of her wealth, had taken to haggling mercilessly until she finally got her way.

BOOK 2
THE MOTHER

Chapter 9

Amid peals of laughter East Indian men were running up and down Alexander Street throwing abeer from open bottles. One woman, unable to get away in time, saw her white blouse so badly stained with the red dye that she kept looking at her chest and the offending man in turn, as if she was uncertain about what had occurred. None of the spectators was laughing more heartily than the creoles, who escaped the attentions of the drunken abeer throwers and stood around to witness the plight of any East Indian who happened to be passing. Another man came out of a back yard with a bottle and, having drawn attention to himself with a series of grotesque grimaces, slowly poured its contents over himself, only to reveal that it contained nothing but clear water.

Lahti, who was standing behind a creole woman for protection, stopped briefly to watch the men, then went off home with her shopping basket filled with cheap fruit Mrs Singh had ordered from someone's yard. At the bottom of the basket were also a few green mangoes she had bought for Rani, who was expecting her first child and did not want Mrs Singh to know of her longing for green mangoes and tamarind. Lahti had bought the fruit, recalling how at the time of her own secret pregnancy she had hankered after sour fruit. Rani shared many secrets with her friend, in spite of the mistrust that lingered since Lahti had betrayed her on more than one occasion.

In fact they had begun to grow apart after Rani's marriage; but Rani's husband could not stand up to Mrs Singh, who treated him like her employee, and she, ashamed at his humiliation, discovered that she needed her friend more than ever. The willingness with which he carried out Mrs Singh's orders caused Aji to name him 'Crapaud' when, in her dotage, she recalled who he was.

Since the doctor's departure the household had remained

outwardly the same, except that one male had replaced the other and patients no longer congregated under the house in the evening. But, in fact, profound changes had occurred. Mrs Singh had begun to take a firm line with Sukrum and Bai, and had told them repeatedly that they would not eat if they did not work. Sukrum, believing that they were in danger of being put out on the road, took to fishing for shrimps behind the sea wall long after the sun went down. Every morning he uncovered his catch to impress his benefactress who, while praising his skill, expected no less of him about the house.

Bai, glimpsing the possibility of their independence from Mrs Singh, persuaded Sukrum to sell part of the catch on their own account, an idea which he fell upon as if it were his own. And so, from month to month the two accumulated savings that came from an enterprise conceived out of desperation.

Lahti's clandestine abortion and the business dealings of Bai and Sukrum appeared to Rani to be the direct result of Betta's departure. Even her husband's obsequiousness suited the atmosphere that had descended on the house like an enveloping cloud. The long conversations with Lahti, when they talked about their hair, about make-up they never put on and clothes they could not afford to buy, belonged to the past which, although only twelve months gone, seemed to have occurred in their childhood.

One night while rubbing her husband's naked back with coconut oil she caught sight of Lahti through the open front door. She was sitting alone on the porch watching knots of strollers in the moonlight which illuminated the pitch road and the empty fields opposite with its wan light. *She* had not changed much, in spite of her clandestine meetings with Sukrum and the assault on her body. As light-spirited as ever she laughed in the same way and would have confined her talk to the same topics that had served their endless conversations since the age of thirteen. In retrospect, Rani mused, it was astonishing that, at the time, she had not appreciated the attractions of her twilight world, where nothing appeared in firm outlines, neither the mornings nor the evenings, nor the tension between Mrs Singh and her son, nor the country's ruined harvests, nor the collapse of its sugar economy in the

world-wide recession, from which the members of the household were protected by the horde of gold Mr Singh had left his
wife. Obliged to fend for herself in matters of money and to sleep
with a bedfellow whose habits she was expected to understand
and accept the moment they were revealed, her confusion at her
new state had gradually given way to a sharpened awareness of
the world she inhabited.

For a month Rani had been dreaming of the unborn infant
dancing in a confined space, like one of the young women who
had performed on the eve of Betta's departure. But on waking
she saw only her husband beside her and through the open
window the silver water tank suspended above the yard. She
would then lie awake and attempt to put herself in focus,
reflecting on the fact that she neither liked nor disliked her
husband, wondering whether the bewilderment at her status as
a married woman was really at an end.

Rani knew that she would move out of Mrs Singh's house, but
felt that any attempt to do so before her husband was able to
establish himself as a jeweller and earn enough money to rent
and maintain his own house could end in a disaster from which
Mrs Singh might be unwilling to save them. Meanwhile she
pretended to be happy and counted herself fortunate to have
Lahti.

Lahti was full of stories of her experiences at work. Mrs Singh
had put her out to learn sewing with the creole seamstress living
in Pike Street, whose girls gossiped endlessly about the elegant
women clients with their exorbitant demands on the seamstress's time, about the seamstress herself and about the clients'
husbands who came to fetch their wives in hired carriages or
motorcars. Lahti was destined to follow an exciting road which,
in Rani's judgement, was full of perils.

Rani no longer wondered what Mrs Singh saw or did not see. It
was inconceivable that she had not noticed some of the goings-
on in the house, her flirtation with Betta, Sukrum's clandestine
business or Lahti's brief pregnancy. As small girls she and Lahti
always confessed under her implacable interrogations, remembering how more than once she had dragged the truth from
them. Their exaggerated respect for her had its source not only
in her wealth, but in these intimidating experiences at a time

when they had never yet met a woman who had so completely defied the conventions of subservience to men. In those days they believed she could see deep into them and even discover their intentions. And if this view had changed with maturity and the return of her doctor son from abroad, there still lingered, until recently, something of that childlike terror at the sound of her disapproving voice or the sight of the ancient wedding sari she had brought from Kerala and which, according to Aji, had been handed down to her through generations of ancestors, back to the time when the veena was still the most popular musical instrument and the sitar, its offspring, was regarded as an extravagance.

From the moment Rani conceived and became aware of the stirrings of another life within her she felt Mrs Singh's spell diminishing, and grew in the certainty that her husband would eventually take her away to a place of their own.

Had she spoken to Lahti about her future in the household the latter would have warned against going out into a world in which people had to rent their own rooms, as the Pujaree did, where neighbours practically lived on top of one another. For Lahti, the world began and ended in Mrs Singh's house and yard where many of its festivities were echoed, and those who were not encouraged to pass through the gates could be witnessed from her windows or heard arriving on the wind. Lahti, like herself, came from a poor East Indian family of numerous children who competed for the right to eat and be educated. Only a fool would leave the sanctuary that was Mrs Singh's home of her own free will. She had resolved to live and die there in a kind of celebration of perpetual immaturity; and even the thought of marriage filled her with terror.

The truth was that, in spite of Rani's need of Lahti, their paths were dividing, through the fact of marriage as much as on account of their contrasting characters, which had once caused endless bickering.

Rani's husband came home every evening soon after the sun went down, when she would eat with him alone at the dining table and listen to the day's happenings at his uncle's jeweller's shop. He was only twenty and was constantly surprised at the things he learned, like the nitric-acid test for checking the quality of gold, or his uncle's dishonesty, which did not stop at using a base metal for the inner ring of the brilliant golden foot rings sold to trusting women. In spite of his travels about the coast to customers who had ordered custom-made pieces, and his dealings over the counter, his two years' apprenticeship had apparently taught him little about people. He had contracted his marriage without any thought that his wife might be indifferent to him. Neither his father nor mother had spoken to him of such matters and every attempt at some form of intimacy elicited the same astonishment that followed the discovery of an irregularity in his uncle's dealing with clients. Indeed, it was his unconcealed pleasure at being served by Rani that encouraged her to ply him with the attentions Aji claimed Mrs Singh used to pay her husband. She oiled his back, pressed and rubbed his feet, washed his shirts with her own hands and reserved one of the camphor-wood chairs for his exclusive use.

When Rani announced that she was pregnant – having dutifully broken the news to Mrs Singh first – he became so embarrassed he was unable to look her in the eye.

'You want me to tell people?' he asked.

'Not yet,' she reassured him. 'Tell your mother in a month. I'll let you know when.'

Aji, after she had been informed of the pregnancy by Rani, threw up her hands in exasperation because her mind had been overcome by the periodic fog that enveloped it. Then, one morning, she seized Rani by the hands and shouted, 'You sure he understan' what the word "pregnant" mean? If I was you I'd tell him so 'e don' think the chile drop out of the Conversation Tree.'

Aji accompanied her observation with a peal of derisory laughter, which she interrupted suddenly to smack her lips before elaborating on her opinion of Rani's husband.

'One thing the chile goin' know to do good is crawl, 'cause the father is a crawl general. One day, you listen to what I tellin' you, a East Indian man goin' rise from awee people, more powerful than Mr Singh and stronger than Betta; an' he goin' knock that crawlin' from we men. It does make you vomit to see big men bend!'

So saying, she spat on the floor and flounced away from Rani who, taken aback by her virulence, could only watch her go through the passage that connected the dining room to the kitchen. And Rani made a resolution that she had made on more than one occasion: never again would she mention her husband to Aji, who had not once pretended that she did not despise him.

But Rani forgave Aji at the first show of kindness on the old woman's part. She forgave her not only because of her age, but because she could not do otherwise. She had often recalled Aji's reprimand on the eve of her arranged marriage, that she was behaving like an animal baying at the entrance to a slaughter-house. None of Mrs Singh's enjoinders to 'show spirit', nor Lahti's encouraging words, could have brought her to her senses as that brief remark had. She felt, immediately afterwards, that she had grown up, that in the brutal observation lay the secret of life ahead of her. Even though her parents, her sisters and numerous relations would not be present to say the ritual goodbyes after the ceremony while she sat in the midst of them, but alone, she drew strength from Aji's presence as the affirmation of her own. Marriage was no better nor worse than any other condition, even to a man she hardly knew. And the months that came and went like the passage of drifting clouds had seemed to bear out the implication of her words. Nothing was as she had imagined it would be. And while thinking back on her first weeks in Mrs Singh's house as a girl of thirteen, when life seemed to stand still in that mansion of strangers where she needed weeks to distinguish inhabitants from visitors, she had no doubt that the surprises of marriage were less harsh than the pain of that first separation from her family.

The infant grew in her womb to the point that Rani was unable to find rest at night; and more than once, driven to distraction by her inability to sleep and the need to remain immobile so as not to wake her husband, she would go downstairs to the drawing room and, opening a window in the gallery, watch the empty pitch road under a wandering moon, the restless shadows of trees hanging low over the white-painted fence and the occasional passer-by who, as surprised to notice an open window as she was to see him at that late hour, would hurry on his way, glancing back from time to time to make certain that all was well. At times, surveying the enclosed yard, as perfect and symmetrical as her old school copy-books, she breathed slowly and deeply until, under the influence of a kind of intoxication, she became convinced that the child sat watching her from the base of her back. Unable to comprehend the extraordinary growth within her, she had fallen prey to her imaginings.

One day she would have to decide whether she was a Hindu, a Christian or nothing at all. If only for the child she was obliged to choose. Her parents were Hindus, but, with little time to do anything but work and sleep, hardly ever went to the temple, even to attend the twice-yearly Kali Mai pujas that attracted believers from miles around. On the other hand her maternal grandparents clung to their customs with a fanaticism that led them to pretend they neither spoke nor understood English. The links with India and its religions were weakening with every generation and now many young parents – especially those who had settled in Georgetown and its suburbs – looked upon the teaching of Hindi with distaste and shunned the society of Pandits, who were never tired of warning against the risks that came with the wrong kind of upbringing.

Rani would have liked to consult the Pujaree, but knew beforehand what his answer would be. Lahti, content to be Hindu, Muslim or Christian, would not take the matter seriously; and as for Aji, she was incapable of giving her a clear answer.

One night while at the window Rani was distracted from her thoughts by the sound of voices coming from under the house. Drawing the bolts of the door softly, she crept downstairs where her attention was drawn to a line of light following the chink between the window and wall of the room where Betta once held surgery. A suppressed outburst of laughter was followed by the sound of a woman's voice which she recognized as Lahti's. Rani, seized with anxiety, turned tail and fled upstairs, where she closed the window and retired once more to bed.

She could not help feeling that Mrs Singh was somehow responsible for Lahti's behaviour, that since Betta went away she had withdrawn her protection from those dependent upon her; Rani, until then unwilling to acknowledge the destructive impulse in Mrs Singh, once believed that she had allowed Sukrum and Bai to occupy the old surgery out of generosity. Now it seemed clear that Lahti's brazen conduct could not be explained simply by her ability to slip downstairs to the men's room when the rest of the house was asleep.

On waking the next morning Rani spoke to Lahti about her visit to Sukrum's room and received the answer that she had not left her own room after they said goodnight to each other.

'But I heard you, Lahti!'

'What you hear?'

'I heard you laughing and talking.'

'It wasn't me, I tell you.'

Rani recalled the uninhibited laughter, the strident remarks that followed it, remarks made incomprehensible in their passage through the pine-board partitions of the surgery.

'You won't change,' Rani accused her.

'Just 'cause you getting child that don' make you Mrs Singh! Is wha' wrong with you at all? You . . .'

Rani interrupted her harshly, 'You had to throw away a child. You're going to keep doing that how long? Who's Sukrum that you're allowing him to do what he likes with you?'

'Who tell you it was Sukrum? I din' tell you was Sukrum. In any case what you got against him? He don' smell.'

'What's wrong with you lately?' Rani asked, almost pleading.

But Lahti turned away in a gesture that seemed significant, as though her youth had turned away from Rani's youth, as though the years they had spent together in the Singhs' household had come to nothing. Until a while ago Lahti's dependence on her had been so evident that Rani often longed for her to go away for a time, so that she might have a few hours to herself, watch the road alone, idle away the evening on her own, even work alone without the possibility of her friend's intervention to impart to her a trivial bit of news or an observation that might have excited her when they were girls. The two women now stood next to each other, Rani in dismay at the discovery of a lost dependence, and Lahti harbouring no more than the desire to stand her ground in the face of a kind of questioning to which she was no longer prepared to submit.

'All right,' Rani said, breaking the stubborn silence, 'don't say I didn't warn you. Whether it's Sukrum or somebody else it doesn't matter. But one day you're going to want to carry a child for nine months and . . .'

Lahti strode off, unwilling to listen.

For a long time afterwards Rani brooded over the certainty of an attenuated relationship that recalled the trailing sound of the sarangi after its bow had been lifted, like the shadow of some obsessive thought. She, with her husband and a child on the way, was more distressed than Lahti seemed to be. And when she told Tipu of her friend's carryings-on he chided her for wandering about the house at night like Aji when she became enveloped in her mist. If Lahti associated with Sukrum it was because like was attracted to like.

'Is her last life that was bad,' he told her, for he believed in an infinity of reincarnations and had no difficulty in seeing Lahti as the victim of a series of misdeeds in a past life. To avoid a similar fate Rani must listen attentively whenever he read from the Vedas and stand by her promise to give him many sons, so that he might discharge his duty to his ancestors.

But it was a long time before Rani came to terms with a loss, the object of which worked beside her and slept in a room on the same floor as the one occupied by herself and her husband, moved around among the camphor-wood furniture with the same assurance as she did, and the scent of whose sweat mingled with hers in the tall wicker baskets where the women's dirty linen was kept. And even after she was able to sit with her at table without experiencing an access of regret at the separation of their ways, Rani continued to have turbulent dreams in which they took turns to comb each other's hair or fought to no purpose like the stray bitches of Kitty with flattened teats.

Chapter 10

The morning after the birth of Rani's child, Aji and Lahti went around the house with baskets to collect the debris of the night before, when the house was filled with the Pujaree's friends. A small girl whose mother had lent her for the day was breaking off faded flowers and dead leaves from shrubs growing in the sawn-off barrels on the porch. The rest of the household was still in bed.

Mrs Singh had just been awakened by the kiskadees calling from the wire connecting her house to the telephone pole on Vlissingen Road and at once recalled with pleasure that there was a new boy child in her house. No one in the 'family' knew what that meant to her, except Aji. Only Aji knew of the five children taken from her by malaria, when in the aftermath of each rainy season she was afflicted with a miscarriage. Two of them were boy children who, had they lived, would have protected her from the terrible thoughts that accompanied her to bed since Betta went away. She could confide in no one how she identified herself with the heroines of destructive myths, who ate their children or slaughtered, for no other reason than an obsessive jealousy which did not grow tepid with the passing months, but rather thrived, attained its autonomy, then took to the subterranean caverns of her thoughts.

When the child was named she would have a celebration just as she did after Betta's birth. Tipu had confided in her that Rani wanted them to leave when he became independent and she, convinced that she was capable of persuading him to stay, had urged him to stand up for himself. He must leave only when *he* saw fit to do so. What kind of man would allow himself to be ruled by his wife? The celebration she had in mind was intended to demonstrate that she considered the couple to be her children.

Mrs Singh had no doubt that her plan would succeed. She

would have her way with Rani, through her husband, just as she had had her way with Tipu's father, who at first had declared that a man could not live in his mother-in-law's house.

Her thoughts turned to other members of the household, to Aji, Sukrum and Bai. The two men had become, for her, part of the family. In the beginning Sukrum's laziness, his over-confident manner, his secretiveness and the way he dominated Bai, had irritated her; but her firmness had led to greater discipline in their work, so that she could no longer reproach them with neglecting the yard. He and Bai had recently painted the elevated water tank, repaired a section of the walaba fence that ran along Dowding Street and constructed an incinerator from an old kerosene tank. The day before, for the first time, the burning saman leaves did not give off the thick, acrid smoke which blew across her yard into the one next door where, her neighbour complained, her cinnamon tree was languishing from the fumes. Besides, their very presence during the greater part of the day must deter thieves who planned to penetrate the compound, she felt.

Although Mrs Singh had settled certain problems arising from Betta's departure she felt the affront of his abandonment deeply enough to seek revenge on someone closely associated with her. And that revenge, consummated with Rani's marriage to Tipu, was strengthened by her growing influence over him. She had decided that that influence must also extend to the child when it was born, over its education and its comings and goings. And Rani would be obliged to yield to the opportunities afforded her offspring as one succumbed to the influence of a debilitating drug that seduced before it destroyed.

When Mrs Singh's husband died, at first she was careful in the use of the wealth he had left. Indeed, she behaved as though she were embarrassed by her control over the lives of those around her. If the assertion of her own independence was swift – she had cut her hair short and taken to wearing men's clothes – she showed herself so hesitant in imposing her will on anyone, Aji was called upon to be firm with the hucksters, the tradesmen and the washerman on her account. But she gradually lost her diffident ways. Her ways, those childlike, guileless ways that masked a terrible will which, long ago, she had known to put to sleep or rouse when the need arose. Her ways, her mother's ways, the ways of certain women of Kerala, the ways of a certain time.

> 'When I was young
> I did a lot of lovin'
> And now I'm old and feeble
> I still got my lovin' ways.'

So ran the words of an American blues song that was played daily on the gramophone of a tailor in Alexander Street for the edification of the neighbourhood, where East Indian men had begun to frequent the rum shops that consumed the wages of improvident men. She had witnessed the ways of the new East Indians whose parents were born in the country, who did not care to model themselves on their elders, and felt a deep sympathy for them, for their children to come and for their offended parents. Had Betta obeyed her she would have performed wondrous works, built a Dharam Sala to rival Ramsaroop's in Albouystown, a house of refuge for the destitute, where the finest musicians played every week and dancing girls performed to the sound of tabla and sitar. She, like Rani, had arrived at the point where the road forked, where good and evil separated. And she had no doubt that it was Betta's conduct that obliged her to take the one leading to the destruction of herself at the moment when she was about to embark on the other.

For the first time she admitted to herself what her actions had already betrayed in the arrangement to marry off Rani to Tipu. The young woman had little in common with a betrothed who had spent most of his youth tending his relations' cows and knew more about carving mango-wood yokes than making calculations with figures that his future bride could manage in her head. And, curiously enough, the discovery of her intentions caused her neither embarrassment nor guilt, only a hardening of the resolve to bend the couple to her will.

Through the open window came the smell of rotting fish from the alleyway separating her house from the one opposite the eastern windows. Her mother, at the time of her periods, used to be affected by tranced images and journeys through unending dawns; and not even her patient father could understand why, at such times, she was unable to suffer the barely audible sound of the wheel that spun rope from coconut husk, when she could endure the drumming of the musician's mridangam. The smell of rotting fish, the call of kiskadees from the electric wires, and cycle bells from the roads before and beside the house on a morning emerging like a moist butterfly from its chrysalis. Had she not been reassured by the coconut trees and innumerable canals that bore such a miraculous resemblance to the Kerala which never ceased haunting her? By the sight of East Indian men plying flat-bottomed boats on the Canje river and their unbrassièred women walking along earth dams with their two-tiered enamel saucepans swinging at their waists? Then her withdrawal into herself when her husband insisted on protecting her from housework, which was the responsibility of a mad housekeeper who fed the rats infesting the house and even called three of them by name because they stood their ground when she set down their food. Here she was, lying in a bed in a land in which she was not born, wondering how so much time had slipped by, how months and years were compressed into brief recollections. Was it not possible that she might return to die in India, in the south where the ashes of her parents and grandparents had been scattered? No, she could not, for she had given birth here. And if she was saddened immeasurably by the realization of her exile she was heartened by the belief that one day Betta would come back to her.

Mrs Singh got up, disturbed by the scent of decay she now recognized as the remains of shelled shrimps Sukrum and Bai must have thrown away in the yard, which she had forbidden them to do time and time again.

The morning followed its customary routine of ritual shower in the bathroom above the kitchen, grooming and dressing, and finally a quarter of an hour spent in the room which the Pujaree had set aside for her devotional prayers in the presence of Kali's painted image.

> 'Mother of all creation
> Who givest and taketh life
> Durga the unknowable . . .'

Mrs Singh begged the goddess to help her achieve her ends, for she surely had not bled to no purpose. And her weekly sacrifices and her good works, had they been in vain? When she thought she was incapable of giving birth to a live child Durga had relented.

At the end of her prayers she decided to consult the Pujaree on the desirability of sacrificing twice a week.

And even in the midst of her prayers she was ashamed of having given in to her mentor's request that she install an image of the goddess in her house. Betta would not approve if he found out, nor would the Mulvi Sahib, who abhorred any representation of humans or any living thing, judging it to be offensive to God.

Before going downstairs she stood before the looking glass, then went and leaned her elbows on the window-ledge, along which was ranged a line of potted ferns. Below lay the expanse of her yard and the neighbour's, divided by a fence above which crowds of midges trembled in the morning sun and dragonflies, mating on the wing, hovered out of reach of pale lizards immobilized by the heat. She heard the first huckster arrive and the lady who sold greens and herbs and the condiments used by Aji for grinding massala. And she recalled how on her wedding day her sisters had decorated her palms and the soles of her feet with henna. She had believed as a child that the old man who sold henna was a supernatural being, just as she thought that Lakshmi, Radha and all the other gods and goddesses lived in the abandoned building where her father's boat tied up. Even here, in the land of shifting river channels, she had changed, continually, until now she stood in the house of doubt after years of guiding everyone around her along *her* chosen road. She had changed, as Aji, who now complained that she saw phantom stars by day. But *she* understood, just as she understood the old woman's dismay when from a seat on the ferry she caught sight of an unusual craft dredging the river mouth. 'For what? For what?' she had shouted, and was pacified only when she was turned round to face south where the river stretched away to the hinterland.

'Yes. I would have lived on sea moss for the rest of my life to keep him and thrown quicklime on the latrine filth with my own hands. All his handkerchiefs were of cambric and silk, yet he spoke harshly of wasting money. But I only wanted to please him, my eagle. . . . And through my indescribable grief I found out what freedom was.'

Mrs Singh went down, and from the landing where the front staircase turned she picked a red hibiscus which she placed in her hair. Then she descended into the yard where the hucksters were assembled with their trays and locked grips.

'Good morning, everybody.'

Her greeting was answered by a unison of voices from the tradespeople.

Chapter 11

The house was full of people and all around and under it coloured lights were strung up and lamps were hanging from nails. A while ago Rani's baby boy was the centre of attention and visitors congratulated both the mother and Mrs Singh, who stood by ready to join her hands in the traditional greeting and enjoin the guests to stay for the music, which was to begin within the hour.

Mrs Singh was anxious about Rani's stony-faced silence. Even the Mulvi Sahib, whom the young mother liked more than any other male visitor to the house, did not suceed in lifting her spirits.

Mrs Singh had hired the same family of musicians, the two girls and their brother, whose expressions had become graver. She had told their father not to bring the sitar, but rather the veena, her favourite instrument.

'You like the sitar for its looks,' she had said to him. 'I like the veena for its sound. We value the veena more highly in Kerala.'

'You talk so much about Kerala. You know very well that the sitar is the queen among instruments.'

'It came from the veena, your sitar,' she objected. 'It looks like a veena, yet gives itself airs.'

So he brought his veena.

All Mrs Singh's friends were there. Beside the Mulvi Sahib there were the Pujaree, the goblet maker and his wife, the creole midwife and the hucksters who came at morning. They were scattered among the hundred or so acquaintances about the drawing room.

By now everyone knew that the infant had been named by Mrs Singh on the advice of a pandit who was also a practising astrologer, that its chiffon swaddling clothes were a gift from her. Tipu was smiling proudly. No one should be in any doubt that he was the father of an infant so handsomely turned out. He was disappointed that Mrs Singh's son could not come, as he had promised, but his uncle, the jeweller, was there, who, like the other guests, had brought a gift, a delicate gold bangle representing a double-headed snake.

Betta, who had visited his mother on several occasions in the year since he went to work in Leonora, had indeed promised to attend the baby's coming-out, but rang the day before to say that he was off to attend a patient. He was going to bring the infant a quinine cup made of lignum vitae bark.

The Mulvi Sahib enquired about Lahti and was told by Mrs Singh that she had gone to an aunt who had fallen ill and would be away for two weeks. Missed by all who knew the house well they did not hesitate to speculate about her absence.

Having handed over his gift of a birdcage he had made himself, the Mulvi Sahib had sat down next to Mrs Singh.

'And how is Aji?' he asked his hostess, half expecting no answer.

'She's upstairs. When I asked if she was coming down she started to talk gibberish. I'll tell you what I won't tell anyone else: I won't be sorry if she died. Now admit that you think. . . .'

'I won't admit anything,' the Mulvi Sahib answered. 'You talk like this only because she won't come downstairs. You're a fine woman and I refuse to judge you.'

'No, you won't judge me. When you lived here you used to avoid my eyes because you saw what no one else could see in them. I'm not ashamed, because my husband had been dead more than a year and I was still a young woman. I've never felt shame, so there's no point in judging me. But there are secrets I won't disclose to you, out of pride, not shame. . . . Lahti's gone away to have a second abortion.'

'Second?'

'She goes to see Sukrum at night. I know and I pretend not to know. I encourage them, you understand. Now judge me. No one who lives here ever ends up begging, or leaves it without knowing to read a newspaper. Rani is a good wife and Lahti'll be a good wife when she gets married. They don't shirk work and they respect their elders and will have as many children as their husbands want. I'm fluent in two languages and am an educated woman yet I knew my place in my husband's home. I was a *good* wife. My husband died and left me alone, without relations. No one is qualified to judge me.'

'Calm down, dear Mrs Singh. When I said you're a fine woman I didn't mean anything else.'

'No,' she murmured, her anger half stilled by his implacable calm. 'I talk about everything except what angers me most.'

And the Mulvi Sahib looked at her in such a way she knew he understood.

'If you were a Muslim lady I would advise you; but how can I say "Do this, do that"? We're separated by our religions.'

'That's why I turn to the Pujaree,' she said, with spite in her voice.

The hum of conversation allowed them to talk without being heard, although the Mulvi Sahib was anxious that Mrs Singh's agitated manner should not attract attention. Never once had he heard her voice raised, even when she was beside herself with anger. He had not forgotten how she once lifted her hand to strike Aji, but at the moment of bringing it down she clenched her fist instead, leaving it suspended above her head.

'It is good that you turn to the Pujaree,' he told her.

'Is it? He keeps upbraiding me when he uncovers these terrible things. . . . He calls them hatred and jealousy, as if such words describe what I feel. When we were first married my husband took me away to the bush. The more he wronged me, the more devoted I became, until he relented and brought me back to the coast. All I remember of that year are goat-suckers wailing after dark. If I listened to the Pujaree I would follow the rules of Suddhi and remain in my room a few days in every month.'

'Yet, without him you're lost,' the Mulvi Sahib remarked, impatient with her for broaching such an intimate subject, and indeed for seeking to enlist his tacit support for her revolt against ancient laws.

Sensing his disapproval, she changed the subject.

'Can you explain to me,' she asked, 'how Sukrum can behave towards Bai as if he was a dog when Bai is so much more intelligent? Why Rani who I treat like a daughter disapproves of me while Lahti worships the ground I walk on, knowing what I think of her bad ways? Can you explain why Aji remains upstairs at a time like this? Why you despise me?'

Her words came precipitately, and as the Mulvi Sahib feared might happen, she appeared to be losing control of herself.

'Please!'

'Yesterday,' she continued, 'or was it the day before yesterday? Ah, yes, it was the day before yesterday, just after he phoned to say he couldn't come. I sat down, determined to be calm; and sitting in that chair in broad daylight it happened, as if I was lying down in a dark room at the dead of night: I saw an enormous mosquito settle on his neck and begin sucking his blood. Its abdomen was curved upwards and its head aimed downwards in an unnatural posture. I was mesmerized by the picture of Betta standing in the middle of the room unaware of what was happening to him. They bite by night, don't they? But the sun was shining on the furniture, on the wall . . . he was standing in the middle of the room. Did you know that they saw through your skin? Like a carpenter sawing through a board . . . until they come to your blood. Betta told me so himself. Then they inject in you something to stop the blood clotting, before they start pumping it up to their stomach. And Betta, who knows so much about this, just stood there muttering, "I've got to go and attend a patient," while that thing became gross with his blood. Oh, Mulvi Sahib, what do you know about life? You go to great lengths to avoid anyone and do everything not to be loved. You have your aviary, you attend the mosque, take care not to enter it with your left foot, prostrate yourself on your prayer mat so many times a day; everything's done according to form . . . ah! and your indulgences, your bright-coloured birds that are freer than birds in small cages and flutter about to please you and flatter your vanity when people say, "Look! A cage full of birds!" I know a great deal about things that fly and bite and suck your blood when you're asleep, then flutter away to rest on walls. But I'm certain you can't find in the Koran what the *male* mosquito feeds on while its mate is lapping your blood.'

'You must go upstairs for a while,' he suggested.

'Yes, I'll go,' she said at once.

'You don't realize,' she continued, after composing herself, 'that you and the Pujaree are the only two men I care for apart from Betta; and both of you demand blind obedience only because I'm a woman.'

She got up from her chair, went over to the musician-father and asked him to begin when she came back down and to demand whatever he wanted from the kitchen.

The Mulvi Sahib took his chair over to the corner where the goblet maker and his wife were sitting with the Pujaree, behind whom stood his mysterious twin nephews, no taller than when Rani and Lahti met them two years before. And immediately the goblet maker's wife, a plump, middle-aged woman with extraordinarily smooth skin, began enumerating for his benefit the presents which could not have been laid out on the cambric cloth for lack of space and were left in a bedroom upstairs. There were two mosquito nets, several celluloid shak-shaks, India rubber balls, a rocking horse, a mysterious game for four players in the form of a cross, and many others. The goblet maker, embarrassed by her loquaciousness, said something to her in Hindi, and at once she gave up.

The Pujaree then began speaking to the Mulvi Sahib of the latest news from India, about the independence movement, which engaged the three men's attention until Mrs Singh came down again accompanied by Aji, who appeared to have been awakened reluctantly from a deep sleep. Then, no sooner had the women taken their seats in chairs offered by two male guests, than the musician and his son struck up a raga. And Rani believed she was in another place where the realization of dreams did not heal, but caused an irrepressible bleeding. Her mother used to go to the cane fields with her breasts exposed, yet refused to accept the gift of her sister-in-law's cast-off sari. Such was her own pride, which she had not lost in a stranger's house, that took away from her the right to name her son. She had no doubt now that she had detected in Mrs Singh a flint-like hardness. As a small girl, while still living with her parents, she often saw the silhouettes of large cockroaches against the moonlight, scurrying along the window-ledge. And for that and much else she had sworn to her brothers that she would live in a mansion when she grew up. But she was certain now that nothing could console her for the loss of her home, where hunger drove the family to bed at sundown. The trade in small girls that had wrenched her and Lahti away before they were of age to give their consent was not regarded as exceptional by anyone. She herself had never thought seriously about it, until she was robbed of the right to name her child.

When Tipu said, 'Laugh a little bit, ne?' she was thinking of her father, a fisherman, who refused to eat before going out in his boat, lest his indulgence attracted bad luck.

'Laugh a little bit, ne?'

And she smiled.

'That's not a laugh. It's a skin-teeth.'

She forced a broader smile, which evidently pleased him, for he turned away to contemplate the family of musicians for whom a pile of sesame cakes lay on a brass platter beside the father, whose face was covered with beads of sweat as he worked his plectrum across the strings of his instrument. Few understood the words of the gazal his younger daughter was singing, for most of them were English-speaking; but they were haunted by the meandering voice and the scatter of familiar words they had picked up from their parents and grandparents.

Nearly everyone had forgotten about the infant lying on Rani's lap. It was sleeping through the heat and the music and the breeze that all but died at the open windows where the humidity on the night air joined the humidity of bodies pressed against one another below the half-dozen electric fans turning on themselves. Some of the children had already dropped off under the constraint of silence and the need to listen to music to which they were not allowed to dance.

Aji preferred to sit on the floor. Tears were coursing down her cheeks, but no one took any notice of her since she went 'off', a term people used to describe her condition when her lucid periods were shorter than those during which she retired into her mist.

Chapter 12

Betta fell foul of the management of the sugar estate when he wrote out a certificate for a field worker who was ill with a fever. A curt letter summoning him to the estate manager's office was delivered by messenger. He went over to the office at once and after waiting about half an hour was asked to go into the manager's inner office.

'What the devil's this?' the manager thundered.

A European – the highest paid staff, down to the overseers, were all Scots, English or Irish – he was so certain that his authority was going to elicit a subservience corresponding to the lowly status enjoyed by someone born locally that he dispensed with the need for preliminary remarks.

'What the devil's this, Singh?' he asked, handing Betta the certificate he had written the day before. 'That's the damn trouble with new men like you: you don't know the ropes. We don't give people certificates unless they have high fevers and are patently sick. This man isn't sick.'

'But he is. I examined him.'

'What's he got? The pip?'

'It's on the certificate.'

'I can't read your handwriting. What's it say?'

'He's got malaria,' Betta said calmly. 'His spleen is unusually enlarged and he has to be hospitalized. It's the worst case I've seen since I came.'

'So, every coolie on this estate's got malaria and you want to hospitalize a man with it. Are you mad? You want every worker to report sick on this estate?'

'I repeat: he has an abnormally enlarged spleen,' Betta said in his quiet way.

'Look, Singh! I'm not going to bandy words with you. Just

bugger off and stop writing certificates. When you feel like doodling with a pen, draw naked women. That's what I do. My drawers are full of naked women.'

Betta left, bristling at his humiliation. Although he had been warned by Merriman what to expect, the last person he believed would give him trouble was the manager. He was not openly contemptuous of him as the overseers and field manager were, most of them arrogant men who strutted about in gumboots and short pants like officers in uniform.

That evening Betta sat at his window waiting for the clock to strike seven, the hour of visiting. Merriman would have had time to close his drug store and take a shower. Meanwhile, he reflected on the incident with the estate manager, turning it over in his mind a hundred times, trying to link it with the things Merriman had told him about the estates' managing staff. He had come into close contact with them, having himself worked on a sugar estate before setting up on his own, and, in the manner of his father, had strong opinions on them, on their lunatic preoccupation with status, and their passion for uniforms.

Betta could hardly wait to discuss the incident with his friend, whom he visited every Friday or Saturday. It was Wednesday, but the thought of keeping the encounter to himself for two days was intolerable. Darkness had fallen rapidly and the Tilley lamps in the police station at the corner were being lit one by one to illuminate the window squares with an extraordinary brightness. Opposite his own yard was a scattering of buildings that housed policemen and their families and in which paler lamps burned. He had still not yet become accustomed to the quarter, the mosque completed soon after his arrival a year ago, the cows grazing in the police compound between a scattering of drays and impounded donkeys and the hum of traffic from the Public Road into which his own street led. In the few days after his arrival at the residence in the windswept street he often wondered what the inhabitants of his old home might be doing, whether Sukrum might be a threat to the good order of that enclosed society with its internal laws, the afternoon retreat of the women that was not to be interrupted except in an emergency, Aji's inviolability and the privileges of his authoritarian mother. In his new home with its overhanging roof there were no gutters, unlike the house in Vlissingen Road, where birds took their dust baths over the staircase at the rear.

On setting out for the Merrimans' home he made an effort to study the layout and buildings in the street where he now lived, and, on turning on to the Public Road, to retain as best he could as much as possible of what he saw.

From a distance Betta could see that something unusual was happening at the Merrimans'. The house was bright and on the porch a couple were standing by the single bench fixed to the wooden railing. Neither of them took any notice of him as he climbed the stairs nor even when he stood beside them, wondering what was responsible for the gathering in the drawing room.

'Is anything wrong?' he asked the man.

'Wrong? Nothing wrong!' the man said.

'Why're there so many people?'

'Is Nen Merriman night,' the man said with some surprise. 'You not from round here.'

'Yes, I'm the estate doctor.'

The man instinctively got up in a show of respect.

'The dispenser inside.'

While he was talking, Merriman, who had caught sight of him through the open window, came to the door and showed him in.

Betta followed him through the door, along the passage between the chairs and the partition separating the drawing room from the bedrooms. Bewildered at the unexpected scene – one lady was holding forth, her words directed at Merriman's wife, who was seated before an assembled crowd of men and women, almost all creoles – he neither caught what was being said nor saw what was happening. Only when he took a seat could he gradually take in the scene, the women fanning themselves, the men with their open-necked shirts listening attentively to the lady's words.

'I did tell him I was goin' home to my mother and he say I could go where I like. Yet when I go he come and pick a quarrel with she.'

'Is that what happened, brother?' Mrs Merriman asked the lady's husband, who was sitting placidly next to her.

'Yes, Nen Merriman; is true. I go and quarrel with her mother, but only after my wife stay away nine months. I thought she was going away for a few days only. She only say . . .'

'I know what he goin' say,' his wife interrupted him, 'but it in' true.'

Betta gathered that Mrs Merriman was holding court and that most of those present were an audience of some sort.

Mrs Merriman had indeed been running an unofficial court for more than five years and its success attracted both litigants and onlookers who came hoping to witness something dramatic. The case being heard had only just opened and immediately caught everyone's attention. Betta sat listening for a while, but his thoughts soon returned to the problem he had come to discuss with his friend, the altercation with the estate manager. Unlike most of those around him, who knew one another and had an assured place in the community, he could not readily forget his own problems by immersing himself in those of others.

Young children were standing next to their parents' chairs or still younger ones were on their mothers' laps, asleep or sucking their thumbs. Most of them seemed healthy, unlike the thin East Indian youngsters with lacklustre eyes he met in the hovel between the back dam and the Public Road.

Just as the couple Betta had met on the porch came through the door there was an outburst of laughter. A portly woman in her forties was addressing Mrs Merriman, accompanying her words with expressive gestures and a wild look in her eye. She kept turning to face a man sitting a few chairs to her left, who, with a fixed smile that belied his status as defendant, kept winking at her as though they were courting.

'My she-goat is a prize goat,' said the woman. 'And Mr Bourne ram goat is a scrawny animal that can hardly stand up 'cause he so weak. . . .'

At this point the defendant winked at the plaintiff fiercely, causing her to turn away and fix her attention on Mrs Merriman.

'He weak like you,' the defendant rejoined.

'That's how he is, Nen,' the woman declared, thinking that she had scored a point against her opponent. 'You kian' talk to him 'bout nothing. I say, "Neighbour, le' we settle this business like Christians"; and he say, "Your she-goat sweet 'pon my ram goat, I kian' help that." "Sweet?" I say, "my goat is a pedigree goat!"'

'But what did his goat do, Miss Ivy?' Mrs Merriman asked, in an effort to bring the plaintiff to the point.

'He jump my prize goat, Nen . . . in front of the children. He crash through the fence and jump me goat.'

The hilarity this remark caused brought the proceedings to an end for the while. Mrs Merriman's husband nudged Betta in the ribs with his elbow and the latter, unable to restrain himself, laughed out loud with the rest.

The defendant, stung to action by the accusation, said in a loud voice, 'Lie! Lie!' but gave up when no one took any notice of him.

Finally, at Mrs Merriman's insistence, order was restored and the defendant was able to say what he had been trying to say against the clamour of voices.

'Nen,' the man intoned, 'the fence had a hole in it already. Two palin' staves was missing. I'm a cooper and I offer to repair the palin' for her. But she say no and I know why she say no, 'cause she sheself want my ram goat to make she-goat pregnant.'

'Oh, me God!' the plaintiff declared in disbelief. 'Me? Me? They got hundreds of decent goats along the coast who would give they right hand to serve my pedigree goat and I goin' glad that a mangy ram that does live 'pon paper an' congo pump leaf jump my she-goat?'

So scandalized was she at the suggestion that she puffed wind into her cheeks and glared menacingly at the defendant.

'Don' wink at me!' she shouted, wagging a finger in his direction. 'Me goat swell up and I want compensation for the damage to her reputation!'

Mrs Merriman stood up in an effort to bring calm to the court. But the onlookers had come in the hope of witnessing chaos and were not to be quietened in the interests of justice. The sleeping children were now awake and those who had sought comfort in their thumbs were laughing with their elders, although few of them knew what was going on.

'Look,' said Mrs Merriman finally, 'it's very serious for those concerned. Please show them some respect.'

She was aware that scenes like this had made her court famous for miles around. But it was the failure of the magistrates and higher courts that had prompted her to take up her father-in-law's suggestion to regularize the counsel for which people had been consulting her since she successfully kept an impending separation out of court; and for that reason alone she disliked the public show the consultations had become.

'Was there a hole in the fence, Miss Ivy?' she asked.

'No.'

'Yes,' the defendant put in.

'You'll have to come back when you can decide whether there was a hole in the fence or not,' Mrs Merriman said firmly.

'There was a small hole in the fence,' the plaintiff conceded promptly, 'is the ram goat make it.'

'Mr Bourne?'

'That's what I say all along. A hole was in the fence! I can't tell who make it 'cause I in' got time to watch the animals courting . . . like some people. All I know is she fancy goat got a thing 'bout my ram goat an' it always wanting to friends with him 'cause she like his style.'

'Style!' shrieked the plaintiff. 'You bring *one* witness to say you ram goat got style!'

'I din' say he *got* style. I say you fancy goat like his style.'

'Very well,' declared Mrs Merriman. 'We're only getting lost. Mr Bourne, is the kid the goat's expecting your ram goat's own?'

'I wasn' there!' the defendant declared. He had given up winking after the plaintiff's threatening outburst and was now sitting up in a dignified manner.

'You see, Miss Ivy,' Mrs Merriman said, addressing the plaintiff, 'it appears one of the goats *did* go through the paling to be friendly. What we cannot prove is whether they were intimate.'

'An' who blow up she belly? The hog? 'Cause if hog start molesting goat . . .'

'Miss Ivy!' Mrs Merriman called out. 'Strange goats come and go in Mr Bourne's yard. I've seen them myself. There's no proof that the ram goat is responsible for the condition of your animal.'

'I see,' said the plaintiff, pretending to be calm. 'From now on he ram goat can butt down my paling, screw my goat an' go back home as if butter won' melt in 'e mouth!'

'No, Miss Ivy,' came the reassuring answer. 'Mr Bourne will have to repair your fence. And in future where it is broken inwards, on your side, I will assume he or his goat did it. Do you agree, Mr Bourne?'

'Seeing as is you, Nen Merriman, I agree. But I want you to persuade Miss Ivy to be good neighbours. I *did* offer to repair the fence, but she say no. I offer to go over and put up she shelves, but she say no. The whole business start 'cause she in' got neighbourly ways. That's the cause of the whole story, I telling you. I'm a student of philosophy and I know a lot 'bout cause and effect. The business goin' start again on account of the background cause bringing about a concomitant effect, like the moon an' the tides, bad mouth an' ruined reputations, evaporation an' precipitation, labia minora an' labia majora. . . .'

'Very well, Mr Bourne. Everything you say must be true. But the important thing is you agree it's desirable that you and Miss Ivy should be on good terms, but no one can force her to be neighbourly or to make her accept your offer to put up her shelves or anything else in her house.'

Then, turning to address Miss Ivy, Mrs Merriman said, 'A gesture from you would help, Miss Ivy.'

And to this Miss Ivy, who was more versed in neighbourly relations than either Mrs Merriman or Mr Bourne, raised her middle finger above her crooked index and fourth fingers in an obscene gesture country folk associated with viragos from town. Then, amidst the murmuring that broke out around her, she made her way between the two rows of seats to the passage along the partition before directing her steps towards the door.

Betta sat through the two remaining cases, pale matters in comparison to what went before. At the end he, young Mr Merriman and his wife went downstairs to see old Mr Merriman while helpers cleared the drawing room and began transporting the chairs back to the houses to which they belonged.

It was only when they were taking their place at old Mr Merriman's cluttered table – the one on which he performed experiments that would 'shake the world', that Betta realized how thoroughly the bad thoughts that infected his mind on arrival at the house had been driven away by the hilarity of an hour ago. He listened to the noise of furniture being moved above him and the clearly audible exchanges regarding the provenance of the chairs on which the onlookers had been sitting.

Old Mr Merriman had been waiting for them and in the twinkling of an eye he had set on the table four glasses and a misshapen bottle of a strong, nameless concoction made from honey he himself had harvested from the hives behind the house.

On one shelf bracketed against the wall was displayed a number of old, hand-made Dutch bottles retrieved from canals. Of different colours and shapes, some of them were so badly centred that they were in danger of falling over.

'That's the one,' old Mr Merriman said to Betta, on seeing how interested he was in the display.

And Betta, still uncertain of his place in the household, got up to inspect the bottles under the supervision of the old man.

'That cobalt colour they can't get in glass any more,' he told him. 'Imagine that! They've lost the secret.'

As interested in the past as he was in his inventions he drew Betta aside and lectured him on his bottles, his collection of aboriginal Indian arrows, his prints relating to the achievements of old Dutch microscopists, who achieved magnifications of two hundred with the most elementary instruments, and on his collection of objective lenses.

'Father,' his daughter-in-law said, 'we're waiting for you and Betta.'

And in that way Betta was spared a lecture that might have 'gone on all night', joked his son.

Mrs Merriman, more communicative than Betta had ever seen her, began relating unusual experiences from her monthly Wednesday-night court; and while she spoke her husband looked on, evidently proud of her reputation as the woman who poured oil on troubled waters.

'She pours oil on troubled waters then sets it alight,' he joked.

'Boy, what's wrong with you?' his father said, knowing well that his son was not speaking in earnest. 'She's got a gift. It's a gift, like teaching or keeping bees. You can teach people the rules, they can either do it or they can't.'

'What about Mr Waithe, the man who taught you?' his son asked. 'You don't think much of him yet he's the best-known beekeeper along the Bank.'

'Anybody can keep bees,' his father retorted with irritation, 'just as anybody can teach. I'm talking about *real* beekeeping and *real* teaching. Some people get a lot of lazy queens; others manage to breed diligent ones. Can you explain that? 'Course you can't. It's a gift, I tell you.'

'Let Doris talk, Father.'

'Oh, yes. Sorry, girl, sorry. When your good-for-nothing husband gets me going you can never tell where I'll end up. Once I start talking about music or beekeeping I can never stop.'

Caught in full flood, his hands gesticulating and his face contorted with enthusiasm for what he was saying, he bowed his head slightly in shame.

'Go on, girl, we're listening.'

And Mrs Merriman, glad of the opportunity to impress Betta, began to speak of her work in an authoritative voice. In the beginning only women sought her out, forlorn creatures who had lost their husbands or been abandoned by their men and wore garments of despair, mourning dresses that gave them a measure of comfort. Her drawing room began to resemble a funeral parlour that attracted women who came to mourn the mourners, and it seemed that all the troubles of the world were heaped upon women. But gradually the men began consulting her, first to redress the balance of a biased account which they were afraid would get about and undermine their consideration in a small community; then with time she was visited by couples whose problems were not yet beyond resolution, and even young people who felt crushed by the weight of a parent's authority or did not believe themselves capable of assuming the responsibilities of adulthood.

Then they discussed the East Indian free immigrant courts and they all agreed that it would be a good thing to make the system a general one.

'Can you see the lawyers agreeing to it?' asked young Mr Merriman.

'About a third of the people who consult me go to law afterwards anyway,' Mrs Merriman said.

So they talked, until the noise of shifting furniture above their heads ceased and the two songbirds began flapping about in their cage above the window and the air grew damp and old Mr Merriman nodded off. And Betta, at the sight of the sleeping old man, was moved to think of his father whom he could hardly recall except for a visit he thought he made with him across the boundary into town where the whistling of frogs was augmented by the disused sewage pipes in which they took refuge; and the same night when, after being served by Aji, he retreated to the gallery where he began to draw on a cigarette with a voluptuous commitment. Here was a different life of which he had little notion. The 'court' he had just witnessed was entirely different from the large gatherings in his mother's house.

He had forgotten why he had come visiting and continued to take part in the exchanges as though that was the purpose of his coming. No one had mentioned that he had come on a Wednesday instead of a Friday, as was his wont. Nor did he bother to disclose his surprise that during two years of friendship with Merriman he had no idea that his wife kept a court. Since things were so they could not be strange.

Under the influence of the mildly alcoholic drink, he desired to speak of his years abroad and regaled them with an account of winter, when snow lay like piles of salt on the fields and crows made brief flights over a forlorn landscape and all the flowers had died, and of summer with its smell of ashes and urine under the railway bridges.

Mrs Merriman got up and placed a cloth over the birdcage before standing in front of the window. Betta came to the conclusion that he would never understand her or her three sons or even the family as a whole, which seemed to function under a total absence of rules. Was this the creole world, in truth? Or were the Merrimans an exception? Their Christian God demanded nothing more than a nightly reading of the Bible at the bed and attendance in church on Sunday. This he had seen on his daily rounds in the hovels and the more substantial houses on the Public Road.

'Take another glass, man,' young Mr Merriman offered, pushing a half-empty bottle towards him.

'Don't force the doctor, Westel,' his wife protested.

She sat down at table once more, beside her sleeping father-in-law.

Then, as abruptly as she had sat down, she got up again. 'I'm going up to bed,' she declared. 'Goodnight, Betta.'

Bravely she pretended that the alcoholic drink had had no effect on her; but on standing up she opened her eyes wide and hesitated before making for the door of the small room. And as soon as the door was closed Betta called to mind why he had come visiting. Yet he could not bring himself to speak about it after such a pleasant evening.

'You can't talk freely in front of the women,' Merriman said, referring to the fact that their conversations were always less constrained when his wife was not present. 'Try telling a sexual joke when they're around.'

Merriman was, in many ways, more serious than Betta, having inherited from his father a love of books and an intense curiosity about the natural world. But he liked to affect a detachment which those who knew him well did not take seriously. The two men liked each other, but had not yet achieved that intimacy which would have encouraged Betta to speak his mind. Besides, Merriman's cordiality, his sympathetic way with everyone, his father, his wife and even the clients who came to the pharmacy, acted, somehow, as a bar to the discussion of his own problems.

Instead, Betta enquired after Merriman's sons and learned that his wife worried constantly about them. The eldest, eighteen years old, kept pestering his parents for consent to marry a girl of sixteen. The second and third, each a year younger, were hardly ever at home. Their conversation shifted from one subject to the other until it came upon the very thing that preoccupied Betta most, the condition of the East Indian community. Did Betta know that the dowry system had all but died out among the poor because for years during the period of immigration there were many more men than women? Now that there was little difference between the numbers of men and women among young people husbands were less indulgent and cases of brutality were not uncommon.

Dead insects lay in a circle round the kerosene lamp on the table, mosquitoes and beetles which had come in through the open window, attracted by the light and the heat of the men's bodies. From time to time one of the two men would slap his exposed arm, occasionally leaving a splatter of blood where a female mosquito had been killed, while pervasive stillness was broken by the croaking of a crapaud from the gutter that ran along the front yard, between the Public Road and the wooden fence. And suddenly, Betta knew that in spite of the problems ahead of him, he was happy in that village, the majority of whose inhabitants were East Indians like himself.

When he bade his friend goodbye he went out into the night under a slate-grey sky and walked rapidly towards the road where his car was parked. Driving past the police station he heard the click of dominoes, like the strident call of a night insect. The sight of a dog picked out by his headlamps reminded him that there were few stray dogs in the country.

'Nor beggars, for that matter,' he said to himself.

The janitor's room beneath his house was in darkness and Betta was seized by the urge to go walking, away from the village on an endless journey west, past the flooded lands where the young rice grew, and the drainage canals that emptied in the sea and the solitary tamarind trees and the endless succession of trenches choked with lotus, and water hyacinth that defied control to the despair of impoverished village councils.

Chapter 13

The janitor had shown the workman who came to repair the cinnamon-green venetian blinds into the gallery, where they stood discussing the price of repairs and what needed to be done. Betta sat alone at the dining table. He could see across the drawing room into the gallery where the two men were negotiating. Knowing nothing about the running of the house, Betta left the business entirely in the janitor's hands and concentrated on his morning meal.

He had not yet been affected by the loneliness that was to oblige him to take a wife, and sitting alone at the unnecessarily large table his thoughts turned to his consulting room, which the dispenser would have already prepared for him. He had put in for a microscope to help in his diagnoses, especially of Bright's disease, the organism that often brought death in its wake and which had been identified by Dr Giglioli three years ago while he was working for the Canadian-American Bauxite Company in McKenzie. He had heard nothing since and was told by Merriman that all Government Medical Officers were once in possession of a microscope, but they had all mysteriously disappeared from their consulting rooms following Dr Giglioli's discovery. In fact the doctor had been dismissed by the company on the pretext that production of bauxite had fallen and consequently his services were no longer needed.

The sirdar to whom he had given a certificate for malaria was able to go to work the day before and was afraid that the estate manager might have it in for him. Betta admitted to himself that he was looking forward to issuing his next certificate, for the manager's attitude had only served to stiffen his resolve to do his work as he saw fit.

Breakfast over, he went down to his car carrying his black bag. On reversing over the bridge he saw the cook arriving from market and waved to her. Like the janitor and the venetian blind mender she was a creole, a lady with a gentle voice, who, apparently, had never smiled in her life. She responded with a languorous wave of the hand, while she stood aside to wait for the car to manoeuvre into the road.

It was the country's boast that no rice had been imported since 1917 and the vast stretches of rice lands south of the Public Road seemed to confirm the claim. In many of the flooded fields East Indian women in head-kerchiefs and ankle-length frocks were bent double to press the young rice stalks into the mud. Postures of work, postures of prayer, of despair and affection, postures of remorse, of envy, of humiliation and tyranny, of incredulousness, of astonishment and dying. . . . He had witnessed them all in the closed world of his Vlissingen Road home. Yet on the West Coast they assumed a significance that, he believed, was connected to the goal he had set for himself. The day before he had treated a woman who was bent double. After giving her a prescription for a bottle of barbiturate for her insomnia she implored him to straighten her again.

'I hear you got medicine for everyt'ing.'

'Not for everything, grandmother.'

'I bet if was you wife you would straighten she out.'

She had come only the week before, complaining of pains in her chest and had pretended she could only speak Hindi, causing Betta to apologize that he knew no more than a few words.

'I got fo' sleep with me foot them in the air,' she complained.

'Grandmother, I don't have medicine for that. Did you work in the rice fields?'

'Yes, Doctor. But I always did pray to Lakshmi. An' I sacrifice 'nuf 'nuf time.'

'The last time you came you said you couldn't speak English, grandmother.'

She paused a while, then said, 'Boy, I old enough to be you gran'mother. . . . Las' time I couldn' talk English. Dis time I remember it. It does come an' go like me chil'ren. You goin' straighten me out or you in' goin' straighten me out?'

'I don't have medicine for that, grandmother. I told you.'

'I gone, then,' she said, turning away.

Yet few old people came to his consulting room. Convinced that their herbal remedies were superior to the doctor's drug medicine they reserved the same deep mistrust for it as they did for banks. And their naiveté was no more disastrous than the naiveté of the educated who would not understand why Dr Giglioli had been dismissed or why the consulting-room microscopes had disappeared from the Government Medical Officers' consulting rooms.

Betta was on the way to the hospital at Uitvlugt estate, a few miles up the coast, where the estate workers were in better health than those in Leonora and Anna Catherina. At the approaches to the village he slowed down to cross the shaky bridge which spanned a trench in which several cows had taken refuge from the morning sun and the insects.

'Doctor, me goin' look after you car!' a little boy shouted as he slowed down just beyond the road that turned off to the south where the estate hospital was situated.

'Me, Doctor, me! He's a big t'ief! He t'ief me okari. He t'ief 'e mother money, too.'

Betta left the car in the care of both boys and went off on foot to work all morning at the hospital before leaving to visit patients in their homes. That day he wrote two certificates. There had been no complaints on that estate that his previous certificates had been unreasonable.

On his way home that afternoon he passed by Merriman's pharmacy, but was content to honk his horn after noticing that there were a number of people in it. He then thought of paying his mother a surprise visit, but reckoned that he would be too late for the last ferry back to Vreed-en-Hoop. So he returned to the big house, threw himself on his bed and slept until eight o'clock when he was awakened by the crickets and the drumbeats of bullfrogs in the grass beneath his window.

The next day Betta arrived at the local hospital on foot with a strange feeling of disquiet. He saw in everyone's face a surly expression and a kind of questioning. To his annoyance the nurse had not put out the jar with water and the enamel cup nor had the screen been pulled out from its recess. And when she arrived, panting and full of excuses, he reprimanded her, simply out of relief that nothing had been wrong.

'All right, all right,' he said irritably, 'get everything ready.'

Soon afterwards the first patient was shown in, a man with an abscess which he had treated.

'It's not yet ready to be lanced,' Betta told him. 'Come back in three or four days.'

And one by one he examined and dispatched patients, some with prescriptions and others with futile advice about a diet beyond their means. Where he suspected malaria there was little he could do since the estate, like nearly all the other estates, reckoned that quinine was too expensive to provide free of charge.

Betta could not suppress the idea that with such a large

labour pool at their disposal the estate owners did not care to spend more than the minimum on their workers' health. In fact he began to take Merriman's assessment of the situation seriously, that the estates' interest lay in having a debilitated work force, so much so that Dr Giglioli was seen as a dangerous scientist who took his research seriously and actually enjoyed identifying parasites that ravaged their workers' lives.

Then one after the other, Betta wrote two certificates for a couple with enlarged spleens. He also arranged for them to go to the Georgetown General Hospital and gave them letters to the Commissary Officer at Vreed-en-Hoop, requesting a pass for free transport across the river. The wife claimed that her husband had been delirious and had had a high fever. She had sent for the doctor, but he had not come. Betta said he had received no message. He suspected that the husband might be suffering from paratyphoid, a diagnosis that could only be confirmed as a result of examination of a blood culture.

After his rounds Betta went home to await the inevitable summons to appear before the estate manager. Strangely calm, he put on his leggings and made a tour of his yard which, though well kept, was neither cultivated nor planted with flowering shrubs, unlike the police compound where policemen and their families lived, and in which ochroe, squash and cassava flourished at the foot of their long staircases. He called the janitor and asked if arrangements could be made to plant vegetables in the yard.

'I suppose so, sir. But I think they does grow bad on this side of the road, seeing as how there's so much water as a result of the depression.'

'And where does the depression come from?' Betta asked.

'It's a mystery, sir.'

'Well, gutters could be dug to drain off the water into the street gutter, couldn't they?'

'I don' think so, sir. We did try that one time, but the water that drained off did come back mysteriously.'

'Couldn't we have deep gutters dug to drain off the mysterious water as well?' Betta asked, intent on finding out how far the janitor was prepared to go with his prevaricating tactics.

'We could try,' the janitor replied, 'but there's a mighty lot of water down there, Doctor.'

That night Betta tried to read, but was unable to concentrate for more than a few lines. His thoughts kept returning to the imminent meeting with the manager, the very circumstance he had decided to banish from his mind as unworthy of serious thought. But the idea had acquired an existence independent of his will and hovered about his reflections like a persistent insect, descending upon him when his attention was momentarily engaged with something else, the janitor's intransigence or the despairing living conditions of a patient and his family, or vultures gathered round a dead dog by the roadside with the aspect of women in mourning. In the end he faced the coming meeting squarely and discovered that the independent idea had grown and taken on a complexity without any apparent decision on his part. By dint of studying the possible consequences of his action he arrived at the resolution that his honour depended on his stand, like a hunter who, after familiarizing himself with the site chosen for his vigil, loses sight of the dangers which first made his venture seem foolhardy.

Betta undressed and went to bed. And it was that night that he decided to take a wife to make his loneliness bearable. The old cook and the janitor, who often had lengthy talks on the back stairs, inhabited a world he could not hope to penetrate, a world he could never understand. Like Merriman they were creoles, but unlike him they were often taciturn and always intractable, and more than once he could not help attributing to them some connection with his loneliness. No doubt they believed that he was beyond the reach of mortal emotions simply because he was a doctor. He could no longer doubt his mother's assessment of her own achievements: she had created a world circumscribed by extensive fences where the aged died slowly, where marriages were contracted, children were born, with its own place of worship, its presiding priest and secret liaisons, where – as she disclosed to him on his last visit – a gaunt abortionist dropped in, bringing with her a bucket and a cake of carbolic soap. Apart from this world within a world he had experienced the sting of loneliness much more keenly than he had done abroad.

'I must take a wife,' he told himself.

Chapter 14

Late the next morning Betta drove up to the estate manager's house, an impressive structure set in grounds next to the sugar mill itself. One of the menservants signalled him to drive his car into the yard under the house, which had recently been painted. The manager himself was at the foot of the concealed staircase that led upstairs.

'Dr Singh,' he said, welcoming Betta with a cordiality that confused him.

'Come up this way.'

Then, as they reached the top of the stairs, he said to another manservant waiting with his back slightly bent in a deferential posture, 'John, bring us two rum swizzles.'

'Not for me, thanks,' Betta said, 'I don't drink.'

'What about a soft drink, then?'

'Thanks.'

'Bring lots of ice, John.'

The estate manager then went over to a corner of the wide gallery where he opened one of the several doors leading into the drawing room and one end of the gallery, beyond which a staircase mounted to the rooms of the upper storey.

Betta wanted to remark on how well the house and yard were kept, but could not bring himself to be pleasant to a man who had showed his hand with so little concern for his dignity.

Along the gallery there were no windows and the view from the house was dominated by a Hindu temple and a small church, separated from each other by the school attached to the church. The overhanging eaves, which kept out the rain, served as a support for small, saucer-shaped marabunta nests, from which a wasp emerged from time to time to undertake an indolent flight into the dusk.

Neither man would break the silence and Betta, who had the impression that the manager was testing him, remained obstinately uncommunicative. Finally, the manservant came back and noiselessly placed the wooden tray on the round table between the two men.

'All right, John,' the manager said. 'Close the door and say I'm out to anybody who wants me. When the mistress comes back tell her I have a guest and do not wish to be disturbed. . . . And by the way the mistress wants you to get wood piled up by the kiln for tomorrow.'

The man went out as softly as he had come in, closing the two-leafed door behind him.

'At last,' said the manager, turning to Betta with a smile. 'It's unusual to meet a man of principle, Dr Singh. I've known five G.M.O.s and none of them had any principles. Admirable men, knew all about survival. Oh, Dr Singh, you disappoint me. I didn't behave well the last time we met, but I *did* give you good advice. But I'm sure you set great store by courtesy, don't you? Well, I apologize for what I said last time. Does that satisfy you?'

Betta mastered his fury sufficiently to think carefully before answering.

'Mr Niven, why did you ask me to come?' he enquired, and saw the effect of his words at once on the estate manager's face, which flushed with embarrassment at what he saw as Betta's insolence.

'If you don't know why I called you here you have no right to be practising as a G.M.O, Singh.'

Neither man had touched his glass and the two drinks stood next to the ice bowl in the middle of the tray, on which a pool of water had collected.

'Will you tell me why you asked me to come?' Betta persisted, unflinching in his resolve to stand his ground, a resolve made easier by the manager's change of style in dealing with him.

'I asked you to come,' he declared, 'because you persist in writing medical certificates, Singh. I wonder if you know that the indenture laws allow us to take estate workers to court if they don't report for work. And that . . .'

'I do my job. I am a doctor, not . . .'

'Damn you! Don't defy me!'

'Defy you! Who the devil do you think you are, my employer? I'm a Government Medical Officer. If you have a complaint about me you can report me to my employers . . . in Georgetown.'

'I'll remember that, Dr Singh.'

The estate manager had got up and was standing between his chair and Betta's.

'I suggest that you get a second opinion on the certificates I issued,' said Betta.

'You have no idea what I'm talking about, have you?' the manager said. 'It's *not* the habit of G.M.O.s to issue certificates lightly, dammit.'

'Lightly? If I issued certificates as I should a third of the field workers would be home in bed. Let me ask you a question: Why don't you buy quinine for the field workers, at least?'

'For a start,' answered the manager, 'we don't take advice from blacks, Singh. Besides . . .'

Betta got up.

'Listen,' said the manager, regretting the words that had slipped the vigilance he had sworn to observe when he made up his mind to invite Betta to the house rather than to his office, where he was in the habit of receiving people from the village.

'Do sit down. I apologize once more,' he said in a conciliatory voice. 'Don't take offence. . . . Um . . .'

Involuntarily he put his hand to his head. Betta recalled how nervous he had been when he arrived, how he told himself that things would go well with him if he remembered all the details of the doors he went through before coming face to face with the manager, a habit he had never managed to shake off since it took hold of him in childhood. But the manager's unusual cordiality on his arrival had disarmed him to the extent of causing him to forget about the doors.

The manager raised his rum swizzle and drank, and Betta followed suit, sipping the sweet liquid in his glass.

Night had fallen and the starless sky had disappeared in the darkness, relieved here and there by lights from cottages and hovels. The manager had not noticed the fading light, nor that the lamplight coming through the transom above the closed door was barely sufficient to distinguish the features of his unwelcome guest. He did not know what to do next. Dr Singh would probably be able to rely on the Immigration Department for support, in which case he would have to resort to other means in order to force him to resign. Did this East Indian doctor represent a new breed of blacks or was he simply a foolhardy upstart whose stay abroad had gone to his head?

'The fact is,' said the manager, 'we can't run an estate with workers at home. . . . Tell me something: Why are you taking this stand? What have you got to gain by it? You live well, you've got the pick of the women on the estate. What do you *gain* by it?'

Betta would not answer, partly because he was offended by the manager's too-familiar tone and partly because he had no idea what to say.

'Under your quiet reasonableness,' continued the manager, 'you're an arrogant man, Singh. Well, that's not unusual. I don't know anyone exercising authority who isn't arrogant. When I was at school I read everything Oscar Wilde had written and everything written about him. Do you know that when the governor of Reading Jail was kind to him Oscar Wilde described him as a saint. Just because he treated him with a *normal* kindness. He'd been treated like dirt in prison until then and normal behaviour appeared saintly to him. Yes, Singh. Ten to one the governor was as arrogant as you, but a man with Wilde's understanding of people was seduced into thinking of him as a saint. . . . I was taken to hospital a few years ago after a heart attack. I wanted to shower presents on the doctors and nurses for their *kindness*, for saving my life. Something had gone to my head and I saw them as saints. *You* are a dangerous man, Singh, because you see *yourself* as a saint. . . . Oh, don't be offended. I don't dislike you; it's just that one of us should not be here. . . . You people! We give you an inch and you take an ell. Trying to reason with you is as futile as. . . .'

The manager, unable to find a suitable comparison, stopped in mid-sentence.

'There's always the fear at the back of my mind,' he went on, 'that one day I'll fall into your hands, that I'll have an attack and you'll be called upon to attend to me. . . . You see, I put my cards on the table. But you tell me nothing except what you *have* to tell me. And that's the trouble with your kind: we never know what you're thinking or planning. . . . Look, damn you, couldn't you cooperate with me? *I* have to answer to the estate owners, just as the field manager has to answer to me and the overseers to the field manager . . .'

'And if . . .' Betta attempted to interrupt.

'You, dammit, don't have to answer to anyone. . . . You think it's easy for me to live in a country where I'm disliked? Where the high point of the month is the party I give for the overseers and. . . ?'

The manager's face had an expression so doleful that Betta took pity on him. He had recently read a report that white expatriates who suffered mental breakdowns were mostly afflicted with delusions of persecution, and the sight of this man, so feared by his staff, the spectacle of his inadequacy and isolation, affected Betta deeply.

He took a long time to reply, and when he finally spoke he could not look the manager in the eye. He stood up once more.

'I would like to cooperate with you, but it would have to be on the basis that sick people go to hospital or are allowed to stay home. Besides, since you've threatened me I'll have to write a report to the Immigration Office . . . to protect myself . . . Can you see me out? I'm not . . .'

'John!' the manager called out, seething with anger that his conciliatory words had not had their desired effect.

The manservant arrived and did not need to be told that the visitor was to be seen out.

Yes, Betta told himself on his way home, I *am* afraid of the estate manager. I'm afraid of his status, of the hold people like him have over us. I'm afraid of my lack of experience in the outside world. I'm afraid of creoles because they are the teachers, the pharmacists, the sick-nurses, the dentists. . . .

His fear, he reflected, was connected with the condition of East Indians, whose children fared badly at school. The Mulvi Sahib and his mother had inculcated in him the need for an inner strength, a fire that burned intensely, that had its source in an inner freedom so complete it was incapable of being smothered. He felt like rushing to the Mulvi Sahib's home and confessing that all his resentments had vanished, that at last he understood: that he understood the importance of physical wellbeing, which could not be separated from spiritual well-being, that he understood the limitation of knowledge, of love and of everything devised or imagined by man, that dense forests grew on poor soils, that human knowledge would always be inadequate for human needs, that there were winters on this self-same latitude where ice was harvested to sell in the valleys, that to wonder at the beauty of birds was not a vanity but a need as deep as their need of illusions; that he understood why the suicide rate among immigrant Indians in Fiji had reached the alarming figure of nine and a half per thousand, even though they were the most prosperous migrants from India, that contentment was like a season of shooting stars which leaves no more than the shadow of a memory, that the true aim of life lay in travelling along the 'way'.

Chapter 15

The following Sunday Betta decided to go and visit one of his patients, a shopkeeper who had been stricken with diabetes and whose business had gone from bad to worse since his illness. In order to accumulate a large capital as quickly as possible he had condemned himself and his family to a meagre diet, having promised them that when he acquired sufficient money he would arrange a banquet at which they and all their relatives would dine on fried bolonjay and curried snapper and sweetmeats from Surinam. Betta was surprised to hear music coming from the shopkeeper's house, a modest cottage on the Public Road raised three steps from the ground, with a rusted corrugated roof from which a pipe channelled rainwater into a barrel beneath a sash window. His curiosity aroused by the contrast between the failing business and the noise of revelry issuing from the house, Betta knocked on the door, which was opened by a boy of twelve, one of the man's nephews.

'Is doctor!'

The shopkeeper's wife came to the door and welcomed Betta effusively.

'Is your husband inside?' he asked.

'He inside, yes.'

'Can I see him? I came to see how he was.'

Betta could tell at a glance that most of those present did not live there, for they were dressed in fine clothes and the women wore jewellery on their chests, in addition to the bangles and foot rings they never took off.

He followed the child's aunt into the bedroom, where he found her husband sitting on a chair next to his bed, his gaunt face no different in appearance from the way it was the last occasion he visited.

'I was comin' to see you tomorrow, Doctor,' the man said, ashamed that Betta should want to come there of his own accord.

'How're you feeling?' Betta enquired.

One of the man's girl children brought in a chair and placed it next to her father.

'How're you feeling?' Betta asked again.

'The same,' he answered, spreading out his hands and forcing a smile. 'You wondering 'bout the fête, ne? Is my nephew. He get a scholarship for a town school and we celebrating.'

He mistook Betta's smile for surprise at a celebration which belied his reputation as a miser.

'I got enough, Doctor. Not enough for the girls' dowry, but enough to feed everybody. And after all when she got education what they goin' want with dowry?'

Betta expressed surprise that the man was even thinking of a dowry.

'The Tamils does still want dowry, Doctor. They got a cripple boy they does call Victor One-Hand, and I myself hear him say he not getting married to no girl that in' got dowry in she hand an' drawers 'pon she tail.'

This information did not square with Betta's experience in his short time in practice in the area, but he did not pursue the matter. He examined the man as best he could without his stethoscope, putting his ear to his chest and then to his bowels.

'Do you follow the diet?' he asked him.

'I got to, Doctor. I in' ready to go yet.'

Betta noticed the bow-legs of the nephew and his brother who had joined him at the door. The condition was widespread among East Indians along the West Coast, even in families where milk was drunk. He promised himself to note the observation in his diary on returning home.

The Mother

'You mus' talk to my young daughter before you go, Doctor,' the man told him. 'Tell she to study good and not to get in with too much friends at school. And not to eat when somebody give she food.'

'I'll talk to her,' Betta promised.

Why did I come here? Betta reflected, when his attention was drawn to the loud voices in the adjoining room. It was the first time he had gone on an unsolicited visit except on the occasions when he looked up the Merriman family. He rejected the thought that the attractive young woman might have drawn him back. Yet, on arriving, he had looked around to see whether she were there.

Then, on hearing the heavy breathing of his host, who had fallen asleep next to him, he thought of his illness and wondered if there could be a connection between malaria and diabetes. He rejected the hypothesis, recalling that diabetes afflicted Indian communities in countries where there was little or no malaria.

Questions thronged in upon him, lingered for a while, unanswered, then gave way to others. Was he, like Dr Giglioli, more gifted for research than general practice? Could the general practitioner make any impact on the health of a community? He desired to love a woman and to be loved, to raise a family in order to justify his existence to his ancestors. But he desired so much else as well. And if tomorrow some effective anti-malarial drug were to be developed what would he make of his passionate wish to contribute to his people's welfare? Was his need to help people a need to help himself?

Now the persistent humming of mosquitoes could be heard about his ears, competing with the voices of unseen faces.

Wherever he went he met respect, at times even adulation, simply because he was a doctor. In some curious way he was drawn to this family, to the boisterous mother and her young daughters, to the sick father who, like so many others, had made a tragic choice in an effort to migrate from the sugar lands. And yet, in the father's slow demise, the house was filled with laughter.

I must marry before it is too late, he thought, and make as many children as would satisfy my forebears before I start dropping off, with some medical label stuck to me.

133

The door opened and the two boys were joined by the shopkeeper's younger daughter carrying a tray.

'Get the table!' she said, frowning at one of the boys, who fled at once.

'You are Meena's younger sister?' Betta said to her.

'Yes.'

'How old is she?'

'Nearly sixteen.'

At that moment the boy came back bearing a round table above his head. The tray was full of food of all kinds, boiled bolonjay, dhal pourri, roti, rice and much else he did not recognize in Tamil cooking.

'You want me to bring Meena?' the girl asked. 'She want to meet you and she was to bring in the tray, but she frightened of you.'

'Ask your mother to come,' Betta said. 'I want to thank her for the meal.'

'Meal? . . . Oh, you mean the cooking? Is I do it.'

'Well, ask Mai to come in any case.'

When the girl came back with her mother he was suddenly covered in confusion because he had called the lady of the household simply to thank her for the meal.

'I wanted to thank you for the food. Do you mind if I ate with my hands? I'd like to.'

'Yes, Doctor. . . . Take away the spoon an' leave the doctor alone. And bring Meena so the doctor can see her. Tell her to stop playing stupid.'

Meena came in, hiding her face behind her raised achal, which was the same colour as the sari she was wearing for the special occasion.

'Your father asked me to advise you about your studies,' he said, addressing Meena's younger sister who had come back into the room. 'You must work hard and not let your parents down.'

He saw how foolish he had been in ignoring Meena, but was helpless to do otherwise. He had grown up in a house of women, and now in the company of women he wished he was out in the open air, at the wheel of his car, rushing away from the house.

'This is your eldest daughter?' Betta asked with apparent self-assurance.

'Say something,' Meena's mother urged her. 'She not shy at all, Doctor. Is she you did hear laughing all the time an' making everybody else laugh.'

The other ladies and one gentleman were led in and introduced to Betta in turn. Aunt, uncle, aunt, cousin and other aunts, all proferring limp handshakes as a sign of deference. And the host slept through the introductions, his head to one side, as serene in ill-health as he had been when he was well.

'Alyou go now,' Betta's hostess said. 'The doctor want to eat with his hands.'

Meena laughed, for that was the way they and their relations ate. The spoon had been an inspiration of their mother's, for she believed that Betta could not be a true East Indian, since he came from the outskirts of Georgetown.

They all left the bedroom, except the two small boys, who stood staring at Betta as he kneaded the rice into a ball before dipping it into the curry and placing it into his wide-open mouth. They were yet too young to be sent away since they were incapable of embarrassing an adult. And indeed the women were in the habit of undressing in front of them, as they would have undressed before a dog or a caged bird.

No sooner had Betta eaten the last mouthful than the older boy ran out to inform the company that the doctor had finished his meal. And this time Meena came in on the instructions of her mother, her diaphanous achal modestly drawn across her mouth and her eyes averted.

'Thank you, Meena,' he said. And she could do no more than take away the tray with unsteady hands.

And Betta's own confusion vanished in the face of the young woman's. He had done the right thing in coming to this house. The facile respect he attracted had contrived to bring about a situation that left him with a feeling of extraordinary confidence.

It would not be seemly to bring gifts soon after his triumph. He must let the matter rest for a while, come back a fortnight or a month later and gauge the effect of his return on Meena and her parents.

Betta, lacking any experience in such matters, was making his plans with a guile and foresight that would have done credit to a rake. And when Meena came back with a basin of water and a towel on which rested an untouched cake of soap, he resisted the temptation to enquire of her if she would like him to come back. While washing his hands and mouth he looked at the contours of her hips through the wine-coloured sari. Until then he believed that love was little more than a strong desire to care for someone else. Now he knew that he wanted to be desired by this strange, taciturn creature.

She took away the basin of water, closing the door behind her and leaving him once more with her two cousins and sleeping father.

From the sounds in the adjoining room others must have arrived. And in truth there were male voices among the women's, belonging to the visiting women's husbands. Even when the two boys went out to see who else had arrived, Betta did not wish to go, but listened for every female voice, in an effort to distinguish Meena's from the others. Suddenly, he felt there was no reason to put off his declaration of interest.

He awakened his host by pulling gently on his short sleeve.

'Is you? I did fall asleep. An' you been here all the time!'

'I'd like to talk to you,' Betta told him, advancing his face as near his host's ear as possible, to avoid running the risk of being overheard.

''Bout what?' asked the man.

'I . . . I'm thinking of getting married.'

'That's good, Doctor,' Betta's host said. He had not witnessed the foregoing scene between Betta and his family and could not imagine that the doctor would condescend to marry into his family.

'Your older daughter . . . her conduct . . . and modesty. Is she promised to anyone? I mean has anyone approached you?'

'No, Doctor. You mean you like her? As a wife?'

'I've been thinking of the matter,' said Betta, 'while you were sleeping.'

'You meet her yet?'

'Yes. I've been speaking to your family.'

'When? Just now?'

'Yes. While you slept.'

'Well, Doctor, I got to say yes.'

'Got to? Why?'

136

''Cause is you,' the man stated, surprised that Betta did not understand. 'Is funny, eh?'

'What's funny?'

'I mean, women does get abused while they sleeping and marriages does get arranged when men sleeping.'

'You don't have to agree because you're my patient. Why not talk it over with your wife?'

'Oh, she goin' be glad! Listen to them. That's all women does think about.'

'Anyway, don't mention it until I've gone, please. Then when we see each other again we can talk about it.'

'One thing, Doctor.'

'Yes?'

'The dowry,' the man whispered. 'It's small.'

Betta assured the man that the dowry would not be a problem.

The shopkeeper rose to see Betta out and as they appeared in the drawing room a silence fell on the company, as though everyone understood that something was afoot. And Betta left, like someone who had just been accused of a crime, without looking to the left or the right, with bowed head.

And once in the road, he could only think of the extraordinary step he had taken, almost on an impulse. Everything pointed to the near certainty that Meena had been sent in to serve him. His host himself said that women thought of nothing else but marriage, and Meena's younger sister had naively disclosed the household's preoccupation. Already, Betta's resolve to marry had weakened somewhat and he drove home muttering to himself that nothing had been settled yet, that, should he change his mind, the family would accept a present in exchange for absolving him from blame.

As Betta was getting out of the car the janitor opened the gate and bade him goodnight. He turned mid-way up the stairs to see him driving the vehicle slowly over the bridge and under the house.

BOOK 3
HANGERS-ON

Chapter 16

The nights when Bai went out on Sukrum's orders he nearly always crossed the train lines into Georgetown, in the beginning with a certain trepidation, but later in the assurance that he knew where he was going and the people he was likely to meet. Less tall than Sukrum, he was as relaxed as his friend was agitated, and the men he met in the Georgetown dives liked him because he talked little and for his pleasant manner. He always took the same route, down Oronoque Street from North Road, and would never have dreamt of passing the saman trees of Vlissingen Road and Upper Regent Street, because he had a mortal dread of great trees in the dark.

Bai felt that one day his knowledge of town might stand him in good stead, for Sukrum's erratic behaviour was bound to land them in difficulties one of these days. Moreover, Sukrum did not bother to keep his liaison with Lahti secret, and every Saturday night he made her come downstairs, even when she was unwell, and forced his friend to go out while they caroused in Dr Singh's old surgery where the scent of disinfectant still lingered. Sukrum once told him that Lahti had not stopped complaining of having to lie on the bare floor and he punished her by forbidding her to bring down the pillow filled with wads of silk-cotton which she used to put under her head in the early days of their relationship. Sukrum no longer spoke about her now and would simply remind Bai on Saturday mornings that he had to go out and not come back before midnight. The days of stealth, when Lahti would slip into his room and allow herself to be fondled while Bai had his face turned to the wall, were over. That first night when Sukrum sent him out with a gesture of the head – no more – and cursed him for coming back two hours later, Bai had walked the streets aimlessly in Kitty and Campbleville and Subryanville, away from Georgetown, with its bright streetlamps and its crowds and its fights and its masked men at Christmas time, all of which Sukrum professed to know well, having lived in a Georgetown dosshouse for a year before drifting into Kitty. The second night he ventured timidly up Church Street and hovered around the entrance to a covered staircase into which men disappeared from time to time and from which no one was seen to come out. The next night he followed a drunkard up the stairs and found himself in a drinking place lit with kerosene lamps. A few weeks later he had made two friends, both of whom lived in back yards and welcomed him into their homes, and when he returned home one Saturday night at the expected hour Sukrum demanded to know where he had been to have got the sweet scent that clung to his clothes. Bai told him that one of his friends was a maker of green pomade, which he sold to the drug stores in town. And Sukrum, angry at the secret that had been kept from him, urged Bai to introduce him to the acquaintance, only to be told point blank that he would not, that it was he who had sent him out. Sukrum's threats were countered by Bai with the warning that he would have to fish for shrimp on his own if he did not leave him in peace. Thus did Bai acquire a measure of independence from Sukrum, for whom friendship was a tyranny over a weaker person. He knew no other way with woman or man and never came to understand why he was either disliked or feared by those he knew.

But Bai had acquired a taste for the dives in the city and often went off on other nights. Occasionally he stood as look-out at the foot of the gambling house which he first visited and believed to be a drinking place and received twenty cents for his pains, the going rate for East Indians who did casual work at night, work which few creoles would take on. His obligingness earned him more offers of work, so that he found himself in the position of being able to pick and choose. And later, recalling his early days as a timid visitor to town, he was surprised at his terror of people and things.

One night, unknown to Bai, Sukrum followed him to town, but lost him in the crowds. Another time he sent Lahti who, frightened by the dense traffic and the incessant honking of car horns and ringing of bicycle bells, fled into a side street where she was molested by three youths. Rescued by a middle-aged man who brought her back to the gate, she was welcomed by Sukrum with a volley of slaps across her face.

'I pregnant,' Lahti told Sukrum. 'I don't want Mrs Singh to know. She goin' to throw me out.'

'I in' payin for it this time, I tellin' you! Ask Bai. He does know people in town. He can get it cheap.'

Bai managed to find a cheap abortionist in Robb Street and Lahti agreed to be taken to her one Saturday night. He and Sukrum had got the ten dollars from their shrimp money, Sukrum agreeing to the arrangement on condition that Bai contribute as much as he did.

Lahti found herself in the company of two young women who sat apart on chairs lined up against a partition. The humidity and want of air in the room, whose windows were closed to reduce the risk of prying, made her feel so faint she asked the two women to tell the midwife that she had gone out for fresh air. And once outside she was so overcome by fear and aloneness she thought of telephoning Rani. At the corner of Camp and Regent Streets she went into Borroughs Drug Store and told one of the co-proprietors that she was ill and wanted to call her guardian. In the back shop she rang Rani, whom she begged not to put the receiver down.

'I frightened, Rani. Is another one. I'm in town at a woman and she got two girls on a chair waiting and it so hot I can't breathe. Come, ne.'

'You know Tipu won't allow me. My God! Why can't you behave? You want me to ask Mrs Singh to come for you so you can do it properly?'

'No! Don't tell her. I got to go now 'cause the man looking at me.'

'Where are you now?' Rani asked.

But the receiver had been replaced.

When Lahti returned to the house in Robb Street only one young woman was sitting on a chair and the two exchanged distressed glances without indicating a desire to speak. The young woman was so shabbily dressed Lahti wanted to ask her how she could afford the money. Perhaps she had no money.

Sukrum had told her that there were men who were prepared to pay for an abortion provided the woman consented to having intimate relations with them. Sukrum had told her many things and she now wondered how she had become involved with a man Rani had despised from the very beginning.

When it was the turn of the young woman to go in Lahti smiled at her and was immediately overcome by a violent trembling. Never again! she thought. She began a silent prayer and started to weep because Rani was not with her and could not speak to her. Was it not since Rani's marriage that her vision became blurred? That things she had spoken of in jest were transformed into uncontrollable urges? Never again! I not going to let him touch me again.

The frenzied barking of a dog in the back yard drew her attention and Lahti clasped her hands in a desperate effort to calm herself. Finding the waiting and the lack of air unbearable she got up and went to the back window which she opened as quietly as she could. There was nothing to be seen but the rear of shops and, beyond, Robb Street with its curved lamps. Her attention was drawn to a rustling sound in the yard and, thinking that it might be the chained dog which had been barking a moment ago, she strained her eyes to see in the dark, but could make out nothing. Then she remembered that the area was known to attract a large number of rats, being near to the Bourda market, where vegetable remains and rotting fruit from stallholders were not cleared away until the following morning. Without being aware of it she was no longer trembling. Her forehead, streaming with sweat while she had been out searching for a telephone, was now cooled by the night air. She pulled over her chair to the window and leaned her chin on her cupped hands like a child lost in thought. She had seen how pregnancy had changed Rani, had made her more serious. She had given up reading the newspaper from cover to cover and seemed to be keeping her at arm's length, as though she risked being soiled. But for her pregnancy meant the deepest anxiety, and as the abortion approached, an indescribable terror.

There was every reason to discontinue her friendship with Sukrum, she told herself. She had made much progress with her dressmaking and would soon be paid a wage; and what was more, Sukrum struck her frequently, especially since, after the first abortion, he was certain of his hold on her. And finally, Rani had been predicting terrible things if the association continued, a prophecy that had been echoed in a dream she had had, the day after she had her first lesson in the secret art of cutting. She had dreamt that she was cutting a piece of organdy cloth and looked up momentarily, only to find, on looking down again, that the lady for whom the dress was being made was lying in the place of the cloth and bleeding profusely from the wound made with the scissors. So terrible had been the effect of the dream that she did not tell Rani, but brooded over it alone. It was the week afterwards that she realized she was pregnant again with Sukrum's child. Had she not been afraid of offending Mrs Singh she would have joined the Evangelist church to which her apprentice mistress belonged, because she was certain the antidote to Sukrum's hold over her lay outside the house.

'It's you now,' the apparition in the doorway said. 'Come on, child, I don' have all night.'

Lahti was unable to move or even answer the stranger; she was unable to think or to suffer and simply stared at the woman. And on recovering her senses the room seemed to be filled with the sound of barking dogs, to which the woman attending her was completely indifferent.

'Rani . . .'

'Who?'

'The dogs!'

'They'll loose its chain soon,' the woman assured her, 'and it'll stop barking. . . . I want you to count up to twenty, slowly. Don' rush, or you'll have to begin all over again. One, two . . . that's right . . . like at school, eh? You did go to school, didn' you? . . . That's it, that's it . . . it's a dream . . . and morning time will come, when the shadows flee away. You remember the words? "When day break an' shadows flee away?" That's right, child . . . I feel sorry for you 'cause you so good-looking with hair down to your waist an' all and the men, the men. All they want to do is mount you. And some o' them don't even want to talk . . . and by the time you learn to handle them they gone off you because you older or they tired of you. . . . Yes, that's it, child, sleep. . . .'

The following morning the household – with the exception of Sukrum – were assembled round the large dining room, and the noise of water rushing through the pipe from the raised water tank drowned the calling of birds and other sounds from Dowding Street on which all the windows were opened to let in the gentle breeze that billowed the dark blinds. Not a word was spoken and everyone pretended not to notice Lahti's empty chair, while Aji dribbled because no one would feed her, out of spite no doubt, because, too, a few days gone when she complained that the dust suspended on the beams of sunlight in the room she shared with Mrs Singh was filling her nostrils and made patterns whenever she waved her hands to disturb it, shapes from the various houses she had lived in with the family in Victoria, Beterverwachting and that place by the sea next to the abandoned house with the shutters intact, she was ignored as if she had already died. No one had spoken to her for several weeks, she noticed, for eleven weeks and three days, and even Rani's infant, who once liked to creep towards her stretched out its arms to keep her at arm's length. Who had taught him to do that? When she said he was an ugly baby that was a long time ago and she was only telling the truth, as Mr Singh did when he was alive and said all babies were ugly and that good-looking children grew up to be ugly grown-ups and those present smiled and said what an observant man he was, that all his utterances should be written down in a book because he had a way of hitting the nail on the head. But whenever *she* spoke people turned away; and what was more, she, who had fed everyone in that house in times of sickness, everyone except the two parasites lodging in Dr Singh's surgery, was only fed reluctantly by Mrs Singh or by Rani after she had spooned food into her child's mouth to show everyone he was able to take solids.

Rani's baby was sitting on her lap, naked, its dimpled arms dangling at its sides. From time to time Tipu turned towards his wife and son. More than ever he looked the part of a father, with his polished shoes and immaculate shirt.

'Aji don' speak no more,' he said. 'You think she want somebody to feed her?'

He cut a slice of bread on her plate slowly, raised it to her mouth; but with a swift movement she knocked it out of his hand, taking Tipu by surprise, although he had been on his guard. Shrugging his shoulders, he replaced the bread – it had fallen beside the table – on the plate in front of Aji.

Mrs Singh got up from the table and Tipu promptly did likewise, following her into the drawing room. But before long he came back.

'I gone,' he said to Rani, who lifted the infant towards him. He took his son, raised him high above his shoulders, then gave him back to Rani.

'I gone,' he repeated, this time to the company generally. But Aji and Bai ignored him as he went off, puffed up with serious intentions as to his work and his status as head of a family.

'I goin' go see what happen,' Bai told Rani, ignoring Aji, who was now nibbling at her bread.

'I don't want to know!' Rani said sharply. 'You and Sukrum and Lahti do whatever you like in this house and you think Mrs Singh doesn't see. But she does see. . . . And why you think I want to know where Lahti is and what happened to her? I've got a family. . . .'

She was so exasperated she was unable to finish. Although she liked Bai she resented his assumption that she was involved, even indirectly, in her friend's escapades and her low life.

'Where is she?' Rani asked, turning to see if Aji understood what was going on.

He told her about the house where the abortions were practised and how Lahti did not want Mrs Singh to know.

'She's going to be in trouble?'

'I don' know,' Bai replied. 'The woman not a midwife, like the one Mrs Singh did get las' time. You think I bad, but I not bad. I does work. I does fish in the week an' does work on Saturday night in town.'

'Everything you and Sukrum do you do by night. Why youal frightened of daylight? And why don't you leave Lahti alone? She doesn't have family to look after her and stand by her.'

'I feel the same, Miss Rani.'

'If anything happen to Lahti God going to punish you.'

When Bai was certain that Rani had finished he went out by the back door. Occasionally she and he had got into conversation at the foot of the stairs or in the kitchen, and she was surprised at his dignified manner. But in the end she associated him with Sukrum who, for her, was the source of evil and an extension of Mrs Singh's influence. Everything she foresaw had come to pass, the belittling role of her husband, the enslavement of her child. But the protection Mrs Singh had extended to Sukrum had compounded her bitterness towards a home where her best friend was being destroyed and in which her powerlessness to persuade Tipu to set up elsewhere caused her to lie awake at night.

Mrs Singh came back to table to finish her coffee and bread.

'Is something wrong between you and Tipu?' she asked.

Rani hesitated for such a long time that Mrs Singh thought she had no intention of replying.

'Nothing wrong between Tipu and me.'

'Then why're you so sour? People who're happy aren't sour. You and Lahti used to talk for hours on the porch. The Pujaree was always wondering what you found to talk about. You and Tipu aren't happy?'

'Nothing's wrong between me and Tipu.'

'Why're you so stubborn? I knew you since you were a little girl and you're not an unhappy person. Not like Lahti, who pretends to laugh.'

'I can't talk about Lahti,' Rani said, trying to seem apologetic, 'until I know what's happened to her.'

'Nothing's happened to her; nothing serious. This morning I got a message that she's staying in the lady's house for a couple days. I didn't know you were worried about her since you got married.'

'Since I got married?' Rani said feelingly. 'What about since Lahti's been carrying on with Sukrum? He's been here less than two years and look at the trouble he's caused.'

'So so!' declared Mrs Singh, speaking quietly. 'You want me to put Sukrum on the road to save Lahti? And suppose she runs after him? Suppose *Miss* Lahti packs her grip and trails along on a leash behind him?'

Rani did not answer, believing already that her revolt was premature.

'You began condemning me *before* you got married, Rani, and for no reason at all. I don't put anyone on the road. If you don't want Sukrum and Bai to share the table with your little family tell me so, and I'll forbid them to eat with us. But don't forget that you'll still be sharing the table with Lahti, who can teach us both about vice. . . . But isn't that what people call love? Isn't that what happens to people who hate arranged marriages? Lahti is free, and why should I interfere with her freedom? I won't put Sukrum out, or her or anyone else.'

'Suppose Lahti dies?' Rani said.

'Lahti won't die; at least it won't be for lack of care. . . . What's the use? You're so young. Secrets are such a burden!'

'If they're in love why don't you encourage them to get married?' Rani asked, more than ever perplexed as to Mrs Singh's motives for her conduct.

'Sukrum doesn't love anyone. He treats Lahti as if he owns her. If they got married he would not need to close the door to hit her.'

The chilling reduction of the condition of marriage to these few words reminded Rani that Mrs Singh was wiser than she was, however devious she had judged her to be. And it seemed to her that the problem of going away was as much her own inability to stand up to her as Tipu's lack of enterprise. The time was not yet ripe.

Mrs Singh left her at table with Aji and the infant on her lap and with thoughts about Lahti lurking at the back of her mind, like vermin in a bowl of rice.

Through the open windows she heard Mrs Singh being welcomed by the hucksters who, since Sukrum and Bai came to live at the house, sold much more than before. Of late Mrs Singh spent longer than ever with them after the cook took away the greens and fruit and fish she bought, and between the hours of eight and nine passers-by in Dowding Street might have thought that the talk and laughter coming from beyond the great saman tree was evidence of an exceptionally large household. The bhajee seller had been coming since the days when Betta was a small boy and, as her strength failed, her trays became smaller so that, from far off, people were able to recognize her.

There was something disturbing in Mrs Singh's words, Rani reflected, something concealed. She had not explicitly disapproved of Sukrum's hold on Lahti. But then she herself was coming increasingly under the influence of the Pujaree, on whom she had lavished substantial gifts. People said she had once been in love with the Mulvi Sahib and once danced to any tune he cared to play. She was forty-six and still attractive. Could it be that she cared for the Pujaree in the same way? He was too ordinary-looking, Lahti had once said. But did she not give him money and buy his twin nephews presents at the time of the big festivals of Pagwah and Divali and Christmas? And who was more ordinary-looking than Sukrum?

Rani put her baby on the floor and began feeding Aji, who accepted the bread absently, smiling without cause whenever she caught the young woman's eye.

'A few years ago you would've told me what to do, Aji, in the days when even Mrs Singh used to turn to you. Poor Aji. When I leave I'll take you if she lets me, and I wouldn' mind if you curse us. You used to plait my hair and the plaits did come apart because my hair's so straight. In those days you used to talk like a book, like Mrs Singh. Everything is silence and intrigue since my Betta went away. When he comes to see his mother I turn aside so as not to offend Tipu. If I could do as I did like would I use my freedom like Lahti? I'm afraid for her and for me. When they gave me my child I didn't know how to hold him, Aji. I was afraid to look at him lest I couldn't love him. But when I saw him lying helpless I felt like crying out with joy that I was his mother. Then horses did come by, galloping down Vlissingen Road; and the midwife said it was a good sign at a birth. You used to tell me how the temple dancers used their feet, soon after I become a woman. Now I'll have to lay up my own stories to tell my son when he grows up. You hardly talk, so how we can know if you're happy or unhappy? Tipu like you, yet you treat him like dirt and you keep grinning at me as if you know something. . . . How come you know so much about India? Listen, they're calling me. Mrs Singh's calling me. You hear? "Raaaaaaneeeee!" I want you to keep my son, but I'm afraid of what might happen to him, because you do the first thing that comes into your head.'

Rani placed her son on the floor and led Aji to the front of the house, the gallery of which was still in shadow.

'Finey!' Rani called to a little girl in the yard.

'Yes, Miss Rani,' she answered in a shrill, unreal voice.

'You're going to look after my baby?'

'Yes, Miss Rani.'

'Well, hurry! Mrs Singh's calling me.'

The child put down her basket and hurried up the stairs.

'Don't bring her outside,' Rani said, leaving the waif to find the infant, who was crawling about the dining room.

Chapter 17

On the Saturday afternoon of the same week, while Mrs Singh was resting upstairs after the midday meal, Lahti appeared in the doorway of the gallery, made up with lipstick and rouge and wearing a new dress with a broad sash tied at the back. A lace frill round the shoulders descended to a V in the front and back and its skirt hung to nothing.

Rani, who was sitting on a mat with her son asleep on her lap, stared at her friend unbelievingly.

'What's wrong?' Lahti asked.

'But I thought . . .'

Lahti laughed aloud.

'You like the dress?'

'How did it go?' Rani asked.

'What?'

'The abortion.'

'What abortion? What you talking about? I jus' come from the dressmaker. I been to work today. . . . You like it? The skirt lined because the material so thin. It nice, eh?'

'Lahti, I'm talking to you!' Rani said angrily. 'Tell me what happened.'

'I telling you. I come from the dressmaker an' she give me a new frock.'

Rani was hurt and said no more.
'Where Miss Singh?'
'She's upstairs.'
'How the baby?'
Lahti bent down to look more closely at Rani's infant. 'I did forget how nice he is. . . . The dress was from a customer who I try it on for, but she din' like it and the dressmaker tell me I could keep it 'cause she say I does work later than the other girls. . . .'

And while she was talking Rani kept thinking of Sukrum and what her attitude to him would be. Lahti went on talking about the day's events at the seamstress's house, about her workmate, who would wait until they were alone and then start jumping up and down on the dress which had been entrusted to them for finishing, partly out of spite, partly because she made fun of everything. She was the one who went home as soon as the clock struck five and was not liked by the seamstress, in spite of the clock being twenty minutes slower than the arrival clock, which told the right time and she was getting nearly a half-hour's work out of the girls anyway. In any case Madame did not like her as well because her hands were calloused from hard work at home and the fine materials got caught on them and drew out a thread. The same workmate had been taken on as a designer because she drew so well, but her work was so bad she was demoted to cutter, then to worker in the finishing section.

'An' the dressmaker threatening to make her sweep the floor, an' if she can't even do that properly she going show her the door 'cause she not running a charitable establishment, she say. . . . I'm hungry. They got anything to eat?'

'Look in the safe, ne?' Rani, told her.

Lahti went off to the kitchen to see if any food had been put away, leaving Rani to ponder on her transformation.

In fact Lahti had been to work that day as she had told Rani. But the dress had been paid for by the abortionist who, frightened by Lahti's weak condition, had refused to allow her to go home and kept her in the room for five whole days, until her fever had subsided and she was her old self again. Mrs Singh had been informed and had given the news to no one except Sukrum. He was made to understand that if Lahti became pregnant again he would have to marry her without a dowry.

Mrs Singh had heard Lahti arrive. Her sleep had been interrupted by a sudden, inexplicable waking. She had always had this experience when her husband came home, in whichever house they lived; and over the last few months it was the arrival of the Pujaree that awakened her.

For four nights she had lain awake wondering whether her ward would die at the hands of a notorious butcher who was known to have spent two years in prison and whose establishment had once been closed by the police and shuttered up for a whole year.

She could never understand why the Pujaree was so calm when they discussed Lahti, while she could not stomach the goings-on in the surgery, where her son had cured so many people of their ailments. For the sake of the infant if for no one else the matter had to be settled, even at the risk of Sukrum's departure. There she was, dressed like a woman of the world, made up with red on her lips. Her own mother used to say that women like that hated cooking and so it was with Lahti, who was incapable of picking a bowl of rice properly or preparing massala or even descaling fish. It was a matter of the greatest surprise when she received an excellent report about her from the seamstress. For finishing and delicate work there was not her like, and she had the finest hands in the establishment, to which Mrs Singh was obliged to reply that the girl did little work at home and it was not surprising that her fingers were unspoiled. Was it normal that a woman's hands were as smooth as the pile on velvet after it had been steamed? Rani, who was worth ten of her, had coarse hands, which told you everything about her honesty and her general character. And the seamstress did not reply, having drawn her own conclusions about Mrs Singh's relations with Lahti. There she was with red lips and a broad sash round her waist, which would not please Rani.

To the gentle knock on her bedroom door Mrs Singh called out to come in, knowing that it was Lahti, who was not certain if she was sleeping.

'Come in!'

And the door opened as though an infant with little strength were pushing it. Lahti, her hand still on the porcelain door knob, thrust her head into the void and said, 'You sleeping?'

'So it's you, at last. How do you feel?'

'I feel good now.'

'Sit down on the bed,' Mrs Singh told her, while she herself made no effort to leave the sash window looking over the fields which stood open at all hours of the day and night, even if rain was falling, and was only hung with a cloth whenever the full moon edged round the side of the house and flooded the room.

'I lost many children,' Mrs Singh said, 'but naturally. What's wrong with you? What's got into you these last two years?'

'Nothing, Miss Singh,' Lahti answered, anxious as to the direction the conversation might take.

'Do you love Sukrum?'

'I don' know, Miss Singh.'

'Do you know what love is?'

'Yes, Miss Singh. Sukrum say he love me.'

'Sukrum!' came the impatient exclamation. 'Do you love him?'

'I don' know, Miss Singh. I tell you, I don' know.'

'Would you like to marry him?'

'No, Miss Singh,' she answered without hesitation.

'But if you don't love him why do you go to his room?'

Lahti reflected before attempting to answer the question truthfully.

'I don' got nothing else to do, Miss Singh.'

'Rani wouldn't have gone before she was married. Why're you so different from her? You don't have any shame, child?'

Lahti wanted to say that she had no idea why she acted as she did, that Sukrum was good company and he was the first man she had known and that his wickedness, far from repelling her, was a powerful attraction, like the forbidden pork they ate in secret and the curse-words he had taught her and which she used freely when they were together. Sukrum was more than adequate compensation for the loss of Rani's company and the long evenings on the porch in the season of innocence when they counted raindrops trickling down the panes and laughed at the old woman huckster who was balding after forty years of carrying a laden tray. How could she know why she did this or that? Did she know why she dreamt what she dreamt, or the reasons for her attachment to Mrs Singh's house? How could she tell why she felt drawn to Sukrum rather than to Bai, who would marry her with the slightest encouragement?

Mrs Singh broke the silence, intent on wringing from Lahti some coherent expression of her condition as she perceived it.

'What man will have you now?'

'I don' know, Miss Singh.'

'Doesn't that worry you?'

'No, Miss Singh.'

'You know that an East Indian man won't marry you unless you're a virgin.'

'How I going know, Miss Singh? Nobody ever tell me.'

'You don't talk about that kind of thing at work? Among the girls?'

'I never hear them, Miss Singh. In any case mos' of the time I with Clara, doing finishing.'

'And Clara never talked about such things?' Mrs Singh pursued.

'No, Miss Singh. Clara's a Christian and don' talk 'bout things like that 'cause her mother would beat her.'

'You would like to bring Clara home?'

'She wouldn' come, Miss Singh.'

'Why?'

'She got to work all the time, till she go to bed at night-time an' don' go out at all. She does go home as soon as five o'clock an' does jump up and down on all the dresses we do.'

'Why does she do that?'

And once more the question struck Lahti as absurd. How would Clara know why she had the urge to jump up and down on the clothes entrusted to her?

'I don' know, Miss Singh. It does make her feel good, I think. An' sometimes it does make her laugh. But she never tell me why she do it.'

'Have you eaten yet?'

'Yes, Miss Singh; there was something in the safe.'

'All right, Lahti. Remember the things I told you. Learn everything you can at work.'

'Yes, Miss Singh.'

Lahti went out, satisfied that Mrs Singh was not angry with her for what had happened, for leaving the house without informing her, for enlisting the services of an abortionist without her knowledge. But, oddly enough, there had been no mention of such things, nor had she forbidden her to visit Sukrum, which she had no more intention of doing than of going back to her parents' house in the country where diminutive hogs competed with lizards for scraps from the midden heaps and the slightest downpour left the land flooded until the kokers opened to drain off the water, leaving a sea of mud, to the delight of the hogs and the misery of people.

Mrs Singh wanted to attribute to Lahti an awareness which had grown in Rani some time ago, but passed her friend's understanding. Lahti was like the grass in the field opposite, which lay down when the wind blew and stood erect again once the wind had gone, without caring to investigate the nature of that wind.

That night Sukrum waited for Lahti to come down to the room he shared with Bai, but she did not come; and when Bai returned at two in the morning with a basket full of shrimps the kerosene lamp was still lit and shadows trembled on the walls.

The following night it was the same, and the following as well; and on Saturday afternoon, when he tried to get into conversation with her she walked off without bothering to answer him.

'You coming tonight?' he called after her.

'No!' she replied, turning to face him. 'Why?'

'That was my child!' he said.

He went after her and grabbed her arm.

'Is my child!' Lahti said defiantly. 'Is *me* who been lying on a bed in somebody else room thinking I was dying and nearly goin' mad with the dog barking in the yard. If you don' leave me alone I goin' tell Miss Singh and you can have it out with her. Leggo my hand.' And with that she wrenched her hand away.

'If you don' come to my room again I going grab you by your hair an' throw you out of the window, understand?' he shouted.

At table next morning he pretended to be indifferent to her and spent the time talking to Bai. Then, as Rani was about to get up, he announced that he was going away and might not come back, to which Mrs Singh replied coldly that he would have to make up his mind soon, because someone else would be replacing him.

In the event Sukrum did not go away and no longer waited up on Saturday nights for Lahti to come and see him. Instead, he went with Bai on the rounds of his occasional jobs and found that his room-mate had made so many acquaintances he was capable of cutting himself adrift and living on his own, which alarmed him, as he was still living in the past when Bai relied heavily on him and was no more than his shadow and could hardly approach a stranger without his help. His dismay at Lahti's behaviour became a kind of panic in the face of Bai's independence. He would have liked to get his hands on the person who had wound her up against him. Either Mrs Singh or the seamstress must be behind her changed attitude. Or could she have met another man? In one week? No, it was a woman behind it, some busybody who thought she knew what was good for Lahti and had advised her that being a working woman she was able to do without him. But he knew she would come crawling back to him.

Bai took him to John's dance hall, where he kept the door and was known by most of the clients, men and women not at all like those who lived in Kitty. Nearly all were creoles, with a sprinkling of Portuguese and one East Indian woman notorious for her independence and generosity towards her husband, who had been out of work for several months.

Sukrum was like a fish out of water and kept returning to find Bai installed on a chair near the door, one leaf of which was closed. Eventually he got himself a seat in the corner of the dance hall and watched couples clinging to one another beneath the coloured bulbs.

His knowledge of Georgetown was confined largely to its dosshouses and cheap cook shops in Lombard Street; and he could only watch, astounded at the freedom of the women and the energetic music. The saxophonist was sitting apart from the other six members of the band. The instrument had only been introduced into the country a couple of years before and its practitioners regarded themselves as an élite amongst musicians. Whenever he played solo he stood up and waved the saxophone from side to side to emphasize the beginning and end of the cadences, his eyes closed and his face streaming with perspiration.

Sukrum remained in his corner until Bai came to tell him that they were going to pay a visit to his pomade-making friend. And the two men walked off side by side along the pavement, Sukrum keeping close to the shop fronts and Bai jostling the endless stream of people. Only a few East Indians were to be seen and each time one was spotted the two men nudged each other and stared. And they walked until they came to the Brickdam Primary School, where the crowds had thinned out and shops were replaced by houses, some of them half-hidden behind trees with thick foliage. Finally Bai turned into a yard in a side street and knocked on a back door. And the welcome extended to him by the man and his wife when the door was opened provided further proof for Sukrum that the Saturday nights he had excluded him from the room had provided the opportunity to learn to fend for himself in the Georgetown they used to watch beyond the train lines from the house gate.

As was his custom, Bai left his friend at one in the morning, accompanied by Sukrum. The two men got home at two o'clock, when the houses in Kitty were all in darkness, except those in which a night light was left burning. But once back in the room the events of the last few hours gave way in Sukrum's mind to the longing for Lahti's company and the Saturday nights when they ate and drank what he bought in the village, and talked endlessly about the goings-on in the house and at the seamstress's establishment.

Chapter 18

The morning train moved slowly eastwards into a red sun and a koker washed in blood. A bull had been slaughtered at the mid-year Kali Mai puja and its blood sprinkled on the kokers and bridges and all constructions built over water. It was the first year that an animal larger than a goat had been sacrificed, because it was the first year that the Pujaree's temple had at its disposal so much money, having received from its benefactress a donation of a thousand dollars. When the gates at the crossing were opened the traffic, which had built up as far as Mrs Singh's gate, moved off slowly, the open carriages and the closed cars, the bicycles and dray carts and donkey carts with their creaking wheels and world-weary drivers.

The Pujaree's nephews, who were sitting on the bridge with their feet dangling over the gutter, could not keep their eyes off the road. They rarely left Newtown, where cars never penetrated, and, unless rain was falling when they visited, spent most of their time on the bridge as close to the traffic as was prudent. The Pujaree himself was at the front door, deep in conversation with Mrs Singh, who was dressed as for a special occasion and wore a red hibiscus in her hair.

As soon as the Pujaree left, she sought out the cook and asked her to take care of the hucksters assembled under the bottom house. Then she asked Rani to tell the members of the household to come to the drawing room because she had an important announcement to make.

In a short time they all met as they were told – all except Lahti. She had gone to work – Sukrum, Bai, Rani and Tipu, and even Aji, who was wheeled out of the dining room by Rani in the new wheelchair Mrs Singh had bought her.

The moment Mrs Singh spoke the baby, who was crawling about the floor in the gallery, began whimpering; and its mother had to take him up and dangle him on her knee. Rani and Aji were the only ones sitting, the men having made a half-circle round the mistress of the house.

'The Pujaree and I,' Mrs Singh declared, coming straight to the point, 'have become spiritual partners. From now on he will be living here . . . in this house . . . with us. He will be sharing a room with me. That's all I wanted to say, except that, whatever you think of him, whether you like him or not, he'll be the master here from now on, and you will treat him as the master. The Pujaree is a remarkable man. Yesterday, at the temple, you had to see how our people flocked to the puja, like in the Courantyne where so many Madrasees live. He asks for nothing and yet people flock to the temple with gifts. And for the first time he sacrificed a bull, and he predicted prosperity for the Indians.'

In her carefully enunciated English – she had been taught the language by her father and her tutor – she described how the Pujaree officiated in the candlelit temple three nights running; how, in the final night, the sacrificial bull was sprinkled with red dye before the slaughter, and all the while the drums were beating; that when he and his helper stood before Kali's statue she was not the only one who began shaking with a trembling that caused images to appear before their eyes.

Mrs Singh was now speaking in a sing-song voice, as though words were being put in her mouth and she was required to utter them in a certain way. And Rani, disturbed by the account, slipped away with her infant to the back of the house, leaving Aji with her head bowed on her chest and grasping the unfinished end of a plaited loaf.

'. . . and he threw water on water and spoke in Sanskrit, in words used for more than a thousand years.

'And those in distress stepped forward one by one in the light of the candles and the Pujaree folded a thick, wet cloth in the shape of a penis and pretended to beat a woman who had not got over the death of her mother, although she had brought up eleven children.

'That's the man who's coming to live in my house, and who certain people don't like.'

She was looking at Sukrum, but she was thinking more especially of Betta, her son.

'All right, go and do your work,' she said in a peremptory voice, as when she was opposed in some action she believed to be important. But no one had uttered a word. She had noticed that Rani had gone and that Tipu, frightened out of his wits by her manner and the curt dismissal, had left the house without their usual short exchange of words. She stood alone, enraged at the lack of enquiry as to the time and other details of the Pujaree's settling in with them. Believing everyone to be opposed to the arrangement, she wanted to have them back to find out why, to say that they did not know him because, unlike the Mulvi Sahib, he was a spiritual man who did not show himself as he really was. How ordinary they were! The Pujaree did not tout for converts as the Christian missionaries did. Everyone in her house was succumbing to the Christian influence. Were they not witnessing the corruption of a soul in Lahti's conduct? Was her degeneration not the degeneration of a way of life?

During the three days past she had spent many hours at the temple and, for the first time since her arrival in the country, she had experienced in the midst of so many people, surrounded by incessant drumming, an indescribable quietness, as when the drone of a solitary bee ceased the moment it alighted. Last night she was unable to sleep for the promise she had made the Pujaree and her impatience to make the announcement before anyone went off. But at the table she felt she could not speak in the presence of Lahti, who had forfeited the right to be treated with the consideration those who had lived under her roof deserved. In truth she longed to put everyone out and start again with the Pujaree, Aji and herself as the first inhabitants of a new house in which Hindi and Urdu were taught and spoken as a duty to counter the disintegration of a people threatened on every hand.

It did not occur to Mrs Singh that her vision resembled Betta's in its zeal and its aim of protecting East Indians. Nor did she admit to herself that her pleasure at welcoming the Pujaree as a permanent member of the household was all the greater because Betta was certain to disapprove. She had always refused to admit to herself that he was not coming back to live with her and so had avoided any action that might lead to a permanent rift. But the Pujaree's endless admonitions to play her part in the pujas finally persuaded her to attend the three-day celebrations and yield to a longing for the music of the mridangam and veena and the dim temple that kept growing like a pregnant woman. Now she was in no doubt that the close association with her mentor, which she had resisted until the latest celebration, would bring about the rift she feared so much. She had reflected long enough on the matter. Now it was so far; and everyone in the household had been informed except Lahti, who would receive the news from Rani by afternoon.

After the Pujaree moved in, the days passed like other days, except that there was one more at table. The noises from Dowding Street and the sights seen from the windows overlooking Vlissingen Road did not change. On Fridays Muslim men dressed in white passed by on their way to the mosque in Church Street, while on Sundays Christian women and their children ambled along on their way to the numerous churches in Kitty, clutching their Protestant hymnals and their hats, in danger of being carried off by the wind which did not abate until it lost its way among the saman and Long John trees bordering the Botanical Gardens. And unfailingly the pale hummingbird with an indigo tail came to drink nectar from the hibiscus and God-birds rustled their wings in the dust baths of roof gutters above which the triangular prayer flag fluttered in the perpetual breeze.

And Aji spent most of her mornings on the porch until the sun turned and she was brought in by Rani or the cook, who would look upwards because of the evil-smelling mustard oil she had rubbed on her hands.

There were good-luck signs on paper scattered about the drawing room, on the camphor-wood tables and chairs; and indeed the house was happier since Mrs Singh got 'married', or so it seemed from the frequent outbursts of laughter and the prayer flag and the motorcar she bought for her husband which could be seen through the trees standing in the yard next to the vat beneath the silver-painted water tank that ensured a plentiful supply of pure water and malarial mosquitoes.

Mrs Singh now only wore saris. She had given her dresses, her trousers and bodices to the women hucksters, who admired her brocade cloth and her transparent achals which gave her an air of great modesty when she sat under the trees bargaining with them. They refuted rumours of her wickedness with a word and would not have it that she detested Lahti with an unquenchable hatred and threatened to put her out for being responsible for a situation engineered by Mrs Singh herself, who no longer had any use for Sukrum because there were now two other men in the house. In the first weeks after her new association she had been beset by nightmares in which her dead husband appeared to her, people said, until the Pujaree exorcized his ghost by ordering him to cross water. They also said the Pujaree had made her get rid of the image of Lakshmi to which she prayed and that she had become docile as in the days when her first husband was alive and she was in the habit of serving him at table before eating with Aji and her friends. It was not important what was true or false, but rather the tone of the house, which had changed for the better, everyone agreed, although the creoles in Kitty did not take kindly to the idea of Hindu prayer flags in the front yard of a mansion with countless windows. But they had no idea what the interior of the house looked like, that it was hung with maidenhair ferns and liberally furnished with chairs. The rumour-mongers speculated to their hearts' content, attributing whatever furnishings they wished to the drawing room where, as one report claimed, there was an out-of-tune piano with yellowing keys by which visiting musicians tuned their stringed instruments. Not having heard of the Vedas or the hundred incarnations of Vishnu or Shakti worship of the feminine principle or that India was a vast agglomeration of cultures on which Christianity had foundered, they could only furnish the house from the accoutrements of their imagination.

The fact was that the great changes brought about by the Pujaree's residence were to come later, after the terrible malarial epidemic of 193x, when the well-to-do began to look at their rainwater vats with suspicion and complaints were voiced in the press about the folly of dismissing Dr Giglioli, who had been well on his way to discovering the breeding habits of the *Anopheles darlingi* mosquito.

If Mrs Singh's happiness was public knowledge Sukrum's rage at Lahti's independence from him had not grown less, nor had Rani's determination to take her family away. Now that Lahti came and went as she pleased her connection with the house had grown even more tenuous and she had told Tipu in no uncertain terms that she would be moving out with her child before the year was out. But he paid her little heed, because he had learned little about her character since his marriage, and could not imagine that she had a mind of her own.

Chapter 19

The horoscopes of Meena and Betta had been matched favour-
ably and they were married in a specially constructed pavilion.
In the presence of his mother and in-laws Betta's garment was
tied to his bride's and the couple walked round the sacred fire
seven times. 'Into my heart will I take thy heart . . .' And he
looked upon her face with a passion beyond his comprehension,
but saw instead a host of images. He looked on her sari trimmed
with gold thread, on her long, black hair, but saw none of these
things through the images that pressed on him in his confusion,
a circling chicken hawk, cocoa beans laid out to dry in the sun,
and the same recurring vision of women in mourning that first
came to him soon after he became betrothed. Betta closed his
eyes to recover his composure and saw the Mulvi Sahib
prostrate on his prayer mat and heard the words clearly intoned:
'La ilah illa allah wa Mohammed rasul Allah': 'There is no God
but one and Mohammed is his prophet.'

Oh, my God, what's happening to me? he thought. Have I
already done something foolish?

But his lapse, which to him had been of endless duration, had
lasted only a moment, and he recovered well enough to see the
ceremony through and witness onlookers dropping dollar notes
in the platter. He felt the warmth of his bride's arm on his arm
and turned to look at her affectionately; and this time he saw
clearly her dark eyebrows. Her sisters and relations had made
elaborate patterns with henna on the palms of her hands, which
recalled the designs in turmeric made by his mother on his body
while she wept behind his back.

'I hear Lord Krishna's instrument,' she had told him. 'Sad, sad,
that you made all these preparations behind my back and her
family knew everything and planned everything, down to the
kind of ceremony. Why couldn't you marry in your home?
There's the space and people enough to help.'

He did not offend her by protesting and now he saw her on the edge of the pavilion, a stranger among his new relations.

His bride called her 'Ma' when the celebrations began and they sat next to each other like sisters. She had given them a perfume container of filigree silver in the form of a peacock and promised them money if they needed it, which caused Betta to wonder, knowing well her need to control the lives of those around her.

The gas lamps, lit at nightfall, hummed incessantly like a horde of insects. Betta would not move from his wife's side and long after the lamps began to burn strangers came to congratulate them, people he had never met, all of whom his wife knew and addressed deferentially with her hands joined and her head bowed. Her father sat in a chair apart, surrounded by friends who flattered him about his son-in-law's status and his daughter's beauty and the faultless organization of the ceremony and celebrations. Businessmen for the most part, they were impressed by the money he must have lavished on the festivities. He, in turn, disclosed his secret: his son-in-law had dispensed with the right to receive a dowry; the couple's marriage was based on love, not an idea he approved, but a deucedly convenient one in the circumstances, now that his health was failing and he had another girl child on the threshold of womanhood.

The company settled to a meal of crab claws, red snapper, curried mutton and boiled rice. And as the stars came out the last birds flew over in formation to their roosting places in the dense vegetation up-river.

'Me goat tek up!' one old man remarked, carried away by the occasion, associating his pregnant goat and the symbolic tying of the bride's and groom's garments which he had witnessed. The men laughed and began to indulge in sexual allusions which delighted the ladies especially, since it was the only occasion they were permitted to be present when their husbands indulged their licence.

Betta's father-in-law ate little and drank bush-tea without sugar, while one friend cruelly reminded him of his love of good fare and an appetite that, early in his marriage, threatened domestic harmony. In truth he used to be insatiable and once confessed to his wife that he was prepared to sleep alone rather than endure the pangs of hunger which tormented him between meals. Now, gaunt and dull-eyed, he watched the others gorging themselves and, momentarily, was tempted to join them at the risk of falling into a coma.

The men sat alone, opposite the women, who, attracted by their laughter, continued listening to what was being said, while pretending to carry on their own conversations.

One middle-aged man related how two East Indians applied for a post as messenger in the Public Works Department at Poudroyen. The one who read and wrote better than the other was appointed, whereupon the rejected applicant complained to the Chief Clerk: 'I'm a Brahmin and in India he'd be an Untouchable.'

'You're a what?' the Chief Clerk asked.

'A Brahmin,' repeated the man.

'And what's that?' the creole Chief Clerk asked.

The disappointed applicant explained his fancied status while the Chief Clerk stared at him patiently. Then, at the end of the detailed introduction to the caste system in India, the Chief Clerk unfolded his arms, thrust his face close to the applicant's, and exclaimed in an affected whisper, 'I don't give a hoot! You can't spell, you can't write like him and you got a discontented look. That's why you didn't get the job.'

There ensued a discussion on the speed with which the caste system collapsed; and one man reminded them of the Brahmin saying that Brahmins lost status whenever they crossed water. They all agreed that that was a good thing, for their forebears were from Madras, where an intense dislike of the Brahmin caste was the norm and the common complaint was of their invincible ignorance.

They continued exchanging stories and experiences, some comic, some grave, all of which were taken very seriously, even where they were the common currency of conversation. So that, inevitably, the story of the East Indian man who bought the larger pair of shoes because they were the same price as the smaller, which fitted him, was related. Then someone spoke of a promising young East Indian lawyer whose father had been recruited in India to work as an indentured labourer on a sugar estate before he was ten years old, a story which was the source of a discussion on the iniquities of the indenture system.

'That's why so much people go back to India when their indenture come to a end.'

'Not many been back.'

'I telling you! A third of the people go back.'

The argument could not be settled, since the man who quoted figures did not have at hand the newspaper from which he had taken the evidence. But the host urged everyone to be still while he recounted a tale that his father had told him when he was a boy.

'He say in those days they din' hardly have no post offices, no postmen in that part; and somebody expecting a letter had to walk miles to the post office to find out if it did arrive. When this man was two miles away he ask a woman walking along the Public Road where the post office was. "You tek de village road 'pon de sea wall side an' when you walk lil bit you goin' see a dog chasing a cat . . ." '

At this point he was obliged to wait for the women to stop laughing, for they had given up the pretence of telling their own tales.

'"Keep goin'," the woman tell the man, "till you get to a lot of bush. Turn round and come back to the Public Road . . ."'

Betta's father-in-law himself laughed and the others joined him, which, in turn, held up the story even longer.

'So,' he continued, 'the man ask the lady, "Is why I got fo' go down the village road when I does have to come back down to the Public Road? In' it better to stay in one place?" So the lady say to him, "If you stay in one place, you dumb-bell, how you goin' get to the post office to collect you letter?"'

Even those who did not understand the joke found themselves laughing, caught up in the general merriment and their host's readiness to forget his illness and entertain them. At this point Betta and his bride, drawn by the commotion, joined the laughing company, and were given two seats, one on each side of the host.

'What about Mrs Singh?' Betta's young sister-in-law asked aloud.

And Betta himself went over to the corner in the shadows where his mother had chosen to sit apart. Then, for no reason, there was laughter when the bride and bridegroom sat together, flanked by Betta's mother- and father-in-law. And Betta's sister-in-law, not to be left out, stood behind her father, proud to be associated with him, because he was her father and made a whole company laugh with stories that had no point; and because at home he was a different kind of man who did not tell jokes but preferred to read Sanskrit texts when not doing his accounts. And she wished inwardly that there were more weddings to attend, when she would see her parents in a different light, her mother expertly painting some bride's palms with henna and her father speaking to a bridegroom-stranger, giving counsel to a grown man who looked up to him. No event had given her a sense of belonging to her family as the preparations for the wedding had and she felt that, should her father die soon, she was protected by his actions in these last hours when he and her mother were the true centre of the extraordinary events which had taken place in her home.

The time came for Betta to take his bride to the house near the sea. And in keeping with the ancient tradition the bride was made to sit on a stool while her parents, relations and friends said their goodbyes. She waited until each stood beside her before she lifted her eyes to the prescribed words that were spoken. And before they departed she and Betta left vermilion prints of their palms on the wall of her parents' house, like fossilized flowers with petals of unequal length.

Bedecked with jewellery, bangles and necklaces and foot rings, the bride left with her husband and mother-in-law, her head bowed modestly, lest those watching should detect a bad omen for the marriage. And at their departure nothing untoward occurred, no one stumbled, nor was there the call of an owl or a goat-sucker or any bird of night which had been looking on with envious eyes as the company dispersed for their homes in the surrounding villages, Uitvlugt, Leonora, Anna Catherina and others, all tied to the cultivation of rice and sugar cane on the polder lands surrounded by a network of irrigation and drainage canals. It was the dry season and constellations were suspended above like ghostly, immobile candleflies. And the voices of two idiot women living in the house next door were heard to converse while they watched the crowd disperse. Betty had lost her memory of childhood days of ribbons. . . . Seven ships were waiting at the bar to sail past fishermen mending their nets. But what did they know of their conversations in port? Did they sing at night and weep on an ebbing tide?

The next afternoon after surgery Betta and Meena took Mrs Singh home and came back by the last ferry. Meena did not feel she knew her husband well enough to ask what was bothering him. She had been touched by the welcome extended to them and by the strange household who came to the gallery to shake hands, by the hibiscus hedge and the wrought-iron gate opening out into the broad, pitch road. The Pujaree had wished her happiness and many children and asked whether she intended to have them taught Hindi, to which Betta had replied abruptly that they had only been married a day. Mrs Singh showed her the room under the house which Betta once used as his surgery and accompanied her round the yard, but neglected to invite her back. And this, as much as her association with the Pujaree, had been the cause of Betta's silence on the way back.

But that night he told Meena of the events that had occurred since he went away; he told her of Lahti's abortions and his mother's recent association with the priest, who had extended his influence in Newtown with her help, even though she knew nothing of his origins. His wife, had they been married a longer time, would have replied that it seemed to her a happy home. Lahti, especially, had made a deep impression on her, not least because she seemed not at all like any of the others. Until then Betta had hardly spoken about his home and in her imagination she had seen his mother in a silent, empty house. One day she would get him to explain how Rani and Lahti came to live there and the others as well, all entirely different from one another, yet living under one roof.

And for weeks afterwards Meena was obsessed with the recollection of Lahti, who, in spite of her East Indian features, reminded her of creole townswomen. Her freedom was reflected in the very range of her gestures and her bold eyes. She herself could not even sustain her husband's gaze, which she still answered with a downward or sideways glance.

Betta's wife did not see her mother-in-law's neglect to invite her as a slight for she knew little of her background. After the wedding she had not said much, but Betta was not talkative either and she believed her to be like him. That must be the way townspeople were. In *her* home the women talked incessantly, restraining themselves only when they went visiting.

Meena reflected that she would have liked to stay for a year or so in the great house, that its vast yard and the asphalt road beside which it stood were an exciting world so far removed from the village that her sojourn there would be like a trip to another country. For a year or so, because she did not believe she was capable of living far from her family, and, moreover, separated by a large river.

During the drive she fell asleep soon after the car negotiated the two planks connecting the boat with the stelling and her perfumed head fell gently on to Betta's left shoulder. He drove along the Public Road through the swirling dust past lone walkers and prayer flags on long bamboo poles celebrating births and other propitious events. And in the thickening darkness nothing was distinct except what was picked out by the headlamps of his slow-moving car. And the thought that he was responsible for Meena's safety filled him with exhilaration and a profound desire to see that she came to no harm with him. He kissed her on her dark forehead and knew that he was her father and her husband and was suddenly afraid that he adhered to no religion, that he was neither Hindu nor Muslim, nor Christian, that the innumerable prayer flags, wayside mosques and churches, the worshippers entering the mosques right foot first, the innumerable pairs of shoes on temple porches, the tolling of Sunday bells, the slow drum in the long Hindu funeral processions, the sermons, prayers, incantations, the midnight masses, the confessions, the pandits with their lotahs of gleaming brass, the ablutions in mosque yards, the belief in an afterlife, in a Muslim hell, the offerings to Ganesha, contentions on the validity of the eucharist, the bleeding thorn-crowned figure of Christ, all these things he saw and heard around, meant little to him, no more than his shadow or the hair cut and discarded by his barber.

Blinded by the headlamps of an oncoming car, he slowed

down his own before pressing his foot down on the accelerator once more. Meena was awakened by the change of speed and asked him which village they were passing through.

'De Kinderen,' he answered.

'We've got far to go?' she asked, betraying her ignorance of the coast where she was born and brought up.

'A hundred miles,' he answered.

'You're fooling me.'

'Of course I'm fooling you,' he said, astonished at her lack of guile. 'You want to drive?'

They laughed, for she could not drive.

'You're in a better mood now.'

'Was I in a bad mood?' he asked.

'Very bad.'

He expressed surprise that she had noticed, thinking he had concealed his irritation with the Pujaree and his mother.

'Why you were in a bad mood?' she pressed him, emboldened by the encouragement he gave her to pursue the conversation, the first unconstrained exchange they had ever had.

'Something that happened at home,' he replied.

'Home?'

'No, not home.'

He kissed her once more and once more she rested her head on his shoulder while he drove towards their home.

The next afternoon Betta took Meena to see the Merrimans. The boys were entertaining their friends with a gramophone they had bought at an auction and the adults were downstairs with old Mr Merriman, who embraced the bride with his usual fervour and gave her a lecture on the perils of marriage, which was like a desert dotted with oases. The secret of a good marriage lay in expecting little. And so on and so forth, until his daughter-in-law protested that Mrs Singh was shy and he should leave her alone. But he insisted on showing her his inventions and would have led her out to see his beehives, in spite of the complaint that the bees were in a vicious mood. But both his son and daughter-in-law insisted that he leave the new bride alone.

'She won't come again if you treat her like that,' his son said.

'All right! All right! Who would think I'm in my own room? Stop fussing!'

But he soon calmed down, for he was afraid that the young woman would be overwhelmed by his manner and might not come again and that the chance to show her his hives would be lost for good.

Betta had visited so often he was now at home in the Merrimans' house, especially in the old man's room, where the impression of a mind in turmoil was reinforced by the disarray of birdcages, spinning-tops, pickled fruit, books piled in the corners and his favourite book of Venezuelan waltzes on the table.

Young Mr Merriman began making fun of Betta, declaring that he must have been nervous at the wedding, to which he replied that it was not a laughing matter.

'I was so nervous my knees were shaking.'

'You ever heard the story of the man at his wedding?' young Merriman continued. 'Instead of saying "I do" he said, "I did"!'

Meena had to restrain herself from laughing as she was accustomed to doing in her mother's home. She was pleased about the visit and hoped Betta would bring her again.

Mrs Merriman tried to encourage her to speak, but since the young woman only answered in monosyllables she soon gave up, bewildered by her lack of conversation. Betta was not very different in the early days, she thought.

When old Mr Merriman got his chance he soon dominated the conversation again, this time harping on the old subject of the inefficiency of the village councils. In days gone by the gutters were well weeded while now they were clogged up with lotus and weeds, so that in the rainy season the yards were no longer properly drained and the flooding that resulted was not what they paid their rates and taxes for. He had ceased paying rates and taxes long ago, since he retired and his son had taken over the responsibility for them.

'In the old days we would've refused to pay for it,' said the old man. 'Oh, no! What could the village council have done? Cut off our electricity? There isn't any. There isn't any sewage. There isn't anything, come to think of it. Nothing except roads that resemble silted-up trenches. So what could they have done? Tell me!'

He was addressing no one in particular, and on seeing the fright in the bride's eyes, he smiled and said, 'No one understands me, my dear. Only my dead wife did, God rest her soul.'

Young Merriman coughed, but his father ignored him.

'She's lying in that waterlogged cemetery. . . . Floating, if you ask me. Floating in that burial ground.'

'Father,' Mrs Merriman interrupted indulgently, 'why are you so cantankerous? If . . .'

'I know. I'll frighten this delicate Indian flower.'

Meena bowed her head and Betta smiled at her discomfiture.

'No, child,' old Mr Merriman said. 'If I don't keep making jokes I'll die of terror. Poor, innocent, little thing.'

And at this point he took her hand, which caused her so much alarm that she looked at Betta for help.

Old Mr Merriman placed Meena's hand against his chest and declared, 'Ah! The commendable modesty of youth.'

'Father, you're going too far now,' young Merriman protested, taking Meena's hand from his.

'You want me to sit in a corner and sulk, don't you? But I'll tell you something: this Indian flower will guide Betta through life with a hand of steel. Gently, mind you; but firmly.'

Soon after the sun went down he fell asleep, as he usually did, and the young people were able to engage in an uninterrupted conversation. Meena learned that the Merrimans got married when he was eighteen and she twenty-two, having been next-door neighbours and childhood sweethearts. There had always been an understanding between their parents that they would marry, for neither of them ever showed an interest in anyone else.

'That's not true,' young Merriman said. 'When you were five you were in love with a santapee dancer. Deny it! Oh, perfidious creature!'

Meena was to say later that she could see both a physical and temperamental resemblance between old Mr Merriman and the young one, while Betta claimed that they had nothing in common.

The two couples went for a walk as far as the adjoining village, knowing that only a few days of the dry season were left and that the umbrella mender would soon be shouting for business under their windows. They went down to the shore where the waves died and listened to the wind which drowned their conversation and shook the mangrove trees.

Merriman spoke to Betta, but the latter could not hear what he said, until the words were shouted into his ears.

'The rainy season's coming soon!'

'Yes, soon!'

Meena had come down to the beach only once before, when a relation from town visited and they took him on a picnic. Now she was on the beach at night! She was out at night like those women who were free and chose their own time for going out and coming in. But she had been happy at home, she recalled, where she could only guess what a certain kind of freedom might be. Yet the exhilaration that the wind brought and the endless expanse of ocean held for her a fascination so overpowering she was certain that, in an unguarded moment, she was capable of leaping into the water as though in answer to a 'call'. And she felt that just because she had not been able to experience the call earlier, she was uncertain what her reaction would be had she been alone. Husband, friends of her own, unfettered conversations, all threatened to overwhelm her in this first week of her marriage, when the marriage ceremony was still fresh in her mind, the taste of baked snapper and her relations' farewell.

Betta and Meena bade their friends goodbye at the gate of their home where their children's friends were still entertaining and the tinny sound of their gramophone could barely be heard on the street.

Chapter 20

Betta invited the Mulvi Sahib to spend a weekend, so that his old teacher could meet his wife. He duly came, early one Saturday afternoon when Betta was out on his rounds and was welcomed by Meena who, to his surprise, was dressed in a sari. At home she wore a frock like most of the village women, but she now dressed as for a special occasion to welcome her husband's former teacher.

She offered him something to eat and took his sandals and umbrella into the bedroom he was to occupy for the time he stayed with them.

The Mulvi Sahib declined the offer of food, but said he was eager to take a look round the house, after which he would go and see the nearby mosque.

Meena called down to the janitor to come and show the visitor the rooms and the yard, and reminded them that Betta was due back at any moment and that they should not go far. She was not as relaxed as she appeared, and had it not been for the well-practised gestures, the joined hands, the modest, welcoming smile she had copied from those around her, she would certainly have succumbed to her nervousness. She prayed that Betta would come home soon. Accustomed to a house full of people, her situation was, in her eyes, so unnatural, she wondered that Betta had not anticipated her predicament and arranged for the Mulvi Sahib to come when he was certain to be there.

Suddenly she heard men's voices in the yard and ran to the window, but she saw the guest and the janitor setting off across the empty field towards the northern boundary of the yard where the sage gave way to courida bushes.

In her agitation Meena kept walking from the windows facing the road to those looking out towards the sea. Then when she least expected it she saw Betta's car turning into the village road, and involuntarily ran out on to the stairs to welcome him.

'Betta!' she called out.

He got out of the car which he had brought to a halt just over the bridge and Meena saw his doctor's bag appear before he did.

'Betta! It's the Mulvi Sahib. He's come!'

'Why aren't you with him?'

And she pointed towards the bushes along the edge of which the two men were walking, the Mulvi Sahib in white tunic and the janitor in a dark working get-up and leggings. Betta waved, but they did not see him. He bounded up the stairs and put his hands round his wife's waist in a deliberately extravagant gesture.

'I thought you were supposed to be made of steel, eh?'

'I thought you weren't coming.'

'I got caught. A patient who wouldn't let me go. Remember I told you about the old lady living by the koker? She said she doesn't sleep any more, so I gave her a bottle of barbiturate. She said she didn't like the colour and I had to explain I wasn't responsible for the colour. Then . . .'

'Well, I nearly died because I couldn't face the Mulvi Sahib alone.'

Then the two men, catching sight of Betta and his wife waving from the window, promptly set off in the direction of the house at a brisk pace.

'You wouldn't think he's over sixty, would you?' Betta said. 'He doesn't look it, but he's over sixty. You should see the way he exercises. . . . Did he bring his prayer mat?'

'Yes. It's rolled up in the corner.'

He reminded her that their guest prayed five times a day, and that she must keep water prepared for his ablutions and never express surprise at anything he did or said.

'Anything else?' she asked, smiling.

Together they waited for the Mulvi Sahib at the top of the stairs and, for the first time since they knew each other, Betta felt confident enough to embrace him.

'My wife was trembling because she had to welcome you alone.'

'It didn't seem so,' the Mulvi Sahib said.

And so began the visit of Betta's old teacher, who saw that, for the first time, his former pupil was speaking to him as a man, no doubt because he was in his own home and 'possessed' a wife.

The rest of that day was spent talking about trivial matters, the way the couple were settling down, the effect of the perpetual wind, the racial make-up of the villages in which he practised and the latest news from Kitty.

The next day the two men installed themselves in the gallery after the midday meal, while Meena retired to the bedroom to rest. At first they said nothing of significance until Betta spoke of his anxiety about his lack of religion, especially since he got married.

'Ah, yes. Why do you think it's important? For your children?'

The old irritation overcame Betta, who thought that the Mulvi Sahib might be making fun of him.

'Not only for my children, but for my wife, for me. Since I've been living over here I have nothing to do at night, so I think about things. Before it was always my studies, then private practice and the business of breaking away from home. I think about everything now. I just sit thinking for hours. . . . I didn't believe it would ever be like that. What is your opinion about religion? Is it dying? Do I need to install it in my house, like a radio or a piece of furniture?' And in saying this he was thinking of the shrines to Lakshmi and Kali in his mother's home.

Betta's head sank. He was surprised that he *did* feel so strongly about the matter.

'I'd like to know your views.'

'My views would only disturb you, Betta. I've got a philosophy *and* a religion. They're not the same . . .'

'But I thought . . . I thought you had definite views on religion. You always said that . . . I'm not certain; but you were always definite about things.'

'I'm definite that I don't want to be anything but a Muslim,' the Mulvi Sahib continued, 'and that it's good for the community that practises it. But the Mohammedans in this country are a minority. If they controlled it I wouldn't hold the same view, because I feel, as in the case of Christianity, Muslims should be kept as far away from the direction of a state as possible. Yet if I told you that religion can be more dangerous than it is useful, would you understand?'

'That's what I thought. Medicine is useful, but would you put drugs into the hands of anyone? Well, would you?'

'Are you saying religion is a drug?' the Mulvi Sahib asked.

'I am.'

'Well, you're right,' the Mulvi Sahib conceded. 'Its appeal rests precisely on fantastical ideas, so its worst enemy is logic. You must believe, that's all.'

'You mean to say you believe knowing that what you believe is wrong . . . dubious?'

'Not wrong, just illogical,' declared the Mulvi Sahib.

'How then do you justify your belief?'

'I don't. I feel that history – biological and . . . whatever history is – it's left me with a need, a spiritual need, which I satisfy by adhering to the faith into which I was born.'

'And what about me?' Betta asked, suddenly feeling that he had been left out in the cold.

'You must have the same need. Everybody does, even the atheist.'

'I asked you first if religion is doomed.'

'Everything is doomed, Betta.'

And Betta detected the same mocking tone he feared and hated.

'I mean, can the world do without it?'

'Ah. . . . There are thousands of people throughout the world who have not religion. They have wealth instead. And it is interesting that Christianity is the most vulnerable to wealth. In fact, in India rich Muslims and Hindus worship as passionately as others. . . .'

Betta shook his head.

'I can't agree with you.'

'Listen to me,' the Mulvi Sahib continued. 'Isn't it a fact you're thinking of becoming a Christian?'

Betta stared at him in astonishment.

'How did you know?'

'Isn't that the way the East Indian community is going, Betta? Aren't there fathers and mothers who abandon their Hinduism and are ashamed to speak Hindi because it is the language of estate workers?'

'Let's stick to the point,' Betta said, making a heroic effort to master his irritation at being caught out by a man whom, apparently, he could never match in wisdom.

'What's the point?' asked the Mulvi Sahib.

'Is religion going to die while society lives on? That's what I'd like to know.'

'I think it will. I see our spiritual side as the contents of a cup, as it were. The cup contains our conscious needs and our spiritual, underground needs. The proportion between them changes gradually at the expense of the spiritual needs, until the moment comes when it will be all but ousted.'

'I can't accept that!' Betta declared violently. 'I'm sorry, Mulvi Sahib. You don't know what it all means to me, you see. Since I got married there are things I must know. I'll be responsible for my family, so I must know. You can speak confidently, but you're only doing what your father did. Nowadays it's harder to be a parent because you have to choose a road and walk along it; and when you discover it's the wrong road it's too late. What choice did you ever make?'

The Mulvi Sahib thought for a while, then replied. 'I didn't say it was not harder for you. I don't even say my views are right. What I say is, whatever you think of religion, it's not a reason for abstaining from it. My advice to you is, join your wife's religion, you'll have the advantage of numbers . . . and other advantages as well.'

'No,' Betta declared. 'I can't do that.'

'Why? Your father was a Hindu and your mother.'

'My mother?' Betta asked, his eyes blazing with anger. 'My mother? You've heard about her and the Pujaree, haven't you?'

'Yes, Betta, everybody knows. For you it's important. Believe me, your mother has so much prestige people see her conduct in a different light. They crucified Christ because he would not condemn the Romans. If he were a rich man they wouldn't have touched him.'

Betta laughed in his face.

'I thought you were anti-Christian,' he said.

'I'm against any state religion. Christ is also a Muslim prophet. My example could have come from Hinduism. But why do you want to quarrel?'

'You're right,' Betta admitted. 'There are things worrying me, about practising on the estates, and about one man in particular, an estate manager. . . . But I've got to settle this business about religion, before my children are born. Somehow it seems urgent. I'm not going to wait until I'm in the middle of that road . . . and I'll tell you one thing, once I've taken it I won't regret anything. But whatever you say about religion I can't believe in a multiplicity of gods and in sacrifice.'

'If I say something, you must promise not to get angry. . . . Do you?'

Betta nodded, but did not look up at him.

'You're a man of science; don't you think that your scientific education is arguing for you?'

'Probably it is,' Betta answered, determined to keep his temper. 'But is it wrong?'

'Yet, you see, science cannot take the place of religion.'

'Not science, but scientific logic,' said Betta.

'And what about the inner need I was talking about? Will Christianity satisfy it?'

'I don't know. You're right about Christianity and status. But I can't revert to Hinduism, neither can I become a Muslim.'

'You know,' said the Mulvi Sahib, 'when I was a young man I used to tell myself I could not teach because I could not love other people's children. Not only I discovered that I liked children, but I was good at teaching them. I'm afraid to be frank with you because I don't think you're ready for it. You want to do the right thing, but does anyone know what the right thing is? People try desperately to educate their children because it's *good* for them, but what we call education, doesn't it take away as much as it gives? Doesn't it heal and bring disease at the same time? Isn't that logical? Can we make *any* advance without going backwards? When I was your age I was incessantly searching, asking myself questions I couldn't answer. And now? Now I know that when I stop questioning myself it will be the moment of my first death. But something's changed; and I don't know if I've been overcome by wisdom or age. And as my questioning became less desperate my faith increased. But the ruler and the fool know instinctively that they don't dare allow the ordinary man to ask questions. Do you realize that in nearly every country drug-taking is allowed? No, encouraged! If it's not alcohol, it's coffee or marijuana or some other drug. In every country except a handful of Muslim ones. And *they*, they are fanatical about their religion, which achieves the same effect, Betta. They feel obliged to strip you.'

'Of what?' Betta asked, fascinated by the Mulvi Sahib's outburst and the complete absence of the mocking tone that made him so angry.

'You know what I mean by *stripped*, Betta. Didn't they strip the Government Officers of their microscopes? But you'll get them back. It only needs a terrible malarial epidemic like the one in 1908 to frighten the life out of our masters, for them to give you them back so that you can keep the workers alive.'

'I had no idea you thought of things like that,' Betta said, in a way disappointed that his teacher did not suffer from the defect he attributed to him. 'With your aviary, your physical exercises and all.'

'I'm more interested in you, Betta, in your *imminent* conversion.'

After a long silence, during which the only noise penetrating from outside was the intermittent sound of a hand-saw from beneath the floorboards, Betta said to the Mulvi Sahib, 'It's nothing to do with status. What have I got to gain. . . ? I've become friendly with a family of Christians, a husband and wife and the husband's father. Oh, we never discuss religion, and they are no more religious than anyone else; in fact they only attend church once a week. But there is something about them . . . their way of living I find congenial. I can't say more than that.'

'I knew a man,' the Mulvi Sahib said, as if he had been waiting for the opportunity to speak, 'who told me he was no longer a Muslim. "Why?" I asked him. "Because it's so inconvenient praying five times a day," he said. "Well, pray once a day then," I told him. "It's better than abandoning the faith altogether." It didn't make the slightest difference because he intended to become a Christian anyway.'

'So he was lying?' Betta asked, far from being annoyed, and particularly interested in the Muslim's story.

'I don't know. But is it important? This continual exhortation to tell the truth only confirms us in our lying ways. In a certain state in the United States the death penalty was abolished and in no time at all the rate of suicide in prison rose sharply.'

'So what do you make of that?' Betta enquired.

'What do *you* make of it, Betta?'

'But is that what we're talking about?'

'Yes,' the Mulvi Sahib answered, this time determined to stand his ground, whatever effect his remark might have on his former pupil.

'You see,' he continued, as Betta gave no indication that he wanted to speak. 'When I'm with the Pujaree or the goblet maker I never get involved in a conversation like this, because the last thing people want is a serious discussion. They prefer to leave that sort of thing to philosophers and historians, the official propagandists.'

'I can't accept your cynical view of life.'

'Ah! At last. Now you see why I never get involved in a serious discussion. That is precisely the vocabulary of our masters. The question is not whether I'm right or wrong. As soon as you get too near the centre you're dangerous and *must* be damned with official vocabulary. But what are *you* afraid of?'

'I'm not afraid, Mulvi Sahib,' Betta answered, almost wearily, as if he had been walking all day.

'If I were you I should become a Christian and not bother to find excuses to justify your conversion. Like most people you act because you feel you're bound to act as you think fit. Even if you try to track down the reason and eventually succeed, you'll deny it hotly if it doesn't suit you.'

The two men looked at each other, convinced they were engaging in a duel put off for too long, that as they had suspected, their paths had diverged long ago, that thinking had brought them no closer together than at the time of their meetings when Betta came home from abroad. Yet Betta would not admit to the Mulvi Sahib that he felt less ashamed now about his decision to become a Christian and that the teacher's advice 'not to feel guilty about it' was just what he wanted to hear. In any case he had finally had it out with him and, like a youth who had just engaged in a fight with an older and stronger tormentor, he felt that there was no longer anything to fear from his opponent.

'Ah,' said Betta, 'how we torment ourselves!'

'Tell me about your practice here,' the Mulvi Sahib asked.

Betta spoke about the hovels he visited, the contrast between practising medicine in England, in Kitty and the West Coast.

'In the London surgery where I was an observer a high proportion of the patients were suffering from pulmonary disorders.'

He spoke of his original impressions, his first diary, begun during his year at the School of Tropical Medicine in London. He fetched it and showed the Mulvi Sahib the first entry which read, 'Black snot from a perpetual rain of coal dust. No one dares hang out washing.'

'I wrote it in winter, when I became convinced that it was impossible to be content in an environment like that. Then came summer and everything looked different.'

It was strange, he said, that he found it difficult to recall much about his practice in Kitty, where there was everything, from malaria among the poor to gout among the handful of wealthy East Indians who consulted him.

'But practising here is like inhabiting a world of demons,' Betta told him. 'Little seems to be real. Whole households suffer from severe malnutrition and I'm afraid to think what will happen when the rain comes. If I write more than a handful of certificates I'm called to account.'

'The clouds're already gathering,' the Mulvi Sahib said, looking out of the window to the overcast sky.

Betta spoke about the East Indians' habit of exhausting every herbal remedy before consulting him about their susceptibility to certain diseases like rickets and diabetes. He told him of villages along the coast where creoles rarely suffered from malaria because the sea wall had not been repaired for years, so that the inhabitants had a reliable supply of shrimps when the tide came in. Besides, mosquitoes could not breed in the seawater pools left behind. He spoke of sickle-cell anaemia, which only affected creoles and afforded a high degree of protection against malaria. And, encouraged by his guest's interest, he spoke of Dr Giglioli's findings that the malaria mosquito could not breed in very acid water and that the creeks in the interior, laden with tannic acid from the vegetation, were often free of mosquito larvae.

'Very few bacteria can live in it too,' he added.

'All of this should be taught in primary schools,' said the Mulvi Sahib, 'instead of sterile subjects like English History.'

'Oh, yes,' Betta agreed. 'In fact I don't see the point in dividing up subjects as they do.'

Without realizing it Betta was repeating one of the Mulvi Sahib's favourite theses, which he had heard so often he believed it to be his own.

They talked until the Mulvi Sahib retired to pray in his room, whereupon Betta went downstairs to see whether the janitor had washed down his car.

The Mulvi Sahib visited the nearby mosque before leaving for home that afternoon. Only a handful of worshippers were there, prostrate on the wooden floor. He listened to the imam, who had just descended from the ornate pulpit.

'We have seen the turning of your face to Heaven, O Mohammed . . . God is great, God is great. There is no other God but Allah, and Mohammed is his prophet.'

The Mulvi Sahib whispered to himself, 'Praise be to God, who has brought us to this.'

He had prayed at dawn, at noon, in the afternoon at Betta's, and now he was glad to be saying his prayers at dusk in a mosque he had entered for the first time, with Muslims he did not know, but who were his brothers because they did the same things he did, prayed in Urdu as he did and prostrated themselves like him, surrendering themselves to a worship whose origins they did not understand and whose justification lay in the fact that it brought them together, unshod and dressed in their skullcaps, and provided for them a celebration of sacrifice and atonement at the centre of the cyclic year, the month of Ramadan, and which ended in a procession of lamps, a thousand lights in the terrible darkness of this world. These practices had struck such deep roots in him, had responded to such a profound need, he was not prepared to abandon them, even if the time came when he was obliged to condemn the use to which they were put. Then his attention was called back to the prayer intoned by the imam, who was speaking in a loud, trance-like voice.

'Thee alone we worship, show us the path . . .'

The Mulvi Sahib returned to the house, pleased that he had come to see his former pupil. And once more on his way to the stelling in Betta's car, he was able to take another look at the mosque standing in a garden of cinnamon trees, with its small dome representing the vault of heaven. In the adjoining plot of land a herd of cattle were lying where they had just grazed, their figures no more than outlines in the dark.

'You had a good day, Mulvi Sahib?' Betta's wife asked him from the back of the car.

'I had a very good day, Mrs Singh. Betta and I argued a lot, so we both had a good day.'

The three laughed, and it occurred to Meena that she had been addressed by her new name for the first time. The cook called her 'Dr Singh wife', while the janitor said, 'Mistress'.

I am 'Mrs Singh', she reflected. A couple weeks ago I was Miss Ramcharran. Today I'm Mrs Singh. And I *do* feel different. I haven't seen my family for two weeks and I am supposed to be mistress in my new home. If Betta had been a different man it would have been unbearable.

And she settled to the long journey to Vreed-en-Hoop, where the ferry boats tied up.

Chapter 21

The rainy season arrived like a thief in the early hours of morning, spattering the panes when Betta and Meena were in bed. Meena had put out Betta's umbrella and leggings on the hat stand, when the clouds drifting inland did no more than threaten rain. Now the drizzle fell noiselessly on the buildings and fields. The cattle first changed position, then one by one they stood up with their rumps to the wind. In the season that was now at an end they had sought out the trenches when the heat was intolerable, but from now on they would make for the well-drained churchyard or the police station compound, and huddle together near the vehicle shed.

The few dogs in the village strayed from the road towards the bottom houses where they found refuge until morning when they would be chased away lest they frightened the poultry. The private, white-painted cottages housing the families of police officers stood apart, separated from one another by an empty space, secretive in their paling enclosures with a gap for gates that had not yet been built.

On the other side of the Public Road the drizzle had already made puddles and runnels of water where the bottom houses sloped away towards the gutters. The rice fields and cane fields, laid out to collect water for fertilization with microscopic organisms, were the places where anopheles mosquitoes laid their eggs, to commence a long metamorphosis that ended in a banquet of blood. These were the vectors of malarial parasites destined to migrate to the victim's liver, and as the more malignant variety, to accompany them wherever they went, for as long as they lived.

The drizzle came down, dampening the air. And when the villagers awoke they saw houses glistening with rain and found that the red dust on the street had thickened and compacted. Soon there was movement, of children on their way to the shops, of cattle foraging for blades of grass that might have survived the baking sun, of lizards on the fences, of sheep being driven to pasture and the passage of taxis on the Public Road.

And in the days that followed the clouds massed and there were times when two inches of rain fell in an hour and the downpour was like a thick veil obscuring the lives of their neighbours. The branches of the cinnamon tree in the mosque yard hung low as though in submission to the inexorable power of the deluge, which brought down the vultures from their perpetual, circling flight, although there was no carrion in the fields.

As the season advanced the new cases of malaria seen in Betta's consulting rooms began to rise and instinctively he placed his hands below his patients' navel in search of the enlarged spleen which signalled an attack of the swamp sickness. More than ever he felt the need of a microscope to examine the blood samples for paratyphoid and other lethal organisms; and he was tempted to write the names of these diseases on his certificates in order to keep his patients away from the sugar-cane fields when they could hardly stand on their legs. He wrote more certificates than ever, confining his diagnosis to the more certain descriptive term 'malaria', so that when the inevitable challenge came he would be able to defend himself.

After surgery hours he tramped along the backlands, leaving his motorcar on the Public Road. He passed farmers ploughing their fields with white-faced oxen, flocks of gaulings scattered along the grey-gleaming furrows. And one afternoon he went by a group of women in mourning, the same startling image that haunted him since he came to live in Leonora. Could they be the same women? Were they alive or had he only imagined their existence? But turning round he saw them in the distance, the unearthly group who did not wave, looked neither left nor right, who refused to acknowledge his existence as though they were blind, he as well, thus explaining the recurrent image that could have no logical explanation. As he was about to enter a yard he turned at the sound of horses' hooves and saw the estate manager and an overseer riding along the back-dam road wearing sun helmets even though the sun was hidden behind the thick covering of clouds. There was something ominous about these men in khaki, their long-maned horses and the assurance with which they sat in the saddle.

Many yards were inundated, forcing the animals under the houses where they were elevated enough to accommodate them. Otherwise the cattle, sheep and pigs stood in the water.

Betta saw three children looking through the panes of a closed window and signalled to them to open up. And once inside he stood, waiting to be shown the sick woman's corner. But no one said anything to him and he was obliged to ask the eldest child, a boy of about eleven, where the sick corner was. He pointed to two walls in turn, both of them hidden by curtains hanging from bamboo sticks.

Betta chose one wall and pulled back the cloth, only to reveal a heap of bedclothes, beneath which a woman and an infant lay. The child was stretched out on its mother's chest, its head turned to the wall and its legs spread apart.

'Who's sick?' Betta asked the boy standing by him.

'All two. They got fever.'

Betta placed his bag on the ground, kneeled down and took out his thermometer, which he placed in the woman's mouth, while passing his fingers across her forehead.

'Where's your father?' Betta asked the boy.

He had come forward and was peering at his mother, who held the thermometer with one hand while the other rested on the infant's back. The boy pointed to the wall.

'Where does he work? On the estate?'

'Yes,' the boy replied, 'but only in the cane-cuttin' season.'

'And your ma?'

'She been sick a year now.'

'She ever worked on the estate?'

'No. She does sell provisions 'pon the Public Road.'

Betta assumed that the boy's father was covered by an indenture and entitled to free treatment. The mother had a severe bout of malaria and associated anaemia, while the infant was suffering from thrush; and Betta left the boy the phial containing quinine which he carried around with him for the worst cases.

'Take this to Mr Merriman,' he told the boy, handing him a prescription for the infant.

'Who Mr Merriman?'

'The doctor-shop man.'

'Oh! Is for who the paper?'

'Give it to Mr Merriman,' Betta said, 'and he'll give you a bottle of medicine for the baby. You must give him just what it says on the bottle. He won't get better quicker if you give him more. It will make him more sick. You understand? You can read?'

'Lil bit.'

'Your mother can read?'

'No. *She* can read,' he said, turning to his younger sister, who was a good two years younger than he.

'Good. Let her go to the doctor shop,' Betta suggested. 'You stay home and look after the family.'

'She frighten to go so far,' the boy declared.

'I in' frighten, Doctor,' the girl protested.

'Good girl,' Betta said, taking out a penny and handing it to her. 'Buy something and share it with the others.'

Betta crossed the room, pulled back the curtain and was confronted with the atrophied figure of a man asleep. He could only be awakened with difficulty. From the dropsy and the enlarged spleen he diagnosed chronic nephritis and judged that there was irreparable damage to his kidneys. He would soon die.

'I'll arrange for your father to be taken to hospital,' Betta told the boy. 'Two men will come for him, so you *must* stay home. Understand?'

'Wha' wrong to he?' the man's son asked.

'He's sick.'

'Bad?'

'He's sick bad.'

The boy, surprised and dismayed at the news, cast a glance towards his father's corner.

'You have any aunts and uncles? Any family?'

'We got family,' the boy answered. 'They livin' by the back dam. So!'

He pointed in the direction of the back-dam road where Betta had seen the horsemen.

'Your little sister must go and tell them about your father when she comes back from the doctor shop. But you must stay home, because when the hospital men come they might go away if no one answers the door.'

'*He* can answer it,' the boy said angrily, pointing to a brother of less than five years old. 'Why I always got fo' do everyt'ing?'

'You stay home!' Betta ordered him.

'Gi'e me a penny, then, like you gi'e she.'

Betta complied, to the satisfaction of the boy, who looked at his sister spitefully.

Betta went away, sick at heart at what he had seen. He had learned from his practice that his sensitivity, even when it appeared to be dulled by a surfeit of suffering, was capable of being aroused with a force which at times threatened his good sense. Instinctively he felt he should assume the role of protector of the family who, apparently, had no means of support. Little by little he was learning the price of commitment to an ideal, the depth of a responsibility which could not be discharged simply by being generous. Perhaps the saintly individual was admired because his efforts changed little and only served to divert attention from the conditions that gave rise to the disease.

The familiar landscape spread out around him, the water in which he now stood, the coconut trees, the gaunt cattle, the odd human who might have been a stranger rather than master of an earth in turn drenched with water and sunlight. The thought came to him that God might have urinated on the world to demonstrate his disgust with humans. And there were humans who, with their passion for honesty, would have caught sight of him in the act but, refusing to believe the evidence of their eyes, would declare that they saw him weeping instead.

Betta walked towards the Public Road, past a line of men with cutlasses; they doffed their felt hats to him. At times like this he was a very important man. He did not shun blackwater-fever houses like other mortals and had been known to save people believed to be not long for this world.

His motorcar had sunk into the soft road verge and had to be pushed into a starting position by onlookers who recognized it from its frequent vigils at the entrance to inhospitable village roads, and sometimes stopped to examine its number plate, its battery and leather upholstery and the housing of its engine, which, like that of all Ford cars, was destined to outlive its bodywork and do service in the rear of a launch for several years.

Betta drove home after arranging with the estate hospital for his patient to be taken there on a stretcher and leaving instructions as to his treatment.

'Cook didn't come to work today,' Meena told him, 'and the janitor went home feeling sick.'

'That's strange,' Betta said. 'Both of them were all right yesterday.'

He went off at once to the janitor's house and learned from his wife that he was at his aunt's home. Whenever he felt ill he went there. But his wife, who would not look Betta in the eye, did not know where her husband's aunt lived.

Days passed without a word from either the cook or the janitor and Betta rang the estate manager's office to ask for replacements for them. So began a cat and mouse game between himself and the manager, who had reverted to tactics for which he and his colleagues were notorious. He left messages that the doctor should telephone at such and such a time, but whenever Betta did call he had just gone out of the office.

Finally Betta lost patience and wrote to the Immigration Office in Georgetown, which had been under constant pressure from the Government of India regarding the death rate of East Indians in the country. Two days later both the cook and janitor reported for work.

Betta reflected that he had had no idea of the problems, both serious and trivial, that would beset him when he came to the West Coast, just as private practice had proved to be entirely different from what he imagined. The diseases he had encountered in hospital during his studentship and internship were all grave, and belonged for the most part to a certain climate. Not once had he come across chickenpox, although it was not an uncommon illness; and as for malaria, it was only recently that Dr Giglioli had identified *Anopheles darlingi* as the carrier. Even at the School of Tropical Medicine he had learned nothing of significance about the scourge that preoccupied the minds of practitioners in the country. His lack of preparation for the altercations with the janitor and estate manager was no less evident. Due largely to his restricted education and upbringing in a house where everything was predictable, it proved to be a severe handicap in his work. He was convinced that the estate manager would not accept defeat in the battle to impose his will on him. Merriman was of the same opinion. In fact he regarded him as an extremely dangerous opponent and told how the sugar estate owners preferred not to enquire too closely how he achieved results.

Was life a series of trivial encounters? Would the country ever have its own university? Even doctors qualified in the United States were not permitted to practise, on the pretext that they were not good enough. Was there a kind of madness at large in the world, a universal folly that could not be apprehended because it was universal? Was there a true morality to which everyone should strive?

That night Betta was called out to a dance hall in the neighbouring village to attend to a police constable injured in a commotion, and after a cursory examination he was able to say that the man's injuries were not serious. Meanwhile he heard a woman giving her version of the events to the police superintendent. The police had been sent for to stop a fight, but themselves became involved in two fights, one on the top floor of the building and the other on the ground floor.

'On the top floor,' the woman witness said, 'the police was

beatin' up the dance men, but on the bottom floor the dance men was beatin' up the police.'

The account went down well with the crowd surrounding Betta, the superintendent and the injured policeman; and the woman, encouraged by the reception of her story, embarked on another tale irrelevant to the superintendent's enquiries. With difficulty he managed to confine her remarks to the dance hall fight.

The injured policeman was soon on his feet and was able to make his way to the superintendent's car, which drove off a few minutes later, followed by Betta's.

However, the crowd hung around to discuss what had happened. There was an argument about who was the best dancer that night, but it was brought to an end by an old man who declared that people did not dance nowadays with their whole body.

'Even I would've beat these jokers tonight. I was a good dance man in me time, but is shoe spoil me foot.'

The conversation then shifted to Dr Singh's work. His swift, expert examination had impressed everyone.

'He's the best doctor 'pon the West Coast,' one man said.

'You talkin' stupid! How you can be good when you been only practisin' a couple o' years? In the nature o' things that in' possible. You got to got *experience*, and he in' got enough experience.'

'Is you who talkin' stupid. Is what you do, not how long you doing it. Some people *born* good screw-men, other people learn to screw good by experience. If you in' know that you shouldn' be discussin'.'

'Is what screwin' got to do with doctorin'? You always goin' off the point.'

'You an' you point! The point is within!'

'Is what you mean?'

'Don' bother. You was always a dunce.'

Another man came to the support of the one with a high opinion of Betta, claiming that he had cured his cousin of a hydroseed which had embarrassed him for years and resisted the treatment of Georgetown doctors, who had charged him a fortune into the bargain.

'Call the thing *goadie*, man,' said the man who thought Betta had not yet proved himself. 'Call it by its name. Hydroseed my ass. An' tobesides, you kian' cure it with medicine. You got to operate.'

'I din' say he cure it with medicine!'

'You did imply it. You say cure! If I say cure it don' mean a operation.'

'Nobody can argue with you,' protested the man whose cousin had been afflicted with hydroseed, 'you too pedantic!'

'What you callin' me?' demanded the man who considered that Betta was not deserving of the praise lavished on him.

'I say you pedantic!'

'Take that back!' he retorted, putting his fists up to challenge the man whose cousin Betta had cured.

'The word mean you splitting hairs,' the other man said calmly. 'Is who stupid now?'

'Is what you laughing at?' the man who was not convinced of Betta's prowess demanded of a woman standing next to him. 'You always grinning as if only you know something.'

'My uncle does teach people how to laugh,' said another man who had until then not contributed to the conversation, and now thought to calm things down.

'How you mean?' a young man asked.

'He got a laughing school. I telling you! He's a big laugh man. When he laugh he does go "Hee hee hawwww! Ha Hoo!"'

'How he does go?'

'Hee hee hawww! Ha hoo! The first thing he does teach the students is how to pull the sides of they mouth like this.'

And by way of demonstration he drew the sides of his mouth into a hideous contortion to represent the rudiments of a smile.

'The second lesson the students got to learn is to say "Aowowow!" like dog when he chase fowl cock and get peck 'pon he eye. He does always tell them students, "Practise! Practise! Everything is practice!" When the students them pass they exam he does give them certificate an' thing. An' in the end he does throw a banquet with the money he earn from the school.'

'Is why you does tell such lies, eh?' someone in the crowd asked him.

'You don' got to believe,' the laughing teacher's nephew said. 'But if you want to learn to laugh you come to the school.'

The crowd began to disperse without having settled the question of the doctor's competence or any of the weighty problems they had been discussing. The fields and yards around the school hall where the dance was held stretched like a lake over which bats flitted like infernal ghosts. There had been reports that the red clay road leading from the East Bank Public Road into Mocha had been washed away by the rains and that no buses were running beyond Bagotstown. Rumours that the river had burst its bank at Ruimveldt had been confirmed and Public Works Department employees had been mobilized to drive bamboo stakes into the banks and pile up sandbags on each side of the large koker. Yet none of these things had come up in the discussions that had just taken place, as though to talk of them would make matters worse and inevitably have disastrous consequences for them all.

Chapter 22

Betta lay next to his wife, whose hair spread over her shoulders and back, in the manner of a dark shawl. As a boy he used to lie in bed and watch the line of light around the door and listen to the voluptuous sounds from the bathroom where his mother was preparing to retire for the night, the splashing of water and the barely audible noise of her toothbrush. She would then come inside and comb her hair, which reminded him of a dark recess where you could make long journeys and from which broke out urgent whisperings and the beating of a muffled drum. And each night, while she believed he was asleep, he looked forward to the sensation of her body against his and its faint vanilla scent. It was not until the age of twelve that he expressed the wish to sleep alone, on the morning following the night he dreamt she stood over him, armed with a quivering penis. And the burden of that dream he communicated to no one, not even to Aji, who was at that time the servant-mother of the house and keeper of its secrets.

It was evident from the moment they met that his mother did not care for Meena. And for that he loved his wife all the more, for that and the knowledge that she had grown up in a house of laughter. Whenever he woke up at night and found her beside him he was astonished that they were indeed man and wife, for it was not long ago that he was visiting her home on the pretext of treating a sick father. As he watched her, arms stretched out, covered by her thin nightdress and dishevelled hair, he wondered how much of his love was physical and how much of it stemmed from a need to protect her from demons, from his mother's possessiveness, from Aji's decrepitude, from the diseases that racked his patients' bodies; and from others, invisible lodgers who entered through the crevices of doorways and the mosquito meshing around casement windows.

They had taken to visiting the Merrimans on the evenings Mrs Merriman held court; and often, when he was kept back on his rounds, he would go and meet her, picking her out from among the audience with a feeling of intense pride. Once a month they went to see her family, taking with them roti she had baked herself, wrapped in damp muslin, and a saucepan of curried mutton. And while he chatted with her ailing father half of his attention was drawn to the goings-on in the adjoining room, the outbursts of Meena's younger sister and the women's talk; and on hearing her voice he felt that his whole life had been a preparation for marriage, for the mysterious relationship which all his medical training could not elucidate.

Betta heard the humming of mosquitoes vainly trying to penetrate the net, and through its innumerable tiny holes he glimpsed the blue-painted partition in his half-sleep, dropping off at the moment the torrential rain began again and the water collecting in the roof gutters gurgled like a throttled animal. Then he heard nothing, neither the mosquitoes nor the rain nor the village dogs barking at the outbreak nor the plotting of those who ride long-maned horses across the back dams.

The next morning Meena got up to make tea for herself and Betta and was struck by the silence, the absence of birdsong and the lowing of cattle. She went to the kitchen window and saw that the water had encroached on the high ground under the houses where cattle were huddled together. It was no longer raining and the branches of trees waved ponderously in the damp morning breeze. The shallow gutter the janitor had had dug to drain the yard had disappeared under the flood, which had invaded the yard and covered the lowest step of the back stairs. Meena immediately thought of her parents' house which was only raised eighteen inches above the ground. Unexpectedly there was the screech of the Parika train, which trailed away into a long echo, like the resonating string of an ancient veena.

They won't be able to open the kokers, she thought.

In her parents' house they frequently spoke of kokers and polders and drainage canals because her father had once been responsible for the great koker at Canal Number One village, where he had opened his first shop.

The knocking on the door was the janitor's. Meena opened the top half and was told that two men were waiting on the front stairs to see the doctor.

Meena shook Betta, who muttered, 'It's Sunday, isn't it?'

'Two men're waiting for you downstairs and the flood's up to the bottom of the back stairs.'

'The flood? In the yard?'

He got up at once and went to the bedroom window through which he saw the glistening dome of the mosque and the flood waters stretching away to the south.

'You know if the Public Road's under water?' he asked.

'I don't know, Betta. Don't forget the men. You want me to ask them to come in?'

'Who're they?'

'The janitor didn't say.'

'Ask them to take their boots off and leave them on the porch. Yes. Let them come in.'

He heard the door being opened and Meena inviting the men in and knew from the careful enunciation of their words that they were born abroad.

Once Betta had taken his bath and dressed he went out to see the strangers; and to his surprise he found the estate manager and the field manager waiting for him by the door.

'I asked my wife to invite you in,' he told them.

Their sunburned faces were stern.

'We didn't want to make a mess on your floor,' the estate manager declared.

Like the field manager he was in short pants, but unlike him he carried no notebook in his tunic nor did he avoid Betta's eyes.

'What can I do for you?' Betta asked.

The field manager looked away as if he had been distracted by a noise or an unusual occurrence.

'I won't waste words,' the estate manager declared. 'I didn't want to have a . . . someone like you working for the estate in the first place. . . .'

'I don't work for the estate,' said Betta sharply.

'We won't go over that again,' said the manager. 'What I want to say to you I can't say here. Why not come to my house?'

'Why didn't you phone then?' asked Betta, nonplussed by the invitation.

'Oh, I forgot you were married. We expected to find you alone, you understand.'

'We'll talk here,' Betta insisted. 'And before discussing anything else I need an explanation about the janitor's absence from work. . . .'

'Ah, you see?' interrupted the estate manager. 'When the people who work for you go absent it's the end of the world, letters to the Immigration Office and complaints. At least you now understand what I mean when I say we can't afford to have our workers off from work.'

He turned to his companion, who nodded in agreement and looked away promptly, for he was clearly under some kind of strain.

'So you see,' said Betta's visitor, 'far from being unreasonable I'm extremely patient. All the janitor's absence did was to inconvenience you. Imagine what it's like for me when I'm presented with a list of absentees first thing in the morning.'

'Neither the janitor nor the maid were sick. I don't meddle in your affairs, but you did in mine. The next time I'll act in the same way.'

'That's what I came to tell you,' the manager said. 'The next time you won't be talking so calmly. I came to warn you that being married you have twice as much to lose as before. And don't blame me if anything happens which you can't put to rights through the Immigration Office. You must know I'm not the kind to let the Immigration Office stand in my way. It's no use looking at the field manager; he didn't hear anything. Now, are you going to get the numbers going into hospital down? Do you intend writing fewer certificates? You see, the next time I'll destroy you.'

Betta recalled the estate manager's well-appointed house, the well-drained spaces between the fruit trees, the sweet-potato patch, the little landing on the canal where a bateau was laid up, the sense of order, the evidence of plenty, and realized that he himself partook of that plenty at the expense of the multitude of workers who could not afford to still their hunger, much less buy quinine to ward off the inevitable malarial attacks. The estate manager understood this only too well, hence his perplexity in the face of such opposition. Accustomed to doing as he pleased with the village women, who went in terror of giving birth to a light-skinned baby in their husband's house, to kicking the men who complained of not having been paid the money corresponding to the loads they had brought in, corrupted by the compliance of underlings and the obsequiousness of mulattos, he had lost all sense of proportion in his relations with creoles, East Indians and his countrymen alike. And, as *he* saw it, Betta had to be brought to heel, lest others learned of his recalcitrance.

'You're afraid, Dr Singh. Not me. I was sick in the bush once, far away from doctors, without medicine, in the company of a river captain and eight crewmen who didn't conceal the fact that they hated me. You talk about the suffering among workers. Well, there's suffering and suffering. Some people take their lives because a wife or a husband dies, some out of boredom. They have no idea what real suffering is. I lay shivering with ague under the tarpaulin of a launch, and no one spoke to me; no one took a spoon and helped me to swallow a mouthful. Day after day all I could see was the brown water trailing by and listen to my heart beating ... a very strange sound. Not a man spoke to me. To this day I've no idea what sickness I had, but the faces of the men seemed distorted from where I lay.'

'It was probably paratyphoid, a complication of malaria,' Betta said. 'And *that's* common on this estate; if you cared to go into the workers' houses you could see for yourself.'

'They have it in their homes, not miles from anywhere, with a crew who would have killed you and left you to the cayman. . . . Since that time I've never been afraid. You're just a . . .'

As the estate manager spoke Betta was filled, not with anger, but rather with pain at the memory of the children in the house of a doomed father and an ailing mother. For the first time he was awakened to a vision of a political upheaval to overcome an evil that had its source in something that went deeper than poverty.

The field manager stood on the top tread of the still-damp stairs, unwilling to leave, while Betta, uncertain what to do next, looked down at him, wondering at his own want of hospitality in neglecting to offer a visitor food or drink. In his home in Kitty it would have been unthinkable to leave a visitor standing at the door.

While Betta was talking to his visitors Meena lay on the bed wondering why he was exchanging words with a European. He had never once spoken to her about his difficulties with the manager, but she knew from the tone of the man's voice and from the visitor's reluctance to come into the house that the call was not a social one. She shared her mother's abhorrence of unpleasantness. Whenever her parents quarrelled her mother used to serve her father with the left hand, while doing everything she could to placate him. *She* was too proud of Betta to quarrel with him. In the weeks before her marriage she had discussed with her younger sister the interminable companion- ship of marriage and it was the twelve-year-old who allayed her anxieties with words drawn from the vocabulary of inexperi- ence: their mother liked Betta, which was a guarantee that things would go well. Now she would find living intolerable without him, without his constant presence at her side in bed or their frequent outings to the Merrimans and her former home. She knew neither of the two men whom she had gazed at through the jalousies, but they were no doubt evil since they found excuses to quarrel with Betta. The short time of her marriage resembled a journey during which she had heard and seen much that was new, the Merrimans' creole home with its artificial flowers, its curtains of grey beads – Job's tears – their visits to the sea by night, birds running along the sand away from an incoming wave, her own self changing, leaving behind old accoutrements like the shed skin of a dragonfly clinging to a stalk. She had heard discussions between Merriman and Betta that would have scandalized her parents, during which Mrs Merriman did not wince or seek an excuse to withdraw. Her mother had told her to be prepared for anything, because Betta did not profess to be a practising Hindu, nor did he claim to be a Christian. She liked Betta, but he was a man. Her daughter must be prepared for anything. Her heart was once rooted in the West Coast and the thought of crossing the river for good used to unsettle her. Now she would accompany Betta anywhere.

At the shouting Meena sat up and listened, but then she heard nothing more than exchanges in a low voice. Her presence outside was unthinkable, yet the urge to go and stand by Betta's side would not abate, and inwardly she raged at her powerlessness as a woman. She could not even go to the door and call out to her husband to ask if all was well, simply because the visitors were men.

Suddenly, unable to bear the waiting, she stood up and went outside. She found Betta standing alone on the stairs.

'Where're your visitors?'

'They've gone.'

'Why were you quarrelling?'

He told her of his difficulties with the estate manager.

'And what're you going to do?'

'I don't know,' he answered, trying at the same time to interpret her expression. 'What do you want me to do?'

'Me? Anything you think you should.'

'That's not enough, Meena. If I were alone I would see the business through.'

'Then see it through, Betta.'

'You think I should?'

'Yes,' she answered.

'I'll think it over. I mean what kind of man would I be if I gave up because I was threatened?'

'Why not go to the police?' Meena asked.

'The police? I've met the superintendent at Merriman's house several times. *He* is afraid of them. He said so himself. According to him about the only thing they can be charged with is murder, and even that's been hushed up in the past.'

Betta told her of the story of the Englishwoman who gave birth to a dark-skinned child. The police constable who used to do her gardening was transferred to the most remote station on the savannah.

'Betta, I'm not worried, you know,' she told him, anxious about the agitation in his voice.

'He came with the field manager. There was something about him, something odd, as if . . .'

'About who?'

'The field manager,' Betta said. 'As if he didn't want to be there.'

They continued talking until Meena went to the kitchen to make chocolate. On Sundays it was she who prepared their meals, and indeed, since the cook's mysterious illness, had taken to helping in the kitchen, as she was accustomed to doing before her marriage and enforced idleness.

Betta decided to speak to his wife about the plan that had been maturing in his mind since his visit to the home of the dying man and his sick wife. He would adopt one of the children if she agreed. Their mother was unlikely to object in the circumstances.

At first he had thought of contributing to the family's support, but decided that as the children's mother was still a young woman the arrangement was likely to give rise to rumours of intimacy with her. Meena at first agreed to his plan, unwilling to voice the objection that she wanted children of her own first.

That afternoon the couple went to see the Merrimans. Betta drove along the Public Road, which was barely above the flood water, in which the carcasses of cattle floated, caught in the once-every-ten-year devastation. Giant buttressed trees rose above the water, darkened by their reflections under a sun setting behind clouds that drizzled an invisible mist. Where were they going? Betta reflected. And why? It was not a day for visiting. No doubt *he* was going to sound his friend on the subject of his dilemma. Meena was afraid to speak her mind, although he guessed she wanted them to flee their home and the pest of hatred. And were they not fleeing at this very moment? In visiting the Merrimans were they not acknowledging their dread of the future in a house that did not belong to them?

Meena touched his arm and pointed out of the window. From the bloated carcass floating at the edge of the Public Road appeared a scarlet king vulture's head to scan the surrounding countryside, while at some distance away a company of lesser vultures, perched on a low tree, waited for the occupant of the corpse to finish its meal. Meena, in an involuntary gesture, waved violently in the direction of the dark companions, who took flight without a sound or even the perceptible flapping of wings.

'Do you think Gopie will get married?' Meena asked. Gopie was the fond name of her younger sister.

'What a thing to ask?' Betta mocked her, while pretending he did not know what prompted the question. 'Not only she'll get married,' Betta continued, 'but she'll go out and choose her husband. Not like a poor creature I know who had her husband foisted on her, eh? Why shouldn't she marry?'

'Because she's so . . . so open,' Meena answered, not satisfied with the word she had chosen to describe her sister's candour.

'That's the privilege of the younger daughter. You were too shy in those days, anyway.'

And she liked nothing better than to hear him talk about the time he used to come courting.

They had not seen a single soul on the road since they left home and they alone had witnessed the corpse being devoured. The scene was a premonition of some loss, she was sure.

They saw a crowd gathered on the road in front of the Merrimans' house and on approaching heard the piano being played by the old man, with the same passion as his conversation. Betta and Meena remained in the car listening to the music, knowing that the old man would not speak until the next day. And on that evening, when night came in waves to the accompaniment of croaking frogs, and the whitewashed trunks in the yard glistened and the limp, celebratory flags announced events long passed, and Death held agreeable conversations with hospitable families, dressed as a sick-nurse who prescribed sea-grape-bark infusion for a persistent itch, and thinkers among men perceived the ambivalence of water, which brought life in the morning and destruction when the sun went down, and the ambivalence of everything they held dear, on that evening a crowd gathered to listen to the man known locally as the 'professor', a lunatic according to some and a mystic according to others, for his way with bees and pianos, who could elicit the sound of bells from two notes played a tone higher than an octave apart and placate a hive by whispering from afar.

Betta and Meena went in after the recital was over, but the old man had already gone downstairs to lock himself in. They found Mrs Merriman over her bible and Merriman crushing a mixture of herbs with a diminutive pestle.

'Betta, man,' came his friend's call when he caught sight of him in the doorway. They no longer stood on ceremony, as in the early days of their friendship, and Betta, after paying his respects to his friend's wife, went and joined him in the dining area, leaving her and Meena to talk.

And later, sharing the old man's honey brew, Betta received the advice he had come for. Mrs Merriman believed that his course of action depended on whether he was prepared to be a martyr or not. If he accepted the role then he should not give up his post. Merriman, on the other hand, had no hesitation in advising him to cut and run, because he was dealing with thugs whom the police would not arrest unless they were ordered to do so by the commissioner of police himself.

'You hear that the Government's authorized the sale of quinine at post offices?' Merriman said, and was surprised that Betta had not learned about the order.

But Betta had no radio and only knew what he read in the papers and the *Official Gazette*, while Merriman's drug store was an information centre, where even notes and letters were left to be picked up by their addressees.

In truth the Government, anticipating a serious malarial epidemic following the worst floods for several years, had authorized the sale of quinine at cost price at the innumerable post offices scattered throughout the country.

Betta did not welcome the news unreservedly, explaining that misuse of the drug could cause deafness.

Meena could still not bring herself to contribute to the conversation when men were present, but the others accepted her reticence as natural and did not urge her to express an opinion. She thought that since people throughout the country already practised medicine in their homes they would have little difficulty in following the instructions on the bottle. She would have liked to say so, but did not know how.

The couple stepped out of their friends' house into a moonless night.

'Remember how bright the moon was the last time you came?' Mrs Merriman called out as Betta and his wife edged down the planks which connected the street to the foot of the stairs. 'It was only a few days ago.'

During the drive home the Singhs talked about the Merrimans, but it had not occurred to them that their spirits had risen during the visit, while, in fact, nothing had changed. The estate manager's threats had indeed occurred, the rain clouds were drifting slowly inland as before and the Public Road was deserted. And when they passed the spot where the carcass eaters had been waiting on the tamarind tree the corpse was still there, with its gaping hole.

Betta sat bold upright in bed, his head and armpits dripping with perspiration. Several seconds passed before the sight of Meena's body assured him that he was in his own house. Looking upwards at the open skylight, he saw nothing but the thick darkness, as palpable as the bushes growing between the house and the sea. He tried to recall the incident that had awakened him, and only when he was on the point of giving up did the image recur, as vivid as the original scene: he was driving slowly along a red-brick road, when he saw them standing at the roadside, the five hooded women in mourning. Unaccountably, he wanted to go back the way he came, but the nearest village street was a half-mile back and it was impossible to reverse that distance. On approaching the women he was struck by the immobility of the figures, all of which were facing south, away from the sea, across the expanse of flood waters interrupted here and there by a tree or a cluster of houses. Then, on drawing abreast of the women, Betta yielded to the urge –aroused in some strange fashion by dread – to stop and speak; for, unlike the previous occasions, when they were far away and walking rapidly, he could now lean out of the car and touch the one nearest to him. Gradually he brought the vehicle to a halt, opened the door and got out. But the women did not react to his arrival; and, indeed, their immobility was exaggerated by the flapping of their garments in the wind.

'Goodnight,' he said, approaching them.

The the woman nearest to him turned her head swiftly in response to his greeting, causing Betta to leap backwards, for her face was the beaked head of a vulture with featureless eyes.

Betta got up and went to the bathroom where he sponged down his face and chest before returning to bed. Soon he dropped off again and did not hear the intermittent showers nor the wind droning incessantly through the jalousies.

Chapter 23

'Is where you goin?' Sukrum asked Bai.

'Out.'

'Where?' Sukrum insisted.

'I in' know.'

'You mus' know where you goin'. You take me fo' a fool? You dress up like a woman and you say you don' know where you goin'. You take me fo' a fool?'

Bai no longer took Sukrum along on his night jaunts because

no one liked him. His pomade-making friend told his wife he would not mind Bai's friend sponging on them if he were more agreeable. Once Sukrum would sit without saying a word all night while he and Bai poured the warm, green liquid into jars; another time he would talk incessantly and fly into a temper if he was contradicted. In the dance hall where Sukrum, on his first visit, had been so circumspect to everyone he met, people had come to dismiss him as surly and quarrelsome. Bai, who in the old days used to hang on to him with a reliance Sukrum had exploited unremittingly, only gradually came to understand how his position had changed.

'Is Christmas time,' Sukrum went on, 'and I stayin' home. You goin' out and that slut upstairs goin' out as if she's a man. Alyou wait; one day I goin' show you. . . . I goin' shine in front of you. Wait, ne.'

'How you know Lahti goin' out?' Bai asked.

'You don' bother how I know. I know.'

'She talkin' to you, then?'

'Who say she stop talkin' to me?'

Everyone in the house knew that Lahti no longer spoke to Sukrum, yet the suggestion that they were no longer friends never failed to put him into a fury.

'The slut goin' out and I stayin' home. She goin' come down the stairs an' see light in the room an' laugh 'cause I in' got nowhere to go.'

'How she goin' know is you in the room and not me?'

''Cause she know you does go out every night to see you Georgetown friends, you big fool.'

He was standing in the doorway, although Lahti had come back from work only a short while ago and was not likely to go out again so soon.

Bai was afraid that whatever he said might cause Sukrum to fly into a rage.

'Rain goin' fall tonight,' Bai observed in a soft voice, anxious to conciliate his friend.

'What the skunt I care if rain fall or if the sun shine at midnight?'

'What you cursing for?'

'Go out, ne. Wha' you waiting for?' demanded Sukrum.

Bai remained silent.

Sukrum continued mumbling and grunting, like one of the dogs, Bai thought. The Pujaree had persuaded Mrs Singh to buy a pair of puppies, which Bai's room-mate immediately took in his charge, excluding everyone from their care.

Sukrum believed that his diminishing influence over Bai dated from Lahti's refusal to have anything more to do with him. For weeks afterwards he used to spend hours shut up in the room re-living the time he and Lahti used to be alone, when they would share food she had bought from the cook shop at the corner of Barr and Alexander Streets and talk about her experiences in the seamstress's establishment. It was unbelievable that it had all come to an end. How could someone who bore his children in her womb twice within a few months ignore him as if he no longer existed? How could someone rely on him entirely then suddenly be able to do without him? In the months before the break it was *she* who used to seek him out. Christmas! He thought he had come to terms with her betrayal until a few days ago, when you could not avoid the preparations for the revelry which would go on until Old Year's night and New Year's morning. Where would she be going? Who would be meeting her? He had never once seen a man in her company or heard that she had been seen with a man. But how could she, who cried whenever they made love, how could she do without a man? He recalled his satisfaction at the discovery of her jealousy. Where had he been on such and such a night? He did not love her any more; and why did he spend no money on her? He had planned to enslave her and was certain that it was only a matter of time before she gave him most of what she earned. Nothing was going to stand in the way of his success, especially since Rani's preoccupation with her child and her weak-kneed husband. One night, believing that the time had come to put his influence over her to the test, he struck her; and when she covered her face with her hands he was seized with a kind of drunken fit at the gesture of submissiveness. While taking off his belt slowly he saw her watching him through the gaps between her fingers. 'Sukoo!' she pleaded. 'Don' beat me, Sukoo! Oh, God! Miss Singh go'n hear when I bawl. Sukoo, don' beat me!' And he remembered his own sister pleading with his father in almost identical words, while he was still a young boy. 'Sukoo, Miss Singh go'n want to know where I get the marks from!' Lahti whined, grabbing his feet. 'All right, Sukoo, give me one blow, then. Jus' one.' And he brought the belt down on her back, content to know that she understood that he had the right to maltreat her. He then took her to the pictures and afterwards stopped on the narrow pedestrian bridge on the way home to watch the moon reflected in the water. From time to time a car or horse-drawn carriage would pass by on Vlissingen Road, then the silence would settle once more around them, like the fall of darkness. She and Bai! Tch! The painful recollection of that time made him turn towards Bai, who was sitting on their canvas bed – a low, simple construction Bai had bought, and which reminded Sukrum of the bug-ridden camp beds in the Broad Street dosshouse.

'Why you don' stay home tonight?' Sukrum asked.

'Who does stay home Boxing Day night?'

'Me!'

'When you come to think of it,' said Bai, 'Miss Singh an' the Pujaree don' go nowhere. Miss Rani an' she husban' too, they don' go out. But some people *got* to go out. I got to go out, I in' denying it. But you does quarrel with everybody, that's why I does go alone. An' these las' few months you worse, jus' 'cause Miss Lahti does dress good . . .'

'Shut you mouth!' Sukrum ordered. 'I know lots o' whores does dress good. She's a slut that throw away two bellies a'ready! What I care if she dress good? An' Miss Singh does dress good, but that don' stop she from living with the Pujaree when they not married.'

'That in' my business,' Bai said, feeling a mounting desire to defy his roommate. 'I don' even pay rent, so what I care what they does do?'

'You's a jackass!' Sukrum shouted. 'You don' see nothing!'

Bai looked outside in order to judge what time it might be from the quality of the darkness. He had made up his mind to leave as soon as it was late enough, and get away from his surly friend. It occurred to him that even if Sukrum's character were to change miraculously he would no longer want to take him to town and his numerous haunts, the cook shops, the dance halls

where he worked, the barber shop whose newspapers were read
by passers-by as well as by waiting customers and the Bourda
market in which his pomade-making friend's wife had a
bookstall.

The sound of a santapee band came up Dowding Street, fife
and drum. Soon the dancers would be under the windows,
gyrating in acrobatic competition, while their acolytes held out
their caps until they were satisfied that the big house had
contributed its due.

'I gone,' Bai said, so abruptly, that Sukrum, taken by surprise,
saw him brush past without uttering a word.

'Go, ne?' he shouted, spitting contemptuously in the direction of the iron gates leading out on to Vlissingen Road, 'you big
asshole! I hope the masqueraders get you skunt.'

Sukrum turned off the bulb and peeped out of the fixed
jalousie looking on to Dowding Street, in anticipation of the
arrival of the masquerade band.

Bai, now thoroughly at home in the Georgetown dives, the
Saturday-night crowds that gathered in Camp Street and Regent
Street, the criminal haunts around the tea house and the secret
back shops of Tiger Bay, made straight for the Regent Street
dance hall where he worked. Beyond Bourda Street the throng
became larger and the noise of whistles and shouting grew,
while knots of men wearing masks appeared from time to time
at street corners and in doorways. On the pavement glistening
from a brief spell of rain the reflections of carbide lamps
fluttered like moths. All traffic had disappeared from the road
except for an occasional intrepid cyclist who was eventually
obliged to dismount and walk among the press of men and
women and young boys armed with cap-pistols. From cake
shops and drinking places opened on the street came the sound
of loud singing, drunken voices celebrating the season in the
district with few churches.

Bai took his place in the doorway of his work-place, installed
himself on the stool which had served several collectors before
him. That night there were many strange faces, of visitors from
the suburbs and country, who danced once a year in the public

halls, attracted by the frenzied celebrations of the dying year. And on being greeted by the habitués whose offhand manner had once intimidated him, Bai nodded in the way *they* did on being hailed, as though courtesy were a burden, exemplifying the popular saying that 'Too much please an' thank you make eye-pass'.

Bai's pomade-making friend arrived with his wife at about ten o'clock and he waved them past without accepting any money. They, in return, brought him a schnapps-glass of rum from time to time and remained chatting with him until the music struck up again, led by the arrogant saxophonist who sat apart. At the end of each piece the men, many of whom wore gloves for the occasion, led their partners to their seats against the wall while they themselves stood. Some of the women left for home between eleven o'clock and midnight to change their dresses, returning an hour or so later, transformed by a shower and new layers of powder, their backs glistening with aromatic oil.

In the houses adjoining the dance hall, people who were standing at their windows listening to the music clapped whenever they judged that a piece of music was particularly successful, while in the yard below couples were dancing on the concrete, as taken by the music as those upstairs. By midnight the hall was so packed, those looking for somewhere to dance had to be turned away. The women had given up their attempts to look tidy and the men, finding it impossible to keep their hands dry in the clammy atmosphere of perspiring bodies, had discarded their white gloves. After a scuffle at the door one of the dancers volunteered to help Bai keep out would-be customers, about a score of whom now stood at the door, hoping that he would abandon it for a while. As the minutes went by the relentless movement of the dancers resembled an ancient ceremony. When the rhythm of a piece was strong the bodies, for lack of space, moved up and down in a restless motion, and the taller men, like giant trees soaring above the canopy of a forest, held their chins slightly raised to emphasize, it seemed, their status as masters of the ritual.

Gradually the streets of the quarter emptied, leaving only the nut sellers with their carbide lamps, immobile shadows caring little for the dancers' stamping feet and the applause at the end of each session.

By one o'clock, when Bai left for home, having counted his takings with the proprietor, the streets and pavements were deserted. In the new concrete gutter the debris of the night celebrations had collected and the pavement was strewn with soiled paper. Bai walked to the top of Regent Street, turning into Vlissingen Road opposite the Botanic Garden gates. Two young boys with a stack of newspapers under their arms were standing at some distance from each other to catch late home-goers. He bought a copy, hoping to placate Sukrum, who liked the papers to be read to him.

Bai stopped under a streetlamp to read the headline: 'Ferry Fares to Rise' – folded the paper once more and, without dwelling on his contented frame of mind, reflected that it was nearly two years since Sukrum had thrown him out in order to be alone with Lahti, forcing him to wander the streets. He looked up each road leading off into Newtown and, on approaching the train lines, recalled his anxiety, indeed dread, at having to go into Georgetown at night on his own.

Mrs Singh's house was in darkness. Any passer-by who did not know its history would have been surprised to see a poorly clad man like Bai crossing the bridge at two in the morning and concluded that he was up to no good, especially as, before being engulfed by the shadows of the trees in the yard, he looked round him in an instinctive gesture of self-protection.

Bai turned the door knob to enter his room, but the door did not give way. He rapped softly, then waited a while before rapping once more with a sharpness that was bound to wake Sukrum if he was asleep. He did not wait long before the bolt was drawn and his room-mate stood before him wearing a pair of pyjama trousers he had bought at a pawnbroker's auction.

'Is you?' Sukrum asked, scratching his dishevelled head and apparently annoyed at having been roused from his sleep.

'Why you bolt the door?' Bai demanded.

Sukrum closed the door gently and remained barring Bai's entrance to the room.

'Listen,' Sukrum said, 'I got Lahti with me.'

Bai stood speechless before his friend and, in some unaccountable way, believed that his evening was ruined by the astonishing disclosure.

'Is what time?' Sukrum asked.

'About two o'clock.'

'Two? Wait, le' me wake Lahti.'

Lahti soon appeared, her hair as disordered as Sukrum's. She pushed by him without a word and went up the back stairs.

'Come in, ne,' Sukrum ordered. 'You goin' on as if you loss something.'

Sukrum was sitting on the edge of the bed, his head cupped in his hands, apparently too drowsy to engage in conversation.

'I din' know alyou two . . .' Bai stuttered. 'I thought you was . . .'

'You thought?' Sukrum said scornfully. 'You mean you would've been glad if she din' come down here no more! You thought? You thought my ass. While you go gallivantin' in town you think I goin' sit 'pon my bed and think 'bout alyou enjoying youself?'

Bai wondered whether it was indeed Lahti and tried to recall the features he had not seen properly in the dark. But from her walk, her hair and her figure it could be no one else, he told himself.

'Is none o' my business,' he said aloud, and started to change for bed.

'Is your business, yes,' Sukrum said, ' 'cause she don' like you. And if she don' like you is your business.'

Sukrum had not forgotten his anger early in the evening when he pleaded with Bai not to go out. He stared at his friend, expecting a response to his remark. But Bai ignored him, while continuing to prepare for bed.

'I say she in' like you! You deaf?'

'That in' my business,' Bai said quietly.

'Is your business 'cause I goin' ask Miss Singh to le' she come and live down here. An' she kian' live in this room when you knockin' around. You hear wha' I telling you?'

'I hear, but wha' you want me to do? Is not my house. . . . It in' your house neither.'

Bai pretended to close his eyes and began breathing deeply so as to be left in peace by Sukrum, who, though disappointed at his friend's lack of concern, was happy enough at the way his reconciliation with Lahti had gone off, and did not wish a serious quarrel with Bai, who stank of liquor in any case. He had persuaded her to leave her petticoat with him, by way of security for her return, he had said. He folded the garment which had been left at the foot of the bed and carefully laid it in the cardboard box in which he kept his few possessions. Before closing the box he lifted it to his face and inhaled the scent that had clung to it from her skin.

'I got you now!' he mumbled to himself, 'you lil slut. When I done with you you in' goin' look down you nose at no man again. You think I's Bai or Rani? You does skin you teeth one day at them an' look down you nose the nex' as if you's some queen or somet'ing. Well we goin' see. Forget? I goin' forget, yes. I goin' forget what you use to mean to me, you lil Courantyne slut. You think I don' know 'bout you? How you use to collect cow dung an' mind the one hog in the yard and only go to school up to ten years? You in' better than me, you pig-minder . . . you collector of shit. Ho ho hoo! I got you now! You skin does smell so sweet, perfume and dry flowers you does thief from Miss Singh. Hooooo! So I does smell o' shrimps, eh? Well shrimps better than cow shit, you Courantyne slut. The same shrimps me an' Bai does ketch you like to eat. Good! Good! When I done with you you goin' be peckin' at them lil stones like fowl that want something hard in it gizzard. You lil slut, you skunt! You forget how much secrets you tell me? I got more o' your secrets than you got fancy dresses. How you does thief Miss Singh money. You tell me all them things an' later want to leave me as if I's some piece o' cloth you does dutty an' throw 'way.'

Sukrum savoured his re-conquest of Lahti in a way he could not while she was with him. When she came down the stairs early that evening after Bai had gone, to his surprise she had taken the back stairs and not the front, and she was not wearing her going-out clothes, but a plain skirt and blouse which she usually put on when at home. He contemplated her without a word, relieved that she was not going out, as he and Bai had thought. He watched her taking clothes from the line, her head raised and the unironed garments spread out beyond her body. It was only when she set her foot on the lowest tread of the long stairway that he spoke.

'Lahti, is what I do you?'

'I din' say you do me nothing,' she replied, her progress up the stairs arrested by the question.

'I got a pain in my shoulder,' he said, trying to assume the air of someone in distress.

'Ask the lil girl to oil it for you, ne?'

Lahti was referring to the girl from the village who picked the dead flowers from the shrubs and swept the yard every morning.

'Tch! You know she in' strong enough.'

At least I got she talking, he thought. I wonder why she stop like that? Probably she an' Rani quarrel so she got to take what conversation she could get.

'You goin do me shoulder? You don' got to do it. I accustom to live alone without nobody to mind fo' me. An' I know you got to do things upstairs.'

Lahti, her arms encircling the pile of clothes and her gaze fixed on the top of the stairs, had the appearance of someone expecting to be called away at any moment.

'I'll see,' she said, and at once started the long ascent to the kitchen.

Sukrum was right in surmising that Rani's attitude had a bearing on Lahti's behaviour towards him. It was Rani's betrothal to Tipu which led her to abandon herself to a temptation which she had never taken seriously until then. They used to laugh at Sukrum, at his clothes, at his high-pitched voice and at the way he lay under the saman tree with his legs crossed and a stalk of grass protruding from his mouth like a man with many servants. He seemed uncaring of his poverty and lack of status in a house frequented by the Pujaree, the goblet maker and the Mulvi Sahib, men of substance or distinction. But when she realized that her carefree days with their endless conversations after nightfall were at an end, Sukrum's flattery, his – to her – ambiguous words and his unashamed glances were no longer comic. The first time she entered the old surgery to see 'his things' she experienced the sensation of an epileptic who was certain that he was about to be overcome by a fit, yet could not say why. Sukrum had made the same request then, to have his shoulder massaged with oil in order to relieve a pain. During the time she had abandoned him he had no idea how she suffered from the separation, how the abortion had terrified her, how for weeks afterwards she would hear the barking of the chained dog when she closed her eyes at night. She wanted to come and see him, because, in that house, which was her very life, she was deprived of conversation. Although Mrs Singh did not celebrate Christmas, she, like Dr Singh, was affected by the carol singing and the festive celebrations, and on returning home in the afternoon fell prey to an intolerable emptiness. Rani had not forgiven her for the manner in which she had been dismissed her enquiry regarding the abortion; Mrs Singh, while allowing her greater freedom than ever, ignored her almost entirely. Only the Pujaree, 'the stranger in the house', as Dr Singh was reported to have described him, was kind to her. Sukrum had misunderstood her aloofness, which she had laid upon herself like a protective garment in the same way that, fearing Rani's contempt, she had pretended that her absence from the house had nothing to do with an abortion. Vulnerable and lonely she had hoped that Sukrum would approach her with the right words.

'I got a pain in my shoulder,' he said.

If he were less crude she would have kissed him on the mouth and told him that she loved him more than anyone else, that she longed for the warmth of his nakedness, that except for Aji, who confused her with a charcoal-burner's wife she had known as a girl and harangued her at table, while complaining that everyone was secretly wishing for her death, she felt that she was ignored by the others because she went out to work like a man and spent her money like a man, without consulting anyone.

Lahti went downstairs at eleven that night, an hour after the lights were switched off and the windows were closed. And Sukrum opened up almost immediately after she rapped on his door, as though he had been waiting with his hand on the brass knob. Without looking at him she said she had come to rub his shoulder and could not stay more than a few minutes because she wanted to do something for Mrs Singh. Sukrum lost no time in taking off his shirt and exposing his wiry body. She made him kneel on the floor while she sat on the bed behind him.

And Lahti was unable to explain why she wanted to cry and why she was drawn to this cruel, inconsiderate man who, on learning that she was with his child, had the same expression in his eyes as when he took his belt to her. She poured a little coconut oil from the bottle she had brought into her cupped hand, placed it on the floor beside him and began anointing his left shoulder. From the village came the sound of drums that drowned the commotion a few streets away and the noise of the sea at high tide and the corrosive humming of night insects in the small room.

An hour later Lahti was still in the room, curled up under a thin blanket against the December night. It was the first time she had undressed completely in her lover's company. Sukrum was standing by the shutter, through which he had been watching for the masquerade band, and with an absent expression was reflecting on the reversal of his fortunes. He was stunned by Lahti's compliance, which, in retrospect, he felt he should have foreseen – did she not linger on the stairs? Did she not come back when the lights had been put out? Had she not made a feeble excuse about being obliged to leave after a few minutes when she had come armed with a phial of oil which must have been taken from Mrs Singh's medicine cupboard? – Stunned by her compliance, his self-absorption resembled the boredom of a man who, having completed a profitable enterprise, is disappointed at the want of excitement that followed his success. He glanced down at Lahti and, imagining her nakedness under the blanket, could only think that he had her in his power once more. And his feeling of triumph was so complete it did not occur to him that he was now in a position to tell Bai that, far from being hurt by the lone Christmas vigil, it had provided him with an opportunity to become reconciled with Lahti.

When Bai did return they were both asleep, Sukrum unintentionally, for he had promised to remain awake in case she was called.

From then on Lahti joined Sukrum every Saturday night, without any attempt to conceal her whereabouts from the rest of the house. She tidied up his room every afternoon, brought him cakes from the village on Fridays and mended his trousers and shirts when they were torn. Sukrum's attempt to evict Bai from the room came to nothing when the Pujaree, who had assumed the management of the household, insisted that he retain his full rights of occupation. And from then on a bitter enmity developed between the two former friends. The whole household, save Lahti, declared itself in Bai's favour, since they were convinced that Sukrum would be Lahti's undoing. If she would not heed a collective warning Bai at least was entitled to their protection.

Bai and Sukrum no longer went fishing together, so that the latter came to depend heavily on financial support from Lahti, while Bai made up for the lost income by working in Georgetown during the week as well. And as the gulf between the two men grew their tense co-tenancy of Dr Singh's old surgery became notorious beyond the yard, for it was known to the hucksters, assiduous gossips who missed nothing.

The day Bai declared that he was moving out everyone was taken by surprise, for his determination to stand up to Sukrum had won the admiration not only of those living in the house, but also of the Dowding Street residents, who knew the two men as the 'morning ghosts', hardly ever appearing on the street except late at night and in the dark hours of foreday morning, Sukrum with a voluminous net and Bai, always behind, carrying a wicker basket on his head.

It was widely believed that Sukrum had driven Bai away by his intolerable conduct. But the truth was that the latter had been courting the pomade-maker's cousin, a young woman with a deformity, whose company he kept for hours on end when the others went out, and whom he had taught to walk a few steps. Now she was able to leave her bed and go to the window alone, an ambition she had cherished since she was a small girl, when she longed to watch the school children on their way home. Bai, always secretive, spoke to no one of the association; and now, fearing Sukrum's vengeance, he preferred to keep silent about the arrangement with his creole friend, who had offered him the room where his unsold pomade jars were stored.

'I suppose you go'n go round telling people is me chase you out the room,' Sukrum told him.

'But you want me to go,' Bai replied, 'so why you quarrellin' with me now I going?'

'I in' quarrellin'. I jus' want to know if you go'n go round tellin' people is me. I glad to see your back, but that don' mean I want you slanderin' me like a dog.'

'I in' got nothing to say to nobody. I goin' away and that's my business. You stayin' and that's your business. Sheep does make nuf noise when he goin' to slaughterhouse. I in' goin' slaughterhouse. I goin' to town, that's all.'

'So is where you goin' then?' Sukrum asked, no longer able to contain his curiosity.

'I goin' to friends.'

'If I in' know now I goin' know later, so why you don' tell me now?'

Bai met his question with a stubborn silence.

'Is you pomade friend?'

The question was met with a vague gesture which said, 'I won't tell you, so there's no point asking.'

But Sukrum's accurate guess made Bai anxious.

'I say I not goin' tell you,' he repeated, judging that his gesture was not convincing enough.

That afternoon he left without much ceremony, having told Mrs Singh and the Pujaree that he was staying with friends in Kitty for the night and would let them know as soon as he acquired a permanent address.

'You've got enough money?' Mrs Singh asked him, knowing that he earned his own.

'I got money, Miss Singh.'

'Why you're going?' the Pujaree asked, less affected by his departure than Mrs Singh was.

Bai was tempted to tell him the truth, but hesitated on the brink of his confession before making up a lie about a permanent job as a watchman at a sports ground.

Both Mrs Singh and the Pujaree came out on to the porch to watch him go, carrying his bundle of possessions as he used to carry the shrimp basket. His Georgetown jaunts had modified his walk as little as they had changed his speech and even from a distance he could have been taken for a farmer returning from his plot near the back dam, his chest thrown forward and his arms swinging in an effort to balance the load on his head. They saw him cross the train lines into Georgetown; and as they turned away the Pujaree remarked, 'I thought he did say he was staying in Kitty tonight.'

Chapter 24

The Pujaree's twin nephews were watching Rani's infant crawling round the drawing room. They knew that she disliked them and were rude to her when she was alone. When the child suddenly bawled Rani came running into the room and took it up from the floor.

'What you do to him?' she asked accusingly, looking first to the one then to the other. 'If you touch him I'll make my husband give you such a beating you won't come round here again.'

They looked at each other and smiled insolently, knowing that Rani would lose her temper. Before they could defend themselves she slapped them both on the mouth and repeated her threat.

'Who frighten' of Tipu?' one of them said, standing his ground. 'Everybody know Miss Singh does beat him when he do bad things.'

'What?' Rani asked disbelievingly.

'We know,' added the other.

'You little liars! So it's you been spreading rumours about my husband all the time. Out! Get out of the house! And when the Pujaree comes home I'll tell him how you been spreading lies. Get out before I hit you again.'

They left, walking slowly. And as one went by he lifted her skirt with a swift action, then rushed out of the front door before Rani could catch him. Clutching her child she was almost in tears with rage and frustration.

The twins looked exactly the same as they did three years ago, when she and Lahti saw them in front of the Pujaree's house. Then, they resembled small men, while now they looked like boys with old faces. Whenever they were asked their age they replied that they had no idea how old they were. The Pujaree was just as evasive, claiming he could not recall the date of their birth or even the year. Today Rani had not heard them arrive, for she never left her son alone with them in spite of Tipu's protest that the Pujaree and Mrs Singh would be offended when they found out how she felt about them.

The 'boys' were twenty and were born to the Pujaree's sister although she had known no man, she always insisted. As the Pujaree's influence in the house increased they visited more frequently and grew more insolent, until Mrs Singh herself felt obliged to send them down to the yard once or twice after consulting their uncle as to what should be done about their conduct. They used to help in the temple, sweeping the earth floor, preparing the sacrifices and advising those for whose benefit the puja was being conducted what was required of them. But they were unreliable and demanded money from those attending the temple, so that the Pujaree, fearing that their behaviour might bring the place into disrepute, asked his sister to keep them away. He would not fail in his duty to support them, he told her.

Rani, unaware of all this, felt that she could no longer put up with their frequent visits and made up her mind to have it out with Tipu about leaving and setting up on their own. The twins' extraordinary lie about the way Mrs Singh treated Tipu confirmed her in the belief that they were not normal and had taken a dislike to her for no reason at all.

Apart from the problems caused by the twins' depredations and her husband's subservience Rani's responsibilities towards the ageing Aji had grown intolerable since Lahti began going to work every day. She was responsible for washing and dressing her, for putting her to bed and feeding her, and even for attending to her needs when she woke up at night, sometimes screaming in terror that she had already died. The child would in turn become agitated and Rani, driven to distraction as much by lack of sleep as by the injustice of the duties she was expected to carry out, would speak to Aji harshly and be met with voluble abuse. Then Mrs Singh would come into Aji's room – she now slept alone – to find out what had happened. On one such occasion Rani turned on her benefactress and confessed that she no longer cared to live in her house, that she and her husband would be moving out soon in order to set up on their own.

'Very well, Rani. You're a grown woman. I should've talked to you a long time ago. Why don't we talk now?'

They went down to the kitchen, where Rani made chocolate, while Mrs Singh lulled the child to sleep against her breast.

The thought of a serious conversation with Mrs Singh, in which she was expected to 'talk', so confused her she took as long as she dared to prepare the chocolate; and even after she had finished she went through the process of cooling the thick, brown fluid by pouring it from one mug into another. How could she *talk* with Mrs Singh, who had fed and protected her, whose power over her she had not dared to challenge even after she was married and apparently independent? The way she thought, and especially the way she behaved, owed much to the utterances and deportment of her benefactress. More than once she described to Lahti how, the day after she first arrived from the country, she was given a mango by Aji. Mrs Singh came downstairs to find her eating the mango skin after she had consumed the rich yellow pulp of the fruit.

'Do you eat mango skin, girl?'

'Yes, Miss Singh.'

'Your brothers and sisters too?'

'Yes, Miss Singh.'

'Well, we don't *have* to eat skins here, child. You can eat as many mangoes as you want,' Mrs Singh had told her with the mixture of kindness and haughtiness she came to believe to be the hallmark of superior women.

And from that day she repressed the desire to eat the tasteless skins she craved.

'If you want to grow up like Mrs Singh,' Aji had told her by way of consolation, 'you got to stop eating mango skin. Tobesides, is hog food.'

Even if she did accept the invitation to talk, much would have to be left unsaid, if only because of that recollection and many others, which pressed upon her now, as they had done on the many occasions when she had all but decided to ask Mrs Singh to encourage Tipu to leave her house and fend for himself and his family.

'Thanks,' Mrs Singh said, as the mug of hot chocolate was placed on the kitchen table at which she was sitting. 'I've got a headache.'

Rani hovered around her, unwilling to sit at such a small table with her or even to look at her now that she was no longer angry.

'Sit down, child!'

Rani could see under Mrs Singh's scant nightdress the medallion she wore round her neck with the image of the goddess Lakshmi on one side and that of Ganesha, the elephant-headed god on the other.

'Now, tell me what you're so vexed for,' Mrs Singh said, knowing well what was troubling Rani.

'I don't like the way you treat Tipu.'

'You think I treat him badly?'

'Yes,' Rani answered. 'You treat him like a boy.'

'But he doesn't complain.'

'That's 'cause he's like that. Tipu is a married man. A married man shouldn' have to ask you what clothes to buy and what he ought to wear. He doesn' ask me.'

'But you said it's the way I treat him,' Mrs Singh reminded her.

'When he talks to you sometimes you don't answer him and when he say something at table you don't pay him the same mind as the Pujaree.'

'Child, I don't know what's bothering you. I treat Tipu no different from the way his uncle or his father and mother treat him. Tipu is a big man, yet his uncle shouts at him. I don't shout at him. I know how you feel, but wherever you go people'll treat Tipu like that.'

'If we had our own house nobody could treat him bad in it,' Rani said firmly.

'Rani, you must do what you think is right. If you go I'll get somebody to look after Aji. . . . But I hope you know what you're doing. . . . Child, I've wanted to talk to you a long time. No, it's not your fault. Long before you married I wanted to have long talks with you, but you were always with Lahti. Every spare minute you spent with Lahti, as if you were sisters. And you don't speak much any more. You're so intelligent, but you hardly see anything. Lahti sees everything, that's why she clings to me, so that people think she was born here. She tortured Sukrum and now he won't let her out of his sight. She's like Keralan women: they let men think they rule them. So you want to go! Go, child. But I'd rather have you here when trouble starts.'

'What trouble?'

'Do you know,' Mrs Singh continued, 'I was waiting for Dr Singh to ask me if he could marry you? I was sure he would come and ask and I knew exactly what I would have said. But he didn't ask. . . .'

If that remark had been the only result of their talk Rani would have suffered twice as much as she had done at the hands of Mrs Singh, Aji and Lahti to earn it. Was it possible that she had misunderstood Mrs Singh so completely? Could it be true that what she herself had considered a brief flirtation was regarded by Mrs Singh as something infinitely more serious? And that she approved of it? Would Dr Singh have married her if he had known how his mother felt? Had Lahti known? Since she saw everything. . . . Lahti, devious, respecter of nothing. She would ask her that very day.

While her mind wandered Rani had lost track of what Mrs Singh was saying, until she heard the word 'confide'.

'. . . to confide in you, especially when I didn't know what to do about Lahti.'

'I'd like to ask you something,' Rani said.

'Go on.'

'Why do you let Lahti and Sukrum carry on?'

Mrs Singh remained silent, causing Rani to think that she had been too presumptuous.

'I didn't let them do anything,' Mrs Singh declared at length. 'But it's not up to you to judge Lahti. In a way she's like you and me, but we'll never do what she does.'

Rani's reaction was sharp.

'No, Mrs Singh, she's not like me!'

'Good, obedient Rani,' Mrs Singh mocked. 'You've never done anything wrong. You look after Aji without complaining, and would never steal from me. Not like Lahti, who stole a gold medallion the very first week she came here. You didn't know, did you? Lahti wouldn't have told you. Aji found it in her drawer. She hadn't even tried to hide it. Ah, but Lahti is pure. The first thing *we* would do if we went anywhere is find out what the rules are and follow them. I never learned so much as in the first year of my marriage, when I used to study my husband as if he was a book: what made him vexed, what he liked to eat, what he liked to see me wear. And that's just what you're like, Rani. And if Tipu died tomorrow you'd cut your hair and start wearing men's clothes, but you'd go to the burial ground once a month to visit his grave. . . .'

'I love Tipu!'

'I loved my husband too. Our husbands were chosen for us, but we love them, because we're that kind of person. When my husband came to Kerala and arrived at our house to negotiate for me with my parents I wasn't allowed to meet him at first. I stood behind the bead curtain listening to him talk and fell in love with his voice. He was my god! But it didn't stop me from seeing myself as his prisoner. You know what people say when a woman is murdered? They say, "I bet it's an East Indian woman." You remember that case two years ago when the husband, a huckster, came back unexpectedly from a trip to Georgetown? You remember? He found his wife with her sweet man sleeping in his bed. And what did he do? He went and got his friend and they came back with cutlasses, woke up the man and gouged his eyes out while she looked on. That sort of thing wouldn't happen to us because we understand our lot.'

'But she didn't love her husband,' protested Rani, for whom the story had uncomfortable overtones, as though she were the threatened, despite her blameless thoughts.

'I didn't say she did,' said Mrs Singh. 'But how do you know she didn't?'

'Because a woman who loved her husband wouldn' behave like that.'

'So you think . . .' Mrs Singh started, only to be interrupted by Rani, whose eyes were blazing.

'Mrs Singh, when you talk I don't know what to think. I hear you speaking to your friends and I don't know when you're joking or when you're serious. I don' joke about things like that.'

Mrs Singh paused, then, deliberately, like someone who had only recently recovered the power of speech, said, 'Neither do I,

Rani. You don't understand because you don't want to understand. Oh, I'm not criticizing you. What I meant was that Lahti is
not like us. Lahti loves Sukrum in a way neither of us will ever
understand. If Sukrum was to die she'd throw herself into his
grave and want to be buried with him. He will destroy her!'

'I'm not sure of things, like you, Mrs Singh. What Lahti's doing
is wrong and you should stop her, especially as you say Sukrum's
going to destroy her. You *know* that and still you does stand aside
and don't do anything? Sometimes I think you hate Lahti. She did
tell me before I got married she couldn't live anywhere else, and
for that alone you shouldn't let her carry on like that.'

'What you want me to do? Chase Sukrum away? Or order Lahti
not to go down to his room any more? You see? You dare not say
what I ought to do, but you want me to do something. What would
please you more than anything is to see them separated. . . .'

'I didn' say that!'

'Then what is this something I must do, child?'

'Send Sukrum away, then!'

'In other words separate them!'

'Yes!' exclaimed Rani, jumping up from the seat that she had
taken. 'Yes! It's disgusting the way they carry on under the same
roof with decent people. You're always praying with the Pujaree
and burning candles and incense, when you tolerate vice in your
house. You don' got no. . . ? You say Sukrum going destroy her,
but isn't that what you want? Who is Sukrum? A lackey that does
stink of shrimps! They're a pair, the two of them!'

Mrs Singh was so astonished at the outburst she was unable to
answer her protégée, who remained standing over her like the
mistress of the house.

Then Rani sat down slowly, as taken aback by her own violence
as Mrs Singh was.

'I wanted to say,' said Rani, 'I wanted you to promise me to help
Tipu to take us away.'

'But, Rani, I told you you can go.'

'I asked you to tell him he ought to go away. He won't listen to
me, but he'll listen to you.'

'Well, go and get him,' Mrs Singh said, believing she read into
Rani's words the implication that the young woman did not trust
her.

Mrs Singh heard the couple's footsteps and their voices arguing. As they approached the door they fell silent.

'You want to see me, Miss Singh?' Tipu asked.

'Yes, Tipu. I think it would be a good idea if you found a house for your little family.'

'What we do?' Tipu asked.

'You didn't do anything,' she replied. 'It's more than two years that you've been living here. Don't you want your own house?'

'Yes, but where we going find a house . . . a good house with my money?'

'That's not for Mrs Singh to tell us,' Rani put in, humiliated by his spinelessness.

'She's right, Tipu. It'll be something small, but you'll be your own master in it.'

'I'm my master here,' he said, turning to look at his wife, who did not hide her dismay.

'Tipu,' Rani said as kindly as she could. 'Mrs Singh say we have to move, that's all. I'll look for a place when you're at work.'

'You'll have to,' he said. 'I don't got no time to go looking for a place to live. All right, Miss Singh . . . Rani tell you we been talking about moving? We been talking a long time about it, with the child and we own furniture.'

When the couple were alone Tipu reproached Rani for crossing Mrs Singh, but she answered not a word, reflecting on how nothing had come of her efforts to find a place of their own, how he rejected every invitation to follow up a newspaper advertisement with excuses, that the rent was too high, that the house was too far from his work-place or that the neighbourhood was too poor. And as Aji spent longer periods awake at night and their son became more demanding the idea of finding her own home became an obsession. She took to accusing Lahti of being lazy and to sulking at table. Everything about the mansion, with its forty-odd windows, its camphor-wood furniture and vast yard disgusted her. Its routine – the cook's punctual arrival and the hucksters' voices early in the morning, Mrs Singh's and the Pujaree's praying, the four meals at the large dining table, Aji's increasing demands – was like the aching of a sick body whose affliction grew steadily worse each day. And while, before her quarrel with Mrs Singh, she was able to apportion blame for their plight between her and Tipu, it became clear that the sole responsibility lay with her husband. The resemblance she had noted early on between him and his mother, the curiously feminine softness of the face and roundness of eyes and chin, meant something after all.

What fascination did the mansion at the corner of Dowding Street and Vlissingen Road hold for Tipu and Lahti? Unlike Aji, who had lost touch with her family, and Sukrum, whose dignity had been eroded by the long sojourns in the Dharm Sala and the dosshouse in Broad Street, Tipu was rich in relations and had never once slept in a stranger's bed until he married. She herself could never tolerate a condition that gave a stranger the same status in her child's eyes that she enjoyed. Was the warmth of Mrs Singh's body and its peculiar scent to compete with her own in her child's affection? Even now she recalled the first experience of that specific odour as something *outside* her, and recoiled in the same way as she had to the taste of samba and massala dosa and other delicacies of South Indian cooking.

Mrs Singh had misjudged her: *she* would not discover the rules in order to live by them. Her benefactress had always made the mistake of believing that she was like her, had always dragged her into her orbit and attempted to keep her there. And this habit, so plain that Rani could call to mind a hundred instances of it, she had only discovered since her marriage and even before Mrs Singh began to spread the web of ownership around her child. Perhaps the difference between herself and Tipu had nothing to do with dignity, but rather with herself as a mother and him as a father. Or perhaps it was the difference between men and women!

Men, women! Would she have been as disappointed if she had married Dr Singh? Everything about marriage had proved to be a burden, except the knowledge that she had conceived, and the sight of her boy child. He was her first experience of exclusive possession since the days of her early childhood, when she considered her mother as her very own and would often push her brothers and sisters away when they approached her, seeing them as intruders in the home. No, she could not countenance the possibility of another dispossession, Rani told herself. And even at the risk of a separation and the loss of Tipu, she would assert her right to her child and a family.

Chapter 25

Mrs Singh served the Pujaree herself. It was eight o'clock in the evening and the others had eaten already. The Pujaree was glad to eat alone, being tired and excessively hungry. Besides, he liked being served by Mrs Singh who, according to his sister, would not tolerate him for long, their backgrounds being so different.

'You always touching people with disease,' the mother of the twins had told him. 'You wash youself and you putting you hand in the fire all the time to purify youself, but a woman like that don' forget what you does touch and where you come from.'

But contrary to her prediction everything had gone well, so much so that Mrs Singh often told him that her life had changed since he came to live with her.

'You want some dhal pourri?' she asked.

'Yes,' he answered. 'It'll be bad by morning if I don't eat it.'

She left him to warm up the dhal pourri and he went on eating his cook-up rice, the dish he had all but lived on when he was alone. He was deeply grateful to Mrs Singh, above all for her substantial contributions to the fund for enlarging the temple, so much so that the puja ceremonies in Newtown were eclipsed only by those on the Courantyne coast, where lived thousands of Tamil-speaking East Indians. He himself came from the savannahs, where his old parents still lived in their low house thatched with rice straw and savannah grass. He could identify every savannah palm and knew how to weave fabric from the ité palm which the Warrau Indians used for making their hammocks. During the savannah storms he used to watch the cocourite palms twisting in the wind like gigantic fans agitated by an unseen hand close to the ground and once saw his parents' house blown away. The move from the Courantyne was an achievement, for he was almost illiterate at the time and possessed little more than a talent for making people listen to him. He knew all the Sanskrit formulae recited for pujas by heart and could recite large sections from the Vedas, so that when he had the opportunity to attend reading classes at the home of a rich Tamil-speaking merchant living in New Amsterdam he learned to read with astonishing speed. The merchant allowed him to hang up a hammock in the shed where his copra was stored and the Pujaree, touched by his kindness, vowed to repay him in some way when he was old enough. But the merchant died three years later. The Pujaree was only twenty and felt that he still had a long way to go before he read English and Hindi expertly. The private evening school was closed by the merchant's wife, who had never taken to the idea of her house being used as a 'fairground'. It was fifteen years later that he met Mrs Singh, who had heard of his work in Newtown and asked him to organize one of her banquets for the poor on the anniversary of her husband's death.

As the Pujaree's influence grew he was tempted to take advantage of her, having waited so long to realize a dream of building his own temple. But the recollection of the three years under the merchant's roof had left him with a vision of kindness and dignity which restrained him. In the end his patience bore fruit and he was invited to live with Mrs Singh, first as a guest and counsellor, then, as their intimacy grew, as her bed-mate. She was two years older, but he discovered that her youthful looks did not belie her prowess in bed, where she performed feats the like of which he had never heard in his years as priest and collector of conjugal tales. It was as though she had been building up a store of energy which, after more than a quarter of a century, was being released in frequent and sustained eruptions. And it was in the aftermath of these experiences that she disclosed her docility, which must have been lurking just beneath the surface of what, for the Mulvi Sahib, was a mannish self-assurance. She bought him a motorcar and made it plain to everyone that he was now master of her house.

The Pujaree, like Rani, saw Sukrum as a corrosive influence, not only on Lahti, but indirectly on Rani as well, whose disaffection was rooted in her worsening relations with both

Sukrum and Lahti. He believed that, deep down, Rani shared Mrs Singh's opinion of her husband: Tipu's character was such that wherever they went he would be the butt of jokes and the family would be constantly humiliated on his account. But the Pujaree took care not to advise Mrs Singh to expel Sukrum, for he sensed her sympathy for him and her curious need to give him Lahti as a sacrifice. Mrs Singh was a woman whose character he could never fathom. The Sukrums, on the other hand, he had met in New Amsterdam. They were only found in towns, just as a certain type of rat was found inhabiting the area around the wrought-iron-fenced markets of Bourda and Stabroek and Kitty. They scavenged on discarded vegetables and rotting fruit and the offal and dried blood of butchers' stalls. They were to be seen lurking in the gardens and yards of houses several hundred yards away, brash, grey inhabitants of a secret underworld that occasionally penetrated the compound of an unsuspecting home. He would wait until his position was unassailable and then whisper to Mrs Singh the word that would be Sukrum's undoing.

She came back into the dining room bearing the Pujaree's dhal pourri.

'Sit down, ne,' he told her. 'The twins been giving a lot of trouble. You think I should send them away?'

'You've got to decide,' she told him. 'They're not rude to me. But I know Rani's vexed with them.'

'When they went to see their grandparents last year they worked nearly all the time and nobody did complain.'

'I don't complain,' Mrs Singh protested mildly.

He waited before replying, in order to make certain that she had nothing more to say.

'I'll send them away then.'

'What'll their mother say?' Mrs Singh asked.

'She didn' want to come. She only did come 'cause I was on my own. In any case town's for young people.'

'Town's for young people,' Mrs Singh took him up, 'but Bai managed. It's town that saved him from Sukrum's clutches.'

'But look what town did to Sukrum. He did end up knocking from pillar to post, weeding one person yard for six cents, carrying some lady bunch of plantains for four cents and sleeping all over the place like a Lombard Street stray dog. How old he is, Sukrum?' he asked as an afterthought.

'He must be about thirty-eight.'

'As old as that? I would've say thirty-two.

'Sukrum wouldn' be surprised if you did ask him to go,' the Pujaree continued after a pause in their conversation.

She answered nothing and seemed to be reflecting on her reply. Then, smiling, she spoke quietly. If he went away Lahti would only follow him. The Pujaree did not pursue the matter. He spoke of the East Indians whose indenture was at an end and who came to Kitty and Newtown, often scantily dressed, in search of work. One of them, a woman wearing no more than a flimsy skirt and a joolah, came to the temple to beg for food. To his questioning she disclosed that she was sharing a room with eight others, six of them men.

'The Immigration Department goin' have to do something about them,' he said, 'or they'll be a army of beggars in a couple of years' time. Already the police had to stop harassing the beggars.'

Noticing his confusion at the rebuff he had received at the suggestion that Sukrum should leave, she encouraged him to go on.

'What the Immigration Department can do?' she asked, thinking of the hucksters, all of whom were originally from the estates and had settled with varying degrees of success in and near Georgetown.

'The free Crosbie Courts still open to them; that's one good thing. But the destitute don' go to court. One town council official been calling for compulsory repatriation to India. After enticing people from their country, some of them little more than children, they now talking 'bout compulsory repatriation!'

The Pujaree had begun to speak with passion, as he often did at the temple. He could not forget his years of poverty, his perpetual anxiety, especially at night when, walking barefoot along a suburban road, he would be startled by the sound of dead leaves rushing along the ground, like brown paper being crushed. He had never become accustomed to that noise on the pitch roads, which he used to haunt in his early days, because they were the best highways. Beside them rose houses with several coats of white and olive-green paint. He knew Mrs Singh's house before she and her husband had come to occupy it, before the sáman tree had been planted. In those days it was inaccessible, except to postmen with their khaki-brown sun helmets and canvas mailbags. A retired manager owned it in those days, who dressed as if he were living in one of those arctic countries where the temperature dropped below freezing point at night. Adorned with a yellow waistcoat and tweed jacket he could be seen every dusk setting out with the call of the six o'clock bee for the sea wall, looking neither right nor left, like a mechanical toy.

'I never thought I'd live here,' he said, suddenly in the grip of his old anxieties.

He could not tell her that he would like the saman tree to be cut down, that he was disturbed by its size and above all by its leaves, especially those strewn about the ground. Sukrum could sweep them up every day. He had little enough to do except weed the yard and maintain the house. The Pujaree carried the Courantyne coast landscape within and the almost treeless savannahs, the sparse grasslands dotted with large termite hills. This was the land in its primal state where long distances could be measured with the eye and even houses and trees were diminished by its immensity. Wherever he went he was haunted by that landscape, obsessed by its absence. There was something odd about people like Sukrum, who chose to lie under the massive saman tree and fall asleep in its shade and ignore its leaves piled against the paling staves. One day he would speak to her at length about that primordial landscape.

They went out on to the porch where it was cooler. Mrs Singh asked him why he thought that he and Sukrum, with similar backgrounds, had known different destinies. He claimed that the difference between them was the difference between inertia and movement. Sukrum was the blunt instrument that lay rusting in the rain. Perhaps it was Sukrum's aspect of decay which fascinated her and Lahti.

The Pujaree spoke again of his stay with the merchant and told her of his first 'experience'. While he was taking the stalks from sweet potatoes in the shed where he slept he fell to the ground in a trance, in which he saw a temple where yellow flames were burning in brass platters. Next to the temple was a creole place of worship with 'Spiritual Church' painted in fresh colours on its façade.

'Weren't you afraid?' Mrs Singh asked him.

'No. I did think I'd been waiting for it to happen all my life. In any case I see it so many times before in the Courantyne, especially people who does live on the savannahs. They does fall and lay on the ground still as. . . . You like that saman tree, eh?'

'Yes, it's my husband who planted it.'

'Oh, well, is so.'

The Pujaree sent the twins away, and their mother followed a few weeks later. But, although Rani welcomed the news at the time, she was later to admit that she felt just as oppressed, that her position in the household had not changed. Mrs Singh did her best to treat Tipu like a man, but managed only to give the impression that she was ignoring him. He, on the other hand, became more obsequious than ever, thinking to placate her with his servile posture; for he was convinced that she had asked him to leave because he had offended her in some way.

One morning he woke up to find that Rani was nowhere in the house. It was unlikely that she had gone to the shops for before she went out she never failed to inform someone. Besides, he had not yet eaten and Aji was still in bed and ran the risk of soiling the sheets.

Tipu ran around the house in a panic, asking everyone where his wife and child had gone. Mrs Singh and the Pujaree tried to calm him down and send him off to work, promising to do all they could to find her. In any case Rani was not the kind to go off and leave confusion behind her. But Tipu was inconsolable. He had never beaten her, they rarely quarrelled, and only the month before he had bought her a new joolah. Many women did not know where their next meal was coming from.

'Calm down!' the Pujaree ordered him, exasperated by his unmanly behaviour. 'Get dressed and go to work!'

Tipu obeyed, jolted by the Pujaree's firmness.

It was a bright, sweltering morning. The hucksters had not yet arrived, but the small girl from the village was already in the yard picking off the drooping oleander flowers. Every few minutes she stopped to watch a passing car or cyclist or to look back at the house. When she saw Tipu leaving – exceptionally early – she greeted him, 'Marnin', Miss Rani husband.' But he passed by without answering her and went right instead of left as was his custom when leaving for work. She took up a position on the bridge and watched him until he turned into Sandibab Street and out of sight. But she remained on the bridge watching everything that moved, the birds alighting with a fluttering of wings on the fence and the vehicles bearing right into Barr Street in the distance. She was tempted to walk along the strip of grass between the fence and gutter, so that she could look up Dowding Street where there was much more movement, but was afraid that Mrs Singh might be annoyed at her idleness. In exchange for her morning duties she was allowed the freedom of the house of which she took full advantage, since she was ignored by everyone. And she herself felt that if she disclosed what she saw to her mother something terrible would happen and she would be barred from the house for good.

Everyone who lived there shared in its mystery, in the girl's eyes, an impression heightened by the remarks she heard her mother make. Lahti's conduct was like that of a creole, on account of the clothes she wore. Rani did not love her husband and Aji would die within the year. Mrs Singh drank a glass of cogue every morning, which accounted for her youthfulness; Bai had left in a fit of anger when Sukrum locked him out and had returned home to find his friend and Lahti in the midst of one of their orgies. They had consumed much liquor and eaten the hallucinatory root Sukrum collected on outings to catch shrimp, and Lahti, dazed and half-clothed, had come to the door herself to chase Bai away. The girl had heard this and much more while listening to her mother's conversations with her father when they thought she was asleep. Fed on such tales she considered everything in the yard to be extraordinary, the flying water tank, the clusters of ripening guava, the painted windowpanes, the stoneware bottles bordering the flowerbed Bai cared for before he left, the Pujaree's new car with its musical horn, the electric bulbs that were illuminated at night when the Delco plant was switched on, the hucksters congregating in the morning, transforming the bottom house into a small market. One of her secret ambitions was to blow the horn of the Pujaree's car which, according to the people of the district, played the tune *'Doctor Wharton Beg Your Pardon'*. The other ambition was to penetrate into Mrs Singh's bedroom, open her make-up boxes and inhale the contents of those blue-tinted jars. Her mother's interest lay in the women.

The girl, on seeing Tipu flee as he seemed to be doing, knew that in some way the equilibrium of Mrs Singh's household had been disturbed, and on returning home in time to go to school, made her first disclosure about the place where she worked. Her mother questioned her closely, but all she could tell was that Tipu had begun shouting after the sun came up and left without saying good morning when, as a rule, he never failed to greet her on his way to work. Her mother, despite the scant information, came to the right conclusion: Rani had left her husband and taken the baby with her. It was 'man' story and all that was left to be established was the identity of Rani's sweet man and his address.

If Rani got man, she thought, then something wrong with Tipu. Is who the child' father, that's what I want to know?

The Pujaree called everyone to come and join him at the dining table while Mrs Singh attended to Aji. He questioned Lahti, but Rani had told her nothing. Sukrum had not heard anyone leave, and the cook, who had only just arrived, was not certain what was going on. Lahti had no idea where Rani might go, although she was certain she would not return to her home. The only thing for it was to wait, in the hope that she might telephone.

The Pujaree advised Mrs Singh that it was best to do nothing until evening, by which time Rani would have got in touch with them, he was certain. He then went off to the temple, promising to be back at midday.

Mrs Singh, unable to face the hucksters after the anguish of the previous hour, gave the cook a five-dollar note to make whatever purchases she thought necessary and then, having installed Aji in a rocking chair by a front window, went to the dining room to be on her own.

Rani had no friend except Lahti; she only went out with Tipu and the child in the evening, when they sauntered up the sea wall road and sat on the stone wall to watch the ebb-tide and departing ships. Mrs Singh was crushed by the realization that the young woman did not trust her sufficiently to confide in her. But how could it be otherwise? she thought. She had seen Rani and Lahti become women and could only continue to treat them as children. Even after the talk with Rani and her promise to encourage Tipu to leave, she was unable to understand why the young woman was so overwrought. It was during that long conversation that she realized how little they understood each other. Until this morning she still believed that the same invisible bonds that attached Lahti to her kept Rani moored to the home as well, in spite of her urgent plea for help. Should not the twins' departure have been enough to conciliate her? Had she not successfully managed her schooling and found her a husband? What did Rani expect of her?

Catching sight of the frail figure of Aji at the window, she recalled how Rani and Lahti used to sit in the same place, waiting for her to come home. She remembered how she had to restrain them from rushing down the stairs to meet her. They were girls then, frank in their expression of joy and hatred. Once, on seeing the young Rani lying athwart the double bed, her thumb in her mouth and her eyes half open, Aji was so struck by the picture of favouritism – Lahti was not allowed to lie on that bed – and by Rani's utter reliance on Mrs Singh, that she was moved to say, 'Why you so open in treating Rani so different?' And Mrs Singh had answered, 'When I'm sick it's Rani who's going to look after me, not Lahti.' How often she had made that remark! The image of Rani as a girl lying athwart the vast bed so touched her, she was caught for a while in the vice of that emotion to which she was all but a stranger. Her numerous aunts and uncles in India, cousins and friends, the visitors, hucksters, neighbours, passers-by made up the warp and weft that stretched across a loom of belonging which, perhaps, could dispense with strong affections. Or perhaps she was of a different generation, a different ilk from these young women whose love ran deep.

Chapter 26

The Pujaree's car was heard on the gravel.

So soon? Mrs Singh thought.

It was only ten o'clock and the porch was still in shadow. Mrs Singh went out front to welcome him.

He told her that Rani was at the temple and refused to come home until Tipu found a place for them to live.

'No, no,' he advised. 'Leave her there. It's better. We must wait till Tipu come back.'

And, an hour later, when Tipu came home for his midday meal, gesticulating even before he got to the door, the Pujaree took him aside, explained the implication of his wife's ultimatum and advised what he ought to do.

'You did promise her to get a place and now it come to this! Why you so hard-headed?'

'My uncle say she got man,' Tipu complained.

'Your uncle! Mrs Singh! Your mother! The twins got more gumption than six of you. You not shame? What use is your uncle if he couldn' advise you to do the sensible thing? And if you don' act fast, is you going to make her get man!'

He agreed to take a house the Pujaree might find for him and to move into it whether he liked it or not.

'She goin' come back?' Tipu asked.

'I don' know. She say she not coming back till you find somewhere. If I was her I wouldn't come back because you does break your word.'

'Talk to she,' Tipu begged, 'and tell she I miss Bhagwan.'

The Pujaree shook his head, wondering whether, in the interest of Rani and Bhagwan their son, it would not be better for her to settle down with another man.

That afternoon the Pujaree brought back mother and son. Only Mrs Singh and Aji were home.

'You mean you couldn't even tell me you were going?' Mrs

Singh said, resisting the impulse to take Bhagwan from her.

'Thanks, my friend,' she told the Pujaree, after Rani had gone upstairs. 'I should have asked you to come and live here years ago.'

And thereafter the Pujaree's word was law in her house. He settled quarrels, made prohibitions, distributed gifts and generally behaved as if he were Mrs Singh's lawful husband. And when he found a cottage in Newtown through the temple janitor, he obliged Tipu to keep his word.

The only person who attempted to challenge his authority was Sukrum. He refused to observe a prohibition as to the use of the Dowding Street gate after dusk and was given the task of padlocking it when the sun went down and the saman tree clothed the yard in shadow.

In the months that followed Rani and Tipu came visiting twice a week. Her transformation was apparent to everyone. Lahti found her to be as patient as in the old days, when she could say anything without fear of being criticized. And even Sukrum could approach her, knowing that he would not be rebuffed. But it was Mrs Singh for whom Rani reserved a tenderness which took her benefactress by surprise. Far from resenting her demonstrations of affection towards Bhagwan Rani gave him over to her as soon as she arrived and, as if to make amends for her surliness during the last months, brought her gifts of creole food she made herself, metemgee, cook-up rice with shrimps and foo-foo soup, dishes the East Indian cook refused to prepare. When Mrs Singh complained that the woman who was paid to look after Aji did not do her work properly, Rani took her old house-mate out to the Botanic Gardens on Sundays to listen to the Militia Band play in the stone bandstand surrounded by palms and gravelled paths where strollers in broad hats walked hand in hand. Aji never kept her eyes off her, in the manner of small children with a parent who had been absent for a few days. And Rani was glad of the old woman's attachment, not forgetting those first weeks in Mrs Singh's house when no one else spoke to her. She taught her then how to recognize the fabrics in the wardrobe, organza, muslin, taffeta and silk-chiffon, and showed her the traditional Indian way of making clothes, measuring the cloth with the palm of one's hand and incorporating waste material into a garment by means of seams. Not having mastered the art of numbers she had never learned to measure with a ruler. They used to listen behind doors to conversations between Mrs Singh and her visitors, the Mulvi Sahib, the Pujaree and the goblet maker, to the Mulvi Sahib's endless exhortations that Mrs Singh should remarry; and these conversations possessed the fascination of the glassy stillness of stagnant water.

And although Rani had moved away her connection with the mansion remained strong, so much so that when the long drought came, the one that people said would never end, she had her water delivered by the Pujaree in the motorcar. But while availing herself of the many advantages the mansion home offered she revelled in the new independence her husband had never wanted. At first Tipu could not forgive his wife for obliging him to embark upon an experience which involved paying rent to a landlord and exercising sole responsibility for protecting his family. But Rani's new attentiveness was more than ample compensation and gradually he grew accustomed to his new obligations, in spite of the threats he saw on every hand. In the end even these proved groundless: the noises in the yard late at night were no more than a stray dog foraging in the refuse bin, and the wandering bees from the hive next door worried Bhagwan in no way when he was left lying in the shade of the ginnip tree.

One night when the little girl who picked flowers in Mrs Singh's yard came round and announced that Aji was dead Rani accompanied her back to the mansion, leaving Bhagwan with his father. She met everyone assembled in the drawing room, the Pujaree, Sukrum, Mrs Singh, Lahti, and the Mulvi Sahib, who had just arrived and was standing by his chair. Mrs Singh, dazed and wide-eyed, as if she were staring at some unusual event unfolding before her eyes, was sitting on a straight-back chair, shunning her usual deep armchair, which stood empty in its place by the wall.

'She got up this morning on her own for the first time in months,' Mrs Singh told the company. 'And when I saw her standing in front of me I nearly dropped with fright. Then she started talking to me. She said that she wasn't sick any more and she was going to pack her things to go away. "To go where?" I was frightened because she looked so well and was speaking clearly, like a bell. "I going to India." Then I began to cry and she abused me. She called me a coward and said . . .'

'Speak, my friend,' the Pujaree urged her. 'Speak and you goin' feel better.'

But Mrs Singh could not bring herself to repeat the abuse Aji had heaped on her, and the foul names she had called her.

'You filly!' she had said. 'You're in heat and you not shame to buy your man. You even dress him up in shoes he never wear before. That's the only reason you don' throw Lahti out! How you goin' show her the door when she doin' what you did always do? You in' shame? You forget I did know you when you was a child-bride. I did watch you from those early days and see how you did do one thing and think something else. Alyou women would do anything they ask you to do: "Married a horse, girl!" and you'd married a horse and take off you veil with you eyes 'pon the ground. Don' look 'pon me like that 'cause I in' drunk. Your husband was a giant. Mr Singh was a prince! An' how he could hoop heself up with a filly like you I jus' can't understand. You pretend you don' know what people get up to in this house, but you know all right. If Mr Singh did know what would've go on here he'd spin in his grave, take it from me! You pretend you so kind and generous when all the time you frighten of a empty house. Is who you think you foolin', you filly! Filly! Filly! At your age you puttin' flower in your hair. Flower in your hair and this in you pants.' And here Aji had made a forceful gesture with the clenched fist of her right hand. 'You is something else! When Betta come here nex' time I goin' tell him everything that happen, in his surgery, in the drawin' room and upstairs. Oh, upstairs! You think I don' know how you oil the bed to stop it from creaking! Creak creak! Oil oil. Creak creak! Oil. I tell you, you is something else with flower in your hair and *umm* in you pants!'

Aji burst out laughing, then suddenly fell serious again. 'I so confused! That's why I goin' back to India and the temples by Ganga Mai. You know they got winter there, and lotus, just like here? And hundreds and hundreds of East Indians, like here?'

She began weeping silently and her quivering voice fell silent, then, as if finding her strength again, she spoke, more quietly than before. 'You come from Kerala, Miss Singh, that's why I never did understand you, 'cause you is something else. You know Betta wife expecting? Oh, you din' know? No, he din' tell me, so you don' got to practise you jealousy 'pon me. I know 'cause I close to Betta and he close to me. And when he go away you *think* you did suffer. He is a prince, but all you want to do is own him, like you own me and Lahti and Sukrum and you did want to own Tipu. The tiger!' She burst out laughing again at the thought of Tipu's name. 'I despise him 'cause he's nothing. Nothing! Like this house, like you empty head and you empty bedrooms. With all you education you's nothing but a filly who never had a thought in you life. It rain last night on the other side,' she said, now speaking with a menacing gentleness. 'No, it din' rain. It did drizzle, so fine it take my breath away. But don' worry, 'cause I pack my grip already an' I taking the immigrant boat, and you can wave goodbye to me if you like. But all them things I say 'bout you is true. . . . When I lay down an' start falling asleep fo' good you must bend down: I got something to tell you. Don' forget, Miss Singh. I got something to tell you.' And she burst out into a grotesque laugh, displaying her bad teeth and mouth red from chewing a leaf she got Lahti to pick for her in the yard. Then, exhausted from her outburst, she suddenly took it into her head to sit down on the floor as if it were a chair. When Mrs Singh lifted her into a standing position she allowed herself to be helped up to the room where she slept.

But Mrs Singh refused to give details of the encounter to those assembled. Instead, uncharacteristically, she complained that she had done nothing to deserve Aji's abuse and that in life people had to expect abuse from those they helped.

Lahti, as the unmarried woman in the company, went off to make coffee and Sukrum followed her with his eyes in spite of the solemnity of the occasion.

'I'll never help anyone else in my life,' Mrs Singh declared, when, in a flash, she saw herself bending over Aji, who beckoned her to put her ear close to her mouth which was opening and closing as though relaying the last remaining breaths with her mouth; and then recoiling from what she heard, the words that Aji had promised her before she died.

'I'll never help anybody again.'

'It's in your nature,' the Mulvi Sahib consoled her. 'In any case the true believer does not expect any reward.'

The Pujaree found the Mulvi Sahib's expression 'the true believer' out of place, but giving no indication that he was displeased, he supported the remark with a nod.

That night Betta, on receiving his mother's telephone call informing him of Aji's death, took the last ferry with Meena and arrived to find the house full of mourners, most of them women with stunned expressions. Meena was taken to see the corpse by Mrs Singh. The young woman stood by the bed for a few minutes, head bowed and eyes fixed on the immobile features of the old woman about whom Betta had spoken so affectionately. Meena had hardly known her, except through Betta, in the same way as she came to know his teacher.

The window and skylight were open and the plaques of darkness on the panes prevailed over the light cast by the kerosene lamp above the bed. It was not appropriate to switch on the electric bulb with its false rays. Meena was surprised that the body was left alone, especially since the windows were open and the pale glow was hardly sufficient to pick out Aji's sunken cheeks. There was a rank smell, which she associated with the bodies of old people. Absorbed in the contemplation of the body, she forgot her unease in her mother-in-law's presence.

'You didn't know her,' Mrs Singh said. 'Betta doted on her and my husband doted on her.'

Meena did not know what to answer or whether to answer at all.

'How old was she, Ma?'

'She was sixty-seven. She never had malaria once in her life, yet by sixty-five she was senile.'

And conversation ceased between them.

The two women went back to the company, bringing the solitude of the dead body with them.

Betta, sitting with the other men, felt nothing, no loss, no pity, for Aji's implacable decline and the suddenness of the news of her death had disarmed him. He glanced around him and the image of an aviary at night in which the birds were asleep with their heads tucked under their wings occurred to him. Did not Aji's death mean more than the passing of a voice?

His thoughts shifted to the relationship between Aji and his mother. He never understood why Aji was permitted to speak to her as she did. Many years ago she was sober, her only extravagance being to exaggerate his dead father's qualities and a dislike of untidy men. She was bound to his mother's home as certain people are bound to the soil. For her nothing existed beyond the gates except on tajah nights when she would follow the glittering tower to the sea along with the crowd and watch its disintegration on the beach in a conflagration of leaping flames. Perhaps he felt no grief because he was unable to believe that she was indeed dead. Perhaps he did not want to know that she was and for that reason had not yet gone upstairs to see the body.

'Paisa na bah,' she used to say in bad Hindi when, as a small boy, he asked for money. In those days she sang like a troupial. And in those days too her teeth were polished like the lotahs of travelling pundits. Aji, grandmother. Had her name given her the right to hold up a mirror to his mother's actions?

Betta got up and said he was going to see the body, hoping that no one would follow him. No one did and he went up the long, familiar stairs, bearing with him the weight of his childhood, his marriage and the manifold experiences that had never borne a name. And it was while he was walking the length of the passage between the bedrooms that he was overcome by the old familiarities which had haunted him in the first and last periods of his student days. The kerosene lamp, blackened where the chimney flared towards its scalloped mouth, had a transparent bowl through which the saturated wick was visible. He wondered why the lamp was lit when the room was provided with electricity, but left it burning nevertheless. Hindu funerals were a common sight in the villages he served and he visualized a long procession accompanied by the dust of shuffling feet and a silence broken at intervals by the single note of a doleful drum.

But Aji's last journey would be along a pitch road for much of its way, across the train lines, past the saman trees and royal palms of well-groomed city roads. The incessant flux of loss and gain was as extraordinary as it was commonplace. Thirteen months ago he was not married and now his wife was pregnant. Since he went away Bai had left, Sukrum, from all accounts, was living with Lahti, and Rani was married and had moved out with her husband when they appeared to be part of the communal life of his mother's home. So much had changed, yet the place was the same, like those beaches which, swept away during a violent storm, are no longer fit for a concourse of swimmers, yet appear to remain the same, with their long stone moles and steps descending to the sea.

Betta switched on the electric light to take his last look at Aji, the grandmother, and saw a face masked with a terrible inertia. Instinctively he lifted her hand and, despite its lack of warmth, felt for its pulse, before lowering it gently.

The urge to do something unusual took hold of Betta, an uncommon need to harangue those assembled in the drawing room or to bring a group of musicians into the death room and celebrate rather than mourn. None of those downstairs with solemn faces would miss Aji as he would, except his mother. Yet, in this hour of meditation, he did not feel the need to meditate. Gopie, Meena's younger sister, would no doubt end up like himself, exercising a dominion over her actions that amounted to tyranny.

When he heard the sound of weeping Betta turned off the electric bulb and, in doing so, became aware of the throbbing of the Delco plant. While going downstairs to rejoin the others Betta decided that he must be more friendly towards Rani, especially as her husband was not there. A marriage of convenience! Smiles of convenience, words, laughter, beds, clothes, greetings of convenience. So it was, more and more so until the time came when they would all be hemmed in and spontaneity would become a term of abuse.

None of those present knew Aji well. One of a family of seven girls, she had run away to Bartica with a man from the neighbouring village, believing that her father would never be able to accumulate the money for her dowry. Her young man, a creole porknocker, had once made a diamond strike, but did not get past the whores of Kurupung. Like the majority of porknockers, life in the bush and the lure of diamonds proved irresistible and, apart from brief trips to his family in the Courantyne and to Bartica to visit friends, he went back to the 'life', leaving the forest from time to time for Kurupung, to sell the stones he had found. When he met Aji he fell in love with her long hair, which she was in the habit of rinsing with henna to banish the lice which had plagued her since childhood. Determined to set up house permanently, he brought her the proceeds from the sale of his raw diamonds, which she invested in a box that gave her first payment, banking the lump sum in an interest-bearing account. But soon afterwards her lover was drowned, along with eight other men, while negotiating one of the rapids on the Mazaruni river in a boat in the charge of an inexperienced river captain. Aji was inconsolable and vowed never to spend the money that was to bind her to the strange man who was not afraid of the forest. She went back to the Courantyne where she was able to attach herself to Mr Singh's household because she knew how to prepare South Indian cooking, which his young wife craved. She bought a necklace with her dead lover's money and the wages she received were spent on bracelets adorned with silver coins. Once, in the euphoria of a wedding celebration that went on for seven days, she was on the point of telling her story to Mr Singh, but held back, restrained by the thought of the mementoes she wore on her wrists and around her neck. She now lay in her bed bedecked in jewellery that for those who knew her had no significance whatsoever except as an investment superior to paper money which could turn to powder. And no one knew of her own bereavement as a young woman in Bartica where the river captains lived and excursion launches fringed with red electric bulbs set out for the coast laden with charcoal-burners and leaseholders in the company of butterfly women, to return at dawn where the three rivers meet and paku fish feed on the corpses of drowned diamond seekers and the forest drives men to the extremity of renouncing the company of humans.

Chapter 27

Gopie insisted that she wanted to go to Mrs Merriman's court. There was no point in her sister relaying her stories from the encounters of litigants if she could not see for herself what it was like. Meena told her to wait until Betta came home; she was not prepared to accept the responsibility. Sometimes the encounters were violent. The last time a man who had agreed to air the quarrel with his wife before Mrs Merriman changed his mind when she began giving evidence. She refused to stop and he, screaming at her from the other side of the room, had to be restrained by Mr Merriman and another man. Mrs Merriman refused to carry on with that case, a show of restraint which did not prevent him from cursing and threatening his wife. The two eventually left together, and a few days later informed Mrs Merriman by letter that they would come back the following week. It was this particular case which interested Gopie, who had already sought and received her parents' permission to attend, provided Meena and Betta agreed to take her.

They waited in the kitchen for Betta to come home, but when the car drew up outside neither of them heard it, for Meena was laughing at Gopie's mimicry of one of her teachers whose clothes were so ill-fitting the pupils had named him 'Old Man Pappy'.

In the year before Meena's marriage Gopie had given her sister a great deal of trouble. Previously obedient and respectful, she had taken to contradicting her and teasing her mercilessly, especially after she became betrothed to Betta. But since Meena's marriage Gopie was obliged to behave properly, out of fear that Betta might bar her from the house.

Betta's appearance in the doorway surprised them both.

'Well, what's wrong?' he asked.

Meena explained that they had been listening for him because Gopie wanted to go to Mrs Merriman's court. He pretended that the question was so serious he needed time to think it over, and Gopie, not knowing if he meant what he said, waited while Meena kept making faces behind her back, certain that Betta had tacitly agreed to the request.

'All right, young lady,' Betta said at length, 'you can come, but you have to drive.'

'You know I can't drive,' Gopie objected, turning helplessly to her sister.

'Sorry, you'll have to drive,' he repeated, as he left the kitchen.

'He's joking,' Meena said, seeing that her sister was near to tears.

The kitchen was grey from wood smoke. Gopie was sitting on a cane-bottomed chair against the wall on which, above her head, dried lengths of orange peel were hanging from metal hooks. Whenever she came to the house she spent much time talking to the cook in the kitchen, the room of her preference when she was at home. As a small child she used to hang around her mother while she was cooking, since Meena hardly ever found time to play with her.

'I tell you Betta's joking, Gopie.'

'You think he likes me?'

'Don't talk stupidness. He's your brother-in-law. He must like you.'

Gopie could not see the connection and neither could Meena; but having made the statement she stuck to it.

'You're coming in?' Meena asked, on the point of taking in a steaming soup tureen out of which a ladle with a curved handle stuck incongruously.

Gopie followed Meena unwillingly to face Betta, who had not missed a single opportunity to tease her of late, giving her what Meena described as a 'bit of her own medicine'.

They set off as soon as Betta had finished his meal. The car windows were open and the hair of the two women flew about their faces. They passed the new cinema, at the entrance to which a crowd was standing in front of a hoarding advertising the current film. Further on the road was once more empty, save for the odd animal grazing by the wayside, a tethered sheep or a cow that had strayed from the fields. Over the fields

to the north flocks of birds were flying in from the sea under a
sky scarred with islands of red clouds.

By the time they had driven the two and a half miles darkness
had fallen. The Tilley lamps in the drawing room of the
Merrimans' home were already lit and although – as it appeared
from the road – none of the litigants or onlookers had arrived,
the bright lights gave the upper storey the appearance of a dance
hall in the hour before the musicians arrived to play tentative
phrases on their instruments. They crossed the bridge over the
wide gutter in which the water was lost among the weeds.

Young Mr Merriman, who was waiting for them, did not
conceal his surprise at seeing Gopie, whom he had never met.

'Well, say something,' Meena told her sister, who remained
standing in the middle of the drawing room.

They performed the ritual of going down to see old Mr
Merriman, who had just come in from the back yard where he
had been looking after his bees. He was muttering about a hive
in which there were orgiastic goings-on and little honey was
made. He ignored Gopie completely, to the surprise of the
others, who recalled his first meeting with Meena. Meena
enquired after his music pupils and he complained that the
gifted ones were philistines while the genuine musicians had no
ability.

'It must be something in the air. The bees are suffering from it
too.'

Mrs Merriman was in her bedroom upstairs, preparing for the
evening, and Gopie now imagined that the imminent encounter
with the forbidding lady would be disastrous.

'You'd better come up if you don't want to miss the start,
young lady,' young Mr Merriman said to Gopie.

Relieved that someone took the pains to address her she
smiled broadly, there and then deciding that young Mr Merriman was even more agreeable than Meena had made him out to
be.

Once upstairs they found that a few people were scattered
about the room. Betta, Meena and Gopie took their place in the
front row while Mr Merriman went inside to see his wife. A
small electric fan standing on the table where Mrs Merriman
was to sit made its semicircular journey on its axis before

starting off again in the other direction with a shudder, as though it were unwilling to change course. More people began arriving and conversations started up.

'Where's Mrs Merriman?' Gopie asked her sister.

'She's inside. She's probably studying the list of people she knows will come.'

'How she knows who'll come?'

'In most cases she doesn't, but some of them write, telling her; and others she does tell to come back at such and such a time.'

'Do they obey her?'

'Mostly,' Meena answered.

'Why?'

'I don't know.'

'What's wrong?' Betta asked, thinking that Gopie might be out of her depth among grown-ups, nearly all of whom were creoles.

'She wants to know why they obey Mrs Merriman.'

Eventually Mrs Merriman came out with a batch of letters in her hand, which she placed on the table before coming over to greet the couple and Gopie. And as she was chatting with them her husband joined them. He had changed his clothes and now wore a pair of short khaki pants and an open-necked shirt.

'I think you can start now,' he suggested to his wife. 'There're more than thirty people here.'

He sat down next to Betta and his wife placed herself behind the table on which she had left the papers.

'Anybody for the court tonight?' she asked aloud before sitting down, using the formula with which she always opened proceedings.

'Yes, Nen Merriman,' a woman said from the back, standing while Mrs Merriman sat down.

'I bring this good-fo'-nothing,' she continued, pointing to a strapping young woman much larger than she was.

'Stand up, let Nen Merriman see you,' she ordered her daughter, who got up at once, so that everyone could see that she was also much taller than the woman who had spoken.

'That's me daughter, Nen. She think she's a woman and does go and come as she like.'

'I . . .' the daughter began.

'Shut you mouth!' exclaimed the complainant. 'You see what I mean! That's how disobedient she is. When I was she age my mother would'a give me one box if I did talk to she like that. I want you to give she a good dressing-down, Nen.'

'How disobedient is she?' Mrs Merriman asked, undismayed by the apparent absurdity of the woman's complaint.

'You see for yourself!' the woman exclaimed.

'Does she refuse to do what you tell her?'

'She don' dare!' the woman thundered, looking up threateningly at the woman standing beside her. 'Refuse? She never do it and she in' going begin now. No, is not that. I tell she that she got to drop her rum-swillin' young man 'cause he not goin' bring she nothing but trouble. She say yes, but now I hear she does meet him in secret. They does meet under the big tree by the koker. What kind of behaviour is that?'

'How do you know the man is unsuitable?' Mrs Merriman asked.

'I know 'cause he mother tell me so sheself. "My Vernon not suitable for your girl. He does drink. He's a stiller at Uitvlugt distillery an' he does thief the key and open the rum vat. He don' got to buy it. Vernon in' suitable for your such a well-brought-up girl like your daughter." She say so sheself. Why she goin' lie to me for?'

There was sniggering at the back of the room.

'She might lie,' said Mrs Merriman, 'because *she* might not want her son to marry your daughter.'

'What?' bellowed the complainant. 'Vernon does drop his aitches and put them on in the wrong place. He does say, "The hegg too 'ot." Vernon is a Portagee and whoever hear of a Portagee who know where to put on a aitch. Not want him to marry my daughter? She too good for him I tell you.'

'My advice to you,' said Mrs Merriman, 'is to go and see the man's mother and ask her if her son stopped drinking whether she would agree to the association or not. If she hems and haws you'll know where your daughter stands. How old is your daughter?'

'Twenty-five, Nen.'

'You expect her to obey you in everything?'

'And is who she goin' obey? She living in my house. When she go an' live in somebody else house she can obey them.'

'Well, do as I said about the young man's mother and try and find out from people who know him if he drinks a lot in truth.'

'All right, Nen. Well, say "thank you", ne?' she said, turning to her daughter who did as she was told from her standing position.

'Who's next?' Mrs Merriman called out.

'Me, Nen,' a man said.

But at the same time an old lady stood up, only to sit down again at once, intimidated by the firmness of the man's claim to be next.

'Who came first?' Mrs Merriman asked again.

'I thought was me,' the old lady said timidly.

'Is me, Nen,' the man insisted. 'I see she when she come in after me. But I's a gentleman, so let she come forward. Stand up, Aunty, an' say you piece. But make it short, 'cause I impatient too.'

The old lady rose, looking round to see if he meant what he said.

Her story was simple: her roof was leaking and she could not afford to repair it.

'Where're you living?'

'By Cayman Walk.'

'Cayman Walk. Mr Gomes lives by Cayman Walk,' Mrs Merriman said. 'Tell him Nen Merriman asks to repair your roof and she'll see he gets paid. Come back and we'll take a collection for what he charges. Tell him I said he must do it reasonably for you.'

'Thanks, darling. God bless you,' the old woman said undemonstratively, before sitting down.

'I got a bad roof too,' the man who claimed it was his turn put in.

'You're not an old woman, brother,' Mrs Merriman said sharply.

'Anyway,' the man said, 'what I come to see you about is the state of the gutter in the village. I don' know when they weed them last.'

There were mutterings of approval when the man embarked on an eloquent denunciation of the village council in the district where he lived. Mrs Merriman there and then drew up a letter protesting in terms outlined by the man. During a ten-minute recess all those present who were not afraid put their signatures to the protest and Mrs Merriman promised that once she was able to verify the condition of the public gutters the letter would be sent off.

During the recess a lady came around selling coconut cakes on her own account and within a short time her tray was empty. She was one of the first to attend Mrs Merriman's neighbourhood court and, to entertain those around her, she regaled them with memorable encounters between husband and wife, neighbours, parents and children and even employers and employees.

Mrs Merriman once more took her place at table and before she could ask who was next the man who had written that he was coming with his wife to continue the investigation into her complaints stood up. But, just at that moment another man, whom most of those present recognized as a foreman unpopular with the workers, shouted out, 'Who gave you the right to stir up trouble? So is this what does happen in your so-called court?'

The man's interruption was so unusual and his tone so venomous, that the outburst was followed by a deathly silence. Then, after a while, Mrs Merriman remarked drily, 'Who are you?'

'That's none of your business.'

'But it is my business. It is my house.'

Once more there was silence as the man searched for a reply.

'I don't want to stay in any case,' he declared. 'But this isn't the last you're going to hear about this.'

'Tell your masters we know who you are,' a man shouted after him.

Business went on as before, with everyone pretending that nothing serious had occurred. Many of those who had put their signature to the petition calling upon the village council to weed the village gutters wanted to ask that their names be scored out, but were afraid of doing so publicly.

At the end of the proceedings those attending dispersed more slowly than usual.

Gopie, on the way back home, asked her sister what all the trouble was about, but it was Betta who answered because his wife, like Gopie, knew practically nothing about what went on on the estates, about people's fear for their jobs, about the suspicion that followed anyone who was promoted, since it was

widely believed that few earned promotion on merit. He
explained that the man was notorious for his hatred of the
workers and cultivated the overseers openly, caring little about
the workers' opinion of him.

'People say whenever he goes into a rum shop conversation
stops. It only makes him worse.'

'What's he going to do?' Meena asked.

'He'll complain to the field manager or the District Commissioner about the petition. I can't see it'll make the slightest
difference. It'll be public knowledge anyway.'

Betta told them about some of the tensions between management and workers, the constant quarrels about the weighing of
the cane carried by the iron punts, an important aspect of the
work, since the field hands were paid by the weight of the load.

Gopie had fallen asleep while Betta was talking, but awoke
when the car came to a halt. While she and Meena went upstairs
he remained under the house on the pretext that he wanted to
see the janitor, who had in fact gone out.

Betta felt that in some way the incident had been connected
with him. Since early February the weather had been fine and all
those months – it was now May – he had seen the estate
manager three times. He had only written a handful of certificates in the period, but he could not suppress the feeling that
the man was waiting for the rainy season with impatience. He
had neither done nor said anything to confirm Betta's suspicions. When he mentioned the matter to Meena she was of the
opinion that the manager's threats were preying on his mind
and that, since they had seen so little of each other, Betta should
not torture himself unduly.

But Betta's misgivings were, in fact, founded on the manager's
calculated coolness whenever they passed each other. Betta got
the impression that if he had spoken to the man he would not
even have bothered to answer. Besides, Cook's frequent absen-
ces and the offhand manner of the janitor, which amounted to
insolence at times, reminded him of the occasion when they
stayed away, reappearing after he asked the department for a
temporary replacement for the janitor. It was the janitor who
enquired, affecting innocence behind a sneer, whether he was
the only East Indian doctor in the country.

With the dry weather and the knowledge that his first child was on the way, with the strengthened bonds of friendship between himself and the Merrimans, he had regained confidence in his ability to foil the manager's contrivances.

Suddenly he realized that Gopie's presence irritated him; her immaturity precluded the discussion of anything serious with Meena when she was there. But, ashamed of his pettiness, Betta tried to cheer himself with the thought that she was still at school and was never able to stay more than a few days, except during the holidays. Sometimes he and Meena would sit for an hour without uttering a word, a feat compared with the constant exchanges in Meena's parents' home and with Gopie's incessant chatter when she came visiting. The many-sidedness of Meena's character never ceased to set him wondering. With her family she talked a good deal, while with him she sensed his need for conversation or silence, like those remarkable dancers who adapt their style to that of their partners, cavorting round the hall during one piece and swaying imperceptibly on one spot during another.

Betta and everyone else forgot the untoward incident at the Merrimans' court. Gopie, like Meena, came to adapt herself to what she saw as the considerable freedom enjoyed by women in the Merrimans' home, and by the same token grew accustomed to Mr Merriman's moods and the strangely heady atmosphere in his downstairs room. She attended the court sessions as regularly as she was able, with the consent of her father, who had himself had recourse to the Crosbie Courts set up specially for East Indian immigrants. He was impressed by the beehives she had started in the back yard under old Mr Merriman's direction. His daughter's association with the creole family was a 'useful' one. Should he not be able to raise a dowry for her she would be in a position to support herself.

While, before, Gopie spoke of nothing else but Betta's large house, now her obsessive conversation was about bees. She intended exhibiting bottles of honey at the cottage industry fair at Cornelia Ida and was certain that she had a chance of winning a prize because of the situation of her hive. Old Mr Merriman said so. She taught her father how to lift the hive frames for inspection and to avoid crushing the bees in doing so. She showed him how to identify the larger cells of the non-workers and to crush any incipient queen cells with his fingers in order to prevent the development of new queens. The neighbours could now see him leaning on a walking stick as he surveyed the wooden box under his guava tree or puffing smoke into the opening at its base or peering up at an exposed frame in search of the elongated body of a queen wandering among her workers like an intruder in the hive. And just as Gopie emulated old Mr Merriman in conversing with his bees, so he, too, began whispering exhortations to Gopie's. More and more he left the running of the grocery to his wife, content to sit in the shade on sun-drenched afternoons and watch immobile leaves floating on the surface of trench water, or listen to the humming of the bees, like an orchestra of diminutive horns.

Chapter 28

When Meena was six months pregnant she suffered from a craving for tamarind, which was out of season. Her father heard of a herbalist at Nismes who preserved the fruit and sold it to pregnant women, not only as a means of satisfying their indulgence, but from a conviction that tamarind possessed miraculous powers and was capable of influencing the sex of a foetus. All his expectant tamarind eaters gave birth to boys! Mr Ramcharran affected indifference to the man's claims, yet paid five times the price when the pods were out of season.

Meena gave birth to a girl, a great disappointment to the herbalist. He insisted that the prescription would have worked in India and promised that the next time Meena was expecting he would deliver the first batch of fruit free rather than see her fall back on green mangoes, which were available at most times of the year.

Although Meena's father was too discreet to comment on the

child's sex, her mother felt his disappointment as keenly as she was certain he did and reminded him of her sister, who began with a girl, only to give birth to a string of eight boys and earn her husband's family a reputation for potency.

After the birth Meena, who in the last hours had not once thought of Betta, looked at him as though he were a stranger when he appeared in the doorway. His presence was incongruous at that time, in that room, the very place their child had been conceived. Betta caught her expression, but, pretending he had noticed nothing and had taken its swift change at face value, he approached the bed and kissed her outstretched hand.

Meena's mother brought his daughter to him while the midwife busied herself in a corner.

'How do you feel?' Betta asked.

'Good. Tired too. And you?' she asked.

'Me? Exhausted. The waiting!'

'The sun's coming up. I was hoping it would be over before morning,' Meena said, somehow embarrassed by his presence and the fact that he had not asked about the child.

'You haven't even looked at your daughter.'

'I can't help it if I'm more concerned about you,' Betta rejoined.

Meena avoided his eyes.

Betta cradled his daughter in his arms, watched by Meena, his mother-in-law and the midwife, who had stopped what she was doing to see how he would handle the child. He was irritated by their belief that he was disappointed that his first-born was not a son, for he was sincere when he declared that his first concern was for his wife. Suddenly he wanted to be alone with Meena in order to explain his attitude, which had nothing to do with the traditional desire for sons. There was no sense in saying anything about the matter to his mother-in-law, who, unlike her husband, was bound securely to Hindu values. He was annoyed most of all because Meena had deceived him into thinking that she did not hold to the old ways.

But in the weeks that followed so much was made of Betta's daughter by his in-laws and their relations that he soon forgot the resentment which accompanied her birth. Once Gopie turned up with five cousins: three girls and two young men.

They all arrived on bicycles, two of the girls sitting crossbar. The baby was lying naked on the table, its arms and legs motionless in the posture of a prostrate doll. But, bewildered at the sudden appearance of six faces staring down at her, she suddenly began flailing the air before emitting a series of short cries, which ceased abruptly at the appearance of her mother.

Nothing brought home to Meena more clearly her change of status than the carefree behaviour of her sister and relations, who laughed and talked and ate without constraint. And after they left, zig-zagging along the rutted, baked-clay street and waving continually until they got to the Public Road, she felt that she had been abandoned and threatened by the same panic that overcame her during the first weeks after the birth whenever Betta left for the hospital in the morning.

Just six months after the birth Meena became pregnant once more and became obsessed with the idea of bearing a son. It was Betta who pointed out to her that creoles did not seem to care much whether they had sons or daughters. But nothing he said, neither his dismissal of the prejudice, nor the assurance that he did not hold to it, could persuade her to dissociate herself from a view she had been led to believe was the very aim of existence.

Chapter 29

Betta heard the janitor come over the bridge and went downstairs to have a word with him about the car. The janitor came to the door of his room and Betta at once smelt the alcohol on his breath. Pretending to have noticed nothing he explained what he thought was wrong with the engine; but when he was about to leave him the janitor remarked, 'Be on your guard, sir.'

'What?' Betta asked, surprised.

'On Sunday, Doctor. Be on your guard.'

'What do you mean by that? Do you know something I should know? Come on, man!'

'I'm drunk, Doctor. I'm so drunk I'm seeing two of you. I did look in the mirror just now an' see three of me. I'm drunk and got to be careful what I say. I don' want to look back an' regret my indiscretions. So I jus' say, "Be on your guard."'

'I ask you again,' Betta said. 'Do you know something I should know? For God's sake tell me if you do.'

'Doctor, I'm seeing three of you now,' declared the janitor, almost pleading with Betta. 'Jus' one indiscretion, Doctor; it'll be just after the end of Ramadan an' the Mohammedans' goin' have a lantern procession. Be on your guard 'cause it's . . . You don' ever get vexed, Doctor? You remember that time me an' Cook was off sick? I wasn' sick, I was *in*disposed. That's what my uncle used to say when his creditors come on a Sunday morning. "Tell them I *in*disposed." I was a small boy an' I thought he did mean he didn' got any money. Half of what people does say I didn' understand when I was in short pants, and is only when I go into long pants I start understanding a lot. I'm sure is the pants did do it. But I know you did suspect my indisposition, Doctor, that I wasn' in debt or genuine sick. To tell the truth, I only talkin' like this 'cause I so shame that you didn' say anything when I come back. You didn' say, "I know you wasn' sick. I know somebody big put you and Cook up to this." But you're not that kind of man, Doctor. . . .'

Betta listened, hoping that his condition would indeed lead him to the indiscretion he feared for himself. The cook said that he drank heavily, but it was the first time Betta saw him drunk, suspecting that in the past he locked himself in whenever he was in that state.

'Get vexed, ne, Doctor? Jus' this one time,' the janitor pleaded. 'Jus' so I could feel good and say, "I was right to do what I do." Anyway, I say already, "Be on your guard." I not saying nothing else because I can feel the indiscretions welling up in me. Now you can't say I did tell you anything. I'll only deny it. An' you can't say I did *not* tell you anything. I do it because when I was indisposed you did act like a gentleman. Doctor, permit me to ask you one question. What the estate manager got against you? . . .'

'Ah,' Betta put in. 'It's the estate manager.'

'Doctor, I jus' want to know what he got against you, that's all. It's estate talk that the two of you had words. That wasn't a indiscretion, it was a enquiry.'

'Tell me what you heard,' Betta asked. 'I won't tell anyone you told me. . . . Do you want us to come to harm because you kept what you know to yourself?'

'Harm, Doctor? I didn' say nothing 'bout harm. Please don' go and say I tell you you goin' come to harm! You're talking 'bout powerful people. 'Bout very powerful persons indeed.'

'Then why must I be on my guard if I'm not to come to harm?'

'Now that's a question, Doctor,' the janitor said, puzzled as to what he should answer. 'You're tying me up in knots, jus' 'cause my head a little kerfuffled. But we all have to be on our guard when you come to think of it. When you're driving the car don't you got to be on your guard? When you eating fish you mus' be on your guard in case a bone stick in your throat. Now I talking to you for instance, I'm on my guard in case my tongue slip. And that time a certain person say, "Do not go to work on such an' such a day" I was very much on my guard. I don' pretend my soul is my own, Doctor. I'm always on my guard, lest I get too uppity and say what I think.'

'Are you going to tell me what you know?' Betta asked, losing his patience.

'No, Doctor, I won't do that.'

'Very well.'

But as Betta turned to go the janitor said, 'Doctor, don' hold it against me. Ever since I was at school I was like this. When my friends used to boast 'bout how many strokes they get with the wild cane I nearly used to faint at the thought of how fine an' supple it was. The teacher didn' have to hit me with it. He jus' had to say "cane" an' I start dribblin' in me pants an' cross me legs with respect for adults who so wise. I'd like to tell you how much I know an' who tell me you got to be on your guard, but I frighten bad. Sometimes I'm impertinent jus' so somebody can look at me severe-like and force me to cringe. The disgusting thing is I does enjoy it, to my everlasting shame. I got to admit it. I like cringing. And the shame I feel afterwards! You're a doctor; is that normal? Suppose I had children what example could I set them? If I had six children that would be six cringers who would get married an' bring up, say, four cringers each. Now six times four make twenty-four. Not to mention their wives, who mos' likely would be cringers themselves, 'cause like does married to like. No, Doctor, I want heroic children, but I know they would either cringe their way through life or despise me.'

'All right, that's enough,' Betta said sternly. 'You're not going to say why I must be on my guard, so that's the end of the matter.'

'Don' hold it against me, Doctor,' he said, his eyes following Betta up the stairs.

The janitor threw himself on his bed and fell asleep soon afterwards, as though the conversation he had just had did not in fact take place.

On Saturday night Betta drove home from his in-laws, where he had taken Meena and their child for a few days. They had quarrelled because she wanted him to stay at her parents' home as well. If it was dangerous for her to remain in the house it was just as dangerous for him.

'If you thought the janitor was lying because he was drunk,' Meena had said, 'why're you sending me away?'

'It's not only that,' he told her. 'I must stay in case I'm called out to a patient.'

Meena was not convinced and hardly responded to his farewell.

On returning home Betta reflected on his situation. In the end he was relieved that things might be coming to a head. Over the last year he had been in a limbo between action and inaction. On his rounds aback the sight of a horse ridden by a European reminded him of his opponent. Since the manager's last visit he had learned that the field manager who had accompanied him was in his power. Betta recalled the odd behaviour of the field manager during the visit, his apparent unwillingness to be associated with the estate manager's threats. He later discovered that the man's secret liaison with an East Indian woman had come to his superior's ears, thus giving the latter a hold on him, for his marriage was at stake should his wife learn of the visits to the woman who lived aback.

He recalled the effect of the janitor's words, 'What's the estate manager got against you?' And in recalling them he wondered what the Mulvi Sahib would do in that situation. When it came to it was he prepared to put his wife and girl child at risk? He longed to tell the Mulvi Sahib he understood how he felt about the idea of an East Indian joining the Christian Church; for now, threatened with the possibility of danger from without and panic from within, it was to the tenets of traditional Indian thought that he turned for guidance.

The mosque yard was filled with a crowd of men and youths, many of them waiting to take their turn at the two standpipes before entering the place of worship, whose interior could not be defiled by the impurity of an unwashed body. What did he have to do with Christianity, which recognized no spiritual difference between the right and left hands, and the Christian Church, which permitted worshippers to enter its places of worship wearing shoes and dressed as though they were on their way to a public dance hall?

And it's precisely why the Mulvi Sahib despises me, he thought, because I can only see clearly when I'm threatened. All these ifs and buts, as if I have a choice. And what of my hatred of the Pujaree, my desire for Rani and all these secret wishes of love and destruction?

Betta could not suppress a certain irrational hostility towards the Merrimans, at the very moment when he was castigating himself for 'not seeing things clearly'. He resented their influence on Meena and Gopie, since it helped to erect a resistance to the dwindling influence of their Hindu background.

Roused by his reflections and the images that crowded one another in his mind – the Indian child Meena had persuaded him not to adopt, the yoga teacher staring down at his feet joined together in an extraordinary posture of repose, Muslim youths leaving the mosque following an hour of instruction, men and women jostling one another by a stretch of trench water after a funeral to perform an act of purification – Betta prayed silently that his waiting should be over.

The next night Betta locked and bolted his back door and sat at his window. He had not lit a single lamp and was able to watch the road without being seen. Red and white lights danced in the mosque yard without any apparent purpose, until, before long, they were seen to assemble in groups. At the windows of the police station the constables on night duty were craning their necks to see the procession move off towards the Public Road.

It moved off silently, the precursor of the next day's celebrations with its mutual present-giving of sweets, sugar cake and goat's milk in calabashes. And he watched without comprehending the significance of the lights and the last day of abstinence.

Betta was taken completely by surprise when a crash resounded throughout the house. He leapt up and shouted, 'Who's it?' But there was no answer. He had not even taken the precaution of arming himself and could now only stand helplessly awaiting the outcome of the assault on his back door. On hearing the second blow he opened the front door, remembering that his porch and stairs could be seen from the police station. He descended the stairs carefully, intending to go to the station for assistance; but on arriving at the foot of the staircase he heard someone shout, 'Look! He at the front!'

Betta ran off in the direction of the sea and later was to ask himself why. Why not towards the station, whose windows were occupied by policemen in a position to help him? He made for the gloom of the bushes between the house and the sea, where not even the animals ventured, leaping across the low bushes until his legs were bruised from contact with the matted vegetation. The trample of feet drove him on until he found himself struggling to keep a hold in the viscous mud to which the firmer ground had given way.

'We got him!' a voice called out. 'He on the mud!'

Betta came to the foreshore where two boats moored close together in a channel were hidden by the bushes, and in a desperate effort to escape from his pursuers leapt into the water separating him from the craft.

'Lef him,' another voice called. 'The mud goin' get him.'

Had the men possessed a torch they would have seen the boat to which Betta was clinging only about twenty feet away from them, beyond the courida bushes, which appeared so mysterious and inaccessible from the house, belonging neither to sea nor land. He had heard the men stop and knew that they were afraid to come out after him. Mystified by their silence he was almost overcome by the urge to call out and ask if they were still there. The intolerable waiting, made worse by the pain in his hands and the numbness in his feet, one of which was encased in the mud, had destroyed his ability to think. And now all that remained was the will to stillness, like an accouri in the presence of a jaguar waiting for the slightest movement to give its prey away.

Finally Betta was able to free his imprisoned feet and hoist himself on to the boat, at the bottom of which was a scattering of hooks and fishing tackle and a broken paddle.

An hour or so later, on hearing the sea lapping against his boat he undid the rope which attached it to its twin craft, reflecting that there was an advantage in allowing it to move with the water, since it was only a matter of time before he became visible to the men as the water rose. The boat began drifting towards the shore with the incoming tide and Betta, fearing that the men had not gone away, used the paddle to propel it along the shore, only to discover that he was so exhausted from running and clinging to the boat that he longed to lie down and go to sleep. He recalled the information in the daily newspapers on the times of high tide, to which he paid no attention whatsoever, and it occurred to him that, had he been chased only an hour before when the water was still far out, he would have had no means of escape.

It was a moonless night and the only light came from houses on shore and the lamps on fishermen's craft further out to sea. And those were the images that accompanied him as he drifted off into sleep, overcome with fatigue.

When he woke up there was only the sea about him, the sea as he did not know it, soundless and inscrutable, broken here and there by metallic reflections from the mid-morning sun; and looking around him he saw no birds, no ships, nothing except the sky and the sea. By mid-afternoon he believed he was going mad from the effect of the sun. He had spent much of the time attempting to keep the paddle athwart his forehead and in a last desperate effort to ward off the heat had undressed and thrown his clothes over his face.

Towards evening, when a breeze sprang up and the sun had fallen away just above the far horizon, he lost consciousness, believing he was about to be overwhelmed by a swarm of flies.

Betta was picked up late the next afternoon by a fishing boat and taken to hospital when it arrived in Parika. For three days he lay in bed, suffering from sunstroke; and when on the fourth day he was able to tell the nurse on duty who he was, she informed the doctor who arranged for Meena to be brought to the hospital.

Meena, her mother and Gopie came to take him home. Mrs Ramcharran and her younger daughter remained in the car while Meena dressed her husband in the pyjamas she had brought him.

'Good afternoon, sir,' said the janitor, who left his seat at the wheel to help Betta into the car.

His mother-in-law and sister-in-law smiled, Gopie with evident pleasure at seeing him again.

After all she's a good child, the thought crossed his mind. And he was ashamed that he had dismissed her unjustly as being foolish and light-headed.

Constrained by the janitor's presence, he did not encourage conversation, and even Gopie seemed to understand.

'Mud, mud, mud!' Betta muttered several minutes later.

'My brother-in-law's sold his property and bought land in the sand hills,' Mrs Ramcharran said. 'He says farming is a lot easier, provided you know what to grow. I see fruit trees growing in sand with my own eyes.'

And so their conversation went, avoiding anything to do with Betta's health. No one even asked him how he felt, believing it would bring ill luck. And throughout, Meena said nothing.

Once Betta was safely up the stairs of his home the janitor drove off with his in-laws.

'Who's looking after Bismatie?' he asked, enquiring after his daughter.

Meena, who was helping him to take off his pyjama jacket before oiling his back, told him that she was with one of her aunts. She opened the phial of aromatic oil, put it down beside her and was about to apply the little she had poured into the palm of her hand on Betta's back when she nudged the table by accident, causing the oil to spill. But, instead of saving what was left of the contents, she stood staring at the thick liquid oozing out of the lip of the phial, spreading towards the edge of the oval-shaped table-top.

Betta leaned forward to right the bottle, but Meena pushed him back then ran into the bedroom to fetch an old cloth.

'What's wrong with you?' he asked, when she had wiped away the oil and taken the table into the kitchen. 'Meena . . .'

But he could see that she was fighting back the tears and did not press her to explain.

'You've been to hospital,' she said, 'and come back and behave as if nothing happened. At Ma's all we could talk about was you and I wanted to tell them that whatever happened you'd brought it all on yourself because you're so stubborn and that I'd warned you, but you never hear. You never hear! You ask about Bismatie. Where else could she be? You want me to bring her back here? Where's Bismatie? . . .'

She was unable to continue and looked at him, waiting for an explanation. He knew that she was against his remaining in the house after the janitor's warning, but he was astonished to learn that she judged him to be stubborn.

'I'm resigning from the service,' he said. 'I'll let them know tomorrow, so there'll be no danger to Bismatie.'

And Meena avoided any expression of sympathy, knowing him too well.

Three months later Betta and Meena stood amongst their scant possessions, all put away in wooden condensed-milk boxes of varying sizes. A brilliant morning sun gave the swirling dust in the street an appearance of a luminous red cloud. Someone had made arrangements for the Public Works Department truck to help the doctor's move from the estate mansion to which he had come as a bachelor nearly four years ago and was leaving as a married man with one child and another in its mother's womb. The dry weather had come again when the slime of roof gutters and the red-brick roads became dust and dung fires made acrid smoke behind the low wooden houses within sound of the sea and the grass wilted and died. The couple left the house after saying goodbye to the cook and janitor, Meena with Bismatie over her shoulder and Betta carrying a small grip which he placed on the back seat of the motorcar. He drove off behind the truck, past the mosque and its empty courtyard and the police station with its windows on two streets.

It was Sunday morning, the day the new doctor was expected to take up residence. Not a single vehicle was to be seen and the car sped along the empty road, slowing down from time to time for an animal which had strayed into the road. They passed the spot where Betta had seen the vultures and further on the Merrimans' house.

'You're not worried about staying at Ma's?' Betta asked.

'No, but I know she doesn't like me.'

'A year or so. It's the only way if I'm to save money for our own place. The house is big and it won't be difficult to keep out of one another's way.'

Betta did not mean what he said, having as little idea how things would work out as his wife. Lahti had answered the telephone and shouted gleefully at the news that he was coming home. Mrs Singh was out, she said.

'I'll tell her you're coming when she come back from the temple.'

Turning towards Meena he smiled and said, 'It's less dangerous at Ma's.'

And she remembered why they were going away and that she should be rejoicing to leave the place where her husband had been attacked.

'Ma,' Bismatie said.

Meena put the child on her lap. It was unseemly to be apprehensive when Bismatie depended on her. She was her mother and belonged to that endless line of women who had given birth and had been changed by the fact of giving birth and by the expectations of those around her. She stroked her daughter's head without knowing why she did so. Betta had said that she would look back on this time and find it difficult to remember details which were now so clear to them, and perhaps even the layout of the house; and the things they would recall most vividly would be nameless.

When Bismatie pointed through the window to a group of women gathering cow dung in a field Meena hugged her and started blowing in her ear, muttering endearments from her childhood.

In the distance a tall locust tree stood at a bend in the road.

'I know!' Betta mocked. 'Be careful!'

Bismatie looked up at her mother and smiled because she was smiling.

Meena recalled how in the months after her wedding when she was still a prey to childish reflections she used to tell herself that the road leading up to the tree was her life while the section beyond represented marriage, for she had never gone beyond that point until she married and used to furnish her imagination with houses and trenches filled ,with huri and painted aeroplanes landing on the river.

Bismatie fell asleep, lulled into a state of torpor by the early-morning heat and an endless succession of trees and houses, having forgotten that they were moving house and would live with her grandmother until she was three years or older if her parents were unable to amass the money to buy a house. And by the time the stelling at Vreed-en-Hoop came into sight Meena had fallen asleep as well.

BOOK 4
THE EXCLUSION

Chapter 30

Betta called several times at the front gate and then at the smaller side gate in Dowding Street. They were both padlocked with thick chains, a remarkable thing because his mother could not stand locks. Just when he was about to give up – thinking that no one was at home and that his mother had forgotten that he was coming – he saw Sukrum approaching.

'What's the matter?' Betta asked. 'Why are the gates locked?'

'Morning, Doctor,' Sukrum said, ignoring the question. 'I can't open. I got orders.'

'Orders from whom?'

'From your stepfather,' he answered, unruffled by Betta's authoritative tone.

'Do you have the key?'

'I got a key, Doctor. They got three keys and I got one. Your stepfather got another one. Miss Singh got one too. But nowadays I does take orders from the Pujaree.'

'Is Lahti home?' Betta asked.

'She home, Doctor. But she not goin' come down.'

'Will you call Lahti, please?' Betta asked, seething with anger at the cool insolence of a man who had accepted and abused his mother's hospitality for years.

'Lahti not goin' come, I tell you, Doctor.'

Betta strode around to the back gate and scaled it with a leap.

'Doctor!' Sukrum shouted, taken by surprise. He watched him go up the back stairs three at a time and only ran after him when he was nearly at the top.

'Doctor, your mother at home!'

Betta opened the back door and saw an old woman shelling peas in a corner. She looked up, paid Betta no further attention and carried on with her work. Through the dining room he went and into the drawing room. He saw the Pujaree and his mother sitting in the corner where they received their intimates. Mrs

Singh stared at her son as though she were suddenly confronted with a burglar at the dead of night.

'Why are the gates locked?' Betta demanded to know.

Neither answered him and his mother's confusion was so extreme she kept turning to the Pujaree.

'Meena and Bismatie are in the car and I'd like to know if they can come in.'

'You see . . .' the Pujaree began.

'Ma, I'd like to know if you're going to unlock the door to let my wife and your grandchild in,' Betta demanded, ignoring the Pujaree.

Mrs Singh rose to answer her son.

'Your stepfather . . .'

'My what?' Betta said with such violence that his mother stepped back towards the chair in which the Pujaree was still sitting uneasily.

'The Pujaree,' Mrs Singh continued, 'the Pujaree and I have decided that we can't have you back in the house. Things are not the same as when you left.'

'And you can't put us up for a few days until we find a place to live?'

Mrs Singh consulted the Pujaree with her eyes, but he remained unmoved.

'You can't stay,' she repeated, half pleading and half angry that Betta should have dared insult the Pujaree.

Betta turned his attention to his 'stepfather' for the first time, but it was the latter who spoke first, remaining where he was.

'I don't want to get mixed up in a family quarrel, but your mother want for me to tell you how things stand now. You leave when she did want you to stay. She suffer all that time when you go to live with strangers and she din' complain. Your mother don' complain . . .'

'When I rang,' Betta interrupted, 'Lahti said she'd tell you I was going to put up here for a while. Why didn't you ring me back? Instead, you put padlocks on the gates and asked Sukrum to tell me you were out. You're a priest and you let me and my wife and child wait while you drink tea. . . .'

And the Pujaree, unexpectedly, yielded.

'Why not let him stay until he. . . ?' he said to Mrs Singh.

'No!' she screamed. 'Let him go and take his wife with him. Go! Run to her like a dog in heat! Isn't that why you went away, pretending you wanted to look after the sick? Is there less misery on the West Coast since you went to live there? Go back to her!'

While she was speaking the Pujaree stood with his head bowed. He had supported Mrs Singh in her plan to exclude her son from the house, but now he stood face to face with Betta, a medical doctor who had practised in the room downstairs and was respected in the district, he could no longer maintain his stand.

Betta saw his mother go to a window overlooking Dowding Street and call out for Sukrum. He had been listening from the adjoining room where he had followed Betta, stopping at a safe distance from the drawing room lest the doctor fell upon him in his rage. Not a word of the quarrel had escaped him and now, made bold by the call of the mistress herself, he showed himself.

'Why did you let the doctor in?' Mrs Singh demanded to know.

'The padlock still on the door, Miss Singh,' he replied. 'The doctor jump the side gate an' run up the stairs.'

It was the sight of Sukrum more than anything else which humiliated Betta. His behaviour towards Lahti, his parasitic habits, the reek of shrimps that accompanied him combined to reveal his own position in its clearest light. Resigned to his mother's decision to keep him out, he said to Sukrum, 'Go back downstairs. I want to talk to my mother.'

Sukrum waited, unwilling to comply unless he received an order from Mrs Singh or the Pujaree. He stared at Betta brazenly, challenging him to raise his hand to him in the presence of those on whom he depended. And it was the Pujaree who nodded towards the door, seizing on what he felt to be Betta's conciliatory tone.

Sukrum left the room; but instead of going downstairs he posted himself in his former position in the kitchen, so that he would not miss a word of an encounter he had predicted to Lahti, who believed that one day Betta and his mother would be reconciled and that he would come back to live in her house.

'I cannot take Meena and my child to a hotel,' Betta told his mother calmly.

'What's wrong with her parents' house?'

'How can I sleep in my mother-in-law's house? I'm not destitute.'

Mrs Singh shook her head, afraid to speak lest she admit her shame at her son's shame. A married woman's place was in her mother-in-law's house until her husband set up on his own. And at the thought of what the Mulvi Sahib would say, taking her conduct as confirming his opinion of her as a man with breasts, she wavered in her resolve.

In fact Lahti had slipped away to fetch the Mulvi Sahib. When Betta arrived she was in the gallery, anxious to avoid him since she learned that he was not to be admitted. But on hearing the unusually harsh tone in his voice she took fright and thought of the old teacher, the healer of rifts. Several minutes after Betta protested that he could not sleep in his mother-in-law's home the exchanges came to an end at the sound of footsteps on the stairs. Mrs Singh went to the window and saw the Mulvi Sahib hurrying up.

'The Mulvi Sahib!' she said, looking round at the others.

Mrs Singh met him at the door.

'Mulvi Sahib . . .'

'Lahti came to get me,' he said. 'Don't be annoyed with her, she was afraid that something might happen. What's the matter, dear lady?'

The Pujaree resented the intrusion and, attempting to reestablish his authority, declared, 'Mrs Singh don' want the doctor to stay here.'

'Why not, dear lady?' the Mulvi Sahib asked.

'Please keep out of this,' Mrs Singh said, avoiding his gaze.

'Dear Mrs Singh, you're not yourself. . . . And Betta's wife and child are outside.'

'Ask the Pujaree,' she rejoined.

'The doctor understand already,' the Pujaree declared, 'that he can't stay in this house any more. He did abandon his mother.'

'What does Betta say?'

'I can't tell my wife I had to beg to stay here,' Betta said.

'Don't go,' the Mulvi Sahib began, taking Betta's hand and fondling it. 'You and your family can stay with me for the while. I'm sure your mother will change her mind.'

The Mulvi Sahib had made the decision while on his way in a

taxi and gave Betta the key to his front door, although it had been left open.

'How can I put you out of your room?' Betta asked.

'Don't keep Meena waiting. She told me she doesn't know what's happened and the baby's getting hot in the car.'

Although Betta would have liked to discuss the arrangement in greater detail he left without more ado, glad of the opportunity to turn his back on the Pujaree, whose pretensions to power had brought him near to violence.

Lahti, from her position behind a pillar, saw the car drive off and was already regretting her action, for which she was certain to pay, she told herself. She looked into Sukrum's room, but he was not there. She found him eventually in his hiding place, only to be ordered out by him, enjoining her to be quiet as she went.

For a long while Sukrum heard nothing and took the risk of looking into the drawing room where he saw the Mulvi Sahib pacing up and down the large room and whispering. It was not evident whether he was talking to himself or not. Sukrum pulled back when an angry voice said, 'It's unbelievable. You're not the same person since this man moved in here. Even after Betta went you weren't bitter. Have you lost your pride? You and your husband have been respected in Kitty. What will people say when they hear you put a padlock on the gate to keep out your own son?'

'How you get in?' the Pujaree asked.

'I came through the loose paling.'

'How you know about the loose paling?'

'Lahti told me. Does it matter how I came in? Since you moved in Mrs Singh's changed. In fact since she met you I've seen things creep into this house by the back door. Look how that man's degraded poor Lahti! She practically keeps him now. I heard he hasn't been fishing for weeks and I've heard much more. Doesn't it mean anything to you?' And here he turned to face Mrs Singh. 'What would your husband have said? You were a woman everyone looked up to. Now?'

'You never looked up to me! The Pujaree does.'

'Because you pay him!'

No sooner had the words been uttered than she slapped him violently. And the assault came so swiftly the Mulvi Sahib had no time to defend himself.

Later she was to understand that behind her horror at striking the priest-teacher lay a deep satisfaction. But now she could find no action or words to convey her revulsion and stood looking straight ahead, as though waiting for something to happen.

It was the Mulvi Sahib who spoke first.

'I know you did not mean what you did.'

'No . . . I'm sorry. . . . You don't understand, you see. All these years . . .'

And she went on to tell him in a bland, unemotional voice that Lahti was her dead husband's grandchild. He had wrung a promise from her to adopt the child after he died. But several weeks later, having failed to comply with his request, he appeared to her and spoke peremptorily about broken promises. The liaison with Lahti's grandmother had been contracted long before they married and she was not to hold it against the girl. The next day she travelled to the village where Lahti lived with her grandmother, who informed her that she and Mr Singh had gone through a marriage ceremony 'under bamboo' and that although it was not recognized by law he always treated her well. Feeling betrayed Mrs Singh went back home without Lahti. And from then on she and her dead husband were to engage in a tussle which drained her until she knew that she would never be at peace until she took her husband's grandchild under her roof. She yielded but could do nothing about her hatred for the young woman. The Pujaree pointed out that Lahti's strong attachment to the house was proof enough of her dead husband's influence and she could only come to harm if she persisted in acting against Lahti's interest. Aji knew about her husband's marriage long before *she* did, and saw her as a usurper, especially as she came from Kerala. Once, anxious to get the older woman on her side, she told her about her feelings for Lahti, only to be scorned for her confidence.

'I had to put up with Aji all this time, with her scornful remarks and her insults. But it's Lahti, Lahti. . . . Oh, my God! To have to sit at table with her, endure her cloying ways, her fawning. And look how she dresses. . . . God knows how many children. . . . But she laughs as loudly as ever. If it hadn't been for the Pujaree . . .'

'Dear lady, don't say any more,' the Mulvi Sahib interrupted, alarmed at the change that had come over her.

'And Betta,' he continued, attempting to steer her away from any further confessions. 'What would your husband have said about what you're doing?'

'My husband?' Mrs Singh asked. 'But this is my husband.'

She placed herself next to the Pujaree, in the manner of someone posing for a photographer.

'What would your dead husband have said?'

'But I can't ask him,' replied Mrs Singh. 'Since I took Lahti in I haven't spoken to him.'

'You *know* he would be against it, dear lady. Why not be courageous and admit it? I've always admired your courage, whatever else I disapproved of in you. Once you used to confide in me . . .'

'But I'm married now. And the Pujaree agrees with me that Betta should only come here as a visitor.'

'And what about your duty to live up to the regard in which the community holds you?'

'Ah! The community!' she exclaimed. 'I take people in from the road. I provide the hucksters with a steady business. I feed the poor once a year and the Mohammedans in the district make their tajah in my yard, and I must think of my duty to the community! Isn't that a strange thing for a wise man to say, Mulvi Sahib? I musn't only support the community; I must be a model for it. A model for whom? For Muslim women who look out on the world from a window and dare not show their faces to men? Or for Hindu women whose husbands keep a gooseberry rod to beat them with when they answer them back? Do you mean the women when you talk about the community, or the men? The men who despise us for being widows and hate us for remarrying. I'm not a model for the community.'

The teacher, resigned to the hopelessness of his pleading on Betta's behalf, realized that any protest or explanation would force her to defend herself with the same desperate energy which, until then, had manifested itself as a single-minded ambition to make a doctor of her only son. He was certain that the view she had just expressed was the fruit of the Pujaree's guidance. He was not a man of words, but his influence showed itself in everything she said. She was no longer the woman in whose house he had lived for several years, whom he had schooled in the need for self-denial. He watched her as a child would watch something transformed into its opposite in the hands of a magician, at once fascinated and bewildered.

'I see you don't wish to talk with me, dear lady,' the Mulvi Sahib said, only to be interrupted by another outburst.

'Don't call me "dear lady"! And when you go home you can tell that woman Betta calls his wife that she's not to go lying to people that I'm her mother-in-law. Tell her if ever she wants to bring Bismatie here she must leave her at the gate.'

Mrs Singh turned away, and as she left the two men there was the sound of scurrying feet in the adjoining room.

'No,' the Mulvi Sahib said to the Pujaree, who was about to speak . . . 'I've known Mrs Singh for years and she was never like this.'

'From the time I know her she always been as she is now. She never was herself with you. She did tell me so. She say you make her feel ashamed about everything she do.'

'Shouldn't she be ashamed of her behaviour today?' the Mulvi Sahib asked scornfully, unable to abide criticism from a man he had known as a wayfarer priest who was to be seen wandering the suburbs of Georgetown with his brass lotah and a cloth thrown over his shoulder. To him he was a disreputable opportunist who gave East Indians a bad name and exercised a fatal influence on a good woman.

'I'm not goin' argue with you, Mulvi Sahib. Words isn't everything. But you must ask yourself if some of the things Mrs Singh tell you wasn't true.'

But as the Mulvi Sahib turned to go the Pujaree saw him to the door and accompanied him down the stairs. And after the two men exchanged greetings the Pujaree went and looked out at the saman tree. Above him he could hear the fluttering wings of birds alighting on the topmost branches and on looking up, saw a hundred swallows twisting and turning in unison under the morning sky. She had given him a pair of sculpted birds with lacquered heads on the evening of Divali after they had put out porcelain lamps on the steps, still haunted by her dream of a flock of birds watching the house from the telephone wires, despite reassurances of his protection during the journey to a tranquil period of her life. This was *his* yard now; its trees were his and he would have them cut down soon. He was responsible for its proper conduct and saw as his next objective the need to persuade Mrs Singh to bring to an end the association between Sukrum and Lahti, which was bound to end in disaster, and felt – something he could not explain – that there was little time left to put the matter right.

Chapter 31

Lahti arrived carrying two paper bags with provisions and fruit, which she left with Sukrum. He did not eat with the rest of the household in the evening and had to fend for himself or wait until Lahti cooked for him at about eight o'clock when she came down again after washing up and performing tasks she and Rani used to finish in about half an hour before the latter went away. The dressers and the greenheart kitchen floor had to be scrubbed for the next day. Wood that Sukrum had chopped had to be cut into small pieces to facilitate the lighting of coal pot fires. The other work – sweeping the house and collecting the soiled linen for the washerwoman – had been done before she went to work that morning.

'Try an' come down early,' Sukrum told her.

'I got my work to do.'

'I know. I say try!'

On her way upstairs she wondered what could be wrong. She hoped he would not be unpleasant to her tonight because she had worked throughout the day without a break to complete an evening dress and was too tired to put up a fight if he became difficult. Her workmate had been shown the door because she abused the concessions allowed them regarding the new and leftover cloth of which they were permitted to take away a reasonable quantity to make dresses for themselves. The new employee was taciturn and resisted attempts on Lahti's part to be friendly. She could not work alongside such a quiet person, Lahti told Sukrum; and it was the main subject of conversation between them since the new employee arrived about a fortnight ago.

Lahti had got into the habit of staying the night with Sukrum, so that they were said to be living together. But the Pujaree put a stop to that when he was no longer uncertain of the power he wielded. She had forgotten the time when she used to slip down to see him at dead of night, sometimes neglecting to secure the back door so that she did not have to force it and run the risk of being discovered. Gradually she had conquered her fear of mirrors which she discovered during those midnight excursions. The looking glass at the head of the staircase gave back little except intimations of another shadowy world, it seemed to her. She no longer remembered the night she went to him after her first abortion when, on returning to bed, she looked into the glass and saw a dog hanging by a rope. In those days she took him bread and ghee. Now, with her wage as an established seamstress, they ate cake with butter spread on the top and sides.

Although Sukrum's conduct had improved since their reconciliation there were times when he acted as if she had never left him and it was she who depended on him for food. More than once he ignored her when she came into his room and would not speak for a long time while she sat on his bed with her hands on her knees and her head pounding in an effort to discover what she might have said to him the day before to put him in a bad mood. At other times he would lift her in the air and swing her round until she was giddy.

'We're happy, Sukrum, eh?' she would ask invariably, blinded by his unusual gaiety.

The more independent she became financially the more she cleaved to him, holding back only because she did not trust her impulses.

Tonight she entered his room with that trepidation that never failed to forecast a misunderstanding between them. Just tonight when she had so much to tell him about her day at work.

'What's wrong?'

'Who say something wrong?' he said gruffly.

Sukrum had been pondering how much he would tell her of what he had heard that morning.

'I got things to tell you,' he said.

'What?'

'This morning when all that happen Miss Singh been talkin' 'bout you.'

'Me?'

He pulled back in time, thinking that if she found out what he had heard their relationship might change in some way he could not foresee.

'Miss Singh say how you gettin' good at dressmaking. She like it when you dress good.'

'She say so?' Lahti asked, with evident satisfaction.

'Last night I see Bai,' Sukrum lied, changing the subject abruptly for fear that he might not be able to keep up the pretence.

'Where?'

'In town,' Sukrum answered. 'I talk to him. He goin' to the dogs. I say, "You goin' to the dogs," but he so stupid he din' know what I talkin' about. . . . If I promise to married you what you'd say?'

Lahti did not reply. Sukrum lost his temper, feeling slighted by the coolness with which she never failed to meet his proposals of marriage. He called to mind the weeks when he almost went mad because she treated him like a leper.

'You hear what I say?' he said.

'I hear you. I don' want to get married.'

'Get out!' Sukrum ordered.

'But we in' eat yet,' Lahti protested.

'We not goin' eat!' he bellowed. 'Out o' my room!'

Lahti rose and left. But when she was halfway up the back stairs Sukrum shouted from the doorway, 'Come back, you fool! I got something to tell you.'

He ran after her and on his grasping her arm she shook free, only to be seized once more and pulled towards a lover who, unknown to her, was as frightened by his action as she had been.

'Come on,' he said gently, 'I was only vex 'cause I love you an' you don' even want to answer when I say . . .'

'You don' love me!' she exclaimed.

'Come an' sit 'pon the bed and I goin' show you.'

And she was lifted by the hands that had never failed to calm her. And they made love on his bed, unaware of the occasional noises that expired on being heard, voices from Dowding Street, a barking dog or a gust of wind. Then, suddenly, the intrusion was palpable, a sharp knock on the door that resounded in the small room, causing Lahti to start.

'I not answering,' Sukrum said.

But she got up and dressed hastily. He eventually opened the door and saw the Pujaree standing before him, stern-faced and silent. Sukrum's impertinent manner deserted him at the unexpected meeting and he stood agape in the open doorway. Then turning round, he said, 'Is the Pujaree.'

'I can come in?' the Pujaree asked.

'Yes, come in,' Sukrum said, weak from the feeling of foreboding that gripped him.

Lahti forced a smile and said that she was about to leave. 'I goin' to see you upstairs,' the Pujaree told her.

Once the door was closed Sukrum pointed to his bed and, having recovered his composure somewhat, thrust his hands in his pockets and stood before his guest with something of his usual jaunty appearance.

'I been thinking 'bout coming to see you about Lahti for a long time. But Mrs Singh tell me I should wait. She got a personal interest in Lahti.'

'I know how personal she interest is,' Sukrum could not help saying.

'If you want to stay you goin' have to marry Lahti.'

Sukrum hesitated while the Pujaree's words acquired their full significance, then, with an outburst of laughter, bared his teeth.

'You want me to married her?'

'Will you or won't you?'

'Yes, man. You tell Miss Singh I goin' married Lahti if she order me to. All she got to say is, "Sukrum, married Lahti," and she won't got to twist me hand before I say yes. . . . But suppose Lahti don' want to married me?'

'She'll marry you.'

'How you know?'

'Don' waste my time.'

The Pujaree did not take Sukrum's question at face value, thinking that he could not resist being difficult.

Believing that it was enough to have said what he came to say he decided to leave the rest to Mrs Singh as she and he had decided. Meanwhile he started to question Sukrum about himself, his background and his relationship with Lahti.

Sukrum

'I see this house from underneath. I know it better from underneath than from outside and inside.'

The Pujaree was to recall – for no particular reason – this remark.

No, he had no regrets about his behaviour when Bai was ill and he often left him for the better part of the day on his own. As a boy he enjoyed looking after his mother and sister when they were sick, but when he grew up he could not stand being in the presence of sick people. Yes, he believed he loved Lahti, but that was his business; he was not concerned about who was in love with whom. Loyalty? What did it mean? Being faithful to someone! Well, Lahti had to be faithful to him. As for himself he was not interested in other women. Whether he suffered or not when Lahti broke off with him was again his business. But she would never do it again. Yes, he was sure! People did not do things like that twice to him. The doctor? He could not understand why Mrs Singh would not allow him to come back and live there, but that was her business. He did not dislike or like Dr Singh. He never did him anything, so why should he dislike him? He once disliked a teacher, yes. He remembered him well. He had disliked other people since the teacher, but not as much. The teacher? He stuck a pair of compasses into his bicycle wheel seventeen times. School? He disliked it. He had no idea why. The teachers were continually examining children's hair for nits and telling them not to use coconut oil. No, he would not come to his temple. He used to attend Kali Mai puja ceremonies in the Courantyne, but a lot of people went who did not go to temple. In fact many creoles went, taking flowers, oleander and hibiscus and animals from their yard to be sacrificed. Yes, he did consider himself to be intelligent. Lahti? Lahti was stupid. He thought he loved her because she dressed well. No, he would not mind if she wore a sari. Why should he mind? He would not mind if she went naked skin. It was not his business. Yes, he might stop loving her. Yes, he would mind. Contradictions? What is a contradiction? Oh . . . but why should he care if he contradicted himself? Odd? He was not odd. Well, if people thought he was odd it was their business. No, Bai did not think him odd. He had not seen him since he left. Yes, he was a bit frightened of Georgetown because there were far more creoles there than East Indians. And the East Indians were either very rich or very poor. No? At least it looked so to him. Yes, he lived in the dosshouse for more than a year and for a time in Ramsaroop's Dharm Sala. He remembered the dosshouse very well. There was a lot of coughing, hawking and spitting. Sometimes he went for weeks without a proper night's sleep. He did not like sleeping in the open because he was afraid of the stray dogs. A man sleeping on his own in an alleyway was attacked by stray dogs, because they thought he was dead. In the dosshouse he was afraid of the rats and outside it were the stray dogs. No, he was not afraid of getting married. He might have to settle down. He liked travelling about from place to place. Once he went into the interior with a team from the Forestry Department. They went to cut lines. His job was measuring the diameter of tree trunks with callipers. He did not like the interior because he was afraid the trees would fall down on him. Fighting? He had been in many fights. He was not afraid of fighting. The scar across his bowels was the result of a knife fight over a bed in the dosshouse in Broad Street. He was taken to hospital to be stitched up. Since then he had been involved in many fights. Why should he admit to striking Lahti? His relations with her were his business! If he treated Lahti badly why did she not leave him? He did not treat her badly. Bai? He had not treated Bai badly either. He never hit him. Yes, Bai was afraid of him, but he had no reason to be because he was his friend. More than once he had defended him. Bai was ungrateful; he preferred Georgetown so-called friends. No, he was not jealous of Bai. He, too, could go and live in Georgetown if he wanted. Sometimes he did go there during the day to buy fish for himself and Lahti. She liked baked snapper, which they ate from time to time. He was not ashamed of being partly supported by Lahti. She would not be ashamed of being supported by him.

The Pujaree recalled Sukrum's expression when he said Mrs

Singh expected him to treat Lahti well if they married. Sukrum stared at him as if he had been insulted.

'I not Bai,' he said in the end, when he could trust himself to speak. 'Lahti not marrying you or Miss Singh. If she married me you. . . .'

Sukrum thought of the conversation he had overheard and Mrs Singh's contempt for Lahti, but resisted the temptation to turn his knowledge to account in the same way as he had held back from imparting it to Lahti, certain that he could take advantage of it at a later date.

'I not goin' let you provoke me,' Sukrum declared, surprised at his success in mastering his anger. He told himself that when all was said and done the Pujaree and he had the same poverty-stricken background, and there was no reason to feel inferior to him. One day he would settle. Meanwhile he must do his best to make him and Mrs Singh believe that he was obeying their instructions. There was bound to be a dowry of some sort at the bottom of the matter.

'All right, Pujaree, I promise to treat she good. You satisfied?'

'We goin' see that she agree to marry you,' the Pujaree said.

The Pujaree relayed his conversation with Sukrum to Mrs Singh, who undertook to find out from Lahti whether she wanted to marry her lover and to persuade the young woman in case she did not.

The next evening Mrs Singh was able to inform the Pujaree that Lahti had consented and that it only remained for them to plan the wedding. They discussed the couple's dowry, which Mrs Singh fixed at fifty dollars. But the Pujaree pointed out that it was a trifling sum compared to what Rani and Tipu had received. Lahti was bound to be offended. Mrs Singh raised the dowry to seventy-five dollars and the Pujaree gave in, pained at her vindictiveness.

Chapter 32

Lahti was not allowed to go down to visit Sukrum for the two-week period preceding the marriage as prescribed by the astrologer, who foretold a happy future for the bride and groom provided they observed the sutras and satisfied the aspirations of their dead ancestors for many sons. The date for the wedding was set by the astrologer, a bearded man reputed to be more than one hundred years old.

The marriage presented Mrs Singh with another occasion to demonstrate her generosity to the inhabitants of Kitty, Newtown and Bel Air.

People commented on the lavish preparations and the generous tables, all for a young woman who was not by any means Mrs Singh's favourite. On the final night of the celebrations there was to be a banquet for those who had once lived in the house, and even Bai, responding to an announcement in a newspaper, wrote that he would come. Mrs Singh herself went to the Mulvi Sahib's house to invite Betta and his wife to a meal of reconciliation. She took a box of sand-coloured flannel vests for his daughter. Visiting the Mulvi Sahib was a pandit who was wearing the Brahminical rope. He was also invited to the exclusive banquet, although he had never set foot in the Vlissingen Road house, but he declined.

The men interrupted their conversation about bondage labour to accommodate Mrs Singh, who sat apart, embarrassed by her son and by the presence of the pandit stranger.

Betta took up the conversation once more. He related how on the West Coast he had successfully treated a man suffering from teh-teh with antimony injections.

'But is it called teh-teh in medical circles?' the pandit asked.

'No, leishmaniasis,' Betta answered.

'And how did you find out about its treatment?' the Mulvi Sahib asked Betta.

'From one of the doctors here. You can't do anything about it when the infection's advanced; but if the lesion is only primary it can be treated successfully.'

They discussed the need for a local medical school and the work of Dr Giglioli on the anopheles mosquito. His strategy was directed to killing the mosquito rather than to curing the disease.

During this conversation Mrs Singh sat with bowed head while Betta stole glances in her direction. The night was dark and the Mulvi Sahib's birds had fallen silent. The kerosene lamps, lit even before the sun went down, had attracted a swarm of insects.

The pandit said he had read somewhere that every culture had its own specific diseases, preoccupations independent of the parasites which caused them, like nahra. Betta agreed, but cautioned that Guyanese nahra and mad blood were almost certainly found in other cultures; they simply carried names baffling to foreigners. In any case he felt that mad blood was no more than an allergy.

Betta believed that he was being questioned so assiduously because the pandit knew his mother by reputation only and was cowed by her presence.

He did not look forward to taking Meena to the banquet for the sight of food had been 'turning her stomach' of late, a good sign, according to her mother, who told her that difficulties of that kind usually meant the child would be a boy.

'What about. . . ?' the pandit began, but Betta cut him short, declaring that his mother never enjoyed conversations about sickness.

'Meena, why not show Ma the aviary?' he suggested.

But Mrs Singh got up, claiming that there was a great deal of work to be done in preparation for the banquet.

Betta and Meena saw her out, while the child held on to her mother's dress.

Betta said goodbye to his wife and daughter. He and the Mulvi Sahib set out at half-past eight. Betta felt much closer to his former teacher since the three-month stay in his house, indeed, since Meena and Bismatie moved out to go and live with

Rani. Rani's son liked taking care of Bismatie; besides, Meena was afraid of the Mulvi Sahib's stern appearance and preferred the company of Rani, with whom she engaged in long conversations about bringing up their children.

Meena usually spent at least one day a week with Betta and, but for the invitation to her mother-in-law's banquet, would have returned to Rani's home that night. She only changed her mind about going with Betta at the last moment, when she began to be afflicted with the sour excretion the child was sending up from her stomach.

The banquet had already begun when the two men arrived amidst cheering from those around the table, disappointed that the family of musicians were putting away their instruments after entertaining them for only a short while. Betta bent down over his mother's shoulders to explain in whispered words why Meena could not come. Her mood was completely different from that of two hours ago and he suspected that she had been drinking. He and the Mulvi Sahib sat next to each other between Rani and the goblet maker, who looked at the old teacher coolly, calling to mind the way he had once been humiliated by him in front of Rani and Lahti.

Betta regretted at once that he came. He could hardly credit the scene before his eyes, Sukrum's open display of affection – Lahti was sitting on his knee – the goblet maker's exposed chest where his shirt had been undone and, worst of all, his mother's tacit approval of the lax conduct.

The Mulvi Sahib was determined not to reprove any of those present. Saddened by Mrs Singh's woolly speech and uncertain gestures, he avoided her eyes lest she read his thoughts in their expression.

Betta turned towards Rani and spoke to her, but as soon as she began to answer Mrs Singh said, 'Kiss her, Betta. Go, kiss her.' Tipu sitting on the other side of the table was smiling foolishly, in no way put out by the suggestion that his wife should be kissed in public by another man.

Mrs Singh got up unsteadily, came round the table and in an impulsive action, drew the heads of Rani and Betta together, so that to those with an imperfect view of what was happening, they seemed to be kissing each other.

'I told you!' Mrs Singh shouted triumphantly. 'They've wanted to kiss for years.'

Betta seized his mother's arm and looked towards Tipu to see how he had reacted. Believing that Rani had kissed the doctor he was craning his neck in case the performance was to be repeated.

'East Indians must kiss more often,' Mrs Singh declared, bowing to the company as if she had made an important announcement and expected to be applauded for it. 'Kiss and do other things.'

Sukrum and the goblet maker laughed aloud and Bai, not knowing what to do, laughed as well, only falling silent when he saw how Betta and the Mulvi Sahib disapproved.

'I'm the mistress of this house and I say we must kiss more often. I speak two languages, Malayalam and English, and I say in both, "Young people must kiss more often!" Lahti is a lucky woman to catch a man like Sukrum, especially with such a small dowry. My husband brought me a dowry! Imagine a *man* bringing a woman a dowry. In his trunk he took to Kerala were brocade and silk and yellow gold from the interior and a tamarind-wood box. My new husband doesn't know about tamarind-wood boxes, but he knows other things.'

She went back to her place and stood before the Pujaree. Then, as everyone looked on expectantly, she kissed him gently on the lips, cupping his head in her hands.

'Let all young people kiss!' she said, raising her voice. 'I married when I was a girl and when my husband died I denied myself all pleasures of the flesh for twenty-five years . . . to what purpose? Twenty-five years that earned me a harvest of in-gratitude. When the rats get at the young rice you know the damage they can do. Rats get children, like humans. Or humans get children, like rats. Brocade . . . a trunkful of brocade and saris shining like kakaralli trees in the dark. My husband said once when he was up-river the house cat came flying in with its hair on end. The man of the house said, "Tiger." And my husband asked, "How you know?" And the man said, "The cat always behaves like that when there's a tiger prowling about." And my husband said, "How does the cat know?" The man said, "If I did know that I wouldn't be here now." So! There are those who know and those who don't. *I* know. . . .'

The Pujaree tugged at Mrs Singh's hand and pulled her down, and, as though rewarding him for saving her from disgrace, she embraced him once more, kissing him this time passionately and long, like a child who, having just discovered the sensual message of kissing, wants to do nothing else.

'I said I wanted to drink,' Mrs Singh said, when she had sat down once more. 'And he said, "No, what would the Mulvi Sahib say?" My first husband would have said, "No." And that would have been that. Rats! Some women breed like rats. I used to breed like a rat, but the mosquitoes would have none of it. *He* is the only one that survived. The ungrateful one.'

Mrs Singh pointed at Betta, her hand trembling.

'Don't go!' she screamed at him. 'Is that all you can do? Go? Even when you go where you want to go you'll have to come back, the Ungrateful One. Now ask the counsellor there. He will tell you what to do.'

Then, addressing her words to the Mulvi Sahib, she said, 'Counsellor! Should he go or stay? Should he listen to me insulting him or should he leave and go breeding?'

'He should stay, madame,' the Mulvi Sahib said quietly.

'Madame? The last time you called me "dear lady". I prefer "dear lady".'

'He should stay, dear lady.'

The Mulvi Sahib was anxious not to be responsible for an even worse exhibition.

'Dear lady, may I make a request?'

'Yes, Mulvi Sahib.'

'Do you promise not to get angry?'

'Yes.'

'Will you please stop drinking?'

'I will, Mulvi Sahib. But I'm already drunk. If I stop drinking I'll still be drunk.'

Then, as many expected he would do, Betta stood up. But far from being angry he smiled indulgently at his mother, placed the palms of his hands together and bowed with that gesture of greeting and respect he rarely used. Then, turning towards the newly-wed couple, who had not changed position since his arrival, he did as much again.

'You're not going,' Mrs Singh said.

'Yes, Ma, I'm going,' he answered, in a voice so gentle he might have been a child.

'Kiss her again,' Mrs Singh said. 'You were once like brother and sister.'

Betta bent down to kiss Rani on her forehead, but she bowed her head and in spite of herself began to weep silently. Tears escaped from her tightly closed eyes to mingle with the sweat on her cheeks and course downwards in an uncertain channel.

Tipu looked on, not knowing what to make of the scene, and saw Betta turn away to leave the drawing room.

Once outside Betta became – in retrospect – aware of the incense-laden air he had been breathing, the heat from the specially hung kerosene lamps the Pujaree found indispensable and the press of bodies in close contact with one another. He reflected on his shame, on the chaos in his former home; yet now he was overwhelmed by a feeling of relief. His animosity at his mother's earlier behaviour passed away at the discovery of her loneliness. Like a musician who has been introduced to quarter tones and found them bewildering, he examined his discovery from every angle, astonished that he had missed what lay before his eyes. She was an exile from marriage and from her country, and the last link with both had been severed at Aji's death, leaving her stranded on the shore of an unrelenting loneliness. Betta suspected that the Pujaree understood her longing for marriage and the accoutrements of a vanished past. The time of abstinence had also been a time of mourning, when her features became marred by faint lines, hardly seen, but perceived in the interrupted cadences of brief reflections. Perhaps the vision of the women in mourning had lost its mystery. 'One makes two; two make three, and three make an infinity of numbers.' Were not the women his mother, rather than figures conjured up by his fear of what the estate manager was capable of doing to him and his family?

Betta thought back on his last year abroad, when he made observations, most of which had since slipped their moorings. He thought back on the absence of extravagant behaviour in that strange culture, except behind closed doors, on the display of fruit in open shops and on the flower seller's stall in the long days of a sparse summer. They had all fuelled the longing for his country. But, in spite of his own experience, he had seen fit to ignore his mother's plea for help, he, who did not hesitate to speak of ideals. 'Choose!' the Mulvi Sahib had advised him. 'But don't deny the destructive power of your choice.' 'Words!' he had said angrily, believing him to be indifferent to the fate of the East Indian community. He had chosen; but his choice no longer carried with it the legacy of a secret shame.

'I'm a Guyanese!' Sukrum shouted.

Mrs Singh had been led away by the Pujaree, vowing that she could never face anyone again. The assembled guests had risen as a mark of respect while she retired, her head resting on the Pujaree's shoulder.

'You's a East Indian,' Bai protested.

'You're Guyanese, too,' Sukrum told him. 'You born here!'

He wagged his finger in Bai's face, daring him to contradict him again.

'You born here,' Sukrum continued, 'I born here. We all born here. How we goin' be East Indian when we born here?'

Now that the doctor and his mother had gone the conversation was carried on in groups. Rani, anxious to benefit from the Mulvi Sahib's knowledgeable talk, listened attentively to what he said. Besides, it was the only way to protect herself from Sukrum's ridicule. He had sniggered while Betta was bowing and now he was not contributing to the exchanges he kept his eyes fixed on her. She had been tormented by him and the twins while she was living there, and although, soon after she went away, she tried to be agreeable on meeting him, he was no less surly. She could no longer even bring herself to greet him when they met on the road or in the yard. Now that he and Lahti were married she gave up any hope that her friendship with the latter might be revived. When Betta attempted to kiss her she thought of Meena, who in the short time she had been living in her home had become attached to her. She would have to face Meena day after day even now that she was certain that her love for Betta was as strong as ever.

The Mulvi Sahib called Tipu over to take the chair Betta had left vacant. He enquired after his son, his work and his plans for the future.

'I goin' open a jewellery business in Croal Street,' Tipu told him.

But from Rani's expression he guessed that the young man was boasting about a project he could not realize in the near future.

'You've got a good wife and a son,' the Mulvi Sahib told him. 'What more do you want?'

'I want my own house.'

'Can you advise him to save his money, Mulvi Sahib?' Rani asked, betraying innumerable quarrels about Tipu's improvidence.

'Don't you save?'

'I do,' Tipu replied. 'Ask her. Is jus' that she don' like me giving my father money.'

'Mulvi Sahib,' Sukrum hailed from across the table, 'you married?'

Lahti, alarmed at her husband's impertinence, seized his arm.

'No,' answered the Mulvi Sahib calmly. 'But if I get married I'll send you and Lahti an invitation.'

Detecting signs of a quarrel Bai edged away from Sukrum, who wrenched Lahti's arm away and went on.

'Is which way you batty does face when you praying?'

'West, Sukrum.'

'West, eh?' Sukrum mocked.

But as he was thinking up another question Mrs Singh appeared once more in the doorway without the hibiscus she had been wearing in her hair, which now hung around her head in a dishevelled mass. She might have been away for twenty years for the remarkable change in her appearance. She had been drinking since taking leave of her guests and was barely able to stand upright. The Mulvi Sahib, thinking the Pujaree was behind her, hurried to assist him in persuading her to retire for the night. But there was no one in the unlit room, and before he could say anything Mrs Singh screamed at the top of her voice: 'Out! Out all of you! And you, Lahti, get out of my house! Go and breed somewhere else, in the rice fields or the cane fields, but get out of my house! Kill the snakes and the rats multiply.

Well this is a decent house. Take your sweet man and your dresses and leave, now!'

The guests scattered as if someone had broken into the room wielding a whip, all except the Mulvi Sahib, who remained close to her while she raged at the married couple who were the last to leave.

'You are drunk, like any common workman,' the Mulvi Sahib said. 'You are drunk like the people you despise . . . a woman! And where is your "husband", the one who taught you so much? Is he hiding behind you? Pujaree! Come down here! Where is he? Or have you left him under your bed? Tomorrow you will hate yourself and there'll be no point blaming it on Betta or Lahti. Did he teach you that your troubles were the wretchedness of the Kali Yuga and that you should not worry about the present or future? I also live my life submitting to the cosmic order, but I'm also responsible for myself. . . .'

'I can't argue with you in my condition. Leave my house . . . I'll send for you if I need you, but I don't think I'll need you. . . . I prayed for all those who went away, you, Betta, Bai, Rani, my late husband, all of you.'

'Can't you see what things have come to? Sukrum was questioning me, talking to me like an intimate. What is this fascination that Sukrum and the Pujaree have for you? They've brought your home into disrepute and will make you the laughing stock of Kitty.'

Mrs Singh stumbled across the drawing room and opened the door on to a bright, moonlit night. It was the season of falling stars and here and there across the sky there appeared at intervals incandescent lines of light that dissolved in noiseless explosions.

'If I need you I'll send for you,' she said, closing the door after he went out and bolting it at the bottom.

It was the Pujaree who had urged Mrs Singh to chase her guests away.

'I will not do it!' she had told him.

'If you don't I will.'

'They won't go if you tell them.'

In the end it was his threat to leave if she did not obey that caused his will to prevail.

'You've not stopped crying since you came up here. Go an' throw them out. Why should these people make you cry?'

For the first time he had been roused to exercise his full rights as her spouse and protector. Standing at the head of the stairs he listened and was surprised at the spirited way she had carried out his orders. The house was now empty but for the two of them.

The Pujaree had been working quietly to this end for years. All his actions had been regulated by his ambition, so much so that it would have surprised him had he been accused of pursuing the very thing that consumed him. Hardly had he taken in the fact of living by her side, in the house that had dazzled him for so many years then he found himself in the position of being able to make of it whatever he chose. He was familiar with every piece of furniture in the drawing room, having admired them during the years of visiting. The bedrooms he had come to know since he moved in two years ago. Tomorrow he would go down and examine the room where Lahti and Sukrum had carried on for so long. They were gone and now Mrs Singh could embark on a new life, guided by him. Lord Krishna created the world with the sound of his flute, the fertilizing element fróm which all thought arose, like bubbles from a stagnant pool. The storehouse had become a surgery, which was later transformed into a room of depravity. If life was change then he would change everything around him beyond recognition.

The Pujaree decided there and then to install in the centre of the drawing room a glazed earthenware model of Shiva, Parvati and Ganesha, garlanded with wreaths of vermilion flowers.

Chapter 33

Betta had found a house to rent in Plaisance, a few miles up the coast. It was near the railway station and, as he had been informed, had to be painted at shorter intervals than houses to the north of the train lines, which escaped the smoke brought by the prevailing winds. Meena was delighted with its appearance and size, and her first remark after going through the large rooms was, 'I can have ten children here.' Betta saw it as ideal, since he could set aside a room specially for patients who preferred to lie down while waiting and – after he had earned sufficient money – take on a sick-nurse and pharmacist to deal with simple cases and write prescriptions in an adjoining sick room. He could use much of what he had learned at the hospitals, given the space and the control he would exercise over the accommodation and conduct of his practice.

The only thing the Plaisance house had in common with the one in Leonora was its size. Meena remembered the latter as cold, continually assaulted by gusts of wind from the nearby sea. The treeless yard, soggy, except at the height of the dry season, was continually guarded by the janitor, a man whose character she was never able to fathom. Here they could start from the beginning, take on whomsoever they chose, plant trees between the house and train lines and, above all, furnish it to their taste.

'Tomorrow I'll start moving our things,' Betta told the Mulvi Sahib, whom he had taken to see the house in Plaisance.

Betta was now driving him home along the East Coast road.

The Mulvi Sahib wanted to speak about Betta's mother. Since the banquet, several weeks ago, he had been planning to choose the appropriate moment, but without success. With only a few days left before the move he felt he had to broach the subject, come what may. The car went by a line of dray carts laden with gasoline drums secured with ropes. The rattling noise of the iron-clad wheels interrupted conversation.

'I want you to go and see your mother,' the Mulvi Sahib said, once he could make himself heard.

'I tried, but the gates were padlocked.'

The Mulvi Sahib did not feel he could pursue the subject and said no more.

It was Monday when Betta went to see his wife at Rani's. He realized, to his surprise, that he had become accustomed to his separation from Meena. His experience on the West Coast had taken him into scores of homes and had taught him much about people's behaviour, which, in turn, had served him well in coping with problems which, on the face of it medical, stemmed as much from tensions at work or those arising from family relationships. He had seen men ailing over long periods, who made swift recoveries on being transferred to another job. He had treated women for malaria or bronchial complaints whose symptoms vanished after their husbands came home from the bauxite mines. While *he* had begun to relish the freedom he had regained, Meena, in her uncomplaining way, seemed to bear a deep resentment at their separation. Plagued with accidents, she had come to be uncertain about climbing a staircase or pouring chocolate from one cup into another. Two days ago she had sprained her ankle while romping with Bismatie and now limped around Rani's house supported by a stick. Those years on the West Coast, an apprenticeship as much in medicine as in the conduct of his own life, had provided him with insights into the murky hinterland of good men's characters. Where did he stand with Meena? He was certain he could not do without her. But what was the exact nature of their relationship? A patient of his who worked in the bush claimed that he had to start all over again with his family when he came back for a holiday after six months away. It was like weeding a trench overgrown with reeds. The children gradually forgot what he looked like and his wife began to grow accustomed to her independence.

Betta and the Mulvi Sahib had talked late into the night on many occasions during his brief stay, but had avoided discussing anything serious.

'We must talk again,' the teacher had often told him. But now that the opportunity had presented itself they both avoided taking it. There must be no dissembling. . . . And that Betta knew to be the most dangerous of all conversations. With his own growing maturity he felt that the teacher's knowledge and wisdom concealed a secret weakness which, should he chance to discover it, would cause him to act like an animal at bay.

The Mulvi Sahib got out and dislodged the part of the fence which he had cut away to accommodate the car under the house. He then went upstairs to prepare the evening meal before leaving for the Church Street mosque where he was to attend communal prayers.

*

Rani's son and Bismatie were sitting side by side on the porch of Tipu's house when Betta arrived. Bismatie shouted out to her father, while Bhagwan remained unmoved by his companion's excitement.

Betta crossed the bridge into the yard. The gate had been taken off its hinges and was resting against the fence where its weight had made a slight indentation against the dilapidated walaba palings.

Both Rani and Meena came out to see who had arrived. Betta, carrying the two children in his arms, greeted the women.

'The Mulvi Sahib likes the house.'

'You took him all that way just to see it?' Meena asked, surprised that her husband should have spent a couple of hours with the teacher when he could have been with her.

'Rani did make something,' she said, 'but it's gone cold. Apologize to her, not to me.'

She put her arm round his waist and Bismatie tried to push her away.

'He's mine!' Bismatie said.

'No, he's mine!' Meena retorted, pretending to be playing a game with her daughter.

'That's what she and Bhagwan've been doing for much of the day,' Meena said. '"It's mine!" "No, it's mine!"'

'They're practising for when they're grown-ups,' Betta teased.

Rani placed a plate of roti and curried potatoes on the table and they all gathered round to watch him eat.

'I'm being watched,' he joked.

'Who's watching you?' Bhagwan asked.

'Everybody.'

'It's mine' were about the only words Bismatie could say apart from 'Ma' and 'Pa', and Rani, taking no account of the difference in the ages of the two children, was proud of her son's fluency.

'Let me see,' she said, 'four twos are eight. Eight eyes are watching Uncle.'

'Why do four twos make eight, Ma?' Bhagwan asked.

'It's just so, that's all.'

'I got two fingers!' Bhagwan said.

The grown-ups laughed.

'Show me them,' Rani urged.

Bhagwan showed them his two hands.

'Show me your hands, then,' Rani said, disappointed that he could not distinguish between his hands and fingers.

Bhagwan promptly ran his hands along his arms.

'Show me your feet,' Meena said.

He pointed to his legs.

And Rani thought it unfair that her son should be the butt of the grown-ups' laughter. But she said nothing and laughed with Bismatie's parents.

After Betta had eaten he took them for a drive in town. It was Easter time and Meena and Rani persuaded Betta to stop the car so that they could show the children a display of chocolate eggs in a shop window at the corner of Camp and Regent Streets. Betta drove along slowly to keep abreast of the women, who had taken it into their heads to 'do' all the shop windows with their display of clothes and Easter kites.

'Ma, Ma!' he heard Bhagwan exclaim, on standing in front of a window in which was displayed an enormous yellow kite, a singing engine, whose tail, decorated with ribbon-like knots to provide stability in flight, was disposed round the floor of the window like the coils of a giant snake. The children pressed their noses to the glass, lost in silence at one of the wonders of the world. Betta himself left the car to contemplate the largest kite he had ever seen.

'Uncle, you goin' buy it?' Bhagwan asked.

'I can't afford it, son,' he answered.

Rani steadied herself against the pane and then instinctively put her arm round Bhagwan.

Betta went back to the car and waited for them. He imagined the Mulvi Sahib prostrating himself in the mosque while he was out with his family and a friend taking in the sights of a festival alien to his religion. He had told him of his father, a 'great man' whom he remembered making seven circles with a slab of 'pure' meat to ensure that he came to no harm and of his grandfather, who stuck knives in his body as a penance, then with covered head joined his hands to form an open flower, before intoning a traditional prayer. The Mulvi Sahib also remembered his mother, who never went out without a dupata round her neck and had dreams that she told no one except his paternal grandfather who acted as her confessor.

Betta felt he knew the Mulvi Sahib much better, a fact that increased his reluctance to argue with him. How he had changed! How they had all changed, obeying the immutable law of refinement and decay. Nothing ever remained the same. And yet the centre never changed; the selfish remained selfish until their death, the rebellious rebellious, their characters obeying a law as immutable as the law of change itself. And in spite of all he had learned about the Mulvi Sahib's background, at times he felt he knew him as little as before, that the centre of *his* character was concealed beneath the evidence of his unswerving faith.

Betta only saw the others coming back at the last moment.

'We were waving to you and you didn't even wave back,' Meena told him.

'I didn't see you.'

The children had grown sleepy just as the shops were becoming more interesting, she told him. And listening to Meena, he realized that she was now more talkative, like Gopie. Had the stay in Rani's home produced the change? Sisters and brothers! The relationship was a mystery to him, he reflected, as strange as the murderous quarrels between fathers and sons he had witnessed on his rounds.

They found Tipu home. Annoyed that he had been left no note about Rani's whereabouts, he sulked for a while, but was soon himself again, being too good-natured to bear resentment for long. He sat and talked with Betta after he had eaten and spoke of his ambition to open his own business. Rani was so familiar with the story that she had ceased to be annoyed at its telling and attributed no greater importance to it than she would to a harmless tick. Betta questioned him about the likely source of capital and wished him well.

He left at eleven o'clock, regretting that he had brought the car when he would have preferred to walk and listen to the croaking frogs and look down into the trench from the new bridge that joined Vlissingen Road to the street in which he was staying.

The Mulvi Sahib was at the window and confessed that he could not go to bed on a night like that. Betta sat down opposite him and told him about the kite and the children's excitement.

'Isn't it odd?' said the Mulvi Sahib. 'We know so little about the child's world, yet we were all children.'

''S'true,' Betta agreed.

'What do you remember from your childhood?'

'Not much,' Betta answered. 'I remember I used to think the train was alive. I believed the crossing was frightening and that no one dared approach it at night.'

He went on to tell how one morning they went to see someone off at the station and he caught sight of the engine driver at the controls. He had got a glimpse of the devil, he informed his mother.

On pronouncing the word 'mother' he stopped, barred by some impediment that lay on his tongue. He glanced casually at his friend who, apparently, did not suspect that anything was wrong.

'I didn't see a train until I was about fifteen,' said the Mulvi Sahib. 'I couldn't understand why you could buy goods with a dirty piece of paper or why no one else liked the smell of locust. . . . I saw your mother, you know. I met her on the way from the mosque. She asked after you.'

'Well. . . . I've learned one lesson from you. There are certain forces you can't control. Once you know it's easier to bear.'

'But is that enough?'

'Is what enough?' Betta asked.

'Is it enough to recognize the forces and come to terms with them?'

'That's what I asked you once,' Betta protested. 'And I said it could be an excuse for inaction.'

'Ah, yes. But even if you diagnosed the forces should you come to terms with them necessarily?'

'Isn't it what you always do?'

'No,' the Mulvi Sahib disagreed. 'I acknowledge the influence the Pujaree has over your mother, but I still try to fight it. Certain things *have* to be done. Lost causes can be as vital as those that can be won.'

'Why?' Betta demanded to know.

'Because you cannot deny the hero in man.'

'You mean it is right for someone to give up his life because he *must* follow his impulse to be a hero?'

'Not right,' the Mulvi Sahib corrected him. 'There is a heroic streak in men that cannot be denied. Children yield to it without shame. When boys go to see a Western they come out of the picture house spoiling for a fight. . . .'

'Boys, yes,' Betta said scornfully. 'But men!'

'Men feel exactly the same way. It's only that they've learned to dissemble.'

'How do you know about how boys feel when they leave the picture house?'

'You forget I'm a teacher,' the Mulvi Sahib answered. 'Besides I see them playing their make-believe games after they've seen a Tom Mix film.'

'Yes. I've seen that rubbish,' Betta said. 'If the horses weren't such good actors I'm sure the picture houses would be empty when they're shown.'

'Ah, but there you are wrong, Betta. Nothing can be further from the truth. It's the guns. Men, especially men, are fascinated by evil. Women have much more primitive characters; put them in prison and they pine away. Yes, Doctor, they pine away. I'm told many of them even cease having their periods. It is the very primitive mind that hates war, my friend. Not our aboriginals. They are planters. No, no, the real primitives, who spend all their time wandering from place to place in search of food, the shy ones! They can't afford to go to war, because they're always living on the edge of survival, in that twilight world between life and death. Once man learned to plant he looked back in search of Death, afraid it had deserted him. Ah, Betta! How perverted we are! When I hear you talk about helping East Indians I have my suspicions. And since you allowed yourself to be chased away from the West Coast . . .'

'I was nearly killed!' Betta exclaimed, his temper flaring. 'Did you expect me to go on and risk the lives of my wife and child? Simply to prove I'm a hero?'

'Why are you losing your temper?' the Mulvi Sahib asked, openly mocking him now.

'If you hadn't put me up these last few weeks I would have

said there was something perverted in the way you provoke me.'

'Ah, well. That's how it must seem to you. From my side, though, things look different. You heard Sukrum's statement at table. "I'm a Guyanese." Or had you gone away already? He said aloud, "I'm a Guyanese." When most East Indians still see themselves as Indians and not Guyanese Sukrum shouts he's Guyanese. Don't underestimate Sukrum. The cane fields can be a great educator. You've never heard him speak of his past, have you? No, he wouldn't tell you. But mark my word, you should show great respect to those who come to town from the sugar estates and survived, the Bais and the Sukrums. They are marked with the sign of the tiger, those the aboriginals would single out as being capable of changing into jaguars. They are not normal men. Sukrum would commit murder and live to be ninety without losing a night's sleep over it. The true warrior.'

'You're making fun of me,' Betta said, almost sadly.

'No, my friend. Do you know he was questioned at length about a man who was killed in the dosshouse he frequented?'

'But that doesn't mean he did anything.'

'He was banned from it by the owner, though. *He* thought he'd done it. I have a feeling your mother recognized the mark on him. Do you know the Pujaree worked in the cane fields as well? Don't worry. Your mother can take care of herself. She punishes and rewards like Kali Mai herself. You're the first person she hasn't been able to have her way with and she still can't understand why. "How is he?" she asked me. You're too much alike to understand each other. It's a pity your father died before you were in your teens. He tamed her, the shadow-bride.'

The Mulvi Sahib had changed the subject because of the effect his personal attack had had on Betta, who now seemed lost in thought, as though he were pondering a question he wanted to ask. Then, quietly, like someone afraid of waking a sleeper, he said, 'You are protected by the respect surrounding you.'

'If you have something to say, say it,' the Mulvi Sahib advised. 'You might not have the chance again.'

'Give me a direct answer: was I foolish to go to work with the estate?'

'No, you weren't foolish. In fact you had an obligation to do

303

so, being one of the few East Indian doctors. You weren't the first East Indian to be a G.M.O, you know. Dr B was one too, but he wanted to earn a lot of money, so he went into private practice. Look, when all is said and done all our plans are nothing in the face of the great manipulator, that tiny centre that remains still when all else is revolving. But when it moves everything else is shaken to a stupor; and the next day, on waking, you're surprised to find you're living in a new world. We call it history just because we have no idea what it is. A story it is not. The odd thing is that in many languages the same word serves for history and story. The great conspirators tell us it is made by people; but the fact is that it makes itself, moving according to its own laws. It has no morals, Betta; that is what is so frightening. It . . .'

'At last I've found out your weakness,' Betta said contemptuously. 'You're no more than a cynic!'

'Cynic! You're falling back on the vocabulary of lost arguments. What exactly do you object to in what I said?'

'Suppose it was true that history has no morals, why do you extol the fact?'

'Have you noticed, Betta, that every time we get to the hub of the matter you lose your temper?'

'Answer me!' Betta insisted, forgetting himself for a moment. 'I'm sorry, Mulvi Sahib. You ram things down my throat and expect me to swallow them. If we're in the grip of historical laws why bother to do anything?'

'But we went over all that once before.'

'So we did,' Betta admitted. 'It's just that I find the doctrine so repugnant I can't run my life like that.'

'Do I run my life like that?' the Mulvi Sahib asked. 'I told you we are obliged to die for lost causes. That's one of the laws of history. My point is that you must be aware of being manipulated. When history begins to whirl and twirl you move with it. But the superior person *knows*. The real hero goes to his martyrdom with a smile.'

'And if the cause is unjust?' Betta asked, genuinely curious to hear the answer.

'That's another discussion with more lost tempers . . . All of this because I'm worried about relations between you and your mother. But then it's all connected, isn't it? . . . Strange that we've never discussed God. Hindus rarely discuss their gods. It's the favourite pastime of Muslims.'

The two men went on to talk about the passive behaviour of the older generation of East Indians, taking care to avoid any controversial remark. The Mulvi Sahib pointed to the contrast between them and the younger generation, whose behaviour was often no different from that of the creoles. Even East Indian batsmen, once renowned for their defensive style, were coming out of their shell.

'Look at D! He made a century in less than two hours. Who would have thought it possible even ten years ago?'

Betta reminded him that the East Indian in the countryside was still very docile, and in saying so he thought of Sukrum's aggressiveness and his mother who, according to the Mulvi Sahib, had chased them all from her house while the Pujaree remained in the background.

'Sometimes,' said the Mulvi Sahib, 'I think that Africa and Europe are the masculine elements while Asia is the feminine.'

Betta preferred to hear the teacher talk like that, giving him the benefit of a deep knowledge of the world, without expecting him to defend himself. The thought occurred to him that the Mulvi Sahib, who belonged to the older generation, was far more aggressive than he was. Yet how could he see him in any role apart from that of 'teacher', the keeper of knowledge, the free intellect who was nevertheless content to submit to the rigid discipline of a repressive religion? Betta questioned himself, despairing at his ignorance of certain matters. If he mistrusted the teacher's discipline, whence his aversion to the Pujaree's sensuality, his partiality for incense and the encouragement of his mother's infatuation?

'When I was abroad,' said Betta, 'I missed the trenches. How can you miss a canal you never noticed before you went away? On my first day back I kept saying foolish things like, "Even the gutters are beautiful!"'

'After you left the dinner Sukrum shouted out, "I'm a Guyanese!" And it sounded like a cock crowing at morning. That's the voice of our new generation. Your "Even the gutters are beautiful" means the same thing, don't you think?'

'It does,' Betta admitted, uncomfortable at the thought that he was bracketed with Sukrum in the Mulvi Sahib's mind.

'Have you give up the idea of becoming a Christian?'

'Yes,' Betta answered, somehow ashamed at being required to answer the question.

'That makes me as happy as a reconciliation between you and your mother would. . . . There's a world of difference, you know.'

'Between what?'

'Between Christianity and Mohammedism.'

'Like what?'

'For instance, we don't see anything wrong in the sexual act when it is not done to make children.'

'Ah,' was the only answer Betta could give.

Brought up on the fringe of creole society and educated outside the public-school system, he was conscious of his ignorance in such matters, and a statement as self-evident as the one just made came as a revelation. But it raised a subject he did not care to argue about. He would never again talk of anything concerning himself with the Mulvi Sahib, for he felt, at last, independent of him. The mystery surrounding his words and actions, if it had not been pierced, had been dissipated by the acrimony of their discussions and the sharp diversion in their convictions about life and individual obligations. They had arrived at a point where the roads they would travel forked. He believed the Mulvi Sahib shared this view, for he had spoken about their 'last chance'. To this day he failed to understand the influence he once exercised over his mother when he lived in her house, like those words he used to hear grown-ups use, which he would repeat over and over again, because they bore a significance as magical as cascading stars: 'Anthropomorphic', 'anthropomorphic', 'anthropomorphic'. . . . He recalled that word, which had leapt out of the monologue of a creole visitor at one of his mother's gatherings, who manipulated his language like the flier of a soaring kite, guiding it among the mass of brilliant tadpole-like constructions over the elegant houses and saman trees in Kingston, where the sea wind drove white gulls to the madness of perpetual motion. 'Anthropomorphic', 'anthropomorphic', 'anthropomorphic', 'anthropomorphic'. He now knew that both the Pujaree and the Mulvi Sahib were the advocates of inaction, the two opposites, which apparently bore no resemblance, but were in fact identical. Between them was the tension of equilibrium, that centre the teacher described so eloquently, the quiet place where convulsions are born. For him it was there that lay the meaning of life.

They had fallen silent, their voices giving way to the great chorus of crickets in the sand-box trees, like watchmen of the night. Betta had grown accustomed to the smell from the aviary, which, at first, used to drive him to the front and a view of the street. He and the Mulvi Sahib were sitting in the dining room, just above the birds, and could see only the indistinct outlines of trees in the darkness outside. There were trees in the yard of the Plaisance house, too, breadnut and sidium. If he got boy-children they could climb them, he reflected, betraying a longing he had denied to himself and Meena.

Chapter 34

Dr Singh and his family had been living in their new home for seven months when they received a visit from Sukrum and Lahti. They came one morning after Betta had left on his rounds.

Meena hurried to the door, thinking that Rani had come. Tipu often brought her on Saturdays, when the children would play on the verandah and watch the last train to Georgetown draw up alongside the station platform, and a few minutes later pull away to the accompaniment of the hissing of escaping steam.

Sukrum did not waste time in disclosing the reason for his visit. He had come to borrow money. Having heard of Betta's success in Plaisance and the neighbouring villages he thought of his benefactress's son before anyone else when he and Lahti found themselves in difficulty.

'The doctor,' said Meena, 'I don't know when he'll be back. How much money you want to borrow?'

'A lot,' Sukrum answered laconically, seeing it as a waste of time to discuss the matter with someone whose natural reaction would be to advise her husband against helping him.

Meena questioned Lahti about her work, and to her surprise, received no answer. Instead, she looked at her husband.

'She don' work no more,' Sukrum said, flattening his hair with his hand, exasperated at the unnecessary interrogation.

Meena's six-month-old infant came crawling into the room and was picked up by its mother. The child, a girl, stared at Sukrum for a moment, then at Lahti for a longer while before transferring its attention once more to Sukrum. They were sitting opposite each other on cane-bottomed, straight-backed chairs, in striking contrast to their public display of affection at the banquet.

'What's its name?' Lahti asked, afraid that Sukrum's attitude might lose them Meena's sympathy.

'Gita,' Meena answered.

Meena left the couple in order to prepare lemonade for them. She heard Betta's car drive up and was so relieved that she went to the window to watch his progress up the stairs. It was the first time she had spoken to Sukrum, but the reality of his presence proved to be more forbidding than his reputation suggested.

From the kitchen she heard Betta's voice, then Sukrum's; and then she heard them speaking at the same time, their voices raised. Then there was a silence. Involuntarily she finished what she was doing as quickly as possible and hurried back to the drawing room with a tray of lemonade. Meena, unprepared for what she witnessed on her return to the guests, did not know whether to go back to the kitchen and put down her tray or stand her ground. Sukrum had ripped off the top of his wife's dress and was pointing at her and gesticulating.

'I'm not one of your intimates,' Betta said quietly. 'Put something on your wife's body and leave.'

Sukrum was trembling with rage.

'Betta, what's happened?' Meena asked.

'Sukrum's threatened to hurt Lahti if I didn't lend him money.'

'You lendin' me the money or not?' Sukrum demanded, ignoring Meena.

'No, I'm not,' Betta said firmly.

'Well, lend me some clothes then.'

'Get Lahti a sari,' Betta told his wife.

'And me?' Sukrum asked, speaking in the same threatening voice.

'You'll get nothing from me,' Betta informed him.

'You know Miss Singh put us out?'

'I heard,' Betta said.

Meena came back with a sari and took Lahti into an adjoining room.

'You think you doin' she a favour?' Sukrum asked. 'You in' doin' she no favour. She's family. She's you father grand-daughter.'

'What nonsense are you talking?' Betta challenged him.

'Ask your mother. Ask the Mulvi Sahib.'

Sukrum waited to see the effect of his words on Betta, who knew instinctively that he had heard the truth. No doubt when he had time to search his memory he would discover clues to the relationship in his mother's remarks and her detachment when considering matters connected with Lahti.

'Go and wait for Lahti in the yard,' Betta told him.

'I goin', but I coming back. You mother put me out an' I din' do nothing.'

Sukrum turned round on reaching the front door and spat in Betta's direction. The resounding crash of the closed door could be heard throughout the house.

'You an' me is cousins by marriage,' he was heard to shout while descending the stairs, and followed his words with a banging on the white pine boards.

He took up a position by the gate while waiting for Lahti, his hands in his pockets and his gaze fixed on some point beyond the train lines.

When Lahti came back Betta questioned her on Sukrum's claim that they were cousins. She herself had heard it from Sukrum, she told him. He had been listening behind a door, unknown to Mrs Singh. The doctor would have to find out from his mother if Sukrum had spoken the truth. Yes, she was no longer working. She had been dismissed because Sukrum had come to collect her wages before Friday and had quarrelled with

Madame, who refused to give them to him. The same thing happened twice. The first time she was told that her husband was never to come there again, but a few weeks later he turned up at the establishment drunk.

'When he drunk he don' know what he doin', Dr Singh,' she told him. 'Long ago he used to laugh and sing a lot when he drink. He does only laugh now when he sober. If only he din' drink.'

No, she was certain she had never heard his mother speak of the alleged relationship, although once she had said in front of her: 'My husband had many bastards.'

She and Sukrum had slept under the wall the first night they were chased out of the house, but they were awakened at foreday morning by the incoming sea. Sukrum went back to the house for his net and basket and every night they fished for shrimps and gilbacker. She told Meena that Sukrum did not find her frocks when he went back to the house.

'We in' got no money, Doctor. We does live on shrimps and fish.'

Betta gave her a two-dollar note and said he would try to find her work. If he did Sukrum would have to keep away.

'Tell him not to come here for money,' Betta said. 'I won't give him any.'

Meena saw her to the door.

'I'm surprised Bismatie didn't wake when he slammed the door,' Meena said, embarrassed at what had happened because she thought he would be embarrassed by the disclosures.

'No sooner things're going well than something happens,' Betta said. 'Did you hear him? "And me!" The damned impertinence. Everybody warned Ma about him, but she was so bent on having her own way she wouldn't listen.'

'Suppose he comes back?'

'For God's sake, Meena, I'll put him out,' he answered testily, for he had asked himself the same question and was planning what he would do.

Meena kissed him on the cheek to show that she understood.

'I agree,' she said. 'Things were going too well.'

Betta's reputation, which followed him in Plaisance, was enhanced by the low fees he charged and by his willingness to encourage proven traditional practices in his patients' homes. And after the successful joint lecture he gave with George Merriman in the local school hall he decided to convert part of his enclosed bottom house into a hospital when he could afford it. Meena had agreed to look after the new herb garden, which he cultivated with the aim of reducing his dependence on imported drugs and pills. The house and its situation next to the railway line were in some strange way conducive to the elaboration of such plans. All this, together with the freedom he enjoyed to conduct his affairs as he chose, had aroused in him a passion for work, so that he was up when the cocks began to crow. By the time the train to Rosignol passed he was at his roll-top desk, making notes on what he had learned the day before, about new poultices, herbs that were effective in controlling diabetes or the young leaves monkeys were reported to feed on. The remarkable knowledge creoles had acquired in the less than three hundred years of acquaintanceship with the environment had prompted him to embark on a compendium of herbal medicines based on their experience.

The East Indians living in the surrounding villages revered him and offered to help with any building connected with his plans for an Indian community for the sick. Unlike his creole patients, they paid him mostly in ground provisions and other produce, or worked for him in his herb garden or cut the grass in his yard.

When Meena's parents and Gopie came on the last day of the allotted period for celebration of Gita's birth there were half a dozen patients working around the house, who had either been recently treated or would be treated at some time in the future.

Sukrum and Lahti made their progress along the village road. He walked about a yard ahead of her, so that she was preceded by a column of fine dust which he continually stirred up with his white shoes. The village women had deserted the street in the fierce mid-morning sun and the only people about were a line of weeders in the overgrown trench. They passed the church and school, huddled together on an unfenced compound, and were soon on the Public Road, where they bore left on their way back to town.

'I tired,' Lahti said, noticing that the gap separating them was getting larger.

'Where we goin' sit down? 'Pon the road?'

In spite of his words he immediately turned off the road and made for a field with a solitary tree, under which a plough was lying on its side.

Three gaulings standing immobile a few yards away, stupefied by the heat, ignored the two intruders; but a flock of ricebirds foraging in the dead grass took to the air with a beating of wings that sounded like a great gust of wind.

Sukrum lay down and fell asleep while Lahti sat staring into the distance beyond the Public Road, towards the sea, concealed behind the pillared cottages and the matted entanglement of courida roots and the stone wall standing on the edge of the land.

What was she to make of her banishment from a house to which she felt attached in the way barnacles were fastened to the stone groin at Kingston? The discovery that she was the granddaughter of Mrs Singh's dead husband only served to add yet another weight to her burden of confusion. She had followed Sukrum from place to place, eaten in cook shops on the thoroughfares of Georgetown in the company of refugees from the estates, whose relations had returned to India or gone on to another stage of an endless migration along the coast, drunk from standpipes in range yards teeming with children and women, wandering in a frock she had not washed for weeks. Why did he rip her frock? When she possessed twenty he had not once gone for her wardrobe in that way. His strangeness was the strangeness of Mrs Singh and perhaps of herself as Rani saw her. Not a week used to go by without him assaulting her, at times on the slightest pretext, as though he had taken it into his head to strike her at such and such a time on such and such a day. Yet, since they set out on this journey without a goal he had not struck her once, content only to punish her with words, constantly adding to his vocabulary of abuse. At the age of twenty-three she was no better than a leper dreaming of the time when her body was whole and her hands were capable of performing miracles. Those evenings spent on Mrs Singh's porch in Rani's company or standing on the bridge listening for rustlings in the grass verge, were they not sisters of the mornings when the same hummingbird visited briefly, half-concealed in the hibiscus of an ancient hedge? She and Rani used to play at laughing and crying at the edge of the placid trench separating Vlissingen Road from the field opposite, imitating the sounds of pleasure and pain. There, so far from the house, Mrs Singh could not hear them and enquire why they were so foolish and did it occur to them that there was anguish in the world and enough of it not to be the subject of a game? They would wail and howl, weep and wring their hands in an orgy of pretending, or double up with convulsive laughter, confirming the opinion of many that the inhabitants of the house with many windows were 'tetched'.

Her involvement with Sukrum could not be placed in time in the same way as her association with Mrs Singh or Rani. He seemed to belong to her childhood, to the recreation ground of her village school, to her departure for the house which she could never leave. The Pujaree had asked, 'Do you love him?', to which she could give no answer, because Sukrum was herself. She could not think as others did, as Rani or Bai, or Tipu, who could separate themselves from those with whom they associated, say, 'I am like this.' 'I want this.' Sukrum's brutality was like the departure of bats from the eaves under their home, or the emptying of the gutters into the kokers at ebb-tide. She accepted it because he and she were inseparable. Even now, when his clothes stank with the sweat of their wandering, she was disposed to lie down by him. But exhaustion kept her awake and the most she could do was remain still and think or call to mind a striking encounter, like the garish pictures painted by creole artist sign-painters as publicity for films to be shown at the great picture houses of Robb Street and Middle Street in Georgetown. She and Sukrum used to stand below their windows to catch the dialogue of the actors, which provided the subject of their conversation while seeking out a pitch for the night.

Lahti yielded to the temptation to keep the two-dollar note for herself. That afternoon when Sukrum visited the public latrines over the Ruimveld drainage canal to relieve himself she intended buying a phial of scent at the La Pénitence market to help banish the shrimp-reek that clung to her person.

Sukrum was sleeping with his face to the ground like a man suddenly overtaken by death. The soles of the white shoes she had bought him only weeks ago were paper-thin and misshapen. They were meant for special occasions! He had worn his first pair of shoes at sixteen, he had told her. For years afterwards he preferred to walk barefooted like most of his acquaintances.

Lahti had kept putting off telling Sukrum that she was expecting again. She had broken the news the night before as they lay down beside each other and he took her by surprise by calmly advising her to drop off, that the following morning the child might have gone back where it came from. It was he who woke her, saying that they were going to see Dr Singh. She wanted to wait for him by the Public Road, judging from his reticence that he was unsettled and that their visit would come to nothing. Afterwards, she dared not tell him of Dr Singh's offer to get her a job, since Sukrum believed he had been humiliated by her working. He had taken her over gradually, first her person, then her time, then her wages and finally the last vestige of her independence. He had swallowed her, so that she could do no more than go where he went, trailing behind him like some kind of waste. In her family the girls used to eat their brothers' leavings and repaid the treatment with blind loyalty to them.

'Where will it all end?'

She recalled Mrs Singh's words when she caught her strutting about in her hundred-year-old sari in which she had got married.

'Where will it all end? Why doesn't Rani do these things? Where will it all end?'

Two days ago Sukrum had caught so many shrimps he was able to sell nearly fifty cents worth. They went to a restaurant in the Chinese quarter near the Stabroek Market. It was frequented by beggars, men and women who hung around like contortionists, with their legs in improbable positions of repose. Sukrum ordered boiled snapper and rice, and afterwards cane-juice wine, which was served in blue-enamelled cups. For more than an hour they sat in a silence broken intermittently by a fit of coughing and the drone of an insect wandering in through the meshed windows. Then, without a word, he stretched full-length on the narrow bench, rested his head on her lap and fell asleep. Clients came and departed while Lahti sat with closed eyes, hoping to be overtaken by a sleep that nearly always eluded her at day time. On opening her eyes at the arrival of a still-young man she gave a start, thinking she had recognized Bai. But when the client put down his bundle of broken umbrellas and looked up she saw that she had been mistaken. The umbrella mender stared at her in turn, thinking it was odd to find a young woman in an eating place of that kind. She closed her eyes once more.

They left the cook shop late at night when the city was in the grip of a deathly silence. She walked behind him through the passage and they could see the pavement lit feebly by the street-lamp. Overhead a strong wind drove the clouds like stampeding cattle. Lahti shrank back at the sight of rats scattering before them on the pavement and across the road on which a group of drunkards were making their way towards the Croal Street canal. They spent the night in one of the dilapidated sheds on the edge of town and fell asleep to the undulating voice of a woman singing in Hindi. That night Sukrum had a dream that men with rakes were searching for him, but was less disturbed about its meaning than Lahti.

They had gone all the way to Plaisance because their money had run out.

Five weeks later Lahti and Sukrum were charged with vagrancy and released after the police had sent them to the public hospital to be deloused and cleansed of the vermin they had picked up in their wanderings. But a few days after that Sukrum awoke in the field to find his wife dead beside him. Hardly able to summon up the energy he went and reported her death at the Alberttown police station and accompanied two constables back to the spot where Lahti's emaciated body lay beneath the tree under which she and he had sheltered from the heat of the sun on leaving Betta's house.

It was Rani who telephoned the news of Lahti's death to Mrs Singh and Betta, having learnt about it from Sukrum, who came to ask for a loan of fifty cents.

Betta was so disturbed by the news that he closed his surgery for two days and left the practice in his sick-nurse's charge. He went to see his mother, who received him dressed in the white of mourning. She showed him a newspaper with a photograph and the piece she had put in in the 'In Memoriam' column of the *Daily Chronicle*, which read:

> The husband, grandmother, uncle and other relatives of the late Lahti of Vlissingen Road, Kitty., E.C.D. wish to thank all those who sympathized with them in their recent bereavement. May her soul rest in peace in the name of Lord Krishna.

'I never once heard her cry,' Mrs Singh said.

Surrounding Lahti's picture were evocations of other deaths, of creoles mostly, Garraway, Sundack, Fraser, Chattergoon, Stewart, Kemraj, all with accompanying photographs.

Betta handed her back the newspaper.

Why did I come? he thought. To witness her remorse?

'I got her her job back,' Betta said, 'but she didn't come as she said she would. Sukrum must have prevented her.'

'It's his fault,' Mrs Singh said with some feeling.

Betta made a gesture to dismiss the observation.

'Fault?'

The single word offended his mother, who read into it implications she did not care to accept.

'Is it my fault then?' she asked. 'Sukrum is mad. He is abnormal. What're you hinting at?'

Betta refused to be drawn.

'Do you know he used to drag her all the way up to Buxton?' she persisted. 'Have you ever heard of anybody walking all the way to Buxton? In search of what? What is there in Buxton? Your father couldn't stand the place.'

Betta wanted to tell her that her voice and manner had become strident.

'Why did I come?' he said aloud.

'Why *did* you come?'

'I don't know.'

'Speak well of the dead,' Mrs Singh said, as though talking to herself.

'Why didn't you tell me that I was related to her?' Betta asked.

'What good would it have done?'

'Did you tell her? No. It wouldn't have done any good.'

'Would it have done any good?'

'I have no idea,' Betta answered. 'But if she is related to us why hush it up?'

'Not to us, to you,' she corrected him. 'I took her in. I didn't pretend she didn't exist.'

'You preferred Rani in every way. Yet Rani has no connection with us.'

'Enough!' she said sharply. 'I did my duty to her! Your father had many bastards. Do you think if we lived in India he would've behaved like that? When he fetched me here he should have said, "I'm the father of many bastards." But he said nothing. *He* was guilty of silence and she was his grandchild. Why do you expect so much of me? When you were small you used to say, "Where've you been?" when I came home, like a husband or father. You weren't entitled to ask me then, and certainly not now. I don't feel badly about not telling her. And as for her death, it's Sukrum's fault. Go ask your great teacher and hear what he says.'

Betta reflected that he had not told her that it was her fault that Lahti had died, yet she was behaving as if he had.

'I must be losing my mind,' Betta said. 'I know why I came: to find out if it was true I was related to Lahti.'

He wondered at his astonishing lapse.

'No, Ma. I'm not blaming you for anything. . . . They came together, she and Sukrum, to ask for money. . . .'

'Did you give them any?'

'Two dollars.'

'You don't know Sukrum,' she said. 'If he knew you were . . . Oh what's the use of all this talking?'

Their conversation went rambling on like a vehicle in need of repair. Finally the Pujaree arrived and Betta felt oppressed by the same distaste for the priest that always overcame him when they met.

'I must go now,' he said.

'Because I've come?' the Pujaree asked.

'I must go.'

'Why not answer him?' Mrs Singh put in.

'No, Ma, I won't answer.'

'Leave him alone,' the Pujaree told her.

Betta took leave of his mother, pained at their inability to speak to each other at a time like this, when both of them suffered the shame of self-revelation, yet could only think of blame. Perhaps the reality of Lahti's death was too terrible to contemplate and could only be evoked in trivial words. Perhaps every action, every word was a feeler put out blindly in an effort to protect themselves and others close to them. 'Forgive'. What an odd word. 'For', the ultimate prefix, and 'give'. Give in excess. Give what?

Betta went to Rani's house to see what more he could learn about Lahti's death. Neither of them had seen her dead body, because Sukrum only came days later to ask for money. He had said no more than, 'She did die under a tree.'

Rani told how she and Lahti had grown apart after she got married, and how, after she had her second abortion, she would not admit to having one, even though she herself had telephoned because she was so frightened.

'When she came back home she do as if nothing happen.'

'What it got to do with you gettin' married?' Tipu asked.

Irritated at being excluded from the conversation, he wanted to say something to impress Betta, but found nothing he considered suitable.

Then, just as Betta was on the point of questioning Rani on the break-up of her friendship with Lahti, Tipu said that according to his uncle Lahti's death was the result of her forgetting that she was an East Indian. She wore creole clothes, had creole woman friends and worked in a creole establishment.

As he spoke Betta recalled the sari Meena gave her, the garment in which she must have died.

He left with a handful of cherries from their back yard while they waved to him from the porch.

Is it we who are alive? he thought, as he drove along the East Coast road. Or is it the town, the villages? What difference does a death make?

And he called to mind the untold tragedies he had witnessed during his years on the West Coast, the collapse and dispersal of families. Yet *life* pursued its course like a river laden with the debris of alarming erosions. And between times there was laughter from the Gopies, the tellers of jokes, from children with time on their hands, from barbers, from women resplendent, from teachers with captive audiences, from frequenters of the Ice House and other notorious establishments. Creoles laughed as they ate, with enormous appetites. And this river, which bore the corpses of their unconscious ineptitudes, where would it flow?

Chapter 35

Gopie was married in Betta's house one Friday afternoon. Her father did not have to find a dowry because the future son-in-law was besotted with his bride-to-be. The couple were married under bamboo, but no one was in any doubt that Gopie was capable of taking care of herself. She was not the kind who needed the assistance of the law if he took it into his head to leave her.

Meena understood how Gopie was not herself, how she would have preferred to kiss her handsome, imperious young Muslim husband full on the mouth and clap her hands and shower those present with good wishes, and how exasperated she must have become when required to endure a ceremony that went on for hours.

Immediately after the formal rites Gopie took flowers to the Muslim girls who were allowed a room to themselves on the top storey, to satisfy the custom of segregation from men. They had brought their own music to which they began dancing once Gopie left. Her husband's family had invited many guests, who arrived in grand motorcars, the men and women separating on the lower storey.

The music of two celebrations was heard in the village, one from the women on the upper storey and the other from the veena and tablas on the lower. And there were those who noted that the music of the cloistered women was distinguished by strong rhythms and a certain frenzy, which caused old men to look upwards without knowing why.

The Mulvi Sahib had declined an invitation to attend the celebrations. Lahti's death had left him in despair, for unlike the people who knew Mrs Singh's household well, he preferred her to Rani, since she was the more vulnerable of the two. He sent the couple a pair of caged birds from his aviary, with instructions regarding their welfare. Only once had he met Gopie and judged her to be one of those people who made their own destiny, unlike her sister.

Gopie the tomboy.

'That's not her real name,' her mother explained to a perplexed guest, who knew it as a boy's name. 'We call her that 'cause she always been climbing trees like a boy.'

'She does still climb trees?' the lady went on, highly suspicious of Gopie's credentials.

'Only low ones,' Gopie's father answered mischievously, coming to the aid of his wife, who was finding it difficult to contain the woman's curiosity.

'How low?'

'Guava trees.'

'Your daughter does still climb guava trees? At her age? Her husband know?'

'Oh, he knows,' Gopie's father confided. 'He say is all right, as long as is not coconut trees.'

'Coconut trees!' the lady exclaimed, scandalized that a young bride with such unsuitable qualifications had managed to catch a bridegroom whose appearance and prospects would be a credit to a family of wealth and standing.

The guest craned her neck to take a good look at the climber of trees now that her veil was up and saw that her expression was not grave enough or modest enough for someone who had just been joined in marriage. She even suspected that her climbing activities extended to loftier trees than the guava and coconut. The poor young man might have been duped!

Rani, experienced in feeding scores of guests, had taken charge of the catering, displacing the lady brought in specially for the purpose. Meena made herself responsible for the Muslim women, who, once their food was brought up, wanted nothing but to be left alone. They had taken off the overgarments in which they had been seen to arrive and were now sitting around in saris, saffron and green, like butterflies quivering beside their abandoned cocoons.

Gopie's parents sought help in the village, so that in the end Rani and Meena were able to sit on the porch and confine themselves to supervising the goings-on, the arrival of the pots and the plantain leaves in which the food was to be served, to dealing with the complaints of guests who had misplaced a pair of shoes or a walking stick, and to tasting food before it was distributed.

'It's our last daughter,' Gopie's mother said, shaking her head with satisfaction. 'My husband say money is no object. What we'll spend the money on when she go away? Especially with my husband so sick.'

The inquisitive guest had not returned after learning of Gopie's character and her place as Gopie's mother's intimate was taken by a middle-aged lady, who approved of everything she saw and heard.

When Betta arrived, escorting Mr and Mrs Merriman between the guests, there was much fanning of bodies among the debris of a meal. A small girl was collecting the soiled plantain leaves while another waited patiently next to a man who was washing his hands in an enamel basin. The Merrimans were taken into the kitchen where Gopie was helping to carve mutton. On catching sight of Mrs Merriman she left what she was doing and rushed to meet her.

'Why you didn't come before?' she said.

'You know what it's like. Anyway, I'm here.'

George Merriman went off with Betta to meet Mohammed, Gopie's husband, who was sitting with bachelor friends on the verandah overlooking the railway station. George knew his father as an orthodox Muslim who acted as cantor in the Leonora mosque and had endowed it handsomely. After shaking hands they stood, embarrassed in each other's company. Merriman had a number of Hindu friends who frequented his pharmacy and often stayed for hours chatting with him. But, apart from two shopkeeper acquaintances whose shops were a stone's throw away, he found the Muslims in the village withdrawn. His wife accused him of having it in for them because they did not drink.

'Enjoy the celebrations,' George Merriman said finally, shaking the young man's hand once more.

He and Betta went out into the yard where they began one of their long conversations. Betta spoke once again of Lahti's death. The hardest thing for him was that she had just vanished. Every day he had been expecting her back to tell her that the seamstress had agreed to re-employ her, and the next he heard about her was that she was dead. He suspected that his mother was deeply affected by the affair, but hid her feelings behind accusations against Sukrum.

There was more to discuss than ever, since their regular meetings were now a thing of the past, what with the river between them and George Merriman's difficulty in freeing himself from his pharmacy.

'You hear they're talking about building a bridge?' George said.

'They've been talking about that since I was a boy,' Betta said. 'Talk, talk! Until Guyanese run the country themselves nothing'll ever get done.'

Meena came to enquire whether Merriman had eaten and although he said he had had a large meal before leaving home she brought him a plate laden with food.

They were soon joined by Mrs Merriman, who joked about how her husband missed Betta.

'He was like a fish out of water for weeks after you went away.'

She looked well, but claimed that she was worried about the future of her weekly court. People attending it had begun accusing one another of spying for the estate management and even she and George had begun arguing about whether controversial matters should be excluded, to avoid giving anyone the excuse to persecute them.

George claimed that incidents had been reported in many parts of the country which suggested that the official censors had become more active in the trade unions as well.

'Isn't there any dancing here, man?' George asked Betta.

'You only want to get at the women,' his wife said, her bantering tone conceding a more serious concern.

Betta explained that the most exciting part of the celebrations was taking place in the top storey where the Muslim women had been playing their instruments and dancing.

They had all heard about the erotic dances performed in secret, in clothes they were forbidden to wear in public.

'They're playing again tonight?' Mrs Merriman asked.

'I don't know,' Meena said. 'They're probably eating. Earlier there was a big crowd at the gates listening to them. From outside you could see their shadows at the window.'

They all waited to hear the young women play their instruments. But when the Merrimans left at half-past eight to catch the ferry no sound had come from the top storey and, for all the guests knew, the women might have been asleep.

The last night of the celebrations was reserved for the family and their friends and they were held in the bridegroom's parents' home in Leonora. Meena went with her parents a few hours after Gopie's departure, but Betta stayed home to attend to his patients whom he had been treating in the open at the back of his yard, where two goats belonging to neighbours were tethered and the ground was strewn with rotting breadfruit. He could not but compare the sumptuous celebrations with the lot of some of his patients and fancied that many of them were judging him, that the unsmiling ones would normally have smiled when he spoke to them, and that the smiles of those who responded to his prompting were full of sarcasm, inspired from the music and the lavish consumption of food. His shame and guilt, quarried from his own imagination, nourished themselves on the deference of these patients.

Betta's fears were groundless. Most of his East Indian patients, however poor, had attended wedding celebrations beyond the means of their hosts and thought it proper that the doctor's family should have used its wealth as it did.

In fact Betta could barely afford to pay his rent and buy gasoline for his car. To his surprise Meena was more contented than she had ever been since her marriage. It was only recently that she confessed to having been unhappy in the previous house, but was unable to say why, whether it was on account of the wind from the sea, or the janitor's enigmatic conduct, or the waterlogged land around it. From the first night she was oppressed by a loneliness that made her welcome the outings to the Merrimans, until she came to see the family as possessing extraordinary powers, which were emphasized by Mrs Merriman's unostentatious skill in dealing with plaintiffs in her weekly court. While Gopie's visits made her long for her mother's house Mrs Merriman's example allowed her to delve into her own self in order to discover resources she associated with the heroism of men like her father and male forebears whose lives were recounted around the kerosene lamps that seemed to magnify them. She understood Gopie's fascination with Mrs Merriman as none of the men did, neither Betta nor the younger Mr Merriman, nor the old man who, for all his wisdom, was a castaway from the previous century.

'How Meena change up!' her mother had told her father, not recognizing in her the diffident betrothed who was unable to hold Betta's gaze. She had approved of her daughter's modesty, for it was the first virtue in a woman, as she had been taught; and, viewing the world as she had been taught, she had worried for her younger daughter, whose open character would bring her nothing but unhappiness.

.

Betta's notebook had grown into a comprehensive diary in which he recorded not only his new herbal discoveries, but his encounters with people, with ailments and even with himself.

November 3rd: Came across a case of buck-sickness for the first time, only having heard of it as a creole term meaning 'fed-up'. A half-Arawak woman from the North-West was brought to the surgery. She had apparently lost the will to continue living. The sick-nurse said no medicine I prescribed would cure her because she was 'buck-sick'. I could prescribe nothing because she had no temperature, no swollen spleen or liver and had a heart as sound as my own. The woman died the following week.

November 7th: Racial sickness map emerging. Rickets more common among East Indians. Those who eat roti as a staple food appear to be particularly vulnerable.

November 12th: Witnessed healer manipulating warm glass on patient's abdomen to cure 'narah' (twisting of intestines!). Merriman spoke at length about such an operation, claiming he has performed it on several occasions with success. Difficult to establish the boundary between reality and illusion. Perhaps they are to be found on both sides of the boundary.

December 1st: Meena's herb garden is doing extremely well. Wonderful intuition, if little logic. (Will show her this. Much wiser.)

December 3rd: Patient tells me he has always used moka-moka to control his blood pressure. The market stallholder from whom he always bought it retired and he can no longer come by supplies. Must get Meena to plant some in her coreilla patch. Will it do well? It grows beside canals.

December 7th: Malaria and anaemia. Anaemia and malaria. The two great scourges of this country. A good diet and a pure water supply is everything.

December 10th: News of another epidemic of malaria among Venezuelan aboriginal Indians. Our Best hospital has a high proportion of aboriginal Indians with tuberculosis. In fact their powers of recovery from the diseases which affected them before the coming of Europeans is impressive. Merriman told me that he knows of more than one case of recovery from the bite of a bushmaster, a snake that usually kills in a matter of hours.

Betta went on recording his reflections and the progress of what he called his *education*. His entries became longer and more introspective, until he discovered that every step across the landscape of his medical experience had been matched by a distance travelled on a path within, with its streets and lamp-posts, its balustraded culverts and decaying bridges, recognized only in retrospect, but as palpable as the landmarks of another road. More than once he had had cause to reflect on the significance of work in his patients' lives, like the Mohammedan wholesaler who, having made a fortune, left the business to his sons, only to find that he was seized by the illusion that he was travelling backwards along a road on which he had come. Meena had changed, too, since she had assumed responsibility for a household. And so, installed – once and for all as he thought – in a place favourable to the realization of his dream of a haven where he and other East Indians could work out their destiny as Guyanese, Betta extended his herb garden, kept a 'diary of knowledge', as he termed it and put aside as much money as he could. And only Meena understood why he began to acquire a reputation for stinginess among her relations who believed that they had the right to descend upon his house and plunder his garden. She, in turn, turned to Rani, who shared their vision, having spent years in a home of uncertain attachments.

The bond between the two families became stronger, so that the unexpected visits Betta disliked when made by his wife's relations, he welcomed from Tipu and Rani. They came whenever they had time, on Tipu's new bicycle, Bhagwan with his legs astride the rear parcel seat and Rani sitting sideways on the crossbar. Occasionally they made the journey on the morning train when Bhagwan indulged in an exercise of pointing out the spot where the train would begin to lose speed.

Bhagwan, Bismatie and Gita often stayed for days in the home of one family or the other and grew to know Newtown and Plaisance equally well, so much so that many people were not certain which children were members of which family, the goldsmith's or the doctor's.

And the months went by, recorded on elaborate calendars of Hindu stallholders decorated with their gods and goddesses, scenes from the Ramayana and Mahabarata which blurred the distinction between myth and history; and on the creole calendars figures of the estuaries of the Essequibo, Demerara and the Berbice, where great islands come floating down, destroying everything in their path; and on the pitted concrete winnowing places weathering with alternate seasons of sun and rain; on children who stand upright of a sudden under the eyes of admiring parents and speak their incomprehensible language, following an irresistible impulse to be like their elders; on spongy moss beds and lacquered finger bowls, on the collapse of boundaries and the blue flux of tides, on silent village funerals, the pale taste of fermented rice for Mandarin speakers; on books collapsing between illuminated covers and on everything under the sun.

One year went by and in that time Bismatie had forgotten the house where she was born, believing what one of the village children had told her, that she had been brought to her home by the afternoon train.

Chapter 36

It was in an atmosphere of growing hostility between his mother-in-law and Betta that he invited the Mulvi Sahib to come and live with his family. The teacher had taken sick while in the mihrab of the mosque during a discussion with one of his acquaintances. On feeling his knees weaken under him he asked instinctively for his shoes, which he had left on the rack near the entrance, the first of a long line of leather footwear.

'Your shoes're on the rack,' one of his friends assured him. 'You're all right? Are you sick?'

In trying to wipe the sweat from his forehead he knocked off the white skullcap which sat so precariously on his thick hair.

Four men helped sit him on the floor on the edge of the mihrab, while one man ran out of the mosque to fetch a taxi.

'My shoes!'

'We'll get you them when you go out.'

'Get them now, please,' the Mulvi Sahib insisted.

The four men exchanged puzzled looks, for none of them knew what his shoes looked like.

From his prone position on the ground the Mulvi Sahib could see the Tree of Life depicted on the dome.

'Why?' he asked.

'Why what?' two of his helpers asked at the same time.

'I don't know. Have I got on my shoes? I can't feel my feet.'

The same thought entered the minds of the four men: he must be dying.

Finally the man who had gone for a taxi came back and announced that one was outside. They lifted him bodily and carried him past the shoe rack and to the waiting vehicle into which two of the men climbed in order to accompany him home. The Mulvi Sahib was not in a condition to recognize his shoes and the others had conveniently forgotten them.

On reaching home one of the men went in search of a doctor. The humidity of the windless night obliged the man who remained to open three windows, only to find himself oppressed by the exhalations from the aviary of sleeping birds.

The next day Mrs Singh learned of the Mulvi Sahib's illness from the Pujaree, who had been told about it by one of the men who kept a grocer's shop in Newtown, on the road to the priest's temple. She telephoned Betta, who drove to the house in Kitty. His examination revealed nothing more serious than anaemia and a slight fever. He prescribed a patent iron tonic and three fresh coconuts every day.

'In my house I can treat you myself,' Betta said, preferring to make the offer in oblique terms in deference to the teacher's independence.

'We'll see.'

'But who's going to cook for you?'

'I can get about,' was the laconic, almost curt reply.

'I'll go now. I've got to get back to the surgery. Try and give me an answer by tomorrow.'

'Why?'

'I don't know why,' Betta admitted. 'Probably because the sooner you can the better for you. You're not God, you know.'

How long? the Mulvi Sahib asked himself, once Betta had gone. How long have I lived? I don't even know my own age. They offered me artificial flowers, me, a Muslim! 'Thee alone we worship. Show us the path.' I remember the mausoleum in a garden of cinnamon, trees with branches touching the ground. To be hitched a lifetime to a Sukrum! Who would believe he was born a Muslim into a family of good Muslims? Dying in a field. . . . Yet they forgot so quickly. She travelled further in her twenty-three years than many of us do in a lifetime. The goblet maker knows it all. I watched him with clay up to his elbows, spreading out his fingers to mould the lips of those pots. He's not the fool he pretends. The singing of the birds and panditji playing a raga on the sitar. . . . They watch without seeing the shadows of those raised frets. Panditji and the goblet maker! If only they knew how I prayed to still my envy of their skill! It's the hour when gaulings fly home from the estuaries. . . .

He tried to get up, but finding that the effort tired him he thought better of it.

How can I go when there is so much to care for in this house? What is death but a timeless calm? Lahti! You were a perfect woman, my mother and my sister. Do not weep! He's your brother. Lean forward and touch him. Ah! We all dress in white and read alone, from right to left, always our index finger barely touching the manuscript.

The Mulvi Sahib recalled how he had heard Mrs Singh saying to Lahti when she was only twelve years old, 'I don't like you. I don't know why, but I can't like you. And anything you say to me won't make me like you.' And he told her, 'If you say things like that you'll kill the child before she's a woman.' And Lahti went on courting her affection, even when she was old enough to bear children. She brought home the first dress she was required to make on her own and demonstrated to Mrs Singh how the hem was to be turned up with pins, how the pleats were to be kept in position and displayed her handiwork when the tailor-tacks were in place.

The swiftness with which she was forgotten seemed so incomprehensible he had pondered over its meaning for weeks. For that and for his strange habits he could not go and live with Betta.

That afternoon Gopie and her mother came to visit Betta's family. Betta told them of the Mulvi Sahib's illness and said that he had offered to take him in. Meena's mother accused him of callousness towards her – he had put a stop to her practice of stripping the herb garden whenever she came – and affection for the Mulvi Sahib, a stranger.

'And a Mohammedan! They does look down on us!' she said. 'Not because I don't complain I don't see!'

No one attempted to cross her, and she was encouraged to go on.

'If I want to take Bismatie or Gita for a few days,' she continued, 'you make this excuse or that excuse. But when is Rani, then is all right. Is Rani this and Rani that.'

'If Meena wants me to stop Rani from coming here,' Betta told her, 'she only has to say so.'

'Gita's too young to spend time away from home,' Meena put in.

'Bismatie's not too young!' her mother exclaimed, putting her in her place as though she was still a girl.

Gopie dared not say anything, having been the victim of her mother's outbursts on several occasions. She had more than once made excuses for Betta and Meena, claiming that they were in fact poor, and was always met with the objection that no doctor in the country was poor.

Once when Gopie reminded her that her father saw nothing wrong in Betta's behaviour she was slapped for her pains.

The quarrel had ended and the children's voices came in from the verandah, as solemn as those of two old women.

Betta was tempted to say something conciliatory, but knew that the situation would arise again and decided to let matters follow their natural course. He excused himself and went off to prepare for his afternoon surgery.

The children, who were on the verandah, noticed the beggar woman collecting money at the gate from shoppers and travellers on the afternoon train, who got off at Plaisance station. She had the swollen face and claw hands of the leper and played endlessly on her comb covered with silver paper she had collected from discarded cigarette boxes. Bismatie had tried more than once to explain to her younger sister that the leper carried, beneath her skirt, a bag filled with silver coins which she had seen her counting when no one was about. Gita saw nothing remarkable in this, but shared Bismatie's curiosity because her sister was infinitely wise.

They saw the sick-nurse arrive with a parcel wrapped in paper, which he held on his handlebar while steering with the right hand.

'Afternoon, Mr Chapman,' Bismatie called.

'Afternoon, Mr Chapman,' said Gita.

He waved to them vigorously.

'Look how he waving and the bicycle driving itself,' Bismatie said, turning to her sister.

'It driving itself? Yes, it driving itself,' Gita agreed, not understanding how a bicycle with a person sitting on it could drive itself.

Mr Chapman dismounted and soon he and his bicycle had been forgotten as other sights engaged the children's attention. He had brought Betta a large portion of beef, half of his trophy from a cow which had been knocked down by the Georgetown train. The accident occurred within sight of his home and he and others in the vicinity had rushed to the spot, armed with knives to carve up the animal, following an old custom of entitlement.

Mr Chapman had failed his chemist and druggist examinations several times and was anxious to keep on the doctor's good side in case he never got beyond the status of sick-nurse dispenser. A distant relation of George Merriman, who had brought him to Betta's attention when he told him of his plans for a surgery-hospital, he had the advantage of knowing the area and its people well. Betta was pleased with his work and it was with him that he first discussed ways of protecting the herbal garden from his mother-in-law. At first his suggestion that a low paling fence should be built round it did not appeal to Betta. Every time his mother-in-law came she would be reminded of the affront. However, Meena thought it was the only way. They had explained to her mother that the plot was indispensable to Betta's practice, but, driven by an obsessive stubbornness, she refused to accept the ban and, on every visit, pulled up some plant, however small, to the exasperation of her daughter and son-in-law.

Mr Chapman took his overalls from the cupboard in the large room on the ground floor which was destined to be the hospital and, as he had arrived ten minutes before time, sat down on a bench, the only piece of furniture, apart from a table in the corner. He could hear the children talking on the verandah and reflected on what he would do if he were a doctor and had the house at his disposal. What was the point in going abroad to study and coming back to treat most of your patients gratis?

Would a baker give away his bread? Dr Singh was mad, he had no doubt. In his place he would allow his mother-in-law to plunder the herb garden to extinction. Most patients wanted medicine in a bottle in any case, especially if it was coloured pink. Or pills. Oval pills, round pills, tiny ones, cake-shaped ones, so long as they were pills. With a pretty wife like that he would dress her in finery and keep her hands soft, instead of having her soil them with mud tending plants that anybody could pick at the roadside. Where he lived there was so much clamacherry the children used it for pasting their kites. And moka-moka? Who in his right senses would cultivate moka-moka? Did he realize what would happen when he furnished his hospital? Every Tom, Dick and Harry would fall ill and seek admittance. But *he* would not complain. It was hard enough to come by a job as a watchman these days, even with the starvation wages they paid. If he was asked what he thought of the idea of a hospital he would be the first to praise it to the skies. Yet he had no doubt that the wrong people had the qualifications. At twenty-seven he felt worn out and bitter at the frustrations he was obliged to endure, the lack of good books and guidance in his studies, the penury of an existence that resembled a forest in which he had been lost since leaving school.

Mr Chapman saw Betta's problems as existing in his imagination. His idealism and tolerance were indulgences that brought no joy.

He got up and opened the door wide to find a group of patients waiting for him. He divided them into two lines, sending one round the house to the door of the adjoining room where Betta was waiting for them. The intention was that the less serious cases come back to him while Betta kept the patients whose ailments he was not expert enough to diagnose. By means of this arrangement he had acquired great skill in diagnosis and felt all the more aggrieved that a rigid system of examinations had kept him where he was.

Meena, Gopie and Mrs Ramcharran were huddled together. Meena had no idea how to console her mother, while Gopie could not understand how a petty difference over a few herbs could have such an effect on her. Impatient at her conduct she said, 'It's a few herbs, Ma. It's not a rice harvest.'

'You keep out of this!' came the warning, as if Mrs Ramcharran had been expecting an impertinence of some sort from her younger daughter. 'You're married, but you're still a girl! He did behave in the same way to his mother. He can't help it.'

'He didn't behave in any way I disapproved of, Ma,' said Meena. 'And I approve of the way he's behaving now. I did tell him so. What is it about the garden. . . ?'

'What is it?' asked Mrs Ramcharran in turn. 'That's what I want to know. If his Mulvi Sahib did want to flatten it he wouldn't mind, but I don' count. . . . And you going let a Mohammedan come and live in your house, knowing how they feel about us.'

'Betta isn't religious,' Meena said.

'What's that got to do with it? Mr Khan don' go to the mosque, but he's not different from the others.'

Meena saw the pleading look in Gopie's eyes and decided to oppose her mother no longer.

She and Gopie went home before Betta's surgery was over. And for some time afterwards there was a coolness between Mrs Ramcharran and her son-in-law's family, which, none the less, healed with the passage of time. Betta's concern for his father-in-law, whose left leg might have been amputated but for him – his diabetic condition hampered circulation in both legs – so touched her, she was to look back on her petulant behaviour in disbelief, thinking that something had got into her from outside, something for which she could accept no responsibility. She had witnessed a similar possession in an elder sister, which was brought to an end not by kindness, but with the brutal intervention of the local pandit, who raged at her for hours. The conviction that Meena and Betta had conspired against her now seemed preposterous. But Gopie wondered if she was next in turn, if her mother had, in fact, accepted that she bore a different name.

Chapter 37

Contrary to Mr Chapman's prophecy Betta's hospital prospered, not least because of his sick-nurse's dedication. Although many of his patients were too poor to pay he earned sufficient money to increase his sick-nurse's wages and buy large stocks of quinine and other drugs. Unable to afford a full-time nurse Betta took on two elderly sisters who lived on the premises and slept in one of the bedrooms upstairs. Surly, taciturn ladies, they demanded that the patients who could fend for themselves should make their beds, do all the washing-up and draw water from the new vat. Bismatie and Gita were frightened of them and kept away from the hospital, until one day a boy of four was admitted. Then they remained standing at the entrance after Mr Chapman arrived to take his part of the surgery in a corner of the room where the permanent patients were housed.

The boy's thigh had been badly mauled by an alligator while he was swimming aback and was bandaged along its length. The day after his arrival Bismatie asked her mother to bandage her leg so that she could visit him; and that afternoon Mr Chapman was accompanied into the room by Betta's two children whose legs were done up so tightly that they had to hop along towards the young patient's bed.

Meena watched her offspring through the half-open door, wondering at what point in their lives they would become adults. And, somehow, the absurdity of their conduct reminded her of Sukrum. The night before she had caught sight of him lurking at the gate and waited for Betta to tell her what she had herself seen. But Betta had evidently not seen him and joked all through the late evening meal about their two children who were now in bed.

'I heard them through the wall,' Betta told her. 'Bismatie asked the boy why the alligator bit him and he said he didn't know. Then Gita said, "Did you get it for Christmas?"'

Meena laughed as well, eyeing him to see if his mirth was genuine or, like hers, marred by the memory of what she had seen the night before through a window of the unlighted gallery. Now she was not even certain whether Sukrum had stood by the gate or on the edge of the unlighted street. Why did she say nothing? Perhaps she was unwilling to arouse memories of the masked men who had chased him at the time of Ramadan.

'How's the Mulvi Sahib?'

'A lot better. But he's not the same. He doesn't go to the mosque. Living alone with no one to clean the aviary. . . . I saw Sukrum this morning.'

'Sukrum?'

'Yes. As I was leaving the Mulvi Sahib's yard I saw him and called out, but he pretended he didn't hear.'

Meena told him what had happened the night before. Betta heard her out, then said calmly that Sukrum had been watching the house for several days.

'Aren't you afraid he's up to something?'

'Why? Ma's taken him in again. He keeps her dogs.'

'She keeps dogs?'

'She has two huge brutes to keep out thieves to replace two tame ones she had before. Got them after she chased everyone away. According to the Mulvi Sahib she and Sukrum do all the work and even the hucksters don't go there any more. Nobody knows how Sukrum got in with her again. The yard is overgrown with weeds.'

'Why don't you go and see her, Betta?'

He dismissed her suggestion with a gesture and they were soon talking about the conduct of the hospital and other matters. Betta told her about the man who had come all the way from Cornelia Ida to be treated and had paid him with a basket of pomegranates. The woman who still displayed the tika on her forehead had moved to another village. What were they going to do when Mr Chapman passed his examinations and left them? Where did Bismatie and Bhagwan learn their kissing game? Children four and five years old did not kiss as often as they did, and on the slightest pretext. Rani told Meena that they behaved in the same way when Bismatie came home to them.

And finally Betta broached the subject he and George Merriman had discussed for a good hour the last time the latter telephoned to consult him about a patient at his pharmacy.

'It's just the people who give little. . . . They, it's precisely they who demand the most,' he said. And she knew he was talking of Sukrum who thought he had the right to his assistance because he used to be a hanger-on in his mother's house. Meena pointed out that people accepted such a claim from their relations.

'But he isn't a relation,' Betta protested.

'I think,' Meena said, 'he's weak.'

'Weak?'

'I can't explain,' Meena went on. 'When he ripped off Lahti's dress it was as if . . . I can't explain. I'm not like you. I *feel* what I say, but can't put it into words.'

'I don't agree. He's not weak. And what would that mean in any case? How many strong people do you know? The Mulvi Sahib, Mrs Merriman, your father? Who else?'

'You.'

'No, Meena. The strong person doesn't quake inside.'

'My father,' Meena said feelingly, 'would not stand up for his principles as you do. And the Mulvi Sahib, what you know of him? He's an enigma.'

'He doesn't quake inwardly. I know that.'

'But what does he stand up for?' Meena demanded. 'His birds? Himself? He does fascinate you because he's an enigma. You yourself said people like that aren't to be trusted. They never say anything definite. Not because he's a brilliant teacher and a good Mohammedan he's strong. Sometimes you vex me so! You tower above these people, yet you still walk with them as though they're your equals.'

'You know I don't believe in that nonsense,' Betta retorted.

'You don't want to admit it you mean. To you Sukrum was always a louse, and he *knew* how you did feel about him. I don' think he came here for money at all. He could always earn enough from fishing. He was bent on destroying Lahti and he wanted you to know.'

'He was in love with her.'

'Oh, Betta. Isn't that what these men who murder their wives say? I was in love with you after hearing Gopie talk about you. What does that mean?'

336

Betta smiled.

'You've changed,' he said, smiling.

'Did you prefer me as I was?'

'I prefer you as you are. I wanted you to be like this. And now I'm a little bit concerned.' And in saying this he made a gesture with his hands the better to convey the meaning of 'little'.

He laughed aloud at her serious expression, thinking that she had taken his words to mean what they said.

'Do you still love me as when we first married?' she asked. 'I don't dress like a doctor's wife and sometimes I say such foolish things.'

'Foolish? You? After putting me in my place you call yourself foolish?'

'Am I the most intelligent woman you know?'

'You're so intelligent I tremble in your presence.'

She struck him with a newspaper several times while he pretended to be afraid of her.

Meena began taking out the eggs from her basket, one by one. She shook each to check that it was not addled, then placed it in a cardboard box. She did not dare shake the eggs at the roadside market as the creole women did, so that from time to time she had to throw away one or two bad ones when she checked them at home. Betta saw that she still had a long way to go in what he called her 'emancipation'.

Betta's and Meena's friends could not understand how they were able to run an institution which impoverished them, and justified their view by pointing to the empty beds. The sick people who were well-off enough to find the fees went to the Public Hospital instead. He was not yet earning enough from his general practice to care for bed-patients without charging all of them. And Betta was faced once more with the reality of his incapacity to take a moral stance while acting alone. Ramsaroop, admired for his Dharm Sala in Georgetown, was a wealthy man. Should he, Betta, first set out to earn a considerable amount of money in order to do what he thought was right? In that case he would have to aim for an exclusive practice and it would be all but impossible to find the way back. Dr K had sought that way and ended up devoting one afternoon a week to treating poor East Indians on the West Bank, to salve his conscience.

At times Betta doubted his own motives and became impatient with his vision of a haven for the sick where they would receive wholesome food and care worthy of a dignity due to them as human beings. Meena spoke of 'not dressing well'. Did she want to wear expensive clothes? He had never once asked. And his children? When they reached secondary-school age he would be obliged to face the choice of buying quinine for his non-paying patients and paying school fees for Bismatie and Gita.

'His hospital's doing well and his children are in rags!' He could imagine remarks being made about his conduct. But he had grown up in a house that attracted public interest from those who had no idea what went on inside it, preferring to feed their imagination on rumour and speculation. It was even now being said that he was receiving assistance from public funds, most of which went into his pocket. He was like all East Indian beggars, who were believed to die on a pile of gold.

In the old days he was wont to consult the Mulvi Sahib when beset by anxieties. The old man was dying slowly and it was he, Betta, who now played the role of consoler as he discovered chinks in his once invulnerable armour. How different things were now! He enjoyed sitting with him inhaling the aroma of Berbice coffee, eating red snapper and toasted cassava bread. There was something about the decadence of his sun-filled drawing room, through a window of which you could touch the pink exora growing in clusters. The prayer rugs, the elaborate calligraphy in Indian ink, in such contrast to the photographs on the walls of creole households or blue portraits in Hindu homes, the ceaseless fluttering of birds encompassed, the suppressed conversations loomed in retrospect like the contents of a vivid dream. The teacher's house was like a derelict photograph with blurred intensities. In so tranquil a place he could no longer raise matters of discord.

George Merriman, with whom he now spoke mainly by telephone, seemed farther away with every month that went by, and at times he longed for those evenings in the company of his family and irascible father, who lived out in the present a bygone age. Mr Chapman's exaggerated respect for 'the doctor' was a barrier to friendship and Betta wondered how he and George could possibly be related.

It was evident to Betta that the measure of success he had at last achieved in his enterprise entailed a sacrifice in personal relationships outside the home. In Leonora, where his efforts had been thwarted by an unscrupulous estate manager and a law which allowed workers to be brought before the courts for absenteeism, his acquaintances had become friends in an ironic reversal of experience. Besides, there was now little difference between his family life and work. He worked where he slept, saw and heard his children at all hours of the day and had lengthy discussions with Meena when, three years ago, he would have been holding surgery at a hospital in Vergnoegen or Uitvlugt.

The occasional visits of the Merrimans and his in-laws only served to emphasize the extraordinary change in his circumstances, which demanded from him resources he was not certain he possessed. Unlike Meena, who had no doubts about the direction her life had taken, his hours of reflection were racked by misgivings, so that at times he envied Mr Chapman's manic interest in forthcoming examinations and his certainty of purpose.

'Egoism'. The Mulvi Sahib had once dismissed his strivings and doubts with that single word, in that time when his remarks were like surgical incisions. The Mulvi Sahib, the Pujaree, the Merrimans, Gopie, Rani, Lahti, old Mr Merriman, his father-in-law, his mother and dead father, the estate manager, the janitor, Meena, his children, Tipu, Sukrum, Bai, Aji, Mrs Ramcharran were all mirrors in which he had glimpsed something of himself, admirable or repugnant, according as he rejected or welcomed what he saw.

Chapter 38

Everywhere spring rice was being sown. Brief showers left a trail of vapour over the edges of flooded fields, and the polder land, crisscrossed with drainage and irrigation canals, shone like an expanse of beaten copper.

Betta got out of his car, having just come back from his first daily rounds which took him beyond the back dams. This was the most strenuous part of the day, for he had to leave the motorcar less than a mile away from the Public Road and walk to the cottages and hovels of his patients. He had just treated a field manager from Ogle whose mule had stopped to scratch its flank against a tree. The man's leg was badly injured and he had to be taken to hospital in one of the estate's punts.

On entering the surgery he immediately noticed the smell of stale tobacco. In order to supplement his income he had rented it out for a party which went on until four in the morning. Before he retired he had looked in at the adjoining hospital, but only one of the ten patients was awake, an old man who claimed he never slept in any case.

The sick-nurse came in to tell him how many patients were waiting.

'Do you smell the surgery, Doctor?'

'Yes. Ask the two sisters to disinfect it for me. I'm going upstairs to have something to eat.'

'I'll do it, Doctor. No trouble.'

'Thanks. You know where the disinfectant is?'

'Yes, Doctor.'

That afternoon Betta wrote up his diary, spending more time on it than usual because he had neglected to make an entry for four days.

'A plague of flies by day and moths by night. East Indians wait too long before calling the doctor, relying overmuch on their herbal cures; and by the time they call me their spleens are swollen badly. At times I want to destroy the herb garden. People believe they have found *the* truth, when in fact they've discovered *a* truth. I am racked with doubt. Went to see Ma at Pujaree's temple. She would not allow me to visit her at home. All the women were required to touch the flame in the building which is not raised above the ground, just as in a Jordanite church. The Pujaree has grown in authority, so much so that someone made him a present of a thousand-year veena – according to Ma, who is completely under his spell now. He read from the Bhagavad-Gita and there was utter silence in the badly lit room. It was very impressive. . . . I felt left out. Is Ma happy? The sick-nurse diagnosed measles for chickenpox and I had to explain that the difference was important, not least because measles can lead to bronchial pneumonia. I must investigate report that exora leaves are effective in treating ulcers. Mother-in-law says that Gopie's husband has forbidden her to keep bees! Poor Gopie. She'll have to learn to curb her enthusiasms in marriage. I cannot get Ma out of my head and find myself thinking about her even when I'm driving. Something is growing in me and I feel it will burst out at any time. Was I happier on the West Coast when I was threatened? Can I not stand peace? Or am I dissatisfied that I am achieving so little? That's it, I am sure. I cannot pretend that ten beds make a hospital or that an individual is capable of achieving much. Yesterday I went to visit a seamstress's husband who had a discoloration in his face, which he thought might be serious. It was only lottah and I told her to dissolve some borax in vinegar and apply it three times daily. On leaving I saw a length of taffeta on a chair and strong memories came back to me – the sound of cloth and the smell of new shoes. How foolish! Sometimes these childhood recollections come flooding back.'

Betta went on to note that the creole belief that much illness was due to 'interference' by someone else was spreading amongst East Indians, as so much else.

Closing his diary he promised to go and visit his mother. It was not good for the children to be told that they could not see their paternal grandmother. It would be worse still not to mention her name, as if she were dead.

Mrs Singh resisted her son's repeated attempts to visit her, protesting that he could always see her at the temple. But the day after Meena told him she was expecting her third child and he rang his mother she invited him to come and see her.

'It'll be a boy, the Pujaree said.'

'And how does he know?'

'Betta, the Pujaree knows many things. You show him so much resistance. If you'd allowed him to help you your hospital would be flourishing. But you go your own way. He said yesterday, "Betta's child will be a boy. He'll pretend he doesn't mind, but he'll be rejoicing in his heart." You're still there, Betta? Betta! Why don't you come and let him help you find it a name?'

'I'll come,' Betta said, seizing the opportunity.

'Come alone, though.'

'Why?'

'Things aren't the same, Betta. . . . It doesn't matter, does it?'

'Don't you want to see your grandchildren? Bismatie is already four.'

'Four? How time goes! When your son is born you must bring Meena and the girls and Meena's family too. Bring them all and I'll show them how I can forget. And you must forget too. We must all forget. I'll have a banquet of forgetting. . . .'

'Forget what?' Betta asked cautiously.

Betta got no reply and began calling her name in the same way that she had been repeating his a while ago.

'Come anyway. When're you coming?' Mrs Singh finally asked without a trace of anger in her voice.

'Any time.'

'Then come tomorrow. After surgery.'

'I'll come after Meena's put the children to bed. About half-past seven.'

Betta replaced the receiver on its hook and went over the conversation in his mind. His mother seemed happier. In her voice, however, there was still that underlying strength that reminded him of forces that have yet to be described.

'Can you remember?' Aji once told him when he was already a man, 'how you did get on when your mother was dressing sheself to go out? You was only seven! You did ask me whether she was a bad-woman! Remember? An' I did ask you where you hear that word an' you say you hear a man call a woman that at the market. You 'member? Alhough you din' go to school you learn a lot of words. Just 'cause she was dressing to go out!'

Evoking the incident of thirty years back he recalled Aji's expression, which was not one of displeasure.

His mother's house was almost empty now. Yet to him it was not empty, and the physical evidence of its emptiness could not suppress the reality within him. Those who died in it and those who went away he associated with the voices of double-gourd veenas and santoors on humid nights, which hung on the air and would not go away. 'You hear the santoor? You dreaming?'

Betta first dropped in to see the Mulvi Sahib before going on to his mother's. He offered to take him to the mosque, but the old teacher declined, alleging a need to pray alone. A neighbour had cleaned the aviary for him. He thought that her motive was not so much charity as the need to clear the air. He smiled and described himself as a 'wicked old man'.

He shuffled downstairs beside Betta and saw him off.

'It's the rice-planting season,' he called after him. 'Not that it means anything to big shots like you.'

Betta's appearance at his mother's gate was the signal for an outbreak of fierce barking from two enormous hounds whose paws came over the top of the gate without difficulty. In the background Sukrum stood with his hands in his trouser pockets, unmoved by Betta's plea to call the animals away.

'It's you, Betta,' his mother called from an upstairs window. 'Where's Sukrum? Sukrum! Tie the dogs up. Can you see him? Sukrum!'

He came forward slowly and without taking his gaze away from Betta gave the dogs a slap on their back, which sent them bounding away under the house. The gate shook from the sudden release of pressure on it.

'I said, "Tie them up!" What's wrong with that man?'

Sukrum walked back to the dogs with the same nonchalance.

Betta waited until his mother signalled him to come up, then, lifting the latch, entered the yard.

'Betta!' she exclaimed, and kissed him warmly on both

cheeks. 'You looked so gloomy at the temple. Aren't you happy? *I* am happy. A burden's fallen away from my shoulders. Don't take any notice of the yard: Sukrum gets lazier every day. It hasn't been weeded for months. He promises, but does nothing. I say promise, but he can't promise anything, poor Sukrum. He's dumb.'

'Dumb?'

'Yes. Didn't you know? Soon after Lahti's death he started stuttering, then became dumb, completely dumb. Have you ever heard an East Indian stutter? We wouldn't be satisfied with that! He doesn't mind, though, so don't feel sorry for him. He probably thinks it saves him a lot of trouble, knowing him.'

'Ma, why are you talking so much?'

She thought for a moment, then said, 'Betta, I've always been talkative!'

'I didn't think so.'

'My little boy,' she said. 'Sit down in the Mulvi Sahib's chair.'

It was one of the indestructible camphor-wood chairs which most visitors did not care to sit in unless others were not free.

'The Pujaree's coming down in a minute. He had to go out, but put it off because you were coming.'

'I don't mind. It's you I wanted to see.'

'Whatever the Pujaree does,' she said, 'show him manners. Whatever he does or says. He may have come from the gutter but he's a gentleman.'

'I've got a lot I want to tell you. . . .'

'No, Betta. The Pujaree's brought me happiness.

'Now's the hour of cripples,' Mrs Singh continued. 'If you go out now. . . . But you know. Nine o'clock is the time for laughing . . . at least in this house when the Pujaree's work is done and we sit to talk about what happened during the day. I was prevented from talking by you. I remained silent and behaved as I was expected for you and did without a man so as not to trouble your mind. Even while you were abroad no man came through my door, except on business, unless it was the Mulvi Sahib. "Why're we quarrelling?" I said when I heard you were expecting a son, "He must come and see me and we must not quarrel." I'll make tea and we'll drink together.'

She went off to the kitchen, leaving Betta on his own. There was so much he wanted to ask her! Why she still wore the white of mourning; why she allowed the yard to fall into such a state; why she did not take anyone in as she once did; whether she allowed Sukrum back because she pitied him, and a hundred other questions. As a child he asked questions without constraint and now it was she who did as she liked and spoke as she liked. But the questions persisted, inwardly, about her and Meena. His devotion to his wife was no less than it had once been to his mother, yet he was continually discovering things about her, like her candour, which made her answer the children's questions, whatever they were. And the Pujaree's influence over Ma? He was certain it did not derive from her understanding of him. Had he not himself changed? Those microscopic seeds strewn about the acres of his character that occasionally exploded into growths of alarming vigour, were they not present in everyone, awaiting some secret demand, some call from outside?

Betta's thirst for reconciliation was quenched by what he saw and felt around him, the overgrown yard, the two hounds, the absence of activity and a pervasive strangeness which conjured up that oblivion of reality he experienced abroad. Like a sloth that comes down to the ground to defecate and clambers up again as swiftly as it can to the safety of its tree-dwelling, he felt a need to abandon his visit to a place where lived a man for whom, he was now obliged to admit, he harboured a terrible hatred. Until then he had refused to come face to face with his loathing, preferring to dismiss the Pujaree as a charlatan or a fool. But his mother's assertion that she was happy proved too much for him.

All about the walls were hung pictures of Indian gods. One of them could only have been the Pujaree's: a purple figure of a kneeling man with a tail which rose sharply behind him. His chest was open and his hands held the two sections apart as though they were the leaves of a door, to reveal a seated couple in the recess. Betta found himself turning again and again to the image in spite of his revulsion and felt that the couple sitting in the kneeling man's chest could only be his mother and stepfather and that the chest they inhabited was the house in

which he came to consciousness, in which his father had died
and Aji too, with her vivid memories that imparted to him a
received experience of things past.

'Indian tea, Betta,' she said on returning. 'Now I only drink
Indian tea. It tastes so much better.'

His mother poured for him and he took his first sip. The tea
was delicious, like none other he had tasted.

'You know everything, Betta. Do you know why Sukrum
doesn't speak any more? Is he pretending?'

'What does the Pujaree think?'

And just as Mrs Singh was about to answer the Pujaree
appeared, more modestly dressed than Betta expected, in a
white tunic and trousers. He and Betta shook hands, but neither
knew what to say.

'Betta just asked if you thought Sukrum was pretending to be
dumb.'

'The doctor don' think so,' the Pujaree said. 'But I knew a man
who pretend for years before they found him out. Anybody can
pretend. In any case is only hard for the first few months.
Afterwards it does get harder *not* to pretend. So it does amount
to the same thing.'

'I'm sorry,' Betta said. 'I'm feeling drowsy.'

He lay back in his chair, looking for all the world as if he had
fallen asleep. In fact he could hear what was going on around
him but had lost the ability to sit up and control his movements.
There was a shuffling sound, like the scurrying of mice, and
then a long, sustained drone. He imagined he saw a swarm of
marabuntas flying about his head, their paper nest burning a
short distance away and the flames abating suddenly to a grey,
curling fringe.

'We only drink Indian tea in this house, Betta,' he heard the
Pujaree saying.

He opened his eyes briefly and saw himself sitting between
the Pujaree and his mother, and all three peering at him.

'Everything here is from India, the food we eat, the instruments. . . .' he continued. 'Look up, Betta, and you going see one
extinguished star. It does look bright, because you expect it to
be. On the houses near the sea all the iron work did rust from the
salt on the wind. They paint them and paint them, but they go

on rustling. While you tinkering with charity East Indians dying like flies. Somebody say the Mulvi Sahib tell you history don' have no morals; and is that the sort of conversation two intelligent men does have? It's the talk of lepers and outcasts and pandits that go with whores. It's the talk of men that abandon their parents and leave them to the flies. You and the Mulvi Sahib think I am dirt, but what you know about me? I give your mother back her peace of mind when I was still living on ghee and roti. We only drink Indian tea in this house and if I had anything to do with it your son would wear Indian clothes and speak Hindi and learn the Bhagavad-Gita by heart. After all, he will be my grandson.'

Betta started from his half-lying position, but was restrained by the Pujaree.

'He'll be a good grandfather, Betta,' Mrs Singh reassured him. 'He's already bought the child presents and planned his education. You will take him to his first Kali Mai puja when he is two so that he can witness the burning of Ravana's effigy. What is there here? They treat us like dirt and children do not respect their parents.'

Betta's mother came over and sat by him, bringing with her the smell of singed hair.

'I went to the cloud forests where quinine grows,' Mrs Singh continued. 'You administer it, but you know nothing about it. He called me Rubeena, a Muslim name, your Mulvi Sahib, and wanted me to run away with him.'

Betta started violently on hearing the last words.

'Oh, Betta, you are naive,' she said. 'Those who make women chaste are fascinated by whores. Doesn't the wheel of Dharma turn and turn? When you realize that the Pujaree is a great man you'll crow like a cook at foreday morning, greater than the Mulvi Sahib and even your father. The day of the night your father moved to this house he dreamt that I had given birth. It was a terrible experience listening to him tell it. And Aji began to cry. He was kind to her and sometimes called her Mai. I could tell you about your father, but you wouldn't believe a word I say. For you people are good or bad, Mulvi Sahibs or Sukrums. He told me I was nothing outside Kerala, because when I spoke Malayalam no one understood me.'

'Betta,' the Pujaree said sternly, 'your mother wants you to bring your son to live here when he born. Is the least you can do after the way you treat her. Two stops on the train, Meena can come and see him whenever she want. . . .'

Betta imagined he could hear the clucking of hens, then the call of an umbrella mender, a man with a young daughter of unimaginable beauty, as dark as Lahti was, who followed him wherever he went, carrying under her arm the skeletons of old umbrellas.

'Now, Betta,' Mrs Singh said, 'we'll have your son, won't we? The Pujaree wants a boy-child. He doesn't have children of his own. His sister's twins don't count, because he's only responsible for them. He wants a boy he can guide without the interference of a doting parent, someone he can make a pandit among pandits, whose tika will shine in the dark like the morning star.'

Betta imagined that his mother had led the figure sitting between herself and the Pujaree out of the room and begun speaking to him.

'If the Pujaree was handsome and dignified like Gopie's husband and wise like the Mulvi Sahib you would not like him any more than you do now. When he was poor you used to think you didn't like him because he wore scruffy clothes. Then when he began to change regularly you disliked him because he sponged off me. If I told you he is rich in his own right would you like him any more? Don't feel ashamed, Betta. . . .'

Betta wanted to ask her how she knew what Gopie's husband looked like, but was unable to express himself. His mother led him upstairs and opened the door of the first room, where Aji used to sleep. Standing over a table in the corner was Rani, who, taking no notice of them, began to pour water from a calabash over her hair, which was so long that half of it lay in the basin collecting the water. Dressed in nothing but a skirt her hair and back glistened in the lamplight.

'Go on,' Mrs Singh urged him, 'she was in love with you before you came back home.'

'I'm married, Ma. . . . Besides, Meena and I have no secrets from each other.' And he realized it was the first time he spoke since he lay down.

Then Rani turned round; but her nakedness was hardly visible under the mass of hair in the wan light of the kerosene lamp. Betta stepped forward and was about to touch her when she drew away from him.

'She's married too,' Mrs Singh mocked. 'Speak to her.'

But Rani turned away to continue what she was doing.

'She's a big woman now. Once she used to obey me. "Yes, Mrs Singh", "No, Mrs Singh", "What you say, Mrs Singh?" She's a big woman, but she hasn't changed. . . . And you know she brings Bhagwan here every Thursday, always with a cooked meal. Aji taught her how to cook Keralan food and everything she prepares for me is done with coconut. And who would think that at one time she was so rude! If I asked her for Bhagwan she would give him to me at once because she's so grateful for what she learned in this house and all. That's her nature, you see. Mind you, Lahti clung to me like a barnacle. It seems to me that children and strangers are not the same. Some children become strangers and you breed in some strangers a special kind of loyalty. And do you know? Sukrum doesn't budge from that room in case Lahti comes back and he misses her. . . . Anyway, come on.'

He and his mother left the room together while Rani was rubbing scented henna paste in her hair and the lamp spluttered for want of kerosene, and from somewhere in the house came the sound of an instrument being played with a bow.

They looked down into the yard and saw the Mulvi Sahib, a young man, leaning against a tree, on the spot where the water tank now was. Immediately beneath them stood a young woman. Grasping an iron handle which resembled a large spanner, she was pumping water to the house and stopped from time to time to wipe the sweat from her forehead. The Mulvi Sahib looked up and saw them, but turned away.

'He doesn't recognize you,' Mrs Singh said, 'because you're so much older. In a minute he'll be going off to court where he's standing in for an interpreter. Why's he standing there? To keep out of the sun. He was vain in those days and his face got blotchy in the sun. He confessed to me once that many days he prayed less than five times, because it was not practical. Doesn't sound like the man you know now, eh, with his rigid ideas and strict obedience to Islamic law? His appetite's shrunk, don't you think? That's all. Haven't you noticed how he smiles when you argue with passion and start gesticulating? Nothing would please him more than to live to be ninety, only to see whether you still hold to your opinions about helping your people. Look! He's going. He won't wave goodbye to a woman. Now come.'

She took him by the hand and led him to a closed door.

'If you give me your son I'd do anything,' she said. 'I'd move out of the house and leave it for you and your family.'

Then, hesitating a moment, she opened the door gently, as though she was concerned not to wake someone who was sleeping. Betta did not recognize the room which was hung with rugs and hessian and gave the impression of being inhabited by a single individual. His mother took him to a door which led to an adjoining room, and then with a sudden, almost brutal gesture flung it open to the screeching of children's voices. Two boys and three girls interrupted what they were doing momentarily, cast brief glances at the two and then promptly carried on chasing one another about the room, a bright, large apartment with a recess where playthings were scattered about the floor.

'They are your brothers and sisters, my aborted children, driftwood, bobbing up and down on the sea; but put out your hands to catch them and they vanish. Say nothing! Just watch. Your father used to dose me up with quinine till my ears rang. The doctor had to stop him because, he said, I would go deaf; but although he understood he couldn't feel for me because men and women are worlds apart. We love and copulate and only the friends stay together in spirit. The Pujaree can feel for us in a way no other man could, for me and those women who go to the temple with nothing but flowers. . . . Don't laugh at him, for my sake. Meena and Lahti used to snigger at the way he talked. "When I catch the train station" and other things he says. He is many things to me and not least he carries a string of narratives on his back, so that I never brood over the departed ones.'

She indicated the children with a nod then went and stood at the window on the opposite partition of the wall.

'I never had to go to a pawnbroker once,' she told him. 'Isn't that something to be proud of? Instead you deny me everything and can't bear the people I hold to most.'

Betta looked at her across the noisy room and was so touched he was prepared to say or do anything to please her and she, sensing her ascendancy over him, asked once more if she might have his son when he was born. He agreed to deliver the child at the end of nine nights and the ritual celebration to commemorate his belonging to this world.

'We must tell the Pujaree,' she said.

Then, after a moment of reflection, she said, 'Not now.'

An outburst of barking from the dogs woke Betta.

'You drugged my tea . . . I don't think I'll be able to crank the motorcar.'

'The Pujaree will crank it for you,' his mother reassured him. 'Anybody passing will crank it for you. Why do you worry about a little thing like that?'

'I can't come here again, Ma,' Betta said.

'Do as you wish, Betta,' his mother said. 'When somebody asks where the burial ground is you know he's a stranger.'

He lay back and said nothing for a long while until his head cleared, when he began to search desperately for something he knew he had to say, convinced that, should he not find it, some terrible occurrence would befall his mother.

'Ah, yes, Sukrum,' Betta said, almost shouting. 'You must tell him to come and see us as soon as he can.'

Chapter 39

'When the baby coming?' the leper woman asked Bismatie.

'It's come already,' she answered. 'It's in my mother's belly.'

'She tell you that?' the leper asked, making a sign of the cross.

'Who say it's there?' Bhagwan said, surprised at what he had heard.

'My ma said,' Bismatie declared proudly. 'She said it begin like a small dot you couldn't even see with a microscope.'

'My ma say,' Gita said, spinning round to give her 'words weight, 'and she show me a grain of dust through a mylosoap and it big, big like that.'

'My ma said,' continued Bismatie, 'my grandmother over the river doesn't snore. She makes a rhythmic snort.'

'You how old?' the leper asked.

'Five.'

'And how you learn to talk like that?'

'Like what?'

'Look,' the leper said, lifting her claw-hand in the direction of the train, which had just arrived, 'the train come. Don' forget! When the people start getting out alyou stand quiet an' look down at me as if you sorry for me.'

'I am sorry for you,' Bhagwan said.

'Don' do like the last time,' the leper reminded them. 'Don' grin all over you face like monkey when parrot shit 'pon 'e head.'

The children looked suitably concerned while the leper whined an incomprehensible litany as the travellers went past. Most of the coins fell beside the tray on to the hard, cracked earth, but the children maintained their rigid posture and expressions of pity until the last person went by.

'I couldn' hold my breath so long,' Gita complained. 'I let it out ten times.'

'I din' tell you to hol' you breath,' the leper said, counting the money in the tray.

Then, when two more travellers suddenly appeared at the station entrance, the children leapt to their positions and the leper took up her interrupted litany once more.

'God 'n 'ven. . . . Go-o-o-o-od 'n 'ven!'

But the travellers, deep in conversation, gave her nothing.

'You father got VD an' you mother got cough!' she exclaimed under her breath.

'You feel sorry for people?' Bhagwan asked, unable to make her out.

'Alyou want me tell you a story?' she asked in turn, ignoring Bhagwan's question.

'Yes,' Gita said, clapping her hands.

The leper had seduced them with her stories and her way of telling them and for that reason they sought her company when their mother was occupied in her herb garden behind the house. Bismatie felt instinctively that she would not approve and took care not to mention the woman, warning Bhagwan and Gita to say nothing about their meetings.

'I goin' tell you a story 'bout a country far, far away.'

And she recounted her tale, accompanying it with grimaces and eloquent gestures and pauses that caused the children to hold their breath and a variety of sounds in imitation of the animals and people that passed before the eyes of their imagination.

'An' the woman take the dog an' loss it away in the bush. Story done!'

'You know any more?' asked Bismatie.

'Nuf more. I know nuf, nuf story. I full o' story. When I lying down I does tell myself them. Jus' for so, when I in' got nothin' to do.'

'You rich?' Gita asked.

Bismatie nudged her.

'Why you pushing me for? I goin' tell Ma you pushing me. . . . You rich?'

'Who say I rich?' the leper woman said petulantly.

'Is she say so,' Gita declared, pointing to Bismatie, whom she had not forgiven for pushing her.

'Why you're so stupid?' Bismatie said.

'I not stupid! I goin' tell Ma you say I stupid.'

'Tell Ma, then, Big Mouth. I'm not your friend any more.'

'The two o' you always quarrelling,' Bhagwan said with that pompous only-child air of superiority Tipu admired in him.

'You brother right,' the leper told the girls. 'Alyou musn' quarrel.'

'He's not our brother,' Bismatie corrected her. 'Our mothers are friends and he's only spending the day here.'

'I thought alyou was brother an' sister,' the leper said, losing interest in the children now that darkness was falling and the likelihood of collecting any more money was much smaller.

'Alyou bugger off now,' she told them. 'I got to collect me belongings an' I don' like alyou watching me. I know you does watch me from up there. Chil'ren is chil'ren an' grown-ups is grown-ups.'

Bismatie led them away, but Gita kept looking back, thinking that the storyteller was about to do something extraordinary now that their backs were turned.

The children went up the back stairs. They were forbidden to do so because the staircase was not provided with balusters, a matter of concern for Meena, who was afraid that Gita might fall off to the ground below. She found it difficult to climb without holding on to the treads and had been slapped on the thighs more than once for disobeying her mother's orders. They crept into the house without being seen and went up to the bedrooms where it was easier to get into mischief; but, having exhausted the possibilities of misbehaving during the long day, they found nothing exciting or new and went downstairs once more to install themselves on the verandah above the leper's pitch. They saw the old woman hoisting herself up by means of her stick. She departed, walking along the train lines where stunted weeds grew between the sleepers, and the rails were barely visible in the twilight.

Gita sat down and fell asleep against the wall, her thumb in her mouth, while Bismatie and Bhagwan watched in silence as darkness gathered and the first candleflies began to wink in a corner of the yard.

'You like her?' Bismatie asked Bhagwan.

'Who?'

'The old lady.'

'She's a leper,' Bhagwan said. 'Ma did tell me so.'

'Is that why people give her money?'

'No! They give her money 'cause she poor. You got to give the poor money or when you come back in the world you're going to be something worse.'

'Oh,' Bismatie answered, impressed by his dogmatic manner.

Bismatie wondered about the old woman and tried to imagine where she lived, whether there were piles of silver coins in her house. She imagined there were children like herself, Bhagwan and Gita running about the house, that she cursed them from time to time, using expressions she shouted after people who neglected to give her money. Her voluminous garments resembled those she had seen on old photographs from a time when women wore dresses that came down to the ground and sheltered under parasols trimmed with lace. Bhagwan told her that the woman was ninety years old, that at such an age everyone became a leper. Would her mother and father become lepers too and hide their money from the eyes of others? The two old women who worked and slept in the hospital did not arouse her curiosity in any way. They were *ordinary* and their actions were predictable: they made the beds, cooked the patients' meals, washed them and remained on the premises at night, unlike the leper woman, who disappeared when the sun went down, skirting the train lines that vanished in the distance into a world of old women, mysterious children and piles of coins. When her father took them out in the car they always went west, in the opposite direction, towards a known world, past the Conversation Tree and endless lines of houses.

Bismatie turned to speak to Bhagwan, but he had gone inside to wait for his mother, who usually came before nightfall. She bent down and woke up Gita, intending to prepare her for bed; and at that moment Meena came looking for them because their evening meal was ready and it was past Gita's bedtime.

'I was waiting for Aunt Rani before we ate,' Meena said, 'but she's late.'

'Why she's late?' Bhagwan asked from the adjoining room.

'She left home late, I suppose,' Meena told him, unaware that his undemonstrative manner hid a secret anxiety regarding his mother, who always kept her word.

But Rani arrived when the family were at table and explained that she had to come by bus because Tipu's bicycle was punctured.

'Betta'll drop you home,' Meena promised. 'He won't be long.'

Chapter 40

Meena's baby was indeed a boy. Betta, unaware that he had promised the infant to his mother, rang her to announce the news. She reminded him that he had given his word, repeating his undertaking in the Pujaree's presence. But Betta denied angrily having done so and a quarrel would have ensued but for the respect he was determined to show her. Mrs Singh told him to ring her at the end of nine nights and they would talk again, and Betta's joy at having fathered a boy-child was tarnished by a vague uncertainty as to what had transpired the night he was drugged.

At the weekend he went to fetch his mother-in-law and father-in-law, who was enfeebled by illness and lack of exercise. Having closed the shop and erected a prayer flag in front of their house they set out with gifts for their grandchild.

Mrs Ramcharran received the visitors who came to see the boy-child and catered for them, while her husband looked on from a corner of the gallery, appearing to be bored, but taken up in the general excitement, the thrill of vicarious fatherhood and the knowledge that his daughter had married well. His waning energies had been channelled into the baby's spirit and now he would not mind to die. Besides, there was little risk to the child's life, since his father was a doctor and a friend of Hindu seers revered in the community.

People wandered in all day from all walks of life, many of them patients Betta had treated, who had contracted an exaggerated respect for his powers.

Betta's mother came too, accompanied by the Pujaree and the goblet maker, who had endowed the Newtown temple two months ago, when his venture as middleman into the commerce of rice proved to be unusually profitable. Mrs Singh and the Pujaree slipped away unnoticed, and everyone was surprised at the discovery of their absence. As the infant's grandmother she was allowed into the bedroom where, according to Meena, she had stared down at her son until he began to toss and shriek as though a centipede was attached to his back.

Betta later telephoned his mother for an explanation of her conduct, but there was no reply. That night he sat up from his sleep in a cold sweat, only to find that the skylight had been left open and the rain which had begun to fall had soaked the foot of the bed. He woke Meena and took her to an adjoining bedroom to spend the rest of the night in the single bed while he removed the mattress and hung the sheets over makeshift racks. The infant slept all the while in its crib, a small presence which had passed almost unnoticed by its sisters, who had heard so much about its existence in their mother's womb they were robbed of the excitement of revelation.

Mrs Singh had reproached Betta for the sacrifices she had made to no purpose. In her private conversations with the Pujaree she harped on her isolation, which was in such contrast to her life in Kerala. But what struck him most was her belief that she was being punished by men for having left the land of her birth. The Pujaree would let her down as well, she was certain. He tried to allay her fears, but she seemed to be obsessed by his future infidelity, which was no more than the punishment to which she was exposed for marrying a stranger.

Months ago, when she confided that she wanted Betta's son – the Pujaree had assured her that it would be a boy – he regretted having predicted the child's sex, for the scandal of abduction would damage his status as a priest. He refused to have anything to do with her plan to seize Betta's child, and said he would desert her if she insisted.

'I told you you would,' Mrs Singh said. 'Go then.'

But on the eve of his departure he conceived the plan to entice Betta back to his old home and extract a promise from him while he was under the influence of a drug he would prescribe.

Now that Betta would not keep his promise the Pujaree advised her to try to understand why she felt the need to have her son's child. If she did it might help her to struggle with the part of herself that was bent on destroying her. He believed it was hatred for Meena which hid behind the desire to bring up another blood-male. He had taught her to be strong and now she proved to be as helpless as Lahti had been under Sukrum's influence.

'I'm so confused!'

He could not forget the days when he came as a visitor and admired the firmness with which she ran her affairs, like a patriarch in the midst of his descendants.

They discussed the matter for several days until the Pujaree, in exchange for her undertaking to convert the lower storey of her house into a temple, agreed to harm the child as a punishment to Betta. And it was to that end that they went to see Betta's son, taking with them gifts, jewellery and diminutive garments. The Pujaree had instructed her what to do when she approached the infant, that on no account she must speak to its mother. Afterwards they were to leave at once, even if it meant abandoning the goblet maker, who was invariably one of the last to go home.

It was Mrs Singh who had sent Sukrum to watch Betta's house in order to catch a glimpse of Meena. He was to report back to her if the daughter-in-law was indeed expecting. Sukrum protested with gestures on each occasion for, as Mrs Singh had told Betta, he was reluctant to go out. Yet, on his way back from Plaisance, he would stop at the spot where Lahti used to accompany him when he went fishing late at night and watch the spray being whipped away from the crest of incoming waves and fish dying in pools left by a receding tide and gulls that stood immobile on the shore, their feathers ruffled by a constant wind.

Each time Sukrum reported that Meena was getting larger round the waist, even when he had failed to see her. One day when he refused to go and keep watch Mrs Singh threatened him and he replied with an eloquent gesture of his fingers, followed by another he was in the habit of using when he indicated that the young Mrs Singh's belly was increasing in girth. Mrs Singh ordered him to do as he was told and he was seen to walk up the road with bowed head and hunched shoulders, like a dog that had lost the will to show fight. From then on he never refused, keeping his contempt for the Pujaree and his hatred of Mrs Singh to himself.

She telephoned Betta on Navaratri, the last of the days dedicated to Saraswati, believing that by then any deformity in the infant would have already shown itself. But Betta was in high spirits, from which she deduced that his son was in excellent health. She heard little of what he said when he spoke of the house which Meena had decorated with dolls and clay figures of gods and goddesses. The clay goblet crowned with a coconut had been knocked over by one of the children and Meena, who had invited a group of girls that evening to sing and dance before it, went out herself during surgery hours to find a replacement. And each word he spoke about his wife increased her rancour.

That night she challenged the Pujaree to deny that he had failed, but he urged her to wait. The child was hardly accustomed to his new world. And so the days went by, during which she was obliged to practise the patience he had sought to inculcate in her.

Chapter 41

When Arjun was nine months old the sick-nurse told Betta that there was something strange about him.

'What?'

'I don't know, Doctor.'

Betta examined Arjun with trembling hands, but could find no defect in his son. He had noticed exactly what the sick-nurse was incapable of putting into words, an expression about the boy's eyes and a peculiarity in his gait as he crept about the floor; but he waited for someone else to point out the fault, telling himself that his imagination was not to be trusted.

'What do you see wrong?' Betta demanded. 'I can't find anything the matter with him.'

'It's nothing I can put my finger on. I'm sorry.'

'In your work,' Betta said harshly, 'there isn't any room for guessing. Facts are facts. Arjun is as normal as any child you'll find.'

And for the rest of the day Betta could not keep his eyes off the boy, watching the way he dispatched a ball across the room, the heavy, awkward turn he made on the palms of his hands. Leaving the surgery to the sick-nurse that afternoon, he took Arjun for a ride through the nearby villages, fondling him at every turn as though he were trying to make up for some wrong he had committed. His grief was indescribable.

The morning Meena asked him a question which contained an oblique reference to Arjun, he knew that she had noticed.

Once Bismatie went off to school and Betta found Meena in the hospital, where she often helped the old ladies with their work. He voiced his fears about Arjun, and Meena, unusually calm, said that they should not jump to conclusions. Since he was not diseased it was best to wait until it was time for him to speak and walk.

Betta wrote to George Merriman that afternoon to tell him about Arjun and begged him to come and see him as soon as he could. He came the following Sunday and the two men talked for hours. They went to see the Mulvi Sahib, who was sitting at a window.

'Courage, Betta. It's not the time for sentimental words. You must attack!'

The Mulvi Sahib was talking as much of Betta as of himself, for he knew that he was unlikely to live out the year. And instead of discussing Arjun's apparent deformity, he took the two men down to inspect the recent acquisitions in his aviary and explained to them the reason for the jerky flight of many small birds.

'They "put away" their wings in the non-flying position every few seconds. Isn't that extraordinary? They don't flap their wings all the time as people think. Mind you, lots of small boys have probably noticed it: the coconut saki does so for fairly long periods.'

And in that manner, between George Merriman's manifest concern and the Mulvi Sahib's practical wisdom, Betta found a relief he would not have believed possible earlier in the week.

'How's your father, Mr Merriman?' the Mulvi Sahib asked.

'He's well enough. He's given up beekeeping and other things because of his arthritis.'

'Ah, the hands, the hands,' said the Mulvi Sahib. 'Your father and I. . . . We're like houses on leaning pillars. People pass them and they don't notice their windows any more or the name on the gate. All they can think is, "When will it fall? It's worse than last year. How much more can it lean?" My hands are in good shape. See?'

And he held up his hands for his visitors to see.

'It's my legs that let me down. You are two medical men. Don't you find it strange that we can be objective when talking about animals, but froth at the mouth if someone makes an objective statement about humans? I read that the harpy eagle, in seizing the head of a monkey, kills it instantly. It grasps it with such force that its eyes pop out; that its own life is at stake if it fails to kill it with a blow, because a struggling monkey would damage its flight feathers. Imagine going on like that about humans! "Murder is essential to the survival of contemporary man."'

'But it's not the same thing, is it?' George Merriman objected. 'The first is a bald statement of a physical fact, but the second is speculation; and, in any case, it contains a moral judgement.'

An argument began, into which Betta was drawn, putting aside his grief for a time. They talked about Mrs Merriman's court and the conditions under which the colonial authorities would allow it to function, and of the lawyers' opposition to it; about the success of rice planting in the country, due mainly to the expertise of immigrants from the Punjab; about Critchlow the trade-union leader, who had frightened the life out of the administration, and about the latest massacre of aboriginal Indians in Brazil. They talked until it was time for George to leave in order to be in time for his West Coast ferry. And afterwards the Mulvi Sahib and Betta continued talking, as though they had been warned that it was their last meeting.

'I've been to see Ma,' Betta said.

'So she relented!'

'It was months ago,' Betta said, and went on to tell him how he was drugged.

'Drugged?'

'I don't know whether it was Ma or the Pujaree.'

Pressed to give details of his experience Betta could not, for he recalled nothing but empty rooms and the sound of a sarangi.

'Who invited you to the house?'

'Ma did.'

'Betta,' the Mulvi Sahib said after a moment's reflection. 'I don't want to know any more. God knows why we're put on this earth. God knows. Do you know? I hope success doesn't destroy you too. Oh I know all about your hospital and your patients who think you're a god. This is the time for vigilance. You're very much like your mother, Betta. You won't find anyone to speak evil of her, except Sukrum. And you know what he is, don't you? But I say he's our conscience.'

'What must I be vigilant about?'

'Everything. Anyway don't let's talk about your affairs: you're not the most important person in the world. In your family your wife's far more important than you.'

Betta, surprised at the change of tone in the Mulvi Sahib's voice, felt the old hostility, but was ashamed of it at a time when he should be showing him the greatest consideration.

'Anyway,' the Mulvi Sahib went on. 'Go and see your mother as quickly as possible.'

'Why?'

'Go and say you were wrong to abandon her. Use the word "abandon". She'll understand.'

'But it isn't true.'

'For your mother it is! Admit you abandoned her and that you accept the Pujaree as your stepfather and have the greatest respect for him.'

'But why?' Betta asked.

'Because your family is probably in grave danger. At Leonora you could have been seriously injured, but now it's your family. . . . Why not do as I say? I warned you about taking up the West Coast job rashly and wasn't I proved right? Now you will lose nothing by prostrating yourself before your mother and saying you were wrong, that you were proud. Why are you so stubborn? There are things you should know which I can't divulge now, things I perhaps should have told you when you came back from abroad. I tried, but you wanted to protect yourself with your arrogance from my "interference". . . . I'm exhausted from speaking.'

He paused for breath, but did not take his eyes off Betta who was lost for words. And still, in spite of the urgency in the teacher's voice, he was unable to humble himself, as he was unable to accept the Pujaree as a member of his family or beg his mother's forgiveness.

Betta bade the Mulvi Sahib goodbye and, when halfway towards the gate, returned to embrace him, a gesture that touched the old man so deeply he hurried back inside to close up for the night.

The next morning the Mulvi Sahib freed his birds. At first only a coconut saki seized its chance to escape, and then in ones and twos they took flight, emptying the aviary gradually, until a single bird remained high up on its perch in a corner, his latest troupial which, like its predecessors, was not expected to live more than a fortnight in captivity. On seeing the Mulvi Sahib enter the cage the bird took refuge in the opposite corner, flapping its wings frantically. But when he wielded a fruit-picking pole the troupial fled, almost colliding with the aviary door. Here and there the ground was flecked with feathers, like islands of shimmering mould, and instead of the incessant chirping there was nothing but an unusual silence. The Mulvi Sahib picked up a tiny feather, turned it over, stroked it between his fingers and then let it fall to the ground in a slow, pendulum-like motion.

He had made his will recently, in which he left all his real and personal property to the mosque, with a special endowment for the construction of a mimba of rosewood and purple heart. Now he could spend the last months of his life in recollection of the demons he had overcome, of the hundred metamorphoses between childhood and old age, and paths he only recognized when they were behind him.

Chapter 42

Betta told Meena of the Mulvi Sahib's advice to make peace with his mother 'at all costs'.

'I should prostrate myself before her.'

'He said at all costs?'

'Something like that,' Betta answered. 'According to him we are in serious danger.'

'What're you going to do?'

'I have no idea.'

'Let me go, Betta. Is only if she accept me that things will be all right. I can't see you prostrating yourself, but I can.'

But he refused to allow his wife to take the risk of visiting his mother, telling her that he was going to think of something.

During breakfast Bismatie asked her father if they could go to Rani's and take their Navaratri presents.

'It's my hospital day,' he told her. 'I thought you'd promised to help in the hospital.'

'I don't feel like it any more,' Bismatie answered.

'When you grow up,' her mother put in, 'you can't break promises like that.'

'She say she not going to grow up,' Gita said, believing she had disclosed some great secret her sister was keeping from the world.

'I *am* going to grow up . . . but slowly.'

'I'll take them,' Meena said, 'if I can have the car. It won't be the same exchanging presents tomorrow when Navaratri is over.'

'If you want,' Betta said. 'But Bismatie must agree not to break her promise next time.'

'I promise, Pa. Never again! And I won't tell a lie either.'

'So you tell lies too,' Meena said with mock gravity.

'I told three yesterday. But from now on I won't tell a lie or break a promise.'

And with that assertion she earned a kiss from her mother.

'I don' tell lies or break promises,' said Gita. 'Can I get a kiss too?'

Meena kissed her as well.

'Arjun just woke up,' Bismatie declared, her head to one side.

'We're taking Arjun too?' came Gita's inevitable question. She did not like going out with the baby because the attention she was once shown and had come to expect, as the younger child in the family, was now lavished on Arjun.

'Yes, we're taking Arjun,' Meena said. 'And if you don't have manners at Auntie Rani you won't come the next time.'

Meena had seized the opportunity to go and see Rani with whom she intended leaving the children while she went to her mother-in-law's house against her husband's wishes. The request to go visiting had come so soon after their discussion and had been made with such eagerness that Betta suspected at once why it was made. And later he was to ask himself why he pretended not to know that his wife was going to a house where he was certain that he had been drugged when he had refused her permission to do so earlier.

'Get Tipu to crank the car for you,' Betta told her when he had

got the engine going. 'I can't stand the idea of him standing by
while you do it.'

'We'll see,' she said.

Gita waved frantically in an effort to make up for the inaction
of Bismatie, who was tending the baby on the rear seat.

Meena took Rani aside and told her what she intended doing.

'And if Betta find out?'

'Oh, I'll tell him when we get home,' Meena said.

'I'll go with you,' Rani offered.

'No. The Mulvi Sahib said that Betta should prostrate
himself. He won't do it, but I will; and you can't be there if I do
that.'

'Why?'

Meena could not answer truthfully and Rani explained that if
she did it in her presence it would be likely to appease Mrs Singh
even more.

'But what can she do?' asked Meena.

Rani finally told Meena what she had hinted at on several
occasions since they became close friends, but had never dared
disclose.

'The Mulvi Sahib think she killed her husband with a tea of
oleander flowers. When I was a girl I did hear them talk. For
God's sake, don't tell Betta I told you. He doesn't know, and
deep down he does idolize his mother. The Mulvi Sahib know
all her secrets and at one time could get her to do what he
wanted. . . .'

Rani went on to explain that when Mr Singh brought his bride
back from Kerala she was so unhappy she wanted to go back
home. She used to go and watch the East Indian women working
in the cane fields and was always complaining that she had been
enticed away from her home. Her husband, fed up with her
complaints, moved to a village where there weren't any East
Indians. Then the children began to come, all of them stillborn,
until she was driven to such desperation she demanded to be
taken back to her beloved Kerala about which she now spoke
obsessively. But a pandit advised Mr Singh to go to Barbados
with her, for malaria was almost unknown there. Three months

later they came back because she could not stand the incessant roaring of the sea and the screeching of doves by night and the absence of canals. Besides, she saw no East Indians there and insisted she could not live in a country without Indians. She was pregnant again, with Betta, who was born a healthy baby and grew up to be a healthy small boy. As soon as he was old enough to understand she began to feed his mind with ideas of saving East Indians from the malarial scourge, although she denied it later. Rani did not know why she killed her husband.

'Didn't the police question her?'

'Yes. It was Aji who told them she and Mr Singh never had a quarrel in the time she was living there and that Mrs Singh loved him deeply.'

Aji had protected her, but despised her for what she had done.

'So,' said Meena. 'How she can interfere with me when she was once suspected of murder?'

Rani was impressed by her friend's argument, but said she would ring at five o'clock to see if everything was well.

Meena was received with a formal hospitality and long periods of silence, during which her mother-in-law ignored her. And when she spoke there were no questions about her grandchildren or the home or the number of children they expected to have. Sukrum entered the drawing room from time to time accompanied by the dogs, which sniffed about her legs while she closed her eyes, praying that they would be taken away. Mrs Singh noticed her discomfiture, but persisted in her reticence, except to enquire whether she wanted Sukrum to bring her any more food or drink. And she found herself eating because she was embarrassed and because the mother was so different from the son and because of the overpowering presence of the distant continent in Mrs Singh's white sari and pictures that decorated the walls.

Seeking out some object on which to fix her eyes in order to avoid her mother-in-law's scrutiny – she was convinced Mrs Singh kept her eyes on her whenever she turned her head – Meena gazed at a smoking incense stick resting in a bronze vase placed beneath an open window. She watched the indolent column of smoke gather speed then disperse to make the picture of a tree.

Suddenly Meena was gripped by an impulse to scream, but certain that she would compromise herself irretrievably in Mrs Singh's eyes she asked for something else to eat.

'Sukrum!'

He came with his dogs, barefooted and ill-clad, intimidating Meena with an expression of unconcealed exasperation.

'Bring some more dossa and bhagee.'

It was mid-afternoon and the only sound from outside was the noise of a passing car dying away in the distance. Meena wanted to plead with Mrs Singh, to speak with her and to explain that she was in no way responsible for Betta's independence, that her only desire was to raise a family.

'As I said,' she tried once more, 'Betta can't forgive himself for not asking for your help in choosing a wife.'

'I know,' Mrs Singh replied.

Sukrum set down the food before her and she noticed the condition of his hands, the long, elegant, well-tended fingers which might have been those of a woman. He took away her soiled plate and left her alone once more with Mrs Singh, who was sitting in a corner of her deep chair.

No sooner had Meena begun to eat than she realized how foolish she had been to ask for more, since she was now obliged to allow a certain time to elapse before taking her leave. She listened for every noise that could engage her attention, anything that was capable of relieving a tension so palpable she could no longer think of it as her embarrassment. All her gestures were misplaced, just as Mrs Singh's, deliberate, but relaxed, were calculated to deepen her panic.

All of a sudden the dogs reappeared at the entrance of the room, unaccompanied by Sukrum. Meena, gripping the arms of her chair, closed her eyes and waited. And just as suddenly as the animals had appeared, so their gasping filled the room and Meena, unable to restrain herself any longer, uttered a piercing shriek which resounded throughout the house, accompanied by the bellowing of the dogs. When all was still once more she opened her eyes to find Sukrum standing above her and Mrs Singh in the same half-reclined position in the corner of her easy chair.

'Oh, God, I want to go home,' she pleaded. 'Please take me to the gate.'

'Why didn't you say you were afraid of dogs?' Mrs Singh asked. 'You frightened them with your scream. They could have bitten you.'

'Please, can I go?' Meena begged, trembling uncontrollably.

'Why did you come here? Why did Betta send you?'

'Betta, Betta,' she kept whispering, convinced of her mother-in-law's madness. Then she remembered that Betta had told her how his mother had consented that the Pujaree should replace her shrine to Lakshmi, goddess of prosperity, by one to Durga, the destroyer. And just thinking of the name struck terror in her heart. 'I don't want to have anything to do with these people,' her mother used to say during the twice-yearly Kali Mai puja celebrations and she was responsible for her own abhorrence of all kinds of sacrifice.

'Please send the dogs away,' Meena said in a hardly audible voice.

'The dogs are gone,' Mrs Singh answered.

She was startled by an incomprehensible cry in the street below and the ringing of a small bell, which was repeated several times.

'It's only the shave-ice vendor. He's calling the children. Do you want some shave-ice?'

'Yes, thank you.'

Mrs Singh asked Sukrum to buy some shave-ice for himself and Meena.

'Tie the dogs.'

Out of respect for her hostess Meena sucked the shave-ice Sukrum brought back, beginning with the side that was soaked in a vermilion syrup.

'You want another one?' Mrs Singh asked, even before Meena had finished what she was eating.

'No, thanks.'

Insects wandered in and out of the windows, some pursuing a noiseless flight across the drawing room, while others hovered indefatigably amongst the endless rain of floating dust.

'I must go now,' Meena said at last.

'Why go so quickly when you've come so far? The Pujaree will be back soon.'

'Please tell me why you don't like me, Mrs Singh.'

'Do you want anything else to eat?'

Meena, stunned at the calm with which the question was put, shook her head.

'Did you celebrate Navaratri?'

'Yes,' Meena answered. 'We always do.'

'And did you buy a lot of painted dolls?'

'Yes.'

'That's why I don't like you, Meena.'

'But why?'

'Because you stole my son.'

The words fell like ice on her neck.

'I know a woman,' continued Mrs Singh, 'who gave birth to deformed babies. First they looked odd round the eyes. Then more and more the weakness showed itself, until everyone could see. . . . I'm frightening you.'

She leaned back in her reclining position.

'It happened in Kerala,' she added in a flat tone.

How can I love him now? Meena thought, searching her memory for the resemblances between Betta and his mother, his at times stilted language, his preference for brass ornaments and a trance-like vision of things as they ought to be. And now, at a time when her mother-in-law had offended her by mocking her innocent child, she called to mind the Mulvi Sahib's counsel, that Betta should prostrate himself in front of his mother in the usual Muslim posture of worship. And, without reflecting any longer on the meaning of the word, Meena stood up before Betta's mother and, to the latter's surprise, knelt before her, then bent her head forward until it touched the ground.

'I beg forgiveness for not coming to ask your advice in all important matters and for being a bad daughter-in-law. You are my husband's mother and I dare not call your name.'

Mrs Singh, confused at the unexpected obsequiousness, had no idea how to react. She needed time to decide whether the young woman was sincere and what she would do in case she was.

'I beg you to forgive Betta. Rani said he dotes on you.'

'Rani. . . . Yes, Rani. Women with small dowries. Did I torment you? Stand up.'

Meena stood up and then sat down again at a nod from Mrs Singh.

'Did I torment you, Meena? I cannot like you. . . . The Mulvi Sahib freed me from *my* torment and then the Pujaree came along and freed me from the Mulvi Sahib, and taught me things I had forgotten. I am helpless without them. This terrible dependence on men. . . . My husband moved as soon as I became friendly with a woman, because she influenced me too much, he said. A stranger always comes along to scatter flowers on your soul. . . . You should hear me talk in Malayalam. I've never become accustomed to English and my husband used to say I can't relax in it. How can I relax in a language I learned from books? You *must* have a close woman friend, somebody like Rani, who will stick to you, for your sake and because of her association with our family. She went through a lot, like Lahti. But Lahti was not up to it. Secrets. . . . Have you got secrets from Betta?'

'No.'

'I forgive you, Meena, but can't like you. Do you want something to eat?'

'Something small, please.'

'Sukrum! Bring Mrs Singh something to eat and take some too. You've tied the dogs? Good. . . .' then, turning back to Meena, she continued.

'In a foreign language nothing you say means what you intend and what *you* think I mean I don't. I have not said what I meant for nearly forty years.'

Then the older Mrs Singh fell back into the same silence with which she had welcomed her daughter-in-law. But now Meena felt she was no longer being ignored.

Sukrum put a plate of sweets on the table and left the two women.

The spectacle of Meena on her knees acknowledging her inferior status had aroused in Betta's mother a strange urge to confide in her. At the same time she could not bear the thought of being addressed full-mouth by her son's wife; and besides, she always finished by resenting those in whom she confided. She was certain she had left some part of herself on the other side of the sea, something that might have come to terms with this endless journey in which she was doomed never to arrive, with is luminous images of clay lamps burning through a long Divali night, of estate chimneys and caged iguanas. 'Did I torment you, Meena?' she had asked, while feeling that it was she who had been the victim of a torment which had its origins in her marriage ceremony. Now she wondered if the peace, indeed the joy, the Pujaree had brought her was not like those cane fires that rage for a short time, leaving the pith untouched. Now, the last evening of Navaratri, she would be alone with her painted dolls, except for the company of a dumb waiter and a man who had persuaded her that there was a state of ineffable contentment attainable through sacrifice. . . .

The telephone rang.

'It's for me, I think,' Meena said, remembering Rani's promise to ring.

'You?'

'Rani said she'd ring.'

'Ah.'

Meena hurried to the telephone, and after a short conversation with Rani said that she would have to go.

'Can I bring the children visiting?' she asked, grateful for what appeared to be a successful mission.

'I'll see,' Betta's mother answered. 'Why not bring Arjun first?'

Meena drove back to Rani's house where the two families exchanged their Navaratri gifts and Tipu told the children his favourite stories, ending with the tale of Ganesha, the elephant-headed god, to whom he was in the habit of praying.

Later the neighbours' three girls called with gifts, and Rani asked the eldest to dance for her as she had done the year before; but in the year that had passed she had grown shy and professed to have forgotten the steps. Rani did not insist, although she knew that her parents made her dance for strangers in her own home where she dared not refuse. The girls stayed for a while, then went away when the minimum prescribed time for visiting had elapsed, for they felt out of place in a house where there were no children of their age and Tipu never ceased telling them that when Bhagwan went to school he was already able to read.

Meena knew that Tipu would not go out and that she would have to wait until Rani came to see her before she could relate what had happened that afternoon. The children had been fed and Arjun was asleep in Bhagwan's old cradle in a corner of the single-storeyed cottage. She was never able to understand Rani's adaptability. She herself had needed months to become accustomed to living in a mansion when she married. Rani, on the other hand, had moved from a mansion to a tiny house and had married a man with few qualities; had made peace with Mrs Singh after having been chased away and seemed as content as she had always known her. Her peace of mind seemed to defy time and circumstance, in the way certain plants are indifferent to sun or shade. Meena was always told she was the contented member of the family, which she never understood, because she was simply what she was, knowing neither Gopie's frenzy for new experiences nor her mother's ambition. But Rani's unstriving contentment changed everyone around her; and often, when she and Betta were separated by some misunderstanding, she would ask herself, 'What would Rani do if she was in my position?' Her mother-in-law, with the instinct of experience, had advised her to seek Rani's friendship, not suspecting that it had already been consummated by a thousand confidences. Yet, in the aftermath of a meeting during which she had been afraid of being devoured by Mrs Singh's dogs, Meena was unable to confide in Rani because Tipu was present. It had taken her several years of married life to discover secret places from which Betta was excluded, as if he were a stranger, and that in this respect Rani was no different.

Rani saw Meena off, full of regret for having divulged Mrs Singh's secret, for she knew how husbands and wives invariably shared information given them in the strictest confidence. What was done was done and she could only hope that Betta would not hold it against her, that he knew her too well to be certain she had not acted from malice.

Rani was expecting her second child and had told Tipu that morning. He enjoined her to say nothing to anyone until his parents knew; but, had she been able to speak with Meena, she would have broken her word. She often wondered about herself and her standing in the eyes of those who could point to mother and father, sisters and brothers as guarantors of their own integrity. And she would wonder why she shared Mrs Singh's past with Meena, and whether she had done so to avoid sharing the burden of another secret which troubled her.

Chapter 43

The pattern of malarial infection had become clear in the previous few years, partly on account of the work done by Dr Giglioli and partly because the indenture labour system which brought immigrants from India had come to an end, thus allowing comparisons to be made between those who came and those who were born in the country. Although the story of immigrants at Mara had often been repeated no one at that time had drawn the conclusions that now seemed obvious. Mara, a small estate on the Berbice river, was allocated twenty new arrivals in 189x and, two years later, applied to the Immigration Department for twenty more, since the others had all died. Within three years the estate was ordered to be closed as the last twenty had perished as well. The health authorities were now certain that children born in the country acquired a partial immunity to malaria by the age of three, so that afterwards they only caught a form of the disease that was less than fatal. However, reinfection did seem to affect the child-bearing capacity of women and exposed the anaemic to the depredations of associated ailments. For Betta and other doctors the problem was now as much political and economic as medical. Even if a miracle drug were to be discovered the poor hygiene conditions on the sugar estates would ensure a high mortality rate.

The longer he practised the more urgently certain questions pressed upon him. All the doctors in the country, save a few specialists like Dr Giglioli, were British trained. This remarkable fact had never been raised in the press, to his knowledge. Not only were medical students forced to study at universities abroad – an absurdity in itself – but they were tied to a single country thousands of miles across the sea!

Then there was the organization of medical practice itself, which was based on the experience of an imperial country, immensely rich, immensely arrogant, with apparently little interest in the health of its own people, unless the labour supply to British factories was threatened. People with the ability and experience of the sick-nurse were excluded from practice, even in areas where there were no doctors. His mistakes were no more grave than those made by qualified doctors whose blunders went unnoticed. More than once he had diagnosed a case of measles as smallpox and had to be told to look for spots on the palms of the hands to eliminate the latter as a possibility. On the other hand he had arrived at the conclusion, independently, that East Indian children with bow-legs had a staple diet of roti.

Now that Betta's aspirations had found expression in his hospital he found himself thinking endlessly on these things and was forced to conclude that the practice of medicine, with its relegation of people like the sick-nurse to a minor rôle, was bound up with much larger problems, like the country's unwholesome dependence on imported flour, corrugated-iron sheets for roofing, and ice-apples associated with Christmas and the manufactured playthings given to children at the December festival. And his reflections made him ashamed that at one time he had contemplated conversion to Christianity, to the Mulvi Sahib's disgust. He now saw his dying teacher as a prophet and tried to call to mind his observations, with their cryptic messages. Like a sleeper in the forest who awakes to a confusion of leaves and forbidding shapes, he was only slowly coming to realize his inadequacies, that he was at the end of one apprenticeship and the beginning of another, that perhaps it would be thus throughout his life. In some ways Meena had come to marriage armed with weapons he did not possess. She accepted Arjun's disability, which became more manifest with every passing week, while *he* could only contemplate his anguish, like the devastation of a landscape in the grip of a drought, and wander through the parched fields plagued by flies and the menace of sunstroke. How was Arjun, with his wandering gaze and imperfect gait? And his mother, whose only visitors were the family of musicians who played for her alone, sad ragas on the veena, while the elder daughter sang in a quivering voice? Arjun's disability had changed him, just as travelling along the road of his choice had changed his mother; and the discovery of his own dilemma gave him a glimpse of what she must have suffered. The practice of medicine had familiarized him with all kinds of degradations of the body and the soul and, in the beginning, he would examine with his eyes people he came across in the street, judging one to have a curvature of the spine, another to be suffering from malfunction of the kidneys and yet another with protruding eyes from thyroid trouble. But only his own woes were capable of bringing home to him the reality of the suffering of others.

Betta grew to love his son excessively, and when he took his family on outings he would sit the boy beside him and benefit from his tranquil ways and instinct for seeing the unseen in the world around him, calling his and Meena's attention to details that had escaped them, the burrs of grass carried away in a sheep's wool, birds pecking at grit, fluttering bits of paper above shop doorways decorated with good-luck signs, the odour of rain on the wind; so that often Meena said, 'You see!' in recognition of a kind of wisdom unusual for normal children. Betta, reassured by Arjun's unawareness of his own abnormality and by his even temper, not only came to accept his condition, but wondered whether it was not for the best, like Meena's appeasing gesture of prostration, which had disarmed his mother.

When Arjun was two he began visiting Rani's house with his sisters, and there he became attached to Tipu, who let him hold pieces of jewellery while he cleaned them with a mixture of lime juice and high wine. Arjun liked the house because it was small, and for its accoutrements, the transparent cachets of coarse material with dried lavender flowers and carvings of animals acquired from Mrs Singh. He was loved because he made no demands and because no one could deny Tipu's son's superiority to him. Yet Tipu's affection for Arjun was enduring, and on days when there was little work he would ride to Plaisance to watch with him for the arrival of the Rosignol train.

The Mulvi Sahib and Meena's father died on consecutive days, the former wasted by age and the latter from complications following an operation on his right leg. Betta attended both funerals, the first one alone and the second with Meena and the children, who stayed in the death house while their parents joined the long, silent procession, enveloped in the red dust of the village road. On the way back from the cemetery many women stopped to have a ritual bath in the drainage canal while the men went to a point beyond the koker, where they cleansed themselves in the muddy waters of a sideline trench. And the performance of these ablutions after a burial brought home to Meena and Betta how far they had become separated from the Indian village community, which held out against assimilation. Each beat of the elongated mridangam, followed by the thud of feet on the dry ground, had stricken Gopie with such terror that she groped for Meena's hand, as though she were still a girl and could not walk the streets alone after dark. And yet, when her mother joined the other women in the canal beside the roadway, she went on with Meena back to the house. There the two sisters waited for their mother and the men, some of whom, like Betta, had congregated under the house.

Betta took the opportunity to strike up a conversation with Gopie's husband, who had not walked with the procession; but finding him uncommunicative he joined a group of middle-aged men from the Essequibo islands. One of them saw Meena's father's death as the demise of the old breed of second-generation immigrants, who had not entirely come to terms with their identity as Guyanese, but thought of India as no more than their religious home. They spoke disparagingly of their parents' shrines, of the rules which isolated wives from the household at the time of their period; yet they attended their local temple and sent their children to Hindi classes. They gave off a whiff of decay, an unfamiliar reek at variance with his experience of their fellow Indians of Kitty and the East Coast, less passive in their behaviour. Even the speech of these merchants from Leguan and Wakenaam was the drawl of those out of touch with the city or estate life, the slow, uninhibited voice of self-satisfaction. Yet, Betta thought, their security was the ideal after which he strove for his East Indian patients, a condition which held at bay leprosy, filaria and the ravages of malaria. He made an effort to contribute to their conversation, but was met by a deferential silence when they learned that he was a doctor, like the traveller who, on discovering that his loquacious companion was none other than Death, decided to answer no more questions, lest his words condemn him.

The Mulvi Sahib's burial was a quiet affair, attended only by men, mostly acquaintances from the Church Street mosque, to which Betta was invited for a memorial service. Copying, like the rest of the gathering, the imam's posture of prostration, he suddenly recalled his wife's prostration before his mother and could not suppress the tears that troubled his eyes, at the thought of her and the Muslim God his friend had worshipped without caring to justify his existence. If the abstract patterns on the wall induced meditation in the minds of the worshippers, they revealed to him the features of the dead man, who had provided him with a model of the man he wished to be and the memory of which still instructed him, even now . . . 'until the day of resurrection'. The words, resounding in his ears like the Mulvi Sahib's own, were answered by the congregation's 'Amin'. Then came the sermon, in Urdu. And Betta was overcome by a feeling of despair, as though the incomprehensible words had some affinity with the procession at his father-in-law's funeral and the thud of the long drum which accompanied it on the village street.

At the end of the service Betta left with the crowd of worshippers and sought out his shoes on the racks stretching the length of the porch.

Meena's mother would close the shop she had run with her husband so many years, for she was incapable of carrying on without him. Unwilling to leave the West Coast, where she was born and grew up among the Tamil community, she waited for Gopie's husband to offer her a refuge. But, while he treated her with great deference when she came visiting, he never once suggested any sort of arrangement, for at the time of betrothal, his parents, who had found out all they could, not only about Gopie, but also about her parents and relations, foresaw Mr Ramcharran's death and advised their son as to his conduct in the event. Mrs Ramcharran cursed herself for her haste in marrying off her favourite daughter to an unfeeling man. She pitied Gopie because her outspoken character would wilt under a yoke designed by her husband's family and turned for support to Meena, who gave her one of the spare bedrooms overlooking the path where passengers entered and left the station and the leper woman sat, propped against her hoard of silver.

And so began a new phase in Betta's life, the accommodation of a second loss. Freed from the tensions of the years immediately after his return from abroad, he had found himself burdened with the first loss, that of the Merrimans' company and the satisfaction that followed his visits to their home. In retrospect the house on the Public Road resembled his friend hardly at all, bearing rather the marks of his father's and wife's personalities, with its white-faced clocks and mahogany boxes in which her 'clients'' letters were kept. The pleasure at the occasional trips Merriman made to see him was marred by his need to keep the sailing of the last ferry in mind, so that their conversations were like the abortive cocoons spun by inexpert grubs.

Many things he desired so passionately as a young man and which once seemed beyond his reach now appeared unexceptional, more especially his family and the hospital. He marvelled at his children's energy, at their indifference to the noonday heat, to the contents of newspapers and to their maternal grandmother with the bulging eyes of a Gemini woman.

Sometimes he would sit at a back window looking down at Meena harvesting herbs in the garden and think of those nights in the early part of their marriage when they lay beside each other listening to the wailing of goat-suckers. She would be fondled nowhere except in their bed, which she saw as her kingdom, in the manner of those women who belong to darkness and can only speak of making love as 'spending the night' with a man. Their life together, like an imperceptibly moving cloud, had now arrived overhead, bright, altered in shape, bearing the residue of countless encounters.

At other times, especially in the evenings, his life would appear to him to be under menace and he would go off to a sick-house as to an appointment with death, through a landscape of brooding crows, zinc sheets rotting in the rain and the ceaseless calling of frogs, convinced that his invalid son and his daughters would wake up the following morning as orphans with no one to support them. And the next day, prompted by the vision, he would make one of his fruitless attempts at reconciliation with his mother.

Chapter 44

After Meena's visit the Pujaree told Mrs Singh that she had lost her ascendancy over her son and daughter-in-law by accepting the young woman's submission.

'If I was there it wouldn've happen. From now on you musn't let them cross your door mouth.'

And so began the final stages of Mrs Singh's isolation. The Pujaree's control over her soul was so complete she even complied with his ban on going out, and her confinement behind the half-closed windows obliged her to cultivate a secret, vicarious relationship with the outside world. She listened avidly for the whistle of the morning train to Rosignol, for the hucksters banging on her gates in the belief that her retirement was bound to come to an end, since no one had ever died of losing a son or of hatred for a daughter-in-law. She watched the young people strolling in the direction of the sea wall and the kite-flyers returning home at dusk and tried to catch the whispered endearments of lovers below her window in Dowding Street, which a massive branch of the saman tree now obscured completely.

One evening, during the festival of Hussein and Hassan, a taja passed by on Vlissingen Road, its glittering edifice borne on the shoulders of a dozen men. An hour later she went out on the porch to witness the flames of its destruction rising above the houses in Kitty and imagined the structure laid out on the shore between the mangrove trees and the Public Road. Of late her dreams had taken on a composite character. Still set in Kerala, they bore the marks of her experience in the country of her adoption. The night she watched the flames marking the culmination of the Hussein and Hassan festival she dreamt that she was sitting on a covered boat drifting along a canal in Kerala. While the voices around her addressed one another in Malay-alam there was one softly spoken man who kept answering his neighbour in English with a marked Guyanese accent. She noticed, too, that she no longer counted in Malayalam, which, the Pujaree pointed out, was a sign that she no longer thought in that language.

'I am nothing, then,' she told him, feeling that her English was more stilted than ever.

'In a way you are nothing,' he answered.

That brief confirmation of her status roused Mrs Singh to rebellion and caused her to plot her extrication from the Pujaree's influence. He might have lied, for in her decline she needed a consoling hand and the illusion of an identity, which had not been eroded by distance and time.

When, during a midday meal, she announced that she was closing the house and going to live with Betta and his family, the Pujaree was so taken aback he fled the table, recalling how she had refused to pray in his company that morning. He delayed his return that night, for fear of discovering that Mrs Singh meant what she had said. He returned long after dark, full of conciliat-ory words and terrified of the consequences of his banishment, and found Sukrum in the company of his dogs, which were lying at the foot of the staircase gasping for breath in the extraordinary humidity of early August.

'What you're hanging about for? Why not go for a walk?' asked the Pujaree.

Sukrum spat into the bushes then turned to stare at him. But the Pujaree pretended to be indifferent to his insolence and went by, judging the distance to the top as he always did before making the long ascent.

The house was empty. After a while the Pujaree gave up searching for his wife and sat down to eat the meal that had been prepared for him and left in a soup tureen on the dining table. While pondering on Mrs Singh's whereabouts he slowly ate straight from the tureen, careful to soil as little of her ware and cutlery as possible. And, with the passing minutes, his anxiety gave way to a certainty of his imminent exclusion from the house with the air of muted luxury he had first glimpsed in the prints of Bakoshi paintings from the Punjab, the home of Mrs Singh's dead husband's forebears.

What had he done her? Had he not initiated her into the secrets of the world around them and saved her from the fate of the Sukrums and Lahtis? Had he not filled the empty space in her large bed where she had lain alone for the greater part of her life in a room haunted by the scent of verbena and mango blossom? She herself had told him how she used to weep when creole minstrels passed by in Dowding Street at the dead of night singing hymns to the accompaniment of mesmeric guitars. Was she not still a child? Like a child she loved listening to stories from the past, about the women he treated, who grew immune to pain, of children named after an ancestor, who came to assume his character, down to the most sullen defect.

So assiduously did the Pujaree feed his illusions of Mrs Singh's dependence on him, by the end of the meal he was confident that she would appear and say how she regretted her words; that she could not do without him by her side, nor could she learn to pray alone. But when the traffic on Vlissingen Road had all but ceased and the croaking of frogs resounded in the trenches Mrs Singh had not yet returned. He prepared to retire and before going to bed scanned Dowding Street and Vlissingen Road successively, but saw no one except a passer-by, a slowly moving shadow between the verges.

The Pujaree had no idea how long he had been sleeping nor why he awoke. There had been no loud noise, as far as he knew, nor was there a draught. But, on turning over, he saw spread out beside him Mrs Singh's wedding sari, its gold thread glistening against the pale hundred-year-old muslin. He slowly rose from his lying position, his eyes riveted on the garment as if it was a nest of serpents. Looking around him he saw no other evidence of her presence, neither her shoes nor her comb, which she was in the habit of leaving on the bedside table after she had loosened her hair for the night.

'Nenny!' he called softly, edging towards the door.

But the whispered endearment only roused the hounds to furious barking two storeys below, which in turn set off the small dogs in the neighbourhood. The Pujaree crept out of the room, leaving the door open. He then tiptoed down the stairs.

His situation made him realize to what an extent he was a stranger in the house, in spite of his influence over its owner. He could hear the animals snuffling as they searched the yard and the dead saman leaves crackling under their paws against the interminable croaking of frogs. Sweat was streaming from his body as he searched the house, ferreting in the shadowy corners and among the pieces of furniture scattered about the drawing room and gallery. But he discovered nothing to indicate that she might have been about, not even the faint, powdery scent of her garments.

Unable to return to the bedroom, he lay down full-length on the floor and fell asleep, even though from time to time the barking of a solitary dog spread throughout the district and grew into an overwhelming chorus.

In the middle of the night the Pujaree was awakened once more by the same obsessive thought that had preoccupied him on going to bed. It was Mrs Singh's passion for her son, an unnatural bond, in his view, which he had striven to destroy. He had managed to stem the flow of tales about her dead husband and oust his authority, and considered it only a matter of time before he freed her from the mysterious fascination Betta exercised over her. It now seemed that he had underestimated his task and called to mind the frequency with which he attacked doctors, their preoccupation with drugs and bread poultices. She had never once shown offence. Yet he should have known how to interpret her reactions, her silences, her oblique retorts, sometimes delayed for days. She often preferred silence to words, in the way the wedding sari had been spread out where she was accustomed to lie. From his own experience of healing he had learned some women's predilection for the language of their bodies and others' for the language of clothes. He recalled a woman's frigidity during two successive marriages; she confessed to him her indefatigable energy in a lover's bed, while seeking his advice on the eve of her third marriage. These gestures, like trees whose extensive roots remain below ground, seemed to him to be the essence of women's behaviour. And yet, knowing this, he had misjudged Betta's mother. He was fond of warning those who sought his counsel of the hold their maya exerted over them, the delusion they had constructed for themselves, like a house of many storeys which they mistook for the world itself. Had he not done the same in his bid for the possession of Mrs Singh's soul? With every victory over her will his grip had weakened, and now he was left to engage in a struggle with her dumb servant.

Day after day the Pujaree left for the temple and came back to the Vlissingen Road house to find that Mrs Singh had not returned. He was obliged to face Sukrum's growing insolence which began to verge on hostility when he was ordered to pay greater attention to maintaining a tidy yard. And by the end of a fortnight after Mrs Singh's disappearance he had become so truculent the Pujaree decided to have it out with him, fearing that, should he do nothing, Sukrum might try to intimidate him with the dogs, which now accompanied him wherever he went.

'You are not to bring the dogs in the house!' he ordered one morning when, hardly up from the mattress on which he slept in the kitchen, he was confronted with Sukrum sprawled in the Mulvi Sahib's chair and the dogs lying beneath the fixed wall-shutters.

'You hear me?' the Pujaree said, raising his voice.

At the harsh sound of his voice both dogs sat up. But Sukrum simply looked at him, apparently challenging him to impose an authority he did not recognize.

The Pujaree glanced at the dogs which were now so alert they reacted to every move he made. Then, as they settled once more into a reclining position, he withdrew, plotting all the while what he would do to get the better of his wife's protégé.

Everything was under the spell of the heavy rain which had been falling for several minutes. The leaves of the saman tree shuddered in the downpour and channels of water ran down the sloping yard under the palings and into concrete-lined gutters. Under shop fronts along Alexander Street people huddled against one another. Among them stood the Pujaree, waiting for a break in the deluge to make a run for his car, which he had left in front of the fruit sellers' stalls. He could see them in the distance under their makeshift tarpaulin covers, surrounded by pools of water. The gutters had overflowed and the sloping shop bridges resembled ramps leading to a river at ebb-tide. Clouds half-obscured by the rain had descended to the summits of the coconut trees in the yards behind the shops and appeared to bear the contents of an entire season. But the shower came to an end as abruptly as it had begun and within minutes the street was filled with passers-by who had been sheltering in the shops and under the awnings. From the surface of the road rose plumes of vapour like smoke from burnt stubble fields and an occasional motorcar slowly making its way through the crowd seemed enveloped in an early morning mist. The Pujaree drove the few hundred yards home and got out of his motorcar to open the front gates; but before he reached the bridge the dogs rushed towards him, growling and baring their teeth. Affecting to ignore them he took a step forward only to be met by such a fierce outburst that a neighbour from the mansion next door came out on to his porch to enquire if all was well, only to go back in when he heard the Pujaree calling out loudly for Sukrum.

Receiving no answer he went round to the entrance in Dowding Street and was followed by the dogs, one of which threatened to scale the low wooden gate. He was now standing no more than a dozen feet from the open window of the little room in which Sukrum lived; but the only effect of his shouting was to irritate the dogs to the point of frenzy.

Disconsolately, the Pujaree turned away, obliged to admit that Sukrum's insolence, the display of Mrs Singh's sari and the free rein given to her dogs to roam the yard at that time of afternoon were unmistakable signs of a decision to engineer a separation she did not wish to discuss.

'Ingratitude! Ingratitude!' he kept muttering to himself as he walked back to the car.

How humiliating it was to be turned away by Sukrum the fisherman!

He drove off in the direction of Newtown and turned into the cinema road which the Georgetown buses once used as a terminus when he first arrived to live as a refugee from the countryside.

The Pujaree parked his car beside the new temple porch which, still damp from the recent shower, glistened between the low trees in the gathering dusk. He called out to the janitor, but he had gone off to the rum shop, contrary to the undertaking he had given. Now everything seemed out of place, the white pine boards enclosing the porch – already too small to accommodate the growing number of devotees – the tiny craters made by the unusually large raindrops, the sheep grazing under the lime trees and the eruptions of light over a communal rubbish heap where fireflies congregated at nightfall. Nothing had changed there, yet everything had changed, so that what appeared symmetrical or attractive only a short week ago was now glimpsed through a distorting glass. The time he was served by his sister and the twins was far off, like a previous life he apprehended, but of which he had slight knowledge, a time of small ambitions when the celestial camphor fires were as dazzling to him as to his devotees. He had borne a twin, a companion with false appetites, whom he must put to rest, together with the objects of fascination he brought with him. His car, fine clothes, presents from his estranged wife, must all be laid aside.

The Pujaree let himself into the temple by the back door and made a bed with discarded garments he kept under the bloodstained altar. He lay down in his day clothes as his father used to do after toiling among the cane cutters. Then, just before dropping off, it occurred to him that Mrs Singh had sought to protect him and not to be protected by him, and that neither of them was capable of playing the rôle of the protected in the manner of the women and men who lived in her house.

Outside, in the narrow street, a gaunt man approached the

temple with two hounds on a leash. He stopped at the entrance and peered into the yard, only turning to go back the way he came when he had made out the motorcar parked under the trees.

BOOK 5
THE RETURN

Chapter 45

'Show me your lo-lo!' Bismatie ordered Bhagwan, who dutifully let down his short pants and allowed her to inspect his penis.

She did so with great earnestness, head bent forward and hands on her hips.

'Show me your thing,' Bhagwan said timidly.

'No!' Bismatie protested.

Bhagwan, angered by the refusal, retaliated by raising his pants with a swift movement of his hands.

'You always like that,' he accused her. 'I always got to do what you say.'

But Bismatie ignored him, her attention attracted by a shadow below the verandah.

'It's who?' Bhagwan asked.

'I thought was the beggar woman. I didn't see her since yesterday.'

'She must be dead,' he said.

'How can she die? Pa would've examined her first.'

They looked across the train lines at the spot where the leper woman was accustomed to sit with her legs stuck out on the path. To the children she represented a permanent aspect of their encompassed world, like the morning sun withering the grass or the debris of a household or the train arriving un-failingly at a certain hour.

It was Bismatie's birthday. Bhagwan's father had brought him the evening before on his bicycle, promising to come back the next afternoon for the party, which was intended to celebrate not only the anniversary of Bismatie's birth, but also her imminent attendance at the local Primary School. Bhagwan, on waking up that morning, had asked for his mother, imagining in his half-sleep that he was still at home. Meena reassured him that Rani and his father were coming late that day.

'I don't mind,' he said, now that he knew where he was.

Rani, who was seven months with child, had told Meena she was not certain whether she would come to Bismatie's party, uncertain whether she could face the long journey on Tipu's crossbar.

Bhagwan, disconcerted by his mother's excessively swollen form, wondered secretly if she was soon going to burst and, despite Meena's explanation of birth several months ago, believed that he had been sent away so that he should not witness his mother's misfortune. It was the first time that he had felt ill at ease in the Singhs' house. His irritation at not being allowed to see Bismatie's nakedness was as much due to a perplexity about his mother's condition as to his belief that she was an own-way person, and he sought refuge in silence while his friend scanned the area around the train station for the leper woman. He wanted to go home but was paralysed by an unspoken law which prevented children from speaking about such things. Like Bismatie, he leaned against the verandah rail to watch the view below them; but unlike her, his spirit was in his own home, where he was watching his mother moving about in a gait she had never used before, her shoulders leaning backwards and her feet spread outwards. He wondered whether she was walking like that now that he was away.

Gita, who was not allowed on the verandah except under her parents' supervision since she had nearly fallen from it two months ago, was keeping her young brother company in the drawing room. He was not permitted on the verandah either, because he did not obey Bismatie. From time to time Gita called out to her sister to complain that she did not want to be alone with Arjun, but received no answer.

Meena had just seen Betta off on his morning rounds, having promised to look in on the hospital on the ground floor. She had got up at five to water the herb garden in anticipation of a fierce heat that would scorch the ground and cause the moisture to evaporate in a couple of hours. Downstairs one of the old women sisters had already taken the sheets from the beds and spread them out on the grass along the palings, leaving the patients to wander about or sit on iron chairs scattered under the shade trees in the yard. She exchanged a few words with the sick-nurse, who had recently passed his examinations, but would not seek work elsewhere because he was too old to 'take a new road'.

'The new patient's gone, Miss Singh,' he told her.

'When?'

'This morning, before the doctor leave. He discharged himself. Is the third time.'

'Are you going to take him if he comes back?' Meena asked.

'Is up to the doctor, Miss Singh. He's a good payer. Every time he goes he does leave a five-dollar note.'

Meena went out into the yard and looked up to see Bismatie and Bhagwan leaning over the verandah.

'What're you doing?' she called up to them.

'Looking,' Bismatie answered.

'When the two of you're so quiet I always think you're up to no good.'

'No, Ma,' her daughter insisted.

'No what?'

'We're up to good.'

She left them to go upstairs.

Since her mother came to live with her family Meena spent more time downstairs, dividing her hours between the herb garden and helping in the hospital, which she could not bear to approach until a year ago, admitting to a dislike of dispensaries and the reek of disinfectant. She endured her mother's strictures with patience, never defending the children when she complained about the noise they made, nor about the soot from passing trains, nor the food, which Meena cooked herself, nor the inferior ground provisions sold at the open-air market where she went shopping. When the sun cast a shadow on the stairs she would come out and sit on the porch, muttering to herself that the East Coast was not like the West Coast and that no one should expect her to be content when she had spent more than twenty-five years running a shop with the scent of raw sugar and ginger in her nostrils. Everyone in the house suffered from her presence except the children, for whom she was a pale reflection of their parents, a grandmother with no power. Both the old women working in the hospital and the sick-nurse felt uneasy whenever she appeared downstairs, not knowing whether she had come to criticize or to talk to the patients, who treated her with the respect owed to anyone from upstairs.

Meena, who had escaped the torment of a mother-in-law, was not disposed to complain about seeing her marriage age under the critical eye of her mother. She and Betta never talked about their new responsibility, believing it to be as natural as the obligations they owed Arjun, who was not only afflicted with a speech defect, but walked like someone being nudged from behind by a malignant spirit.

For Bismatie's seventh birthday Betta had arranged a concert of East Indian music by the family who used to play for his mother. The girls were both married now and it was not certain whether the husband of one would allow her to dance in public, in spite of the fact that it was common knowledge that he had married her for her dancing. Meena explained that the party was for Mrs Singh's granddaughter, and that they had hired a pianola for the occasion, the first ever seen in Plaisance and possibly on the East Coast. Besides, they were churning their own ice cream and the musicians would be the first to be served. These assurances, far from pleasing the possessive husband, caused him to object that the celebrations were a creole arrangement and that creoles disliked Indian music. It was only his father-in-law's intervention which made him delay giving a final answer. Betta felt wounded by the jibe, while understanding the musician's reservations, for he recalled his mother's censers and the pervasive scent of akiari incense on those grand occasions in his mother's home.

The Saturday passed like most other Saturdays, since the preparations for the party were in the hands of the women working in the hospital and an East Indian fruit seller at the roadside market, who was accustomed to being entrusted with the organization of all kinds of fêtes.

After the midday meal the whole family lay down to rest in beds and hammocks scattered about the house, in the torpor of a September afternoon, with the silence broken by humming electric fans. Even the sick-nurse, who liked to evoke his insomniac nights in the same affectionate terms he used when speaking of his relations, succumbed to the effect of the heat and fell asleep while reading one of Betta's medical textbooks.

On the top storey where Betta and Meena were, a fine rain of dust drifted past the window, above which birds were taking their dust bath in the metal gutters.

Bismatie, the first to be awakened by the sound of clothes being beaten by the canal, went upstairs to see if her parents were awake and found them talking. Without a word she slid into bed between them and promptly fell asleep once more with her thumb in her mouth. Meena sat up with a start.

'What's wrong?' Betta asked anxiously.

Meena, almost ashamed to look at him, let a few seconds pass before answering.

'I felt . . . I don't know . . . as if Ma was in bed with us.'

She had confessed to him that since her mother had come to live with them she had woken up more than once at the dead of night, convinced that she was lying between them.

'It's broad daylight!' Betta objected.

She leaned across her daughter's sleeping form to kiss his arm, an unfailing sign that she wanted to make love. They lay down again, unwilling to continue the conversation, even though Bismatie was fast asleep.

Betta dropped off like his daughter while listening to the uninterrupted pounding of the women's clothes. But Meena lay awake, reflecting on the effect Bismatie's appearance had had on her. The lack of superstition in Betta and the Merrimans had shamed her into pretending to her children that she was not afraid of the dark and into avoiding any involvement in conversations about experiences described as spiritual or even those relating to practices abandoned by immigrants after crossing the ocean.

Unable to discover the significance of the reaction to Bismatie's behaviour, Meena's attention was drawn to the diminutive form lying on her side, a thumb in its mouth. The day before she had noticed her preoccupation with the arrival and installation of the pianola. Long after Arjun, Gita and Bhagwan had gone off to play she remained to stare at the exposed innards of the instrument until she was dragged away by the old woman who came upstairs to fetch ware for the patients.

'In which part of the pianola is the man sitting?' she asked the old woman.

'Which man?'

'The one who plays the pianola.'

'It does play by itself,' the old woman said, and smiled in a way that was the equivalent of an outburst of laughter for a normal person.

Bismatie did not believe her because she had seen the keys go up and down with her own eyes when the transporter demonstrated how it worked. Meena's confirmation of the old woman's observation did not appear to convince her either; and the same night Bismatie was disappointed that her father should give her the same answer.

Meena was convinced that her eldest child was no different from other children and that her talent for disturbing grown-ups was no more than her candour, which had not been held in check by the rain of prohibitions Gita and Arjun took more readily to heart. She studied her features as she had so often done before and found the same deeply arched eyebrows of Betta and the same uncompromising will that had made her so anxious in the first weeks of their marriage. Was Bismatie abnormal in a way that was different from Arjun's incapacity to walk and talk adequately? And if that was the case, was it a condition for the success which appeared to be within her grasp in everything she did?

It was not the first time Meena had put her eldest child under the microscope of her reflections. They had so little in common that, had she been a man, she would have been convinced that Betta's child was not hers. *He* adored Bismatie and aroused in her the same jealousy that she fought to conceal whenever Gopie came to visit them before she got married.

How can I be jealous of a small child, my own daughter? Meena questioned herself, comparing the disparity in length between the two figures lying next to each other. She had once heard a cantankerous patient of Betta's scream at her unruly daughter, 'I wish you din' born!' Perhaps it was the anxiety about finding a dowry for Bismatie that deepened her unease and incipient hatred. Yet her feelings for Gita were entirely different.

Betta sat up in bed and asked what time it was.

'Must be about half-past three,' she told him.

'Half-past three! But I've got to do things in the hospital before the party. You'd better wake Bismatie soon.'

Bismatie was to take the children down and share out packets of sweets among the patients, who would have a party of their own to celebrate the doctor's daughter's rebirth. By touching her they would increase their chances of recovery and repatriation into their families, most of whom lived far away along the coast and had preferred to bring their relations to Betta's establishment rather than leave them in the dreaded New Amsterdam hospital or in one of the sugar estate 'morgues'.

The children filed into the hospital with Bismatie at their head. Bhagwan came behind, his serious expression followed by Gita's fixed smile. And last of all came Arjun, apparently in imminent danger of falling on his face. They went among the patients sharing out their sweets in brown paper their grandmother had taught them to wrap.

The hurricane lamps hanging on nails in the corners of the room were unlit, although it was almost dark and the whirring of the six o'clock bee had begun to dominate the twilight sounds.

'Such nice chil'ren!' one middle-aged woman said. 'Is how ol' you is?'

'Seven,' Bismatie answered.

'Seven? When I was seven I was sellin' oranges in the road market at Mahaica, y'know. An' one day a man been goin' to Rosignol in 'is carriage. He din' know the road and instead o' turnin' left he turn straight an' end up in Cane Grove.'

The patients laughed, to the surprise of the children. Even their parents would not have appreciated the coastal joke, which depended on the contrast between Cane Grove and Rosignol.

One old man attempted to seize Gita, but as she withdrew out of his reach Arjun was caught. He was obliged to sit on the man's knee and allow himself to be bounced up and down while the others completed their rounds. Finally the patient let go, faint with exhaustion, and the children filed out again through the rear door, all the while stifling their giggling until they were upstairs in the kitchen, where a village girl was churning the ice cream in a can packed with ice and salt.

At table Bismatie ate as little as possible, having an eye on the cakes and sweets to be consumed during her party. She received permission from her mother to go and look out for any children who might be arriving. In fact her mind was set on the pianola which her father had promised to play when a large enough number of guests arrived. She went and stood before the polished instrument, wondering why there were any keys at all, recalling her father's explanation that no secret player lived inside. Occasionally she looked at her reflection, half-mirrored in the upright like the shadowy mass of an unfinished portrait.

The drawing room was decorated with paper figurines made by Meena, who had stayed up working the night before last, while Betta entertained the goblet maker and a companion who had accompanied him. The stranger, embarrassed that Meena was not expected to dance attendance on them, offered to help her and proved to be adept at cutting out fantastical shapes from the coloured paper she had bought. Bismatie was sitting in the gallery under a circle of cut-outs when the first guests arrived, a mother and her five young children. She suddenly realized that she needed her mother to welcome the guests, who did not know the house. But before she could run off she was surrounded by the children, who began examining her, in the belief that no one else would appear. The three girls among them began picking at her dress, so that she seemed to be the visitor and they the hosts. Unrestrained by their mother, they said whatever came into their heads and might have stripped Bismatie had not Meena appeared, attracted from the adjoining room by the strange voices.

'Mrs Narine!'

'I didn't know it was so early. You said seven o'clock and I came at seven.'

'But it's all right,' Meena assured her. 'Bismatie, say thanks.'

Bismatie took the three presents from the mother and whispered an inaudible 'Thanks'.

An hour later all the guests seemed to be arriving at once, children with their mothers or big sisters, whole families of three generations, neighbours and finally the musicians with their husbands and ageing father, as erect as ever, carrying a veena in a container of rigid material. And Betta embraced him in memory of those nights long ago when Rani and Lahti served the guests samoza and saffron-coloured cakes.

Finally Rani arrived with her husband, when the children were gathered round the pianola, watching the embossed roll turning and the keys falling and rising of their own accord. Bhagwan, lost in contemplation of the instrument without a player, had not noticed his parents, who separated, Tipu joining the men and Rani seeking out Meena, with whom she wanted to speak about her pregnancy. Her features had coarsened and all that survived of the attractive girl was the *memory* of her beauty.

As Meena had promised the musicians were the first to be served with ice cream. Soon after Betta sat down with the men to eat the pianola stopped, attracting the attention of the grown-ups, who had become accustomed to the background honky-tonk sound some of the men associated with cowboy films from America with their performing horses and mild absurdities. The children, who were served ice cream last of all, remained standing beside the silent instrument. Meena and the goblet maker's wife – she arrived a long time after her husband – gave out split-peas soup in enamel plates and immediately afterwards glasses half-filled with rice wine, an extravagance donated by a Chinese wholesaler who had set out to reform the drinking habits of Guyanese.

Occasionally the voices would suddenly fall silent and the whirring of electric fans could be heard across the packed drawing room and the guests would contemplate one another as though they were strangers and had met for the first time. And just as suddenly people would start talking again, with no recollection of the interludes.

Bismatie came over to her father, pushed in turn by Gita and Bhagwan, and asked him to start up the pianola again. Even Bismatie was afraid of interrupting the men's conversation and could hardly bring out the words. Betta got up to do as the children asked and at the tinny sound of the mechanical piano he could not help feeling that having fought to save his people from a disease that went hand in hand with exploitation on the sugar estates he had fallen prey to the seductions of its tinsel music.

When Betta thought that the children had listened long enough he invited the family of performers to play them 'real' music, anxious not to offend the old musician's son-in-law.

After much preparation and a number of whispered exchanges the father began to pluck his instrument. Bismatie and other children sat down on the floor beside their parents and grand-parents to listen, more interested in their reaction to the music than in the music itself, which haunted the older people, who sat with glazed eyes, with the same expression Betta's mother wore when she spoke of her dead husband who would visit her in the company of a crowd of hucksters carrying a tray full of combs and artificial flowers. They listened while clutching their grandchildren in a kind of desperation, perhaps anticipating the events that would descend upon them twenty-five years later and grieving for the younger generation, who were unable to understand even terms of endearment addressed to them in Hindi.

The sick-nurse cast his eyes round the room, mystified by the effect of the music on the listeners. He found it mortally dull and thought that the doctor, being an educated man, must share his distaste. But when the women began to sing he was touched by their gestures, which conveyed experiences apprehended but not understood. The only creole in the gathering of East Indians, it seemed to him he was a spectator at a ceremony of strangers. For were they not strangers in a country of creoles? The meandering voices belonged to remote back dams in the season of dusty roads where he had ventured as a boy on swimming excursions. Here he was in their presence and that of an indolent instrument which mimicked the human voice.

Bismatie called her mother over to a window where she had taken up position when her neighbour complained of her fidgeting. Meena, irritated by the interruption, signalled her to come away, but was obliged to comply when she persisted. In the moonlight she could make out the figure of a woman squatting by the gate.

'It's the leper woman,' Bismatie told her. 'Can I invite her in?'
'No.'

'Why?'

'Pa said you can't.'

'Why?'

'She's got a bad disease.'

'Then we can put her in the hospital.'

The woman stirred and her rags seemed to flutter like the leaves of a bush disturbed by the wind, and Meena felt the same cold foreboding as when Bismatie took her place between her and Betta in their bed.

Meena pushed Bismatie in front and made her sit on the floor beside her chair. But she no longer listened to the music. The urge to go back to the window and look at the woman who had not been seen for several days was so strong she kept turning her gaze across the listeners, imagining the huddled lump of rags half-hidden by the gate post. Betta looked at her questioningly and resolved to find out what was amiss as soon as the music stopped. But it went on endlessly until the moon began to show through the wide-open window and sweat was pouring from the listeners' faces and most of the children had fallen asleep.

When the music finally stopped Betta asked Meena what had happened.

'Bismatie wanted to invite the leper woman.'

'I thought she was sick.'

'She's at the gate,' Meena said.

He reflected for a moment.

'Let her take some food down.'

Betta and Meena went to the kitchen together to prepare something as quickly as possible. Until tonight they were relieved that the leper woman had not appeared for some time and that the relationship with Bismatie seemed to be at an end.

Once Meena and Bismatie disappeared through the front door Betta rejoined Tipu and the other men, who questioned him about Meena's agitation. Both the goblet maker and Tipu were unable to understand why he did not forbid Bismatie to associate with the leper woman in the first place and Tipu complained that his skin had begun to itch at the very thought of a leper in the vicinity. Their conversation centred on the subject of leprosy. Betta explained that those afflicted with the disease were being allowed out of the leprosy asylum at weekends in Trinidad, following the new practice; but he decided to say as little as possible when a group of men joined them, attracted by the earnestness of the conversation and the word 'leper', which held the attraction of all repulsive things.

Meena, walking ahead of Bismatie, could see that the woman had not moved. Moreover, as they grew closer to the immobile form it became clear that she was not clad in rags, but a voluminous garment which was neither a dress nor the amorphous garments the beggar was in the habit of wearing.

'It's my birthday,' Bismatie said, bending down slightly. 'I brought you some food.'

The head turned slowly, its features barely distinguishable in the moonlight.

'Ma,' Bismatie complained, 'it's not the leper woman.'

Meena bent down in turn, then drew back in horror before she could scrutinize the features.

'Call Pa!' she ordered. 'Quick!'

Bismatie ran up the front staircase to fetch her father. Meena, who had withdrawn a few feet, kept looking from the woman to the house until she saw Betta hurrying down the stairs, followed by the sound of voices and the appearance of guests at the window.

'Oh, God, Betta, it's your mother.'

Betta dared not look away from his wife for fear that her words might mean much more.

'You are wrong!' he said firmly. And, unaccountably, he felt like humiliating her.

'Go and look for yourself,' she told him.

And Betta, even before he drew aside the achal covering the head, whispered, 'Ma –'

He picked her up bodily and walked through the gate and under the house, between the whitewashed brick pillars and up the back staircase overlooking his wife's garden of herbs. And it was only while carrying her that he understood how he had lied to himself, that much of what he had done was not of his own choosing. And in carrying her up the stairs he was overcome by the feeling that he had done so once before in the identical way and in similar circumstances before he was married. At no other time – except in childhood when, alone in a room, he was oppressed by the size of the bed and his own insignificance – had he been so overwhelmed by a conviction. He felt unable to impart his experience to anyone at the time just as he did now, for it belonged to that shadowy part of his self that appeared to be surrounded by a wall of shame.

Betta laid his mother on the bed in which he and Meena slept, then he went downstairs to telephone a colleague to come and examine her.

Meanwhile Meena and Rani went from group to group, explaining that the doctor would be down as soon as he had attended his patient. Bismatie, who could not understand the need for the grown-ups' deception, repeated the lie to Arjun and Gita, who would have failed to recognize their paternal grand-mother, even if she had not been enveloped as she was.

The father-musician began playing alone, for his daughters had been taken away by their husbands. He sat cross-legged with his instrument on his lap, his iron-grey hair falling over a forehead where all his passion seemed to reside and bring forth beads of sweat which gathered beneath his chin. Eventually he packed away his instrument and left, and before he had gone through the gate he heard the pianola break the silence, like the spiritless laughter of a malicious child.

After the children went up to bed and the last guests had gone away Meena and Rani sat together in a corner sipping green tea and exchanging confidences. Betta came down once to see the doctor to the door, but went back up in order to remain with his mother for a while, he said. Tipu fell asleep in a spare bedroom, where he had dragged Bhagwan, who had been refused permission to sleep with the other children.

Chapter 46

The friendship of the two women had grown so slowly they themselves had no idea of its strength. But Tipu had watched its growth, approvingly at first and then with a certain unease.

Betta had entirely approved of Meena's acquaintanceship with Mrs Merriman, whom she used to visit only on a certain day of the week. Her relationship with Rani he had once seen as auspicious, since it brought the latter to his house and recalled his old infatuation at a time when he had not yet known a woman intimately. Then his resentment declared itself suddenly. He had heard them whispering and, surprised at his distaste for their intimacy, had upbraided himself for the unworthy resistance. Thereafter, he refused to entertain his envy of Meena's independence and rejected any reflection about it. Tipu, on the other hand, had openly quarrelled with Rani, accusing her of neglecting his household and dragging Bhagwan to Plaisance on the slightest pretext.

'Is where you living? There or here?' he would ask with sullen voice, only to relent when she took his protest seriously and gave up her visits.

And the friendship grew because neither husband would forbid his wife to see the other.

Meena told Rani of her dismay at Mrs Singh's appearance out of the blue. It was difficult enough coping with her mother, who had been sulking upstairs during the party because she was not allowed her own way in organizing the children's activities.

'I pretend nothing's wrong, but Betta does see how she's spoiling everything. Before she came we were happy. But she interferes in how we bring up the children. She went on about the beggar woman so much I stopped Bismatie from going over to talk to her . . . only to get peace. And she does see everything, everything. She knows when Betta and me quarrel, what his patients suffering from. She's become obsessed with disease and won't even let anybody wash her cups and plates. She's always talking about the next malaria epidemic and that I should talk to Betta about stocking up with quinine because it isn't the likes of Dr Giglioli who'll cure people of malaria by cutting up mosquitoes and naming them like dogs. And she never was like that, you know. . . . She asked me how I know Betta didn't have an outside woman. I have to put up with that; and now this. . . .' and her voice trailed off as if she had fallen asleep on the straight-backed chair.

'I didn't know,' Rani said, touched by her friend's confiding.

Rani felt that Meena was repaying her for all the secrets *she* had shared with her concerning Tipu. He had become as corrupt as his uncle, whose malpractices in making and selling jewellery had so surprised him in the beginning.

'I didn't know because you don't talk . . . I mean about the things that worry you,' Rani said.

'Betta's going to keep his mother here, I'm sure. And what can I say? After all he allowed Ma to come and live with us. What can I do? . . . And Bismatie's becoming . . . I can't explain. She's not a child like other children. You saw her with the pianola? She does treat it like a person. . . . This morning Gita saw her trying to feed it. . . .'

'She's only a child. Bhagwan's just like that. He plays with the trees in the yard and calls them by name.'

'It's not the same. . . .' Meena insisted. 'You may be right. She prefers grown-ups to children and remembers everything they tell her. The beggar woman's filled her head with stories about things she shouldn't be learning yet, and I can't talk to Betta about it any more because he's more worried than me.'

Rani never interrupted her when she spoke of Betta and would even tactfully attempt to bring the conversation round to him.

'I believe,' Meena went on, 'he never wanted to leave the West Coast even though he used to be tormented by the estate manager. It's the Merrimans he does miss, you see, and the poverty.'

'The poverty?' Rani asked in surprise.

'Yes, the poverty. He's drawn to the poor and diseased like a magnet. And me? I can't stick dirt. . . .' And in saying so her mother's obsession with clean crockery came to mind.

'He used to like going into those long yards,' Meena continued, 'and listen to the complaints of the estate workers. . . . You've ever been to the West Coast? No? It's another world. He used to say that one day a great man would come and sweep away all the poverty and filth among us Indians. And I couldn't stand him delving into those yards. God made rich and poor and it'll always be so. He goes on as if he discovered poverty.'

And suddenly Rani realized that a rift had grown between Meena and Betta, that the disagreements of which she had spoken in the past were symptoms of a profounder malaise. And

her satisfaction at the discovery was so palpable she did not try
to suppress it, for in all these years she had not ceased loving
him. He was her husband and his children were her children.
Was not Tipu right about her attachment to the house, without
appreciating its extent?

'The Mulvi Sahib always did tell him,' Meena said, 'that he
was trying to save himself, not East Indians. You understand
that? And Betta used to get so vexed. But the Mulvi Sahib did
always turn things upside down. Then one day I did understand
what he meant, when I heard Betta talking to his mother on the
telephone. Although he says she must live her own life he was
suffering because she kept him out of the house. It did take me
all these years to find out that Betta was no different from other
East Indian men and that all he did give me, all the freedom I
had, only come from his head. . . . I want to go far away, from
poverty, from his mother, from all these things that haunt
him. . . . Why did she have to come here and cause confusion?'

Rani, who had been the last outsider to visit Mrs Singh since
she shut up her house after the Pujaree was expelled from it,
could see her in no other light except that of benefactress, the
great provider, her son's godmother, presider over a house once
famed for its celebrations and where, even now, the last of its
hangers-on lived with his two hounds. Meena must have sensed
a lack of sympathy in Rani's expression and searched for some
way to convince her of Mrs Singh's disruptive influence. And so
she spoke of her wedding, when her mother-in-law sat apart,
aloof, unresponsive to the hospitality of the country people
surrounding her. She spoke of Mrs Singh's lack of interest in the
children, of her implied threats to disinherit Betta and of her
disgraceful liaison with the Pujaree, which had caused Betta so
much distress. She spoke of Gopie, her sister with a man's
name, who came to her in a dream. She had promised her all her
saris, but on opening the wardrobe she found that it was empty.
And she continued to speak, leaving the trail of her preoccupation with her mother-in-law's misdeeds to evoke matters
entirely unconnected with them.

'Betta's too proud to make me unhappy. He's a man of
principle. . . . I'm talking too much. All these years I wanted to
talk my heart out to you, but I was afraid you were in love with

Betta. The first year of our marriage I did as Ma told me and studied Betta so as to please him. Now I look back and wonder why I couldn't see that his character was there, for everyone to see.'

'What d'you mean?' Rani asked, shaken by Meena's suspicions about a secret she thought to be protected by an impregnable discretion.

'But he's just like his mother!' Meena answered.

'I can't think of two people more unlike!' Rani said.

'How are they unlike?' Meena asked.

Rani could not answer, for her brief explanation of Betta's character revealed striking similarities, like their terrible will.

'As a child I used to see so many things,' Meena continued, 'but now I have a cluttered mind. I remember whenever Ma was sick with anxiety she'd go on and on about something else that didn't worry her at all, and my father could never get the truth out of her. You know, whenever they quarrel he punishes her with silence.'

'Who?'

'Gopie's husband. With silence! Gopie, who can't bear to be ignored!'

And Rani thought it strange that she should repeat the thing that could not preoccupy her most.

'What is he doing up there?' Meena asked, clasping her hands in despair. 'Oh, God! If only he'd tell me where I stand. Mai! Mai! Our mothers name us to destroy us.'

Rani got up and stroked her friend's head in an impulsive gesture, giving her what she had longed to receive from Mrs Singh when she first came to her house in a headlong flight from poverty. All the wisdom of the Pujaree's Vedas and the Mulvi Sahib's Koran was incapable of protecting them from time and chance. The child growing in her could protect or destroy her and there was nothing for it but to wait, just as she could only wait to see what effect Meena's suspicions would have on their relationship.

'You must come to my house,' said Rani, 'and stay for a few days. Leave the herb garden. Let the plants wither. It's not the end of the world.'

Just then Meena's mother appeared in the doorway wearing a crumpled dress. She had watched Betta taking his mother up the stairs and now, overcome by curiosity, she wanted to find out what had happened.

'Who was the woman Betta did bring in?'

''Twas his mother, Ma. There're two mothers in the house now. Aren't you glad?'

'What you mean? She's staying?'

'Yes, Ma. She's staying. Can't you laugh a little, Ma? From time to time. The children play with the leper woman because she does laugh and tell them stories. Can't you laugh a little?'

'Since you married,' her mother answered, 'you say what you like to me. We'll see how you talk to your mother-in-law. Is there any food for me?'

Meena got up without a word and left the room to prepare something to eat.

Her mother quickly went to the opening leading to the back to see if her daughter was listening. Then, like an actress playing a part on the stage, she leapt back to join Rani.

'Who was the woman Betta brought in?' she asked. 'Was it really his mother? His mother from Vlissingen Road?'

'Yes,' Rani answered, put out by Meena's mother's obsequiousness.

'You're big with child. You can't lie to me. You think she does want me to stay here?'

'She must do!' Rani answered.

'If Betta did give me the money to open a shop you think I'd hang around their necks? Girl children only drag you down!'

Meena's mother, interpreting Rani's silence as insolence, sat down in an easy chair and placed her right elbow on the armrest. She wanted to remind Rani that she was a nobody, that her son put on airs like the child of rich parents, but, afraid of what Meena would say if she learned of the outburst, remained silent. She had fawned on her parents, and later on her husband, and since she had come to live in Plaisance had fallen into the habit of fawning just as assiduously on her daughter whenever she was uncertain of her position.

'Can you ask her to treat me as a daughter should treat her

mother?' she asked imperiously. 'Is only because the house got no religion that she go on like that. Wherever you turn you see temples and mosques and churches, but as far as the children concerned they could be dance halls. . . . Well, you yourself see how they does behave. Ask Meena if she could go an' talk to anybody who did come out of a train station in her small days. The other day Arjun and another boy did tie two pigs together by they tails. Ask Meena if I telling lie. You call that bringing up chil'ren? How they can respect anything when they see how their mother does neglect me?'

'Meena respects you,' Rani said. 'I know that.'

'And the children?'

'Times changed,' Rani answered. 'When I was with Betta's mother I had to do as I was told. I don't expect Bhagwan to be like me. As long as he respect me I am content. The children respect you.'

Meena's mother stared her up and down as if she had pronounced an obscenity and, deciding that there was no point in pursuing the conversation, fell silent. When Meena came back with a large piece of birthday cake and a glass of ginger tea she nodded, but took no notice of the tray laid on the table beside her. Rani and Meena tried to include her in their conversation, but she did not respond. Neither felt that she could speak while the older woman sat near them, stone-faced and defiant; and when at last she got up and took her tray with her they knew that their conversation had foundered on her ill will. Sometimes Meena and Rani would sit without speaking and watch the iridescent pawn-flies settle on the telegraph wires. But that was an altogether different silence.

Eventually Betta came downstairs and found the two women sitting alone, looking through the window at the lights in the village and the outlines of the houses and the station across the road.

'I can't get a word out of her about what happened,' he said, almost absently. 'For all I know Sukrum might have driven her out.'

'I don't think he'd do that,' Rani said.

'I'll have to go and see for myself.'

Meena heard the latticed gates to the bottom house opening and a few moments later the sound of the car starting up.

Why had her mother become a child again? Had Gopie bowed her head out of love or terror to a husband who looked like a god and behaved like a demon? Would she herself ever recover the tranquillity of the early days of her marriage when she and Betta discussed at length a forthcoming weekly trip to the Merrimans and their eccentric father? Betta thought they were as happy as ever. But then she had always seen ahead of him to the debris that followed the jollification, after the dancing was over and the instruments were put away. He did not realize that he had begun to withdraw, until, she was certain, his face would be hidden from her. How could they survive the arrival of *his* mother, who had never forgiven them for marrying?

'Everything'll be all right, you know,' Rani said, concerned that the events of the day might have overwhelmed her.

'Yes, I know. Why shouldn't it be? Are you hungry?'

'No.'

'I don't know what I'd do without you. You're like a rock.'

Rani fell asleep on the chair, fatigued by her sitting position and by the child feeding on her blood.

Meena wondered about the leper woman, who had not been seen for days. No one thought of her since Betta's mother had been identified. In the grip of the ultimate affliction, she never failed to draw the children to her, with her storytelling and, like all her kind, her refusal to look within. Was she not a model for them all, for the pandits and the imams and the priests who would refuse to bury her on the pretext that she belonged to no church? For the decent folk who would condemn her for concealing her cache of money in a voluminous skirt? Perhaps she had fallen into the abyss on her way to her begging pitch, or drowned in the back-dam canal where her body lay among the reeds, forever suspended between the bottom and the surface, its presence unsuspected by passing boatmen and weeders tramping the dam, decomposing in the eternal cycle of life and death.

Meena watched the moon drifting in its inverted sea and

wondered what her husband could be doing that he had not returned, and, to console herself, called up images of her sleeping children and the house in which she lived, her remote childhood, Gopie and her mother, the landscape in which she grew up and the mirrors that told her what she looked like and her garden of sweetbroom and piaba, the bride who begged Betta not to hurt her when they slept together for the first time, the frightened wife who lay down to give birth when the rain drowned her screams, and was certain that she was what Betta made of her during the years of their marriage. Her fears were therefore groundless. Meena consoled herself with this reflection and recalled that Rani, married to a thieving jeweller, travelled along her pre-ordained road with a dignity that could not fail to please her ancestors. She watched her sleeping friend and, imagining her coarsening features exposed to the sunlight and a brush covered with tufts of falling hair, her anxieties were allayed for a while.

Nearly all the lights in the village were extinguished; but here and there among the coconut trees candleflies flared like the wicks of spluttering lamps. Meena got up and woke her friend, who followed her upstairs.

Chapter 47

Mrs Singh could no longer stand up to Sukrum after the Pujaree left. She quarrelled with him constantly about the cost of provisions, which he was now responsible for buying, about the state of the fences surrounding the yard and about the dogs which were becoming unmanageable.

'You should loose them sometime during the day,' she had told him frequently, 'or they'll get so bad-tempered you won't be able to handle them.'

When he began bringing his friends into the house – an assortment of vagrants drawn from the afflicted of Kitty and Georgetown – she threatened to get rid of him. But as she failed to carry out each threat Sukrum grew in boldness until the number of his acquaintances visiting the yard after dark so alarmed her she sought the assistance of the police. Two constables in khaki who came to see what help was needed were so impressed by her hospitality and the faded magnificence of her dwelling that, after eating at her table, they decided to seek out Sukrum and teach him a lesson. But they were afraid of the dogs which sat up when they entered the room.

'I hear you dumb,' one of them said to Sukrum. 'Well, I in' care if you deaf an' dumb! If you give Miss Singh any more trouble we goin' hawl you ass off to the station an' teach you a lesson, you ungrateful good-fo'-nothing.'

The constables had to be content with aggressive words and, when they left, were not in a mind to retaliate on hearing the door of Sukrum's room slam behind them.

Mrs Singh urged them to keep an eye on the house in their spare time, for which service she rewarded them with money and a sumptuous meal whenever they called on her. Sukrum retaliated by allowing the dogs to roam the yard during the day and refusing to let the constables through the gate when they came. And each time Mrs Singh was obliged to leash the animals herself or shut them away under the threatening glare of the ever-silent Sukrum.

She permitted him to entertain one friend, an umbrella mender, a gaunt creole of no fixed abode, who had never been seen without his defunct umbrellas tucked under his arm. This character of forbidding appearance spoke on Sukrum's behalf whenever one of the constables came calling and had to be escorted up the stairs by Mrs Singh.

''Cause you got on a uniform you piassin'! But we watchin' you. Why you don' climb the stairs alone? You got fo' walk in front o' woman now?'

'There's no point keeping dogs,' Mrs Singh told the younger constable on one of his visits, 'if he brings all his friends to the house.'

''S true,' he replied. 'An' most of them been inside before, Miss Singh. They're the scum of Kitty. Why you don' get rid of this Sukrum an' take on a good watchman? Constable Cadogan can find a lot o' people would be glad to do a job like that.'

'Ah, yes,' was all she replied, unwilling to answer that she would only be happy with an East Indian.

Indeed, in the last five years a number of small Indian-owned dry-goods shops had opened in Georgetown and their employees, who could be seen standing among the bales of coloured cloth, like newcomers conspicuously out of place in a residential district, were all East Indians.

'I uses to come to your yard as a boy, Miss Singh,' he told her, 'to help make the tajah with the men. An' I did always walk down to see the men burn it 'pon the beach. An' people did complain 'bout the ashes when it blow back 'pon the land. The Mohammedans stop making tajahs now. Why?'

'They aren't allowed to,' she told him, touched by the evocation of that period of her life.

'You remember Aji?' she asked the young man.

'Yes, Miss Singh. She had a hot mouth.'

A breeze parted the strands of the maidenhair fern and the throbbing Delco plant drowned the early evening noises.

'Why you cryin', Miss Singh?'

Tears were coursing down her face, which nevertheless remained expressionless, like the immutable features of a well-groomed doll.

'Why you cryin'? He givin' you trouble again?'

She shook her head and looked at her young visitor with his uncommonly pleasant manner.

'Are you married?' she asked him.

'No, Miss Singh. But I courting.'

'You're courting. It's the best time of all. My husband went across the ocean to court me. At first I wasn't allowed to see him, and then later he courted me in the presence of my parents and my aunts and uncles and neighbours and strangers who came up the stairs to look in at the window. Young people now won't understand that. . . . He was my God! What's your name?'

'Ivor.'

'They say you can tell us East Indians by our voices. Is that true, Ivor?'

''S true, Miss Singh.'

'And by our names, of course. My mother's name was

Lakshmi, the name of a goddess. I used to pray to Lakshmi once. Do you ever quarrel with your sweetheart?'

'Sometimes.'

'Do you call her names?'

'Is she does call me names, Miss Singh.'

'Does it hurt?'

'No, I does laugh when she start cursin' me.'

'You laugh? . . . I can't bear anyone calling me names. What a strange young man you are!'

After a short silence the constable, more concerned to maintain the flow of words than to seek information, asked, 'Is true Dr Singh got three children?'

'Yes. Didn't you know?' she asked, surprised that everything about her son was not common knowledge. 'He's got three children and a wife.'

The constable could not hide his surprise, but felt that the bitter tone was aimed at discouraging further questions of the kind and searched for some other way to prevent the conversation from dying.

'Constable Ivor,' Mrs Singh said solemnly. 'When are you going to come again? The more often you come the better Sukrum behaves. I know he's a coward, but I'm mortally afraid of him. He does all the work around the house, you know. . . .'

'Miss Singh, I goin' send you somebody, a reliable man. If you don' like him I goin' send you another one. An' I goin' keep sending them till you satisfy.'

'I'll see,' Mrs Singh told him. 'You don't have to leave now. I'm just going to lie down a bit.'

What was she to make of him, this obliging young man? There was no doubt that her husband had decreed she was not permitted to have close relations with any man, and his spirit hovered above her, surveying everything she did and said. She was certain of this the first time the Pujaree made love to her in the conjugal bed, when, momentarily, she felt she was being ridden by two men. Hers was the curse of widowhood, with which she had been made familiar since childhood from the women's conversations that often came to an abrupt end at the approach of a man.

One evening the constable's colleague came alone. Unlike his friend he paid no heed to Sukrum's friend's taunts; but his hatred of the dogs and their master, bred of frustration, grew with every visit. He came, and, as usual, was met at the gate by Mrs Singh, who escorted him up the overgrown path towards the stairs. Sukrum, hearing the barking of the dogs, came out with the umbrella mender. Catching sight of the constable, the umbrella man sniggered contemptuously before turning to go back to the room with Sukrum. But the visitor, as if he had been waiting for the challenge, spun round and ran down the stairs after them. Hardly had Mrs Singh begun her descent to see what was happening than a sharp explosion rent the afternoon silence and resounded in seemingly endless echoes. She found Sukrum and his friend kneeling over the prostrate body of one of the dogs. The constable was standing apart, a pistol held at the ready in case he should be attacked by the other animal. Then, with the utmost calm, the visitor said, 'The nex' time I'll shoot the other one. An' the nex' it'll be one of you.'

The sergeant forbade the two constables any further visits to the house except on his orders. And Sukrum's unbridled behaviour could be traced to that fateful afternoon when his dog was shot and Mrs Singh found herself cut off from the outside world. And her longing to be with Betta grew in intensity, but, unable to overcome her hatred of his wife, she could only wish for his eventual release from the bonds of marriage.

Sukrum, once he saw that the constables no longer came visiting, opened the yard once more to his unemployed acquaintances; and from mid-morning the sound of dominoes and loud talking could be heard by passers-by in Dowding Street. The side gate, more convenient for visitors from Kitty, was now kept open and a hardwood table was placed under the saman tree, the branches of which now spread far beyond the paling fence above the street.

Mrs Singh used to watch Sukrum and the visitors from an upstairs window. There was no doubt that the umbrella mender was the dominant one among the strangers, and she saw that in the chaos of her yard there was a certain order. The women who were allowed past the gate usually paid their respects to him and Sukrum before joining the other men; and amidst the gaming at dice and cards, the shouting and rollicking, the bad language and the threats of violence, she felt that one of the two was at hand to settle matters.

Sukrum, since he had lost his speech, attracted people more readily, and there was an ease in his relations with the umbrella mender which had been entirely absent in his friendship with Bai.

Mrs Singh gradually came to accept the situation she had so dreaded in the beginning; so that the morning following a drinking bout after the umbrella mender had repaired two damaged paling staves which had been broken in an altercation, she came down and spoke to him. Addressing her as 'Mistress' he asked if she was pleased with the work. To her suggestion that he should come up and eat something he declined, declaring that he was only an umbrella mender and that his clothes would soil her chair.

'Mistress, if I was you I wouldn' let any o' these people in you house,' he told her.

She was on the point of asking why, but realized that she knew what he meant. They were marauders, night folk who only left her alone because she was useful to them. And yet the need to have people around her was so strong she delivered herself up to the torpor of inaction and pretended to be unaware of suspicious comings and goings in the early hours of the morning when the houses nearby were shrouded in darkness or lit with faint nightlights.

In the morning the umbrella mender would set out, barefoot, on his wanderings through the nearby town, shouting his incomprehensible words, like a bird with a single call. And in those words was a smouldering tone, a voice at once powerful but mute. And Mrs Singh wondered if he ever slept, whether he was not a whim of her imagination which, of late, was beset with images from a buried time. Her dreams had all but abandoned Kerala now and were full of associations from her adopted home, of kokers and municipal markets with wrought-iron fences, of churchyards and tilting gravestones, of bandstands by the sea, of flooded lands and drunken boats, of inscrutable creoles, of pitch roads glistening in the wake of torrential downpours, of schooners with folded sails and gardens visited by iridescent birds. The umbrella mender, she had no doubt, was the bearer of a message concerning herself, a premonition of events that would befall her with the inevitability of the season of rains.

In the days that followed Mrs Singh ferreted around in every chest and cupboard in search of objects that were connected in some way with Betta's childhood or early manhood. And everything she found, old exercise books, a pair of diminutive leather boots, a scalloped cotton reel, two primers on anatomy and a clouded photograph taken on the day before he went abroad, was displayed on the altar of her abandoned shrine of Lakshmi. And determined to await as calmly as she could the anticipated event, she looked out on to the world outside through her gallery windows, confining her dealings with it to her contact with Sukrum and the washerwoman who came on Friday mornings to deliver what she had collected the week before in her shallow, wooden tray.

The night when revellers were celebrating the end of Pagwah, dressed in garments stained with red dye thrown on them during the daylong celebrations, Sukrum appeared upstairs at the door of her bedroom. Quietly he shut the door behind him, then crossed the room to close the wide-open sash window through which the water tank could be seen in the bright moonlight. When his back was turned she leapt out of bed and opened the door before he could reach her. She made for the kitchen, thinking of the two bolts securing the door; and in her headlong flight she stumbled, only to recover at once. Drawing one bolt after another with swift, economical gestures, she stepped on to the staircase. Then, taking care not to run her hand over the new greenheart rail, she started descending the stairs by twos.

'Mistress? Is where you goin'?'

'Oh, God!' she exclaimed, throwing herself into the arms of the umbrella mender who was standing in the middle of the staircase. 'It's Sukrum. He came into my bedroom.'

'Go back up, Mistress. If you fight it goin' be worse. He does worship the ground you walk 'pon.'

Mrs Singh turned round to see Sukrum looking down at her.

'Go back up, Mistress. . . . Sukie! Don' hurt she, understan'? Don' hurt she, I tell you!'

Mrs Singh tried to slip past the umbrella mender, but he grasped her firmly with both hands and held her until Sukrum joined him.

'If you scream, Mistress,' the umbrella mender warned, 'Sukrum goin' hurt you.'

Mrs Singh accompanied Sukrum to her bedroom, whimpering, bewildered by a distress she had foreseen but did not believe she would experience.

She stared at the roof while Sukrum kissed and fondled her with pounding heart. And neither of them heard the revellers in the yard, the screams of the women or the occasional periods of silence under the drifting moon.

It was the season when the buttressed silk-cotton lost its leaves in order to survive the dry season and the sky carried a burden of glittering stars, and hummingbirds ceased visiting the garden where all the flowering plants had died for lack of care. She must bathe, she remembered thinking, and stand naked over a small fire to cleanse herself. Above all, cleanse herself in the manner of temple dancers after they had soiled their bodies with strange men. And when she regained her senses it was the first thought that occurred to her; and images of bathers crowded her mind, men and women with wet saris like a thin skin over their bodies, and of small fires scattered along a dun-coloured beach. Opening her eyes to see if she was alone on the bed she found that the moon had waned.

'Betta!' she whispered. 'What will your father say?'

Finally she got up and took her shower and then made a fire in the bathroom with the wood she had prepared for the next day. She stood over it at intervals until she believed herself cleansed by the flames. She then put on her wedding sari and over it a large, shapeless garment Aji once wore, before picking up the receiver of her telephone to call the police and report the rape. But the impersonal voice that answered threw her into confusion and she replaced the receiver. Then, without any warning, she was seized with a fit of trembling. She let herself fall into an easy chair and clutched her knees in an effort to still the uncontrollable shivering which left her cold and exhausted. But, as she was about to get up in order to make for the nearest bedroom upstairs, the trembling ceased as suddenly as it had come. She went and stood before a mirror to examine herself, but saw that she was no longer the same person, that something essential had deserted her features.

Before leaving the house she turned the looking glass to face the wall and looked around her, undecided whether she should take anything with her. In the end she left empty-handed by the front door, reducing her chances of being spotted by Sukrum or his friend.

Betta found his mother's house empty. There was no evidence of the Pagwah celebrations, neither in the yard nor in Sukrum's room, where the bed was made and the floor was swept; and the fresh scent of the wind through the open window on Dowding Street gave him the impression it had not been occupied for several days.

Upstairs, his mother's bed, like all the others, had been made and the only unusual sight was the remains of a wood fire on the concrete bathroom floor.

Betta, having no key to lock the house, could only bolt the back door. He decided to return the following day with a locksmith unless his mother could tell him where the keys were.

EPILOGUE

Chapter 48

The leper woman was sheltering from the fierce sun under an umbrella anchored to the ground by an arrangement of stones. She had been absent from her post for five months and Bismatie, as soon as she caught sight of her, ran out to engage her in conversation.

The streets were empty and only the odd, desultory call of a bird broke the mid-afternoon silence.

'Where've you been?'

'You jus' as full-mouth as ever,' the woman said, ignoring the question and Bismatie's evident pleasure in seeing her again.

After a while the old woman gave a belated answer to Bismatie's question: 'I been sick. . . . Is where you sister?'

Then without waiting for an answer she declared, 'You growing fast. You goin' get you father long legs.'

'I've got two grandmothers and one is getting old.'

'Which one?'

'My father's mother.'

'Well everybody does get old,' the leper woman remarked, as if she were irritated by Bismatie's observation.

'But she's growing old fast,' Bismatie insisted. 'There are things on her face.'

'Alyou young people ignorant bad. Everybody's get old. Listen! Listen to this story. It true, so help me God! Is a story to show how ignorant people is nowadays. Listen good!'

And she went on to tell the well-known story of the inspector who visited a primary school for the day. He was specifically keen on religious instruction and told the tale of Joshua at the battle of Jericho to each class he visited in turn. When he came to the sixth standard, certain that the children would be familiar with it, he asked a tall, intelligent-looking boy, 'Who brought down the walls of Jericho?' The pupil, trembling like a leaf, rose respectfully and blurted out, 'Is not me, sir! I don' know nothing 'bout any wall.' 'What's your name?' asked the inspector? 'Crozier, sir,' the pupil answered in a pleading tone of voice, by way of confirmation that he bore no responsibility whatsoever for the collapse of the walls of Jericho. Just then the recreation bell rang and the inspector, after dismissing the class, made straight for the headmaster's corner. 'Look here, Mr B!' he thundered, 'your sixth standard is the most ignorant I've ever come across in my whole career. I asked a boy who brought down the walls of Jericho and he insisted he had not.' 'What's the boy's name, inspector?' asked the head teacher, who had risen as a mark of respect. 'Crozier.' 'Crozier? Oh, inspector! That's the fifth Crozier who's passed through this school and they're all of impeccable character. I can vouch for this boy. He would never touch a wall, much less bring it down!' The inspector kept his counsel, judging that ignorance was endemic in the school and that the only way to tackle the problem was to complain to the chief inspector. Armed with his damning report on the school he first went to the office of a high-ranking official at the Education Department and complained, mentioning specifically the incident about the wall. '. . . And the headmaster himself defended the boy. He had never even heard of the walls of Jericho!' The high-ranking official, surprised that the inspector should take the matter so seriously, did not wish him to carry it any further. 'Look, inspector,' he said, 'the Education Department will pay every cent towards the cost of rebuilding that wall. I beg you to leave the matter in my hands.'

'Eh, eh!' the leper woman said in conclusion. 'Them high-up people din' know as much as me 'bout the Bible.' And she burst out laughing, amused by her superior knowledge.

'Is why you not laughing?' she asked Bismatie.

'I've never heard about the walls of Jericho,' Betta's daughter confessed.

'Jes. . . ! You mean. . . ? An' all this time you fool me 'bout how bright you is!'

Bismatie thought that the leper woman had changed, that the five-month gap since their regular conversations had hardened her. She scrutinized her features and body under the incredible mass of rags, to verify that she was in the company of the same person who, in spite of her curse-words and short temper, she knew as a warm, desirable companion. Suddenly the leper woman's clothes were monstrous vestments, like the pustules that had broken out on her paternal grandmother's face, which she took to be signs of age. Her breeding would not allow her to run away on the spur of the moment as she was tempted to do, and she stood watching the physical wreck with clawed hands. Were all old people the same? Would she, one day, wear a mask as her grandmother did, to terrify the children who came into contact with her? A cardboard mask lined with brown paper smeared in soft grease and charged with a terrible mystery? And why this long tale about the walls of Jericho?

Bismatie was certain that the reason for the sudden fear of the woman lay in that tale which, far from being comical, made her think of disasters in the home.

'When two grandmothers livin' in the same house,' Bismatie heard the old woman say, 'one of them does get old fast. . . . An' I tell you something else, never married a man a lot older than you'self.'

'Why?'

''Cause you goin' grow old fast to catch him up,' the old woman answered.

Everything the leper woman said and did seemed ominous. Sitting near her pile of rocks, surrounded by the withered grass and furrows made by cart wheels, she was a witch, Old Higue, who lived in a corner house and was responsible for the untimely deaths of children.

'Is wha' wrong with you, chile? You mother din' tell you not to stare? If you don' wan' fo' talk haul you tail and lef me alone.'

Bismatie went off, relieved that she did not have to find an excuse for leaving. On reaching home she took up a position at a window and stared out at the leper woman, watched her place her right hand from time to time on the bag containing the cache of silver coins or change position to remain in the shade of her umbrella.

Something had come to an end for Bismatie, like the culmination of an apprenticeship. She now stood, bewildered, unable to comprehend her loss or why the leper woman, who once fascinated her, now aroused only the deepest revulsion. Until now she could never understand why her parents and other grown-ups spoke about the old lady in whispers and were evidently disturbed by an association which, to her, was as natural as asking Bhagwan to let his trousers down. Bismatie's eyes were blurred with tears as she no longer took in the scene across the road, but looked out on the verge in front of her house, where the dead grass had been flattened by a succession of cows in search of pasture.

Mrs Singh, like all the women in the house, was in bed. Beside her, on a low table, lay her mask, which she never failed to keep at hand in case someone should enter the room unannounced. No one ever did, not even the children, who avoided her for her forbidding silence and the rigid, featureless mask. She only permitted Betta's wife to serve her; and she, in the beginning, always entered the room full of dread. In her view Betta's mother had lost none of her power, despite the evidence of destitution in the tiny room overlooking the back yard. The only furniture was the bed, a small commode and a table. The partitions were bare, apart from an image of the goddess Lakshmi, and in the wardrobe hung a half-dozen saris Betta had bought her. A stranger might have taken her for a servant or a relation who had fallen on hard times, especially as the bunch of purple buck-bananas attached to the rafter was hanging directly over her bed. Did they not belong in the kitchen, with the orange peel, the condiments and phials of vanilla?

She had, indeed, grown old in the few months she had spent in her son's house, and her features, disfigured by an infestation of pustules, resembled a parched, forlorn landscape. The mask she had had made after Betta confessed that her complaint was incurable and a number of other designs had been tried and discarded. When she first noticed the deepening lines and the first pustules she took to examining herself for long periods in a looking glass behind her bed; then one day she made Betta take it away, unable to bear the evidence of her decline.

During the bright hours she spent much of her time at the window, but in moments of intolerable loneliness she would open the door just as much as was necessary to call for Betta's wife, only to stare silently at her through her grotesque disguise.

The respect Meena had once shown her vanished under the repeated displays of apparent contempt; and now every peremptory call was answered with greater unwillingness than the last.

The daylight hours became for Betta's mother a kind of imprisonment, relieved occasionally by the sound of raised voices, when she would put her ear to the partition and listen avidly for signs of dissension.

At night she had taken to looking down through a jalousie into the herb garden, the part of the yard from which Lahti seemed to have come to pay her two brief visits, dressed in a winding sheet. The last, about a week ago, had been an event as important as the day of her marriage or her son's birth, she thought.

'Why don't you ever complain?' Mrs Singh asked her, after Lahti had stood by the bed for several minutes, unable to look her in the eye, like those villagers who behave as if they had an obligation to be poor.

Receiving no answer, Mrs Singh said, 'Why did you come?'

'I been to the old house. It's the house, Miss Singh. I not happy anywhere else.'

Mrs Singh felt the same irritation at her presence as in the old days, the same inclination to put her down.

'What you want me to do?' she asked.

'You can't move back?' Lahti begged. 'I not goin' come again if you move back.'

Mrs Singh looked at her former charge kindly, but could only shake her head in answer.

'You must go back,' Lahti declared.

'Must?' Mrs Singh asked in surprise.

'Miss Singh, I got to return.'

'You mean to the room where you and Sukrum used to carry on!'

'No, Miss Singh,' Lahti said urgently. 'I was happy before Sukrum. . . . It was since Sukrum come that I start dreaming 'bout the man with a grass-knife.'

'What man?'

'I dream a man with a grass-knife use to cut up children in the rice field at harvest time. . . .'

'You never told me about that!'

'I use to tell Rani. . . . We din' tell you 'bout a lot of things.'

'And what did the man do to you?'

'I use to run away an' only one time he nearly catch me.'

'Children in North India have that dream,' said Mrs Singh, as though disturbed by the revelation. 'My father came from there and I was married by North Indian customs. . . . How helpless we are!'

'You still so good-looking though,' Lahti said.

Mrs Singh instinctively put her hand to her face to touch the unyielding mask. She smiled bitterly at the remark, thought for a moment to take it off so that Lahti could see the pustules and deep-lined flesh. But she resisted the impulse and examined, instead, the dead woman's features.

'You've always disturbed me, child. I've done terrible things to my husband on account of you. . . .'

And in a flash, as the unhappy spectre stood before her, Mrs Singh understood that she had been contaminated by the tyranny of conscience, that Lahti's death had affected her so deeply at the time, she had felt obliged to dismiss the Pujaree, and later, to remain in the house, offering herself to Sukrum as a sacrifice to her past.

'You know that Sukrum raped me?' Mrs Singh said.

'Sukrum?' the young woman asked in amazement. 'But he din' dare come near you, Miss Singh. He tell me one time he din' believe you would let the Pujaree touch you.'

'I let him. Now I know I let him. I saw how he used to look at me with hatred in his eyes after your death, and yet I let him stay in the house. When the umbrella mender was kind to me I told myself that nothing was wrong, knowing exactly what he would do.'

'But why you let him, Miss Singh?'

'Because of what I'd done you.'

Lahti wanted to protest, but Mrs Singh silenced her with a gesture.

'I used to lie in bed dreaming of going back to Kerala, until I took to forgetting, little by little. First, the people who used to visit my parents. I confused those who came on Mondays with the ones who came on Saturdays. Then I forgot the faces of my relations, and in the end my parents. . . . Did you know that my dowry was a boat? A dhony that plied the coast and went as far as Ceylon? I only saw it once, but my father said the finest Tamil craftsmen built it and that it was unsinkable. I had an unsinkable ship manned by sailors who hardly ever went ashore. I exchanged everything for a husband and a casket full of jewellery, my parents, my unsinkable boat and all else. . . .'

'I never hear you complain before, Miss Singh.'

'Ah, Lahti! I am bleeding to death slowly, spilling my blood in invisible drops while I watch children do as they please, little girls come and go like grown-ups, seeing everything, judging everything. . . . So you had such dreams, Lahti! And you told me nothing! Tell me more about them.'

She broke off confiding in the young woman, thinking that by doing so she was demeaning herself.

'I use to dream one thing all the time before I came to live with you, but it did change afterwards.'

'After you came to me?'

'Yes. A fair come to my village one time and after that I dream I was in a fairground listening to the music and watching the crowds. And all of a sudden I did smell the ink from a book the Pandit use to bring with him to our house. Later I dream 'bout the wooden horses, but nothing else. . . . What 'bout your boat, Miss Singh? And when you done talking 'bout your boat say you goin' take me back.'

Mrs Singh obliged, as if she had been waiting for Lahti to make the request.

'When I watched men stitching the sails of my boat I was proud. You know sailors can tell when a storm is coming up by the cry of sea birds. . . ? There is a little girl in this house, my granddaughter. I detest the child! Oh, God! If I was to tell you. . . . Something's wrong with me, Lahti. If you hadn't died I would have given the Pujaree all I possessed, and he would have been my master! I worshipped him as I worshipped my husband for a while. That I can love like that and yet be able to destroy someone. . . . Why did you come back to torment me?'

In a sudden, unpremeditated gesture, Mrs Singh took off her mask, exposing her deformed features to the dead protégée, who looked on, unmoved.

'Take me back, please,' Lahti begged.

'Go away!' Mrs Singh screamed, leaping from her bed.

There was a sound of voices in the house, and a few seconds later Betta flung open the door. He found his mother looking through the window into the night. One of the panes was broken and blood was dripping from her right hand, soiling the sheet.

Mrs Singh turned her back when she saw her son.

'Get some dressing and my bag!' Betta told Meena, who arrived a few moments later.

'What happened, Ma?'

But she remained silent. So swiftly had the incident developed that Mrs Singh had no time to put on her mask, which lay on the bed a short distance from the end of the bloodstained sheet.

'I don't want Meena to see me bleeding,' she said. 'Keep her out of the room.'

'I . . .' he began, then turned to open the door, on which his wife was knocking sharply.

Taking the bag and bandages away he signalled her not to enter.

Betta stood over his mother, despairing that he could not get a word out of her. A strong scent of ink came from the corner of the room, where the soiled sheet made a crumpled mass. Unable to find out why she had screamed he imagined the cause to be a nightmare or some fright, for she had told one of the old women who looked after the patients in the hospital that she found the house disturbing and was certain many people had died there.

Time and time again Betta had tried to draw her into the activities of the household, believing that, like Meena's mother, her opposition would come to an end; but from the beginning it became clear that unless she was able to exercise complete control over what went on she would remain cut off. The gradual deterioration in her features had provided her with another reason for her continued isolation.

Betta knew that his mother liked Gita, her second granddaughter, but the latter was terrified of the mask and would not be reassured that her grandmother did not put away her face at night.

He closed the window and thrust a hand through the broken pane, not knowing why he did so. Tomorrow he would get the sick-nurse to mend it, he told himself.

An unusually bright moon, which cast a vague, eerie light on the floorboards, added to his feeling of uneasiness. He reflected on his early efforts as a boy to master the contents of school textbooks in order to please her and the Mulvi Sahib, on the harsh conditions of student life in a country with brief, uncertain summers, and on his determination to free himself from her indomitable will.

Now he could take pleasure neither in his mother's helplessness, nor in the fulfilment of his own ambition to found a hospital of his own. And if he denied a more secret ambition to overcome her, it gave him no joy to witness her utter dependence on him.

The next morning Meena took up her mother-in-law's breakfast and found her standing in a corner, her face to the wall.

'Mother-in-law, I've brought your tea.'

Mrs Singh turned to face her.

'What're you staring at? Betta said I musn't be ashamed of my appearance.'

Mrs Singh had not bothered to put on her mask and Meena was certain that she was deliberately trying to frighten her.

'I've come for the sheet. Can I take it?'

'You are too deferential, daughter-in-law,' Mrs Singh screamed. 'I do not trust you! You must have ensnared Betta with your niceness. I can imagine him in your home, and you with your gaze fixed on the floorboards. "May I marry your nice daughter, Mr So-and-So?" "She's a virgin and has never known a man, not even slightly!"'

Meena was so intimidated by the unexpected fury of her mother-in-law's attack and by the open display of her unmasked face that she dared not move towards the sheet.

'My husband went to India to find a *nice* girl. None of these Guyanese East Indians had the qualifications he was looking for. Most of them did not gaze at the floor in the presence of a man. They had learned too much from black women. But do you know that black men go abroad to look for wives as well? They go to Barbados in search of *nice* wives. The flower from Kerala that closed modestly in the dark was only part of a plant, dear daughter-in-law. But when the root became exposed it was a revelation not only for my husband, but for me. . . . I heard you begging Betta not to increase the number of free hospital beds, that he had to save the money for your children's education. Is it money you want, daughter-in-law? Do you want me to dispose of my house and give your family the proceeds? After all, what good is it to me now? Ah, your eyes light up! Admit you married Betta because you thought he would be rich one day. I remember when you came to me and prostrated yourself in your deferential way. And what is left of that respect?' she asked, grinding her teeth with rage. 'What happened to that floorboard gaze? When you come into this room your look is averted. Why? You should have been here last night and you'd have witnessed a scene of genuine subservience, a subservience so complete I lost my temper at it. You only know subservience from one side, but I can tell you, from the other it's as revolting as the duty to lie down under a man you despise. Your best friend Rani knows all about that, but then she's not subservient, and learned to fight, to master her husband and tame him before he started believing in his invincibility. She is vastly superior to you. . . . Yes, every crab-dog can dream of love and the subservience of love.'

'I'm sorry,' Meena said, shaken out of her complacency about a mother-in-law who, since her arrival, had kept to her bed.

'I've tried to do my duty,' Meena continued.

'I've tried to do my duty!' Mrs Singh exclaimed, mimicking her daughter-in-law cruelly, with no pause between the remark and its repetition. 'I knew a young woman who was so afraid of her husband's mother she walked into the sea at Cove-and-John. You must go and see the spot one day. They say it's at its best when you go alone.'

Mrs Singh went and lay down, then got up once again to don her mask.

Meena fetched the sheet from the corner, hesitated as though she had something to say, then left the room, closing the door behind her.

Chapter 49

The household routine had been so disturbed by the 'incident' that new arrangements were made for feeding Mrs Singh, cleaning her room and attending to her personal needs. One of the old women from the hospital took over Meena's duties in exchange for her assistance in the morning hours, when the patients who were not bed-ridden sat outside under the trees. But Betta's mother fell back into her old ways at once, speaking to no one except when Rani came. Then, on hearing her voice, she would ask to see her and her children.

Meena, when she looked back on Mrs Singh's outburst, welcomed it, since it freed her from the obligation of going to the room.

Betta, as the months went by, was seized by a sort of frenzy for work. He had an annexe built and extended his non-fee-paying treatment, to the point where people began to see the house as a free institution, rather than a paying hospital which accommodated a certain number of free patients.

Occasionally he would take his family and Rani's on an excursion up the coast; and once they even went to a Georgetown picture house in Robb Street – the same one under whose windows Lahti and Sukrum used to stand and listen to the actors' words and dream of the luxury of sitting on one of its bug-infested benches in the pit. Betta, Meena, Rani, her husband and two men relations, the five children, took up a whole row in the dress circle. Gita enquired whether the actors had arrived yet from America and was surprised to hear that the film consisted of photographs strung together. Bismatie pretended she had known all along, but was to meditate on the matter for several days.

After the show Betta, while driving Rani's family to their

home in Kitty, went out of his way to pass the house in Regent Street where he had courted the mender of cane chairs. The unlit building, mysterious in the swift passage of the vehicle, seemed to be urging him to stop.

'Why you slowed down here?' Meena asked.

'Nothing,' Betta answered, roused from his reverie by the unexpected question.

Back home he ate with his family, then went for a walk alone. It occurred to him that he, and perhaps others, rarely made any conscious decisions, that his actions were dictated by a series of images so brief, he was almost entirely unaware of them. The act of passing the unlit house in Regent Street had left in his mind a retinue of unfulfilled longings, and he was to question whether his life had been his own.

Sometimes there would be a banging late at night or early in the morning and Betta would get up to find a stranger at the gate, who feared the worst for a sick relation. And Meena would invariably declare that East Coast people, who were irresponsible, did not care tò learn the elements of house medicine, but preferred to waste the doctors' time. Besides, after driving himself all day, how could her husband be expected to go out on foot to houses aback and cross planks over canals with God-knows-what lurking in them?

Betta would nevertheless go off with the stranger, enquiring on the way what the patient's symptoms were, in order to arrive at a tentative diagnosis. Meena was incensed at the interruption of his sleep and the assumption that he was at the beck and call of the community. He, on the other hand, found a perverse satisfaction in the way East Indians discounted his entitlement to a private life. Looking forward to acquiring some experience which might add to his knowledge of his people, he entered the hovels of the poor with a feeling compounded of pity for their condition and trepidation at what he might discover between the bedclothes. He became acquainted with dwellings by muddy canals, stilted shacks afloat in the barely penetrable night, children with the preoccupied expression of adults, the crowing of cocks intoxicated with visions of a false dawn, the portentous shrieking of goat-suckers behind the most isolated sick-houses; and all this combined to imbue him with a passion for trips which his wife detested from the bottom of her heart. Often he only returned hours later, his trouser legs caked in mud and his hands marked with the blood-evidence of mosquito bites.

To assuage Meena's anxiety Betta would bring home anecdotes he collected during these visits: a mother placed a pair of scissors under her daughter's cradle so that the child would come to no harm; a boy smiled continuously because he was so short-sighted he was unable to recognize those he knew.

His thoughts returned to his mother's alarming apathy at unexpected times, in the midst of examining a patient or at some unusual sight, like a tamarind tree in flower or a turning in the road where the ocean came in view. He invited a colleague to see her, but the examination betrayed no ailment and he went away as mystified as Betta was.

And from then on he abandoned his efforts to communicate with his mother, just as Meena and her mother had done. Even Rani was ignored for the first time one afternoon in March when she came to report that she was pregnant with her third child. On subsequent visits she was treated no better and, as it became clear that her erstwhile benefactress no longer wanted to be seen, she, too, abandoned her.

Mrs Singh began to furnish her room with dolls which she bought through the old woman who cleaned her room. In the beginning they were disposed on the recess of the Demerara window, then on the floor against the partitions, so that the old woman complained that tidying the room was no longer a simple business. Betta, fearing that he would not be able to replace her, increased her wages and urged Meena to help once or twice a week.

It was during one of these visits that Meena, seeing her mother-in-law stretched out on her back, immobile, corpse-like, wished, indeed, for her death. The night before – the Divali festival – Betta had entertained friends from the village, and the sound of her own and their guests' children running up and down the front stairs, the uninhibited laughter of their guests and the flickering of tiny clay lamps supplied by the goblet maker, had recalled the time immediately following her marriage, the delirium of courting. Old Mr Merriman had remarked in jest that creoles courted before marrying because they could not wait. She had had Betta all to herself then, he who had taught her the secret of caresses in those interminable nights. Of late he had begun to be himself again and she could only pray that he, like the rest of the household, had all but forgotten his mother and her solitary life in a house of so many voices. When the guests had gone she wanted to remark on the success of the evening and on his gaiety, but was afraid she might break the spell of her newfound contentment. The acrid smell of the extinguished lamps, some of which were still burning under the house and in the back yard long after the guests' departure, trailed after them on the rising air.

Yes, Meena thought, she'll die and Betta will get over her death as he has overcome our son's handicap.

'Ma, you want anything?'

But Mrs Singh turned away, to the relief of Meena, who left the room.

The next time she went up early one afternoon when Betta was on his rounds and the children had gone back to school and nursery after their twelve o'clock meal. Finding her mother-in-law's bed empty she hurried over to the window, afraid that the older woman might have leapt to the ground below in a moment of despair. But before she could cover the short distance she was seized and held in a vice-like grip from behind, while a hand was placed over her mouth. The sensation of being submerged in the sea lasted several seconds before she became aware of the damp hand on her neck and, on opening her eyes, a pair of scissors pointed towards her face.

'You and your mother,' Mrs Singh said in slow, clearly enunciated words, 'and your vulgarity. You know who Betta is? He is a prince! Look at those pictures of Lord Krishna on sale at the stalls and you can't fail to see the resemblance. He's never once raised his voice in my house or in this; but every day I hear your mother bawling like a market woman and your children rampaging through the house. I will cut out your tongue and feed it to the carrion crows, and then they can mourn for you in silence. But knowing them they'll wail like black women at a wake, in an endless lamentation that will rouse me to more violence.'

Mrs Singh dragged her daughter-in-law over to the open window and turned her head upwards to look at the powdery blue of a sky under which vultures were gliding in wide circles.

'You see them?' Mrs Singh told Meena, pointing with a finger at the vultures. 'The bucks call them "The Mothers". . . . I saw you peeping at me through the half-open door, hoping I was dead.'

Mrs Singh tightened the grip round Meena's neck in an incredible display of strength. Then, muttering to herself, without relaxing her grip she spoke of her own character.

'The Pujaree said I was generous, but my generosity is not mine. Keralans are hospitable *as a people*, so I don't know what I'm really like. The Mulvi Sahib said I was own-way and wanted to be a man, yet the Pujaree saw me as the most feminine of women. I can't bear the sight of blood, but I admired the Pujaree for the orgy of blood-letting in his temple. I don't know what I am.'

Then, raising her voice, and addressing Meena once more, she said, 'But you and your mother, who grew up with the jabbering of the illiterate and half-literate in your ears, are certain of everything.'

Mrs Singh pushed Meena towards the bed and the young woman tried to turn and look at her, only to feel the masculine grip tighten even further. She was made to sit on the bed and stretch her legs, so that her mother-in-law remained behind her. Mrs Singh then began cutting off Meena's long hair, still pressing a hand against her mouth. The black strands fell to the bed, and as they accumulated Mrs Singh experienced a deep satisfaction, as if she had excreted some encumbering waste. And Meena, torn between relief that she was not to be killed and terror at what might be a preliminary act to her killing, sat trembling on the bed. Her face, covered with an inexhaustible stream of perspiration, glistened like a kusha of beaten copper. She dared not beg that her life be spared for her children's sake, because of her fear that Mrs Singh, in a fit of anger, might attack her with the scissors. Convinced that her mother-in-law was mad when she began talking of Lahti's visits, Meena gave up any notion of trying to pacify or humour her. But Mrs Singh was speaking the truth. Lahti's appearances had multiplied in the last week and her requests to be repatriated to the Vlissingen Road house was the only subject of her conversations. Mrs Singh had grown afraid of her, for she knew that visitations by the dead usually became less frequent with time.

When Mrs Singh finally let Meena go she ran down to the hospital to seek the protection of the sick-nurse and wait until Betta came home. Collapsing in a fit of uncontrollable weeping, she was immediately surrounded by the patients and the sick-nurse, who stared down unbelievingly at the devastated head and the uncharacteristically undignified behaviour of the doctor's wife. The patients were dispersed by the sick-nurse, who then urged Meena to pull herself together and tell him what had happened. In the end she gave him her account of the attack and begged him to bolt the back door and keep watch on the front.

Betta, who came home before the children, felt at once that all was not well. The knot of patients standing at the gate turned away when he got out of the car and went back into the hospital, only to place themselves at the windows, as though his arrival were an extraordinary occurrence.

The sick-nurse came to meet him and the patients saw the two men look upstairs before hurrying into the hospital where Meena was sitting on one of the beds. Betta sat down next to her, placed her head on his shoulder and comforted her with inaudible words. Then they saw her restraining him as he got up to go.

Meanwhile the sick-nurse had returned to guard the unlocked front door, which was usually left wide open. The afternoon silence would be broken in a few minutes by the noise of children and the shave-ice man intercepting them on their way home. Five minutes past three, ten minutes past three, days of predictable occurrences, like the chiming of a reliable clock, to be interrupted by incoherent Saturdays and mute Sundays.

It was a quarter past three. The patients saw Betta leave his wife, heard his footsteps on the stairs and on the floorboards above and almost felt the silence that followed.

Betta, on entering his mother's room, saw her lying on the bed, surrounded by a carnage of mutilated dolls.

'Ma!' he said sternly.

But his mother did not answer, for she was dead. It was the act of taking her hand which disclosed the pair of scissors covered by a wad of cloth. She had preferred not to hold the naked metal before plunging it into her chest.

Dr Singh closed his mother's eyes and contemplated the masked head, and he, who had seen scores of patients die, glimpsed for a moment the true significance of words fraught with shadows, beds and veils and leprosies that leave the hands intact. How often had he not heard bursts of laughter from a neighbouring cottage the moment a spirit fled, or become aware of the extraordinary calm of the world outside, without flinching? Now, when the silence was broken by the shave-ice man's clanging bell, he was jolted into the realization that his was a private grief, for his mother was a stranger to the community of Plaisance. Away from the Vlissingen Road house, its hucksters and hangers-on, its priests and teachers, its visitors, its trees and nearby fields, its memories of glittering tajahs to be burned on the seashore, she had lost an identity nurtured in the wake of her marriage and voyage across the ocean. Incapable of coming to terms with his desertion, she had installed herself in his house with defiant gestures. Her death was his doing, but he could not have acted otherwise.